STUART PAWSON had a career as a mining engineer, followed by a spell working for the probation service, before he became a full-time writer. He lives in Fairburn, Yorkshire, and, when not hunched over the word processor, likes nothing more than tramping across the moors, which often feature in his stories. He is a member of the Murder Squad and Crime Writers' Association.

Also by Stuart Pawson

The Mushroom Man
The Picasso Scam
Last Reminder
Deadly Friends
Some by Fire
Chill Factor
Laughing Boy
Limestone Cowboy
Over The Edge

The Judas Sheep

Stuart Pawson

This edition published in 2005 by
Allison & Busby Limited
Bon Marche Centre
241-251 Ferndale Road
London SW9 8BJ
http://www.allisonandbusby.com

First published in 1996 by Headline Book Publishing.

A catalogue record for this book is available from the British Library.

10 9 8 7 6 5 4 3 2 1

ISBN 0 7490 8314 X

Printed and bound in Great Britain by
Bookmarque Ltd, Croydon, Surrey

The Judas Sheep

Stuart Pawson

Chapter One

The tyres of the Rolls-Royce hissed on the wet road as it pulled into the kerb, splashing dirty water against the legs of the old woman on the pavement. She turned and glared at the driver, unimpressed by the noble origins of the cold spray.

'You sploshed me,' she remonstrated in a low accent, as he walked round to open the rear passenger door.

Mrs Marina Norris swung her cover-girl legs on to the pavement and stood up. 'Wait for me, Harold – this won't take long,' she told her chauffeur, with no attempt to hide her distaste.

'He sploshed me,' said the old lady as Mrs Norris swept by.

Harold watched the wife of his employer trot up the wide stairs and vanish through the revolving door of the Town & County department store, and wondered if she were wearing tights or stockings today. 'Yes, ma'am,' he said after her retreating figure. 'Don't worry about me, ma'am. Presumably your old feller owns the double yellow lines as well as the bleedin' store.'

'Young man, you sploshed me,' the old lady repeated.

Harold glanced at her ham-shaped legs, mottled red down one side through sitting too close to the fire, and flecked with brown down the other, like a thrush's breast.

'Sorry, love,' he told her, as he slid back into the driving seat. In a lifetime starved of apologies it was more than she had expected.

Harold lowered his window and lit a cigarette, holding it outside the car and half-heartedly trying to blow most of the smoke that way. One good thing about this job – there were always plenty of cigs available. Two or three times a week the boss would leave him a carton in the glove box, or a couple of packets with just one cigarette taken. He gazed across at the shop doorway and wondered about Marina Norris.

Every Friday morning he would drive her to Town & County and she would do her rounds, blowing through the store like a February gale through an orchard, picking fault and criticising at every counter. She would purchase, although that wasn't the right word because no money ever changed hands, several items of clothing that she would never wear, and, her week's work done, allow Harold to drive her back to Lymm for a well earned g and t.

And then there were her Wednesday afternoons . . . Harold dropped the half-smoked cigarette on to the road and lit another. They were the type designed for office workers who snatched a quick drag outside their smoke-free zones. Heavily loaded with nicotine at the front end, they gave an instant rush to calm the frayed nerves of chairman and typist alike, before fading into blandness.

Every Wednesday afternoon for the last six months, Mrs Norris had been in the habit of going off in her own car – a sporty little Honda coupé. Apart from that she rarely drove; Harold would have to reverse the car out of the garage for her and leave it pointing in approximately the right direction. Where she went he did not know. Until this week.

Two days ago, Mrs Norris had driven the Honda over the

fleur-de-lys shaped wrought-iron edging around the flower beds in the grounds of the Royal Cheshire Hotel, puncturing the front nearside tyre. She rang Harold and asked him to collect her in the Rolls.

Surprisingly, she said she would ride in the front with him. As she swung her legs in he dropped his gaze deferentially, as all randy chauffeurs do, and was rewarded with a glimpse of stocking tops that nearly gave him a cardiac arrest. He confused R with D on the automatic gearbox and almost reversed the Rolls into the Royal Cheshire's ornamental pool. When she asked him to light her cigarette he could smell the alcohol on her breath, over the perfume and smoke, and her eyes were big and black and sparkled like he'd never seen before.

So, he thought, Mrs Norris spends her Wednesday afternoons at a posh hotel, gets popped up, and wears stockings for the occasion. There was no cabaret at the Royal, and they were much too genteel to employ Bunny Girls, so there must be another reason. Knowledge is power, he said to himself, and this knowledge could be very good for my job security, very good indeed. He'd taken her home, then gone back with the gardener to collect the Honda.

''Ello, Harold. How are you?' said the voice.

Harold jerked out of his daydreams, dropping the cigarette, and turned to the face that had appeared at the window of the Rolls. 'Hey! Who the hell do you think you are?' he protested, for the man was now leaning on the windowsill, his head almost inside the car. He was holding a rolled-up plastic carrier bag in his hands.

'A friend, Harold. I'm a friend.'

Harold's hand moved towards the ignition key, so he could raise the electric window, but the stranger slid the plastic bag back to reveal a large automatic pistol. His voice now had iron in it. 'Don't do that, or I'll ventilate your friggin' spine. Now put your hands on your knees, where I can see them.'

Harold wasn't a brave man. The colour drained from his face and the palpitations in his chest brought the taste of bile up from his stomach. He had to look down before he could place his hands on his trembling knees. 'What . . . what do you want?' he ventured. If the man had told him: 'The car,' he would gladly have vacated it.

'First of all, a little talk,' the man replied. 'Just so as we know where we stand, if you'll be following my meaning.' He was wearing ex-Army camouflage clothing and had a concave face, as if he'd been born without a nasal bone. Or modelled from plasticine and then given a good thump.

Harold swallowed and nodded. He felt certain he was about to die, possibly from a heart attack.

'You have a little daughter, I believe,' the man said.

Harold spun to face him, eyes wide and mouth hanging open. 'You . . . you . . .' He tried to speak, but nothing came out.

'Charlotte, I'm told. A bonny wee thing. Now would you be knowing if she arrived at school this morning?'

Harold raised his hands towards the man, but the gun slid from under the bag, pointing towards him. 'If you so much as touch her . . .' Harold began.

'You'll what? Tell the police? We're not interested in you or your daughter. We may have her, or we may not. Can you afford to take the risk? That's what you have to ask yourself, Harold my boy. Now here's what you do.' The man stooped low alongside the expensive car and gave his instructions to the chauffeur.

Marine Norris emerged from Town & County accompanied by the manager carrying her purchases. She'd castigated a girl behind one of the perfume counters for looking bored and bought six blouses, three skirts and four pairs of shoes. Harold didn't notice her until the manager knocked on the car window.

'Sorry, ma'am,' he muttered as he opened the door for her.

Mrs Norris was annoyed. She didn't like being seen outside Town & County with a bunch of their bags. 'We'll put these in the boot,' she told him.

The manager stood on the pavement and waved as they pulled away. 'Arrogant cow,' he mouthed through his smile.

'We'll go to Claire Louise's now, Harold. I haven't an appointment, but she'll fit me in.'

'Yes, ma'am.'

Three hundred yards down the road was a large junction controlled by traffic lights. Harold's instructions from the man with the flat face were to stop at the lights in the left-hand lane. He cruised towards them at a snail's pace, as if part of a motorcade transporting some dignitary to an important function. Mrs Norris enjoyed travelling through town very slowly in the Rolls-Royce.

'You're in the wrong lane, Harold. It's straight on to Claire Louise's.'

'Yes, ma'am.' He'd seen the man making his way towards the lights. He walked with a limp.

'Harold! The lights are at green. Why are you stopping?'

'Don't know, ma'am.'

She, too, had noticed the man on the pavement, waiting to cross the road, and wondered with distaste what sort of hooligan he was. She judged everyone on first impressions, but for once she was on the conservative side. The car stopped alongside him and he yanked the rear door open.

'Move over,' he hissed, and bundled her across the seat.

Mrs Norris screamed and kicked, but the man poked the

automatic into her side and pulled the door shut with a *clunk* that had cost a fortune to perfect.

'Keep quiet!' he told her. 'Dead or alive doesn't make any difference to me.'

Harold took the left turn as he had been instructed.

'Follow the signs towards the M6,' the man told him.

Mrs Norris huddled in the corner, as far from him as possible, her arms wrapped round herself for protection in a manner that was older than mankind. Thoughts of murder, rape and kidnapping tumbled through her mind. What she had previously only heard of briefly in TV newscasts was now happening to her. She clutched the lapels of her unborn-calf jacket and felt her breasts trembling against her forearms. She wanted to shout, to protest, to reason, but terror had rendered her mute.

Harold tried to see her in the rearview mirror, but she'd sunk low into the leather seat. 'He made me do it, ma'am,' he whimpered. 'They've got Charlotte. He made me do it.'

The man pressed the muzzle of the gun into the junction between Harold's left ear and his skull. 'Just drive!' he ordered.

Fifty minutes later, the Rolls-Royce turned off a B road into a narrow cart-track. Winter branches dragged along each side of the immaculate coachwork and the vehicle tipped and rolled as the wheels sank into mud-filled ruts and climbed out again. In half a mile they came to a clearing, surrounded by stark brown silver birches. A red Ford Sierra was already parked there, its boot-lid ominously open.

'Terminus,' said the man. 'Everybody out.'

There was a greeting party of two more men, but they could hardly be called welcoming. Their coat hoods were drawn up, concealing the lower parts of their faces. 'All OK?' asked the bigger one.

'Like a dream,' said the first, as he dragged Mrs Norris

from the car. 'You too,' he told Harold.

Marina Norris, now on her feet, pulled her arm from his grasp. 'You bastard!' she hissed at him. 'You—'

His fist hit her on the side of the head, hurling her to the ground. Harold shrank at the ferocity of it. It wasn't a slap or a punch; it was a blow. He didn't think a human being could take brutality like that.

She lay on the wet grass, propped on one elbow, with a look of hurt bewilderment on her face and a trickle of blood coming from her nostril. The man unzipped his camouflage jacket and concealed the pistol somewhere within it. He walked over to the Sierra and lifted a Kalashnikov assault rifle from inside the boot. 'Put her in there,' he ordered.

The other two grabbed Mrs Norris and manhandled her into the boot. They pinioned her arms and legs with plastic ties and stuck a length of duct tape over her mouth. She blew the blood out of her nose so that she could breathe, and realised that she was wetting herself. The boot-lid clunked shut, switching her off from the outside world as abruptly as turning off a television, leaving her in total darkness.

The first man, he of the concave face, caught sight of his own reflection in the Rolls's paintwork. His legs were truncated, but the curve of the bodywork gave him a barrel chest. He posed for a few seconds, holding the gun at exactly the same angle as Lee Harvey Oswald held his rifle in the photograph he used to have on the back of his locker door.

He wrenched himself away from the image. 'You, over there,' he said, swinging the Kalashnikov towards Harold and then in the direction of the trees.

Harold was speechless and paralysed.

'Don't worry. We're just going to delay your progress. So we'll have a head start, if you'll be following my meaning.'

He jabbed Harold with the gun, propelling him towards the undergrowth.

Five yards into them he said: 'Kneel down.'

Harold's knees gave way and he sank to the ground.

The man placed the barrel of the gun against the back of Harold's head and pulled the trigger. The Kalashnikov was only set for single fire, but it was enough to blow his brains through his face.

'Good morning, Mrs Wilberforce,' I said brightly as Annabelle opened her door to my knock.

'Good morning, Inspector Priest. You look wet-nosed and bushy-tailed for this time in the morning.' She held the door wide for me to enter and I followed her through into her kitchen. 'Have you had some breakfast, Charles?' she asked.

'Yes, thank you.' I didn't have much to say, relying on a beaming smile to convey my feelings.

'I've made us plenty of sandwiches, and that's a flask of soup,' she said.

'Terrific.' I tested the weight of the parcels. They were heavy. 'Do these go in your rucksack or mine?' I wondered.

'Yours. You're of the stronger sex.'

'Since when did you start believing that?'

'Since I felt the weight of them. It's my fault, I made the bread with strong flour.'

I looked doubtful. 'Are you having me on?'

'Having you on? *Moi?*' she chuckled.

Annabelle was wearing a big Aran sweater with jeans and a pair of trainers. She looked as if she'd just stepped off the 'Outdoors' pages of Grattan's catalogue, except I knew she could deliver the goods. She'd climbed Mount Kenya a couple of times and her rucksack and hiking boots near the door were the pukka-gen items.

'I left my sack outside,' I told her. 'I'll just pop these in yours for the time being. How did the conference go?'

I hadn't seen Annabelle for a week. Once upon a time she lived in Africa with her late husband who eventually became a bishop. He died of cancer. Now she did a lot of work for a variety of overseas charities, and had just attended a conference in London, aimed at trying to direct their various contributions more effectively.

'Oh, so-so,' she replied. 'I need to have a word with you about it, when we have a chance.'

'I expected you to come home bubbling over with enthusiasm,' I told her.

She looked concerned. 'I ought to be, but – I'll tell you later. What about you? Have you made any decisions yet?'

'Probably. As you say, we'll talk later. C'mon, let's wait for the bus at the end of the street.'

I'd parked my car on her drive. We gathered up the stuff we needed for a day's walking in the hills and padded silently to the end of the cul-de-sac, our anoraks flapping open, rucksacks hooked over one shoulder and hiking boots held in our hands. It was eight o'clock on a bright January morning.

'This will keep the neighbours guessing,' Annabelle declared, glancing up at their still-closed curtains.

'You worry too much about your neighbours,' I said with feeling.

'I have a confession to make.'

I turned to her. 'What's that?'

'I've never been on a coach-trip before,' she confided.

'Really?'

'Really.'

'Gosh. I never realised how deprived you were. You don't know what you've been missing. Bus-trips are an important part of our heritage. We'll have community singing on the way back, and a collection for the driver.'

'Honestly?'

'Honestly.'

'Community singing?'

'Sure. There's always a sing-song on a bus-trip.'

'Now you are teasing me.'

'Teasing you? *Moi?*'

It was the first outing for the newly re-formed Heckley CID Walking Club. I'd had nothing to do with the organisation because I was off work due to so-called ill-health, and was grateful for the invitation to go along. A big shiver shook my body and I zipped up my jacket. The forecast said bright but cold, and looked like being right for once.

'I've decided to go back to work,' I said.

She looked at me for several seconds without speaking, then said: 'I don't think you should rush things.'

'I'm starting to feel restless,' I told her. 'I've decided that retirement might not be the state of bliss that I'd imagined it would be. I need another three years' service to qualify for full pension; I'll do that at least.'

'Oh Charles, start thinking of yourself first, not the job. Don't go back this time until you're certain you are ready to. Have another few weeks off.'

'And what about you?'

'Me? I'm as fit as a fiddle, now.'

'So am I. Bet I beat you to the top today.'

'No, Charles. Skin and bones mend easily, but you had been working a sixteen-hour day for six months, without any breaks. You became emotionally involved with a case. It's probably bad medical practice to say this, but I think you were close to a breakdown, and you are the type that it hits hardest.'

'And what type's that?'

'The type that thinks it can't happen to them.'

That made it Gilbert Wood, my Superintendent; Sam Evans, the Police Surgeon; and now Annabelle all thinking that I ought to have six months' sick leave and then quietly retire. It felt like a conspiracy, so I decided to change the subject.

'Gilbert has offered me the loan of his cottage in Cornwall. I thought I'd maybe go down there for a week or two. He won't take payment, so I could do some decorating or something to earn my keep.'

'That sounds like a good idea. Cornwall in winter can be delightful. Gilbert is a good friend, Charles, I'm sure you don't have to earn your keep. Why not just go there and relax for a while?'

'Chill out, as we say in Heckley.'

'Precisely.'

'Yeah, you're right. I was thinking – it's a big cottage, well, big enough. But not too big to lose that cosy feeling. Has all the amenities. If you liked, if you wanted, what I'm trying to say is: if I did go, it'd be nice for you to come down for a few days, too.'

Annabelle opened her eyes wide, in mock horror, but after a few seconds her nose wrinkled like it always does when she smiles. I could hear the noise of the bus's engine, toiling up the hill. She said: 'Charles! Are you suggesting an . . . assignation?'

'Mmm . . . yes,' I told her. 'Or to put it another way . . . yes.'

'Is it a nice cottage?'

'Very nice.'

One of Carter's Luxury Coaches came round the corner and headed towards us.

'Roses round he door? It must have roses round the door.'

'Floribundas. In floribundance.'

'Oak beams and an inglenook fireplace?'

'I'll fix it.' I was smiling now; this was sounding promising.

The bus stopped in front of us and the door folded back with a hiss of hydraulics. I picked up my rucksack and boots and stood aside to allow Annabelle on first.

'I'll have to consult my social diary,' she said as she passed in front of me.

'Ratbag!' I snarled, and followed her up the two big steps.

The bus was only about half-filled, but it still had a few more calls to make. 'Morning, all,' I hollered to the familiar faces.

'Morning, Charlie,' they chorused cheerfully.

'This is Annabelle,' I told them.

'Morning, Annabelle,' they chanted back.

'Good morning, everyone,' she responded.

'Never knew you had a daughter, Charlie,' someone said.

We put our stuff up on the luggage rack and found a seat about halfway back. The bus did a circuit of Heckley, picking up the remainder of the passengers. Dave Sparkington is one of my Detective Constables, the one I usually work with, and I was looking forward to Annabelle meeting him. We stopped near his house, where he was waiting with two of his children, but he didn't get on the bus. The kids were wearing bobble hats and anoraks, but Sparky had his raincoat over his shoulders.

His daughter, Sophie, came down the aisle, looking for me. 'Good morning, Uncle Charlie. Dad says can he have a word with you.'

'There's been a murder,' his son, Daniel, informed me, and was promptly reprimanded by his big sister for listening to other people's telephone conversations.

I felt Annabelle tense in the seat beside me. Her body language was saying: *Oh no, not again*. 'Don't worry,' I told her. 'I'm not working.'

'Morning, Chas,' Sparky greeted me when I stepped off the coach. 'Sorry about this, but something's cropped up. Do you mind if the kids come with you?'

'Of course not. Why, what's happened?'

'Farmer out shooting rabbits in Heckley Wood a couple of hours ago. Found a body. Patrol boys report that his head was nearly blown off, no gun around, so it looks like we've a murder on our hands.'

'Sugar. Sounds as if it could be a gangland job,' I said.

Sparky read the disappointment on my face. 'Aha,' he laughed. 'So you have a nice day out with my kids while me and Nigel catch the villains, eh? He sends his apologies. I've told the two of them to behave and said you can clip them round the ears if they're cheeky.'

'Great, thanks.'

I climbed back aboard and we lurched away as I introduced Sophie and Daniel to Annabelle. Dave is one of the best policemen I know, even if he is as Yorkshire as Harry Ramsden's and as blunt as a punt. Nigel is just the opposite. DS Nigel Newley was standing in for me and on the accelerated promotion scheme. He hailed from deepest Berkshire and had the manners of a P.G. Wodehouse flunkey. They were an ill-sorted pair, but after an uneasy start were beginning to work as a team. It was interesting to observe how they influenced each other: Nigel had started wearing crew-neck sweaters and Sparky had bought some aftershave.

Ingleborough Hill used to be 2,376 feet high, but now it measures a mere 723 metres. It sprawls like a sleeping lion, dominating the landscape. It is not the highest hill in Yorkshire, but it is the most majestic. Legend has it that the Brigantes held out against the Romans here. Remains of their dwellings and fortifications are plainly visible on the summit. We like to think that this bit of Yorkshire, like much of Scotland, was never conquered by the Romans, but that's bunkum. Today the top was lost in the clouds, as it so often is.

The bus parked in the Hill Inn car park, where we donned our gear and stuffed ourselves with sandwiches to lighten the loads in our rucksacks. Sophie's and Daniel's would have taxed a paratrooper yomping across Dartmoor, so I made them off-load most of it. We milled around, stamping feet and rubbing hands to keep warm, criticising each other's clothing. There were several pairs of navy-blue serge trousers on show.

'They look nice,' I told one wearer. 'Do they sell them in camping shops?'

'I can let you have a couple of pairs. Trouble is, they only walk at one speed,' he replied.

Nigel had organised the trip, so in his absence we were leaderless. I waved my arm like John Wayne at the start of a cattle drive. 'Let's go!' I shouted.

Nobody stirred.

'The pub's open!' I tried. Several faces turned towards it.

Slowly, we moved off. At the first stile we were reduced to a long straggling procession, winding sluggishly towards the mountain. Our route took us up the lion's armpit, where it was steep and rocky, and then over its mane.

Sophie and Daniel had latched on to Jeff Caton, one of my Detective Sergeants. He knew them well enough and was twenty-odd years nearer their age group. I looked back every few minutes to make sure we weren't leaving anyone behind.

Climbing is a private activity, however many of you are together. You lift your feet forward and suck in air and try to let your mind wander away from the tiredness in your legs. I let my own mind focus hungrily on Dave Sparkington's news.

They'd be making a fingertip search of the murder scene about now. An incident room would have been set up and the body moved to Heckley General Hospital for a PM. Identifying the victim was a priority. If he carried any ID the enquiry would make an immediate leap forward.

I usually do the murders that come into Heckley nick. Mostly they are domestics, and we have someone in a cell within twenty-four hours. There's nothing glamorous about it, just sadness and a sense of gratitude that we were born at the other side of the tracks, or had the wit to drag ourselves across them. But then there are the others . . . I had an overwhelming sense that this was one of the others, and I wanted to be a part of it.

As we crested the brow on to the summit plateau, the wind hit us like a buzz-saw. I pulled up my hood and helped Annabelle with hers. 'OK?' I yelled above the roar.

'Mmm, super.'

We bent into the gale and headed, hand in hand, towards the stone wall that provides some shelter up there.

It's not the ideal place for a picnic, so we just snatched a quick sandwich and a cup of soup. By the time everybody arrived we were chilled through, but as we dropped off the summit again the air felt unnaturally calm and it was possibly to hold a normal conversation.

'Phew,' Annabelle said, pulling her hood back and brushing her fair hair from her eyes. 'This is better. Is it always like that on the top?' Her cheeks were pink and her eyes shone like sapphire pools.

'Always,' I told her, 'but the windswept look suits you. How are you feeling?'

'I feel fantastic, thank you. And you?'

'OK, thanks. I was puffing a bit at the top, though.'

Our descent was via a slightly different route. As we

moved off the hill, the Batty Moss viaduct at Ribblehead came into view, three miles away. The sun was punching a hole through the mist, illuminating the curving masterpiece of railway architecture.

'Look,' I said, pointing and tugging at her sleeve.

'Oh, what a beautiful view,' she replied.

'It's a watercolourist's dream,' I declared. 'Or maybe a Turner's.'

'Is that the line they are always wanting to close?'

'Yes. The Settle to Carlisle.'

'Why don't *you* paint it, Charles?'

A long time ago I was an art student. I still dabbled, occasionally – mainly posters for police dances. 'Yep. Could do, one day.' I remembered that I had my camera in my bag. 'Hey,' I said. 'Let's capture it for posterity.'

I took two pictures of the viaduct and one of Annabelle. She tipped her head to one side and smiled, and as I framed her in the viewfinder my stomach turned to mercury. I swore that I'd do anything I could, go anywhere I had to, to make her mine. No, that was impossible. Spend the rest of my life with her, share her bad times as well as the good, that's what I wanted.

'That was a smasher,' I enthused as I lowered the camera. She insisted on taking one of me.

Jeff Caton and his charges caught up with us. They were making a race of it. 'Hi, boss,' Jeff gasped. 'When are you coming back?'

'You don't need me, from what I've heard.'

'We don't need bellybuttons, but we'd miss them if they weren't there.'

Sometimes I wonder if I trained them all wrong. I said: 'Did you hear any more about that drug addict who injected himself with curry powder?'

'Yes, he went into a khorma,' Jeff replied. Sophie and

Daniel clasped their hands over their ears and staggered about making rude noises.

When they left us, Annabelle and I trudged across the fell towards the Hill Inn with our arms across each other's shoulders. 'Your staff are obviously terrified of you,' she said.

'Does it show?' I asked.

'Yes. You must be really cruel to them.'

'I like to think I run a tight ship.'

She gave me a squeeze. 'It's been a lovely day out,' she told me. 'It's good to blow the cobwebs away. We should do this more often.'

'It's not over yet. First there's the pub, then there's the community singing. They're the best bits.'

She was quiet for a few moments, then she said: 'Charles?'

'Uh uh.'

'What we were saying, this morning . . .'

'Mmm?'

'Well, now I think I understand why you don't want to leave.'

'Thanks. I'm glad you do. But we can only postpone things. One day I'll have to go.' I looked across at her and pulled her closer. 'That's why I'm trying to develop other interests.'

She dropped her arm so it was around my waist. 'I see. So I'm just an alternative to night classes or trainspotting.'

'Some of the happiest days of my life were spent trainspotting,' I replied, and kissed her, out there on the moor, somewhere between Hardrawkin Pot and Braithwaite Wife Hole.

In the pub we couldn't find a seat near the log fire so we leaned on the end of the bar and I ordered two halves of Old Peculiar.

'Mmm, that's good,' Annabelle confirmed as she took a sip.

'Not bad,' I agreed after a longer draught. We stood and smiled at each other, pleased with our morning's exertions and enjoying the rewards.

'So,' I said. 'What went wrong with the conference?'

Annabelle looked away from me and gave a big sigh. 'Oh, nothing went wrong. I suppose, in fact, that it was a huge success. We certainly made some good decisions. It's just that, well, they want someone to go out to Africa to assess the effectiveness of our programmes. They've asked me if I'd consider going.'

'Oh. How long would it be for?'

'Initially, four weeks.'

'When?'

'Quite soon.'

'Sounds right up your street. You said "initially". What happens after four weeks?'

She was fiddling with her glass, turning it in circles on the bar. 'That would depend on what we found. If necessary, it could turn into a permanent posting.'

I felt as if I'd woken from an anaesthetic to find they'd amputated the wrong leg. I said: 'Oh,' again. A couple vacated two stools amongst the throng near the fire. I sipped my beer and went on: 'So, do you think you'll accept?' I could hear that my voice was an octave gruffer than normal.

'I don't know what to do, Charles.'

After a long silence I said: 'If someone goes for a month and decides that it ought to be a permanent position, does it have to be the same person who gets the job?'

'No, I don't suppose so.'

'Then I think you should go, if that's what you want.'

'Is that what you really think?'

I shook my head. 'No, but—'

A hand touched my arm. It was Jeff. 'Excuse me,

Annabelle,' he said, 'but there are two seats over here.'

We joined the rest of them until it was time to get back on the coach for the journey home. It was dark soon after four, so we couldn't see anything through the windows. After a while Annabelle went to sit with Sophie and they had a long and earnest conversation. Sophie will probably go to a decent university in a couple of years, so I imagine Annabelle was explaining her options to her. Annabelle was accepted for Oxford when she was seventeen, but went to Africa instead. I like women who are brainier than me.

Young Daniel came to sit with me. We discussed England's prospects in the World Cup and then had a serious talk on the chances of Martians landing in Trafalgar Square and paying off the national debt for us. There was no community singing on that trip, so I had plenty of time to wonder how the murder enquiry was going.

Chapter Two

Nine-thirty Monday morning I was drinking the first cup of tea of the day and reading my mail when Gilbert rang. My only letter was a not-to-be-missed offer of a decorative plate that would enhance any room, as well as becoming a sought-after collector's item. It depicted a wooden bald eagle hovering over a lake. The blurb said that if you looked carefully at the mountain in the background you might see the spirits of the timber wolf, the elk and various other creatures of the West, skilfully portrayed by the artist. I hadn't realised it was a mountain. I thought it was a pile of dead creatures waiting to be skinned. I projected *Call of the Wild* into the waste bin and answered the phone at the same time.

'Good morning, Charlie. How are you?' Gilbert asked.

'Sleepy. And hungry. I also appear to be out of milk and what's left of the loaf has mould growing on it. But thank you for asking.'

'Don't mention it. The Assistant Chief Constable has just had me on the phone and—'

'That sounds precarious.'

'What does?'

'The Assis . . . Oh never mind. What did he want?'

'He wants you on this murder enquiry. Seems to think the moon and the stars shine out of your backside. Otherwise he's going to take it off us.'

'Recognition at last. Why can't Nigel handle it?'

'Too inexperienced. And it's looking as if it could develop into something interesting. Plus we had three ram raids last night and I'm expecting to catch hell from the Chamber of Commerce. It's the fourth time Binks's Hi-Fi has been hit.'

'He could always call it a crash-and-carry.'

'Don't you know when to give up, Charlie?' He sounded exasperated.

'Sorry, Gilbert, but I'm supposed to be off sick.'

'I realise that,' he replied, 'but it's not proper sick, is it? It isn't as if you've broken your leg or got appendicitis. It's just this stress thing, isn't it?'

'That's what I keep saying. It's *you* that keeps telling me to resign!'

'Right, but this is important.'

'I thought you wanted me to go down to the cottage?'

'I do – so how about coming back here for a few days, just until the pressure dies down, then throwing off again?'

'Doc Evans won't wear it.'

'He'll do it for you. Maybe just part-time, to begin with.'

'Mm, we'll see. So bring me up to date.' I popped the used tea bag back into my mug and re-filled it with hot water.

'Good lad. I want you to nip over to Liverpool and talk to a man called Norris. He's a multi-millionaire; right up your street.'

When did all the millionaires suddenly become multi-millionaires? I stirred two sugars into my tea and took a sip. 'Tell me all about him.'

'Coming up. First of all, we've identified the body as a man called Harold Hurst. He had *Wendy* tattooed on his arm, in a rather tasteful hearts and flowers design, and a lady of that name walked into a nick in Liverpool on

Saturday morning and filed a Missing From Home report. She's described his clothing and we're checking the fingerprints, but it looks like poor Harold. He'd been shot from close range in the back of the head by a single shot from a seven-point-six-two millimetre. That's Kalashnikov calibre. It exited through his face, hence the lack of a visual ID.'

'But you found the bullet?'

'Yes.'

'It sounds like an execution. What else?'

'It does, doesn't it? Tyre tracks. The last three vehicles up the lane into the wood were a Vauxhall Astra with a blue light on top – they're in for a bollocking, a mid-range vehicle with a popular tyre size, and something big and expensive.'

'Any ideas what?' I asked.

'Possibly a Rolls-Royce. Hurst was employed as chauffeur to the aforementioned Mr Norris, who owns a Roller. That's why I'd like you to demonstrate your undeniable charm and rapier-like interviewing technique on him.'

'How could I refuse? Where do I find him?'

'Are you coming in to look at the file?'

'No. Since when did I let the facts influence me? Where does he live?'

He was American, with an accent that could have lured a gopher out of its hole. I hated him from the start. 'I'll be in my office at Shenandoah Incorporated from eleven a.m.,' he drawled into the phone, 'but I have an important meeting straight after lunch. If you can make it any time before, say, one o'clock, Inspector, you'd be mighty welcome. It's a nasty business and I'll help in any way I can. Harold's death has been a shock to everyone at Shenandoah.'

It wasn't until I found the factory, on a new trading estate at Halewood, that I realised that Shenandoah made Red Wing cigarettes. Norris had thoughtfully informed Security of my impending arrival, and I was soon being ushered into his office.

His handshake was like being caught in a car-crusher, reinforced by his free hand on my elbow. For an uneasy moment I thought he was about to drop on one knee and flying-mare me over his shoulder. Not that he'd have far to drop, as he stood barely five-and-a-half feet tall. His hair was a silver mop, highlighting his tan, and the suit was immaculate.

'Inspector,' he said with practised warmth.

'Good morning, Mr Norris.' I flexed my fingers and was relieved to find they still worked. 'Thanks for seeing me at such short notice.'

'No problem. Please, take a seat.' He asked the woman who'd brought me in to rustle up some coffee and cookies.

His desk was the ugliest piece of furniture I've ever seen. It looked as if it had been carved out of a solid tree-trunk using Stone Age implements. Primitive. No, that wasn't it. Pioneer. He barely peered over it, six feet away from me. Apart from an ashtray, a cigarette box and a lighter it was bare. It's my ambition to have a desk like that.

'So how can I help you, Inspector?'

'First of all, when did you learn of Harold Hurst's death?' I asked.

'Just this morning. My secretary rang me at home. Don't ask me where the information came from.'

'So how long had he worked for you?'

He pursed his lips in thought for a moment. 'Best part of a year, I guess.'

'And what was his typical working day?'

'Pick me up in the morning, bring me here and take me home when I finished. In between he might ferry my wife,

Marina, about. Just general chauffeuring duties, nothing hard and fast.'

'So when did you last see him?'

'Friday morning. He brought me here – we live at Lymm, in Cheshire – and continued on to Town & County department store, in the town centre.'

'Liverpool?'

'Yeah. Marina does consultancy work for them, calls in every Friday. Actually, I'm the major shareholder; as good as own the joint. They left there about half an hour later. That'd make it about eleven. After that, nothing.'

'What does Mrs Norris say?'

He lifted the lid on the cigarette box and leaned across with it. 'Cigarette?'

I shook my head.

'Mind if I do?'

'Of course not.'

He lit up with the big gold lighter. 'Fact, is, Inspector, Marina hasn't been home since. I don't know where she is.'

I was taken aback, knocked out of my stride. The coffee had arrived so I took a mouthful. It was strong and satisfying. Good stuff. After a few moments I said: 'You realise the implications of what you are saying, Mr Norris? This puts our investigation on a different course altogether.'

He shook his head, disagreeing with me. 'No, sir,' he insisted. 'The two events are not linked.' He nipped the cigarette into the ashtray and left it there. He'd only had one puff. I sat waiting for him to find the words, to expand on his last statement.

'Marina and I . . . we . . . the fact is,' he began, 'we are on the rocks. She has a boyfriend; meets him every Wednesday afternoon at the Royal Cheshire Hotel, near Northwich. Friday evening I decided I'd had enough. I was sitting here about seven o'clock, wondering where the hell

Harold was, and I rang this number for a private investigator that someone gave me. Left a message on his ansaphone. Then I had to send for a taxi. To say I was annoyed is like saying the Pope is a Catholic. A goddamn Rolls-Royce and a chauffeur, and I had to send for a taxi.'

I could see his point. I think I'd have been pretty miffed myself, but I'd never know. 'So how can you be certain that she made it to the department store, and left when she did?'

'I dropped in there, Saturday morning. Unexpectedly. I like to do it now and again. The manager had his usual gripe to me about her interference.'

'I see. And you didn't report your wife missing,' I stated.

He shook his head. 'That's not a crime here, is it?' he asked.

'No.'

'I thought not. She's not missing, just gone.'

'Have you reported the car stolen?'

'I'm coming to that. I was waiting for Security to tell me my taxi had arrived when the phone rang again. Someone very politely informed me that my Rolls-Royce was at the Burtonwood services, on the M62. Eastbound. Would I please collect it? I was relieved. I thought there must have been an accident or something, and everything could be explained. I collected my spare keys, in the taxi, then had him take me to the services. The Rolls was there, as promised.'

'And you have no idea who it was on the phone?'

'I assumed it was you guys – the police.'

'What was his accent like?'

'Bit like yours, I guess.'

Husky, but with a hint of sophistication. 'There was nothing in the car – no message?' I asked.

'No, sir.'

'And nobody has contacted you since?'

'Uh uh.'

'OK. Do you mind, Mr Norris, if I ask a local SOCO – that's a Scenes of Crime Officer – to give the Rolls a thorough going over; see if we can find some evidence of who's been in it lately?'

'I'm afraid there could be a problem with that, Inspector.'

'Why's that?'

'Well, you see, I was wondering the same thing myself. I felt uncomfortable in it, and it was covered in mud. So after I left Town & County on Saturday I took it to the garage and had them give it a full valet service.' He said *g'rarge* and *v'lay*. 'Now it's as spick and span as a West Point cadet's boots on graduation day.'

Fantastic, but I still needed some plaster casts from the tyres, to prove it was in the lane where Hurst's body was found. 'Pity,' I said. 'I'd still like him to have a go, though, if you don't mind.'

'You're welcome, Inspector. The car will be in the garage here all afternoon.'

I asked him a few questions about his wife and her friends and quizzed him some more about Harold. He gave me various names and numbers and I thanked him for his cooperation. As I was about to leave I said: 'Mr Norris, can you be absolutely sure that nothing was going off between your wife and Hurst? That they weren't having an affair?'

He shook his head and gave a little smile. 'Out of the question, Inspector. Marina liked her men either rich or built like Sylvester Stallone, but preferably taller.' The last bit made the smile a full one. 'Harold was neither.'

'What was he like?'

He pursed his lips in his thoughtful mannerism, and I wondered if he was about to give me a description of the back of his chauffeur's head. 'Hard to say. Not the type of person you'd notice in a crowd. Kinda . . . faceless.'

I already knew that.

This was the kind of enquiry I like. It was out of the ordinary – something was going off that was difficult to fathom. Rich man's wife missing, his driver found dead. What was the link? It was easier when you didn't know the people, didn't feel sorry for them. I called at the local police station and told the Superintendent why I was on his patch. I also used their telephone and had a look at the street plan.

The PI that Norris said he'd tried to contact had received the message, so I advised him against following it up. Then I visited Town & County department store.

The manager was early middle-aged, about ten years younger than me. He smiled a lot and pumped my hand eagerly. At a guess he was worried about his job, being too young to be one of the old school, yet too old to be a whizzkid. I knew the feeling.

I refused a coffee and thanked him for seeing me without an appointment. 'You must be very busy,' I crawled, and he told me all about the tribulations of sales and stock-taking. He'd last seen Hurst on the previous Friday, when Mrs Norris left the store. The manager had walked out with Mrs Norris, carrying her purchases, and had seen her into the car.

'I don't suppose she told you where they were going next?' I asked.

'I'm afraid not, Inspector.'

'But everything appeared perfectly normal?'

He thought about it. 'Well, yes. Harold was asleep, or deep in thought, and didn't see her coming. That annoyed her, but it wasn't unusual. We shouldn't speak ill of the dead, but he was a bit of a doylem.'

We shouldn't, but we usually do. He told me that Harold

had been happily married, with a seven-year-old daughter. Maybe he wasn't too bright, but somebody loved him, was mourning for him. I thanked the manager for his assistance and headed south, out of the revitalised city and into the leafy towns and villages of Cheshire. Except that they're not very leafy in January.

Mrs Norris wasn't officially missing, so I hadn't mentioned it at Town & County. At the Royal Cheshire Hotel I said that I was trying to piece together Harold Hurst's last movements. 'I understand he brought a lady called Mrs Norris here every Wednesday afternoon?' I said. Faces turned hunting pink and eyebrows shot up like flushed grouse. The register was sent for.

A Mr Smith had a regular booking, with a table for two at lunchtime. 'We do not let rooms by the afternoon,' I was assured. 'We are not that sort of establishment.'

'Yes, you are,' I replied. 'You just charge overnight prices.'

The staff were more forthcoming, and knew exactly who I meant. She wasn't brought in a Rolls, they told me; she drove herself there in a smart little Honda. The bloke came in a Daimler and gave good tips. I bet he did. Nobody could put a name to him other than Smith, and he paid in cash. Somebody's got to be called Smith, and no doubt a few of them are having affairs. I promised to send someone round for a fuller description and headed home. It had been a long day.

Somewhere on the Tops, up near Scammonden dam, I wondered if the Town & County security cameras had captured Mrs Norris's last visit. *The Archers* finished and a programme about gamelan music came on Radio Four. I hit the off button so hard I nearly pushed it through the dashboard. The local traffic police had been asked to examine their films for shots of the Roller, but I couldn't imagine what we could learn from a few frames of grainy videotape showing her in the store, and decided it wasn't worth pursuing. That was my first big mistake of the day.

The choices were wide and cosmopolitan: was it to be fish and chips, pizza, curry or Chinky? Or maybe a few slices off one of those big lumps of reconstituted meat that rotate perpetually, so the grease never quite makes it to the bottom, like the base of some horrific 1960s table lamp? I decided to stay with the faith and pulled up outside the chippy. They also sold floury bread-cakes there, so I stocked up with half a dozen of those, plus a Special and chips and a portion of mushy peas.

I dashed through the house, turning on lights, kettle and gasfire, and within five minutes was tucking in, a large steaming teapot before me. It had been a good day, but I hadn't come to any conclusions. Strictly speaking, that's how it should be. First of all, we gather the evidence. Then we form theories and put them to the test, just like scientists do. Non-judgemental. Personally, I'd rather have a confession, or a gun with fingerprints on it. Failing that, it's useful if there's someone in the frame that you've taken a dislike to. Norris, for instance.

I placed the teapot within easy reach and telephoned Gilbert, to give him an update. When we'd finished he said: 'So Doc Evans said it's OK for you to start work?'

'Er, no. I haven't had time to see him.'

'Bloody hell, Charlie, you're out of order working when you're supposed to be off sick.'

'I'll get him to backdate it.'

I flicked my radio over to Classic FM and caught the end of the *Enigma Variations*. I was just wondering whether to type my report before or after I showered when the phone rang. It was Annabelle.

'Hello, Annabelle,' I said brightly. 'This is a pleasant surprise.'

'Oh,' I heard, followed by silence.

'Er, hello. Are you still there?'

After a moment she said: 'Yes, I'm still here, Charles. I was expecting you over for supper.'

Oh God! I'd clean forgotten. I fumbled for words. 'I . . . . I'm sorry. I thought we said Tuesday.' It was a lie, and it pierced me like a corkscrew as I heard myself saying it.

'No, I'm sure we said Monday.'

'Oh, I am sorry, Annabelle. I must be confused. You know how easily that happens.'

'Yes. Well, it won't spoil for a few minutes – unless you have already eaten?'

I rubbed my stomach and ran a hand over my bristly chin. 'Er, no, I haven't.'

'Good, so are you coming over?'

'Yes, please, if I'm still welcome.'

'Mmm. We will have to consider that.'

'Turn the flame down low and give me twenty minutes.'

I put the phone down and dashed upstairs. That made it two mistakes so far today.

Bradley Norris had some thinking to do. He eased back a cuff to look at his gold Vacheron Constantin and drummed his fingers on the red oak desk that had belonged to his grandfather. They should be ringing any time. The visit from the detective wasn't a surprise, but he was a cautious man and the stakes were high. He hadn't lied about the call on Friday night that told him where the Rolls-Royce was parked, just been rather selective about the content of the message.

He always worked late on a Friday. It was his habit to call a progress meeting for four p.m. That way he stopped his managers sneaking off early for the weekend. 'Poets' day', he'd once heard one of them call it. 'Piss of early, tomorrow's Saturday,' the manager had candidly replied when asked what he meant. Well, that attitude wasn't good enough for anyone who wanted to keep working for Bradley T. Norris. The meeting usually ended around five, but Norris liked to stay behind; wander around the production lines; create the illusion among the workers that he was a twenty-four-hours-a-day man. If he was so keen, they should be, too.

It had been a good week for Shenandoah Inc. (UK). The new factory had exceeded production targets for the first time and was on course to go into the black, proving that the move to Britain from America had been a shrewd one. The anti-smoking lobby was almost as rabid here as in the States, and sales would be in decline were it not for aggressive marketing, but attractive incentives and a compliant labour force made this a good place to build a new plant. Eastern Europe, where sales were burgeoning, was barely the flick of a butt away, and the vast market of the Third World was yawning just over the horizon. There were no Surgeon General's warnings there, and *Made in England* was often more acceptable than *Made in USA*. The only cloud in the sky was a zealous politician on the campaign trail, but there might be ways to deal with him.

He'd wondered where Marina could be. She was good for his image and for the company's. She was young – more than twenty years younger than him – was glamorous and fashionable, and she smoked like a New England kipper factory. But when you said that, you'd said it all. He'd met her when she was a model, used by Shenandoah in a highly successful advertising campaign. They'd had to come to England to find her because there was nobody similar back home who could draw on a cigarette and make it look as if they were having a multiple orgasm. Her American counterparts were heavily into half-marathons and born-again virginity. Marina's pouting lips, wreathed in blue smoke, said volumes more than: 'My, this is a good cigarette.' The young and trendy fell for it, and so did the President of the company.

Norris had looked up the number of the private investigator someone had recommended, and left a message. Marina would take him to the cleaners, but it would be worth it. He'd sent for a taxi, and when the phone rang he'd assumed it was Security at the front gate, to say it was waiting for him, but it wasn't.

'Mr Norris?' the strange voice had enquired.

'That's right. What can I do for you?'

'I'm just ringing to tell you that your Rolls-Royce is at Burtonwood services, eastbound, on the M62. Could you collect it from there, please?'

'Why, sure. What's happened? Who is this?'

The voice had droned on, ignoring his questions. 'There'll be no charge for the Roller. You also have a wife, Marina. A good-looking lady, if you don't mind me saying so.'

Norris realised it wasn't the public services informing him of some inconvenience with his car. It was something far more sinister. 'Y-yes?' he stuttered.

'She, unfortunately, won't be in the Roller. If you want her back it'll cost you a hundred thousand pounds, cash. Cheap for a bird like that, I'd say, but we're not greedy. You get the money together, we'll be in touch on Monday. Oh, and don't call the police. If you do, I can't guarantee she'll stay in one piece.' *Click*.

Norris had stared at the silent instrument for a few seconds before replacing it. He'd taken a Red Wing from the ivory box on his desk and lit it with the solid gold, gas-fuelled reproduction Zippo lighter. He'd sunk back into his Texan leather chair, inhaled deeply for the first time in ten years and sent three perfect smoke rings spinning towards the ceiling.

Nothing had changed, he decided. His wife had disappeared, but there was no way that the police could link her with Harold. His plans were half-formed, and a lot depended on the people he would have to deal with, but there was no need to abandon those plans.

Norris busied himself with balance sheets and private accounts and wrote several cheques, the largest of which were to pay off Marina's credit cards. Then there was her bill from Town & County. He'd picked it up from the manager, Saturday morning, when he'd called in and surprised Security by asking to see the tapes from the twenty-four-hour surveillance cameras. He didn't have as long to wait as he'd expected. At two thirty-five the phone was ringing. 'Norris,' he said quietly.

After a long silence the same voice as before said: 'Did you get the money?'

'Yes.'

A longer silence. He was obviously disconcerted – a period of negotiation had been expected. 'All of it?'

'Yes. All of it.'

'Okay. Stay where you are.' He rang off.

Twenty minutes later he was back. 'What's the number for your portable phone?' Norris gave it. 'OK. Here's what happens. Nine o'clock tonight you put the money in the boot of the Roller and sit there waiting for us to call. Understood?'

'I understand.'

'And listen to this: the person who collects the money will only be a messenger. He won't know where your old lady is. So if I were you, I'd play ball. It's your only chance to get her back.'

So far, so good. They'd kept their word Friday night; now he'd find out if they could deliver the goods again. But the goods he had in mind didn't include Marina Norris.

It was raining, turning to sleet, as Bradley Norris placed a small bundle in the boot of the Rolls. The clock on the dashboard, which no longer had a tick to disturb the discerning driver, said five to nine. Six minutes later his phone rang.

'That you, Norris?'

'Yes.'

'Is the money in the boot?'

'Yes.'

'Good. Here's what you do. Drive south on the M6 to the Knutsford services. Park the Roller about two spaces away from the end of one of the rows of cars, pointing outwards. Know what I mean?'

'Yes, I think so.'

'Right. When you get there walk into the restaurant and order yourself a nice meal. Take at least an hour to eat it. Then go back to the car and drive home. OK?'

'Yes.'

'Good. I reckon you're about ten miles away, so be there in fifteen minutes. Any later and it's off. Understood?'

'I understand.'

'Oh, and you can leave the boot locked. We have a key.'

And he was gone.

The phone call was made by Frank Bell, the big one, and leader of the gang. He was the brains behind their schemes. He folded the little Motorola portable phone acquired earlier via a teenage car-thief and placed it in one of the pockets of the camouflage jacket he wore. 'He's on his way,' he said, looking at his watch.

The man seated beside him was similarly dressed, except his jacket bore the insignias of several crack regiments, not all of whom had fought on the side of the Allies in World War Two. He was called Shawn Parrott, and was further distinguished by his unprepossessing physiognomy. Parrott was only average height, but he had steel cables for sinews and a pair of hands like excavator shovels. He was the action man, the Mr Fix-it, the killer. The only emotion he'd felt when he blew Harold the chauffeur to Kingdom Come was inside his jeans, but that was his secret.

Norris, never a fast driver, made it well within schedule. He was fussing over the unfamiliar light switches and other controls when the phone rang again.

'Yes!' he barked into it.

'Our mistake,' said a new voice. 'Drive down to the next junction and back up the other side. Then follow the old instructions.'

Fifteen minutes later Parrott and Bell watched the Rolls creep tentatively into the northbound car park, feeling its way like a new rat in a laboratory maze. Norris turned down an aisle, then changed his mind and headed for the next one. He paused, saw a better space, and moved forward again. He drove through one bay and parked with the car pointing outwards, exactly as ordered. After a few seconds the lights extinguished and the door opened. The two men watched him walk purposefully towards the restaurant.

The third member of the gang was called Darren Atkinson. He'd followed the Rolls down the motorway in a battered Bedford van. He pulled into the space behind it and switched off the ignition with a screwdriver. Then the three of them left their vehicles and walked towards the toilets, Atkinson in front, Frank Bell and Shawn Parrott about fifty yards behind. They all had pees, without acknowledging each other, and walked back the way they'd come. They were confident the American wasn't under surveillance.

Frank Bell started the Sierra and drove it across the car

park, stopping next to the Rolls. Darren Atkinson was already lifting the boot-lid.

'Hurry up!' Bell urged him.

The upper half of Atkinson's torso vanished inside the cavernous boot of the Roller. He emerged holding the bundle, which was wrapped in a Town & County carrier bag. 'This is all there is,' he hissed.

'Are you sure?'

''Ang on.' He dived inside again. 'There's nowt else,' he declared.

'C'mon, then. Let's go.'

Atkinson jumped into the back seat of the Sierra and Bell let the clutch out. He drove quickly but without any visible fuss, careful not to attract attention. They left the stolen Bedford for the police to find.

Atkinson passed the package to Parrott, in the front seat. 'Bastard's done us, if you ask me,' he said.

Parrott fumbled with the wrapping until he reached the contents. 'What the fuck's this?' he cursed. He was holding a video cassette.

Bell, driving, looked across at it. 'What else is there?'

Parrott lifted a manila envelope out of the bag, stuffed full of something. 'This looks more like it,' he said, pulling a bundle of notes from it.

Bell eased the Sierra into the middle lane, keeping a careful eye on the speedo. 'What are they? Twenties?' he asked.

His partner-in-evil flicked through them. 'Yeah, all twenties.'

'Can't be more than a few thousand there. Anything else?'

Parrot groped around in the bag and found a sheet torn from an A4 pad. Printed on it in block capitals were the words: WATCH THE TAPE, THEN RING ME.

'Yeah,' he replied. 'He's sent you a fuckin' love letter.'

None of them owned a video machine. They drove slowly up the M6, towards the next junction.

'My mam's got one,' Darren told them.

'Where's she live?'

'Sutton Coldfield.'

'Fat lot of good she is, then. What about that bird of yours?'

'No, she sold it.'

'What about you, Shawn? Any ideas?'

'I'm thinking.'

'Well, hurry up about it.'

They'd reached the junction. 'Off 'ere,' Shawn ordered. 'Towards town.'

'Where are we heading?' Frank Bell asked.

'Just a friend's. Where I get the phones. He'd prefer it if you didn't know 'is name.'

Frank Bell smiled with satisfaction. At last he was going to meet the mystery man who supplied them with an endless supply of portable telephones and ringed cars. He needed Shawn Parrott for his connections in the underworld, but he didn't trust him any more. At one time, on the streets of Belfast, he had preferred to have Shawn guarding his back rather than anyone else, but now he wasn't so sure. There, the lines of authority were clearly defined, but now they were blurring at the edges. Shawn Parrott was growing cocky, and that meant dangerous.

They drove up the Chester Road, past Old Trafford and picked up the Stretford Road. Parrott's directions were terse. 'Straight on,' or: 'Right 'ere,' were the limits of his communications.

'Maybe you should ring him,' Bell suggested.

'Yeah, lend me the phone.'

Bell removed it from an inner pocket and handed it over. The contact was at home.

'Hi, it's Shawn.' The other two listened to half of the conversation. 'Do you have a video-player?' 'We have a video we need to watch.' 'It's important.' 'Fuckin' important.' 'I don't know what sort of video.' 'Thanks. I've got the Skipper with me. Do you mind?' 'Cheers. We'll be there in five minutes.'

He closed the phone and handed it back. 'He said it's OK. Turn right 'ere.'

Frank Bell swung the car round the corner, down a narrow street of workers' cottages whose doors opened directly on to the pavement. The mill-owner obviously hadn't expected his tenants to have the time or energy for even a minimal amount of gardening. He'd never dreamed that one day they'd all own cars, but now the streets were lined on both sides with parked vehicles of every size, colour and economic status. A good-looking black girl was standing under a street-light. She was wearing hot pants over suspenders and stockings. Sprayed on a wall was the message: *Welcome to Moss Side*.

Parrott wasn't sure of the house. They drove right round the block and up and down several similar streets, past the black girl again, before he said: 'This is it.'

'You stay in the car,' Bell told Darren. 'Any problems, drive off and come back in half an hour. And stay away from the tom.' They stepped between the parked cars and pressed the doorbell.

It was answered by a man of mixed race, much younger than them. He was pale-skinned, but his curly hair and facial features revealed his family history. 'Hi, man,' he said, beaming, as he and Shawn exchanged a 'gimme five' handshake.

'This is the Skipper,' Shawn said.

'Frank,' said Bell. 'Pleased to meet you.'

'Hello, Frankie. Come in. Make yourselves at home.'

They went through into a sitting room. It was furnished with a big suite covered in flowered material, and a pair of massive hi-fi speakers, from which a drum rhythm thumped like an overdose. A peroxide-blonde girl was sitting on the settee.

'Business, sweetheart,' he said to her. 'Can you find yourself something to do?' She stood up and sulkily left the room. 'Now, what's this about a video?'

Shawn handed it to him. He examined it, as if expecting its outside appearance to betray its message. 'How are you getting on with the phones, Frankie?' he asked.

'OK. No problems. You do a good job for us.'

'Which one are you using?'

Bell removed it from his pocket and showed it to him.

'Oh, that one. Nice little job. How many times have you used it?'

'Five, maybe six. Just short calls, though.'

'Mmm. Better let me swap it for a re-programmed one. They're getting better all the time at putting a stop on them.'

'Thanks.'

'I see you're still using the Sierra.'

'Yeah.'

'Got a nice Cosworth in the pipeline, if you're interested. Full set of paperwork. Belonged to a dentist in London.'

'Not at the moment, thanks. Can we see the video?'

'Sure. It's part-way through. Do you want to watch it from the beginning?'

'Er, no. From where it is now.'

'OK. Here we go.'

He thumbed the remote control. There was the usual snowstorm of noise on the screen, then it cleared to show a stretch of pavement and road, wet with rain. Vehicles and pedestrians moved silently across the picture, and an occasional figure turned towards the camera, looming large before disappearing beneath it. Frank Bell and Shawn Parrott leaned forward, hypnotised by the flickering image.

A Rolls-Royce came from the right, and stopped in the centre of the screen. An old lady pulling a shopping basket on wheels was in the foreground. She turned, as if to speak to the chauffeur as he walked round the car to open the rear door, letting the elegant figure of Mrs Marina Norris out on to the pavement.

'What shit's this?' Frank Bell cursed through his teeth.

Shawn Parrott sat like a statue, his ugly face slowly turning the colour of bird droppings. 'You said there wasn't no fuckin' camera,' he hissed at Bell.

'There wasn't. They must have put a new one in.'

They watched Harold the chauffeur get back into his seat, and a few seconds later a pair of legs appeared at the top of the screen. As they approached, the unmistakable figure of Parrott was slowly revealed. The camera zoomed in on his face.

'Oh man! Oh man-oh-man!' the owner of the video machine sniggered, slapping his knee. 'Ha ha! If you could see your face. I don't know what you've been doing, Shawn, old buddy, but I'd say someone has you bang to rights.' He fell back into his chair clutching his sides with laughter.

Shawn wasn't amused. He was aware that Mrs Norris would be able to give a description of him, but the rantings of an hysterical woman were worthless compared to this. It was a picture of his face, in close-up. He'd be identified within hours.

Outside, the black girl had wandered across to talk to Darren in the car. He wound the window down and leered at her. 'Hello,' she said. 'I could make a nice white boy like you very happy. Asda prices.'

She'd been beautiful, once, but now had a livid scar from her left ear to the corner of her mouth. Darren shuddered at the sight – he'd heard scars like that called Jamaican telephones. 'Sorry, love. I'm just the driver,' he said.

'Some other time, maybe?'

'Yeah. Definitely.'

They were exchanging good-natured banter when the other two spilled out of the house. 'I said leave the tom alone,' Frank Bell snapped at him as he climbed into the front passenger seat and slammed the door. Darren shrugged his shoulder at the girl and wound up the window. As they drove away she saw the pale face of Parrott, in the back seat, turn and watch her until it was lost in the reflections of the street-lamps. There was something in his look that she recognised, and she pulled her thin jacket tighter around herself, as if it would keep out the fear, as well as the cold.

Chapter Three

There were about twenty of us at Tuesday morning's big meeting. Superintendent Gilbert Wood outlined the strategy and progress so far, leaving Acting DI Newly to fill in the details. I think my chief purpose was to keep the Assistant Chief Constable off his back.

The body was now positively identified as Harold James Hurst, aged thirty-nine. He'd been shot at close range with a single bullet to the back of the head, and little attempt had been made to conceal the body. A retired couple out for a walk in the woods had heard what sounded like a shot at about three o'clock on the Friday afternoon, and that tied in with the pathologist's estimate of ToD.

The tyre tracks and the bullet, found in the mud underneath him, proved that he'd been brought to Heckley in the Rolls, alive, and killed where he lay. It was a long way to come, and somebody obviously had local knowledge. Straws like that can be important. I told everybody about my little talk with Mr Norris and my visit to the Royal Cheshire Hotel. We agreed that finding his wife, and her boyfriend, was a priority.

I didn't feel terribly well, probably due to overeating on an empty stomach. After the meeting, Nigel despatched the troops and I wrote the reports that I'd intended doing before Annabelle rang. I tagged them for the computer and concentrated on reading the print-outs to see if anything leapt off the page in a blaze of clarity. Nope, just the usual spelling mistakes.

Gilbert came up behind me and put his hands round my throat.

'Aargh! The Profiterole Strangler strikes again!' I croaked.

He gave me a shake and moved round to sit next to me. 'So what did the doc say?' he asked.

I shoved the print-out away and downed my last drop of coffee. 'Nothing. I couldn't get through.'

'Did you try picking the phone up?'

'OK, so I haven't tried. Shove it over.' I looked up the number in my diary and two minutes later I had an appointment to see Sam Evans at his Wednesday-evening surgery.

'Bet you feel better already,' Gilbert said.

Bradley Norris was watching CNN news at home when the next call came, more or less as he'd expected it. He'd guessed that they would take all night to digest his message, and smiled with grim satisfaction. He was beginning to read their minds, know what they'd do before they did. It was a technique that had served him well in thirty-five years of business.

He waited until an item analysing the fiscal situation amongst the Pacific rim countries had concluded – it took twelve seconds from start to finish – and picked up the phone.

'Norris here,' he said benignly.

'What do you want?'

'Ah, hi there. I'm so glad you called. I want to do business.'

'What sort of business?'

'Big-money business – what other sort is there? The goods I left you were a gesture of good faith – I could have you in the can by tomorrow, if I wanted. I think we ought to meet.'

'Where?'

'That's up to you. You're calling the shots.' The smile returned. No, they weren't – *he* was calling the shots.

'We'll ring you back.'

He'd expected it to be a short phone-call, if they were smart. It's possible, by triangulation techniques, to trace the approximate location of a mobile phone. They might think he was setting them up.

An hour later they were back on. 'We meet in Liverpool. Cunard Road, near the back of your store. There's a big pub on the corner, called the Empress of Canada. Be in there about three o'clock. Should be quiet then.'

'Good. You don't waste time. I like that.'

'See you then.'

''Bye.'

Norris chuckled. Already they were saying polite farewells to each other. He watched an item about the movements of players between baseball teams, then wandered down to the kitchen to tell his housekeeper that he would be in for lunch.

At exactly three o'clock the Rolls-Royce slid to a standstill in a sidestreet off Cunard Road. 'Wait here, please, er, Ron. I don't think I'll be too long,' Norris said.

'It's Rod, sir,' said his new chauffeur, sent by the agency. He had lank greasy hair and an earring. Norris was determined that their relationship would be a short one.

'Rod, right,' he said.

As before, he was in the wrong place. It wasn't the sort of establishment he would have dreamed of entering normally, and he didn't feel safe, even though it was nearly empty.

He'd ordered a pint from the unshaven landlord when the phone behind the bar rang.

'Norris? I'll ask,' he heard the landlord say into it.

'That's me,' Norris told him, and the landlord passed the phone across.

'Make it the Blackamoor,' said the voice. 'Turn left out of the door, it's about a quarter of a mile. The beer's better there.'

Norris paid for the pint and apologised to the barman for being unable to stay to drink it. 'You have it,' he suggested.

'Cheers,' the barman said to his retreating back, and downed it in one long draught.

The Blackamoor was more intimate. Lunchtime drinkers had staggered back to their employment and only a couple of heavy-session regulars leaned on the ornate Victorian bar. An old man in a flat cap sat at a table near the window, studying the racing page of a tabloid, a hardly-touched glass of Guinness in front of him.

Norris gazed round in a mixture of appreciation and disdain as the landlord pulled him another drink. He registered the contrast between the gleaming glass, copper and brass of the bar, and the shabby brown and green of the public areas. This was what he regarded as a typical English pub: quaint and interesting, but also inefficient, unhygienic and a waste of a prime site near the city centre. He carried his beer to a table in a corner and sat facing the room.

A man in an Army surplus jacket came in and ordered an orange juice, leaning on the bar. He looked familiar. After five minutes, when his glass was not quite empty, he walked over and sat at Norris's table.

'Mr Norris?' the man asked.

Norris thought that a man this ugly should be capable of anything. Anything out of step with the norms of society was what he meant, and he was a good judge of character.

'Yes,' he replied. 'Who are you?'

The man shook his head and drained the dregs of his orange juice. 'It doesn't matter,' he said.

'Would you like another drink?'

'No.'

'Right. So are you interested in this job I have for you?'

'Save it.'

'Pardon?'

'Save it.'

'I don't understand.'

'Save it for the Skipper. I'm just a piece of cheese.'

'A piece of cheese? I'm afraid I'm still no wiser.'

'Bait in the trap. In case this is a set-up.'

Realisation dawned on Norris. 'Oh, I see. No, it's not a trap. I'm totally alone.'

The man in the Army jacket, Shawn Parrott, sat in sullen silence. Norris said: 'You must be very loyal to the Skipper, taking a risk like this.'

'He's a good bloke.'

Norris examined the insignias on the ex-Army jacket and pondered on the wearer's conflicting loyalties. He looked for a common denominator, and after a few seconds he found it. Violence.

'Were you a soldier?' he asked.

'Yeah.'

Norris's own military service consisted of two years in the National Guard, marching up and down a schoolyard in Richmond, Virginia, at weekends, courtesy of having a grandpa in the Senate. 'I was in Korea,' he lied. 'Fighter pilot. Flew fifty-seven missions.' He briefly wondered if fifty-seven had been a convincing choice.

Parrott showed a flicker of interest, but didn't follow it up with conversation. Norris dived in with a question: 'So which regiment were you with?'

Parrott stiffened, his head erect and shoulders clicking back. 'The SAS,' he boasted.

'Wowee!' Norris sounded impressed. 'The tough guys. Boy, they're the crack regiment of the British Army. Were you with them when they did the Iranian Embassy Siege? That was really something.'

Parrott looked embarrassed. 'No, I, er, wasn't with them long. They wanted me. Came top of my selection group, but my mob wouldn't release me. I qualified for them, though.'

He's a bigger liar than I am, Norris thought. He had the measure of his man now: he was a turkey, a turkey with the scruples of an alligator.

'Oh, what a shame,' Norris sympathised. 'That doesn't seem fair. Your own mob must have needed you pretty bad.'

'Yeah.'

'Who were you with?'

'The Paras.'

'The Parachute Regiment! Well, they've got to be some of the finest soldiers in the world. Did you see the siege on TV?'

Parrott was grinning now. 'Yeah! And seen it on video. They were crap. Did it all wrong. I'd have been in twice as quick,' he enthused. 'In and out, no survivors. Got what they deserved.'

'What do they call that,' Norris asked, 'when they come swinging down the buildings?'

'Abseiling,' Parrott blurted out, eager to impress. 'Anyone can do that, it's dead easy.'

'Jeez, I couldn't do it. Would you believe it –' he leaned over and tapped Parrott on the arm '– I'm an ex-jet jockey and I'm scared of heights?'

They laughed, like two old buddies sharing a joke.

Norris had noticed two new customers come into the bar.

One of them was big, and had a military bearing about him, with neatly-cropped hair. The newcomer had slowly consumed a pint of beer, while possibly surveying them through the ornate mirrors that decorated the wall behind the bar.

Parrott got to his feet and said: 'I'm going now.' As he walked away Norris noted that he had a slight limp.

The newcomer came over and sat with Norris. Norris said: 'You don't take chances. I like that.'

'Can't afford to. You said you wanted to talk business.'

'That's right. First of all, do you have a name?'

'Frank.'

'OK, Frank. Your buddy thought that I might be setting you up. How do I know that you aren't doing the same to me?'

'You don't, so let's cut the crap. We've got your wife; you've got a video showing Shawn in all his glory. Let's call it stalemate.'

Norris gestured with his thumb after the vanished figure of Parrott. 'Is that your buddy's name, Shawn?'

'That's what he calls himself.'

'He looks some mean hombre.'

'He is. So what's this business you need doing?'

Norris finished his beer and placed the glass back on the table. He studied it for a few seconds, adjusting its position so that it fitted neatly into the pattern of the tiles. 'Was Shawn really in the SAS?' he asked.

Frank Bell shook his head. 'No, they wouldn't have him.'

'Why?'

Bell smiled for the first time. 'Too violent for them,' he replied.

'I can believe it. What happened to his face?'

'That? Oh, he was mixed up in a riot in Belfast. Silly prat was off-duty. He'd infiltrated the other side and was right there with them, confronting the troops. We let go with a few baton rounds – plastic bullets – and Shawn caught one, full in the face. It should have killed him; blinded him at least. He just shook his head, grabbed two of the ringleaders by the throat, and dragged them across to our lines.'

'Jeez. Did they give him a medal?'

'No. Thirty days in the cooler.'

'Now ain't that just typical of you Brits. So I'd be correct in saying that Shawn has a chip on his shoulder?'

'Yep. A bloody big one. Shawn has a dream. Do you know what it is?'

'Go on.'

'One day, he says he's going to do something so bad that they'll lock him up and bury the key. He'll spend his declining years in jail, watching TV and basking in his reputation. He calls it his pension plan.'

'Wow! But he'd follow you through thick and thin?'

'He's saved my life, more than once.'

Norris nodded his approval. 'So what's your main line of business, Frank?'

'Import and export. Mainly import.'

'Bit like me, eh?'

'More than you'd imagine, Mr Norris.'

'Ah ah! I know what you mean. People want a little fun, a little . . . stimulation. We fill the need. That's what I call good business.'

'Except that you operate within the law.'

'So far, Frank. So far. But times are changing.' He leaned forward and lowered his voice. 'I want someone removing, Frank. You know – permanently.'

'I guessed you might. Anyone we know?'

'A politician. A famous politician. How do you think we should go about it?'

Bell pursed his lips and whistled softly with concentration. This was the kind of big-league contract he'd always wanted. He'd spent many a sleepless hour planning such a thing. 'First of all,' he said, 'I'd create a smokescreen.'

'A smokescreen? Why?'

'Remember Kennedy?'

'Sure, I remember JFK.'

'Oswald was unlucky. Or betrayed. With all this shit that's been created about a conspiracy, he could have got clean away with it. Another few hours and he would have done. The FBI would have been chasing Cubans, the KGB, the mafia, the . . .' Bell waved his arm in the air, thinking of likely suspects '. . . the Teamsters, everybody and his dog, while the lone gunman sat at home watching it on TV, sipping a Budweiser.'

Norris was impressed. 'That's an interesting theory, Frank. What about doing the actual deed?'

'Ah, that's the hard bit. Somehow, you've got to know where he's going to be at a certain time. That means surveillance, which can be dangerous. And expensive,' he added as an afterthought.

'Not necessarily so, Frank,' Norris told him. 'Mightn't it be possible to control his movements, call the shots, get him where you wanted him?'

'How could you do that?'

'I've a few ideas. So far you haven't asked what's in it for you. I like that in a man, Frank, but I want it to be worth your while.'

'So, what's in it for us?'

'I'm glad you asked. First of all, Shawn gets to show the SAS that anything they can do, he can do better. Something really spectacular. For you, Frank, how about a million pounds cash – payment on delivery?'

Bell inhaled audibly. 'Jesus. I'd say you had a deal, Mr Norris.'

'Good. Good. We all need a pension plan, y'know. You

and me also. This could be ours. With a million pounds, minus a few expenses, you could set yourself up nicely. Either live fairly modestly for the rest of your life, or go for the big one. I can't really see you settling down, Frank. What's the profit margin in your line of importing? About five thousand per cent? With your enterprise you could soon make that million into fifty million.'

Bell sat back in his bentwood chair, head nodding slowly. Fifty million sounded better. Much better. This was what he'd been waiting for. 'So when do we start?' he asked.

Norris had read his man correctly: make the numbers obscene enough and you could hook anyone. He said: 'Welcome aboard, Frank. We won't shake on it, here in the pub. Look too conspicuous. The two thousand in the envelope was for immediate running expenses. As you can imagine, raising money like that isn't easy – I have accountants and auditors to deal with. If you need any more I can advise you on a simple way of stealing a certain highly marketable commodity. I'm insured, so it'll be no skin off my ass.'

Bell had been struggling to suppress his elation, but was suddenly looking grave. 'There's just one point, Mr Norris,' he said. 'Your wife, Mrs Norris. Shawn was a bit rough with her. She's all right, but can we be sure, when we bring her back, that—'

Norris raised a hand, silencing him. 'Sorry, Frank,' he interrupted. 'Did I forget to mention that? Part of the deal is that Mrs Norris *doesn't* come back. Let's call it a gesture of seriousness of intent. Oh, and I'd prefer it if there wasn't a body. I won't be in a hurry to marry again, and I hate funerals. Give me a ring when it's all over, then we'll do some serious planning.'

He stood up and walked out, back to his chauffeur-driven

limousine, and Shenandoah Inc., and his big, quiet house in Lymm.

I'd fallen into the juggling act again. Private life and work were up in the air, with me wondering which to catch and hold on to. Last night Annabelle had been her usual understanding self, and that made me feel a hundred times worse. She'd cooked spring chicken *bonne femme*, with new potatoes. In January! The fish and chips had blunted my appetite, and I struggled with it, even though it was one of the best meals I'd had in years and I refused a helping of apple pie for the first time in my life. Annabelle hid her disappointment, but I could sense it.

A quick result would solve my problems, but it was looking doubtful. Nigel was over in Liverpool, trying to arrange a reconstruction of Hurst's last movements, using Norris's Roller. Maybe somebody's memory would be jogged. After that he was visiting the widow. At this end of the enquiry we were still knocking on doors. Heads were being shaken and lines drawn through lists of addresses. Nobody had noticed a luxury limousine being driven up a cart-track, and mud-spattered Rolls-Royces are as common as pink flamingos around Heckley. Maybe we'd have better luck at the Burtonwood services on Friday, but I doubted it.

Poor Harold Hurst's death had all the hallmarks of a gangland killing, but we couldn't find the links. His lifestyle was modest and his friends few. Nobody knew much about him and fewer cared. Maybe he saw or heard something while he was driving Norris around. Something to do with the disappearance of Mrs Norris. I was certain that our investigations should be concentrated around Bradley T. Norris, and Shenandoah Incorporated, until Gilbert walked into the office like Neville Chamberlain, waving a piece of paper.

It was a fax from our ballistics boffins in Huntingdon. The

bullet that passed through Hurst's head had travelled down the barrel of an AK47 Kalashnikov, as we thought. The news was that it was a decent match with a similar one that had despatched a suspected IRA informer to the big shindig in the sky, in Belfast in 1988. A sudden piece of information like that is usually just the breakthrough you have been waiting for. Our euphoria didn't last long, though. We soon realised that it only heaped confusion upon confusion. Gilbert rang Special Branch and I decided to have a relapse.

Like ten million prisoners before her, Marina Norris made another mark on the wall with the heel of her shoe. She'd felt stupid when she did it for the first time, but quickly realised it was the only way she could measure the passing of the days. She counted the marks, touching each with the tip of a chipped enamel fingernail. Saturday, Sunday, Monday, Tuesday. They'd said she might be freed Tuesday, if her husband played ball.

She'd nearly choked to death in the boot of the Sierra. Each time the car had accelerated or braked she'd rolled one way or the other, unable to brace herself with her hands and legs pinioned. She was certain Harold was dead, and that she soon would be.

Eventually they'd arrived, and she was dragged and carried into a building with linoleum on the floor and smelling like a house from her childhood. A dirty, unpleasant house. They went through another door and down some stone steps.

She'd felt a blow, not fierce this time, and fallen backwards into a soft armchair. They'd unfastened her hands and ripped off the gag. There were two of them, and they were wearing masks – balaclavas – with holes to see through. Marina had seen similar ones on television, worn by terrorists and protestors and bank robbers in second-rate films. If they don't want me to see them, she'd thought, they mustn't intend to kill me; and she'd begun sobbing, partly from fear of what their intentions might be, partly from relief.

As they'd turned to leave her, the door at the top of the stairs had opened and she'd seen the third member of the gang standing there. He wasn't wearing a mask, and she recognised him as the man with the ugly face who had kidnapped her. He threw her shoes down into the cellar and held the door open for the other two. A key turned and bolts slid across. She'd stared down at the shoes with their four-and-a-half inch heels, and was for the first time struck by their ridiculousness.

They fed her ham sandwiches, which she hardly touched, and sweet milky tea. The cellar was large, with newly whitened walls, and reminded her of the one at her grandma's in Croydon, where she'd lived for a year after her mother died. She'd escaped from that prison, she told herself, but this one was different. There was nobody here to help her; these men were looking for different rewards.

On the second day she'd had to use the Elsan toilet, and had dragged it under the stairs, where she couldn't be watched through the peephole in the door. The two in the masks were relatively OK, and she'd even struck up a rapport with the thin one, who was definitely number three in the pecking order. She'd asked him for another blanket and a towel, and he'd brought them. But the ugly one scared her. Each time the door opened and she saw it was him something inside her would turn to ice. He'd put the food on the dirty little coffee table and stand looking at her, wet-lipped and slack-mouthed. She'd feel his eyes fumbling with the buttons of her blouse, then with her bra strap, and item by item her clothes would drop to the floor. Then he'd give a little smile and walk awkwardly back to the stairs.

According to her wristwatch, matching partner to her husband's, it was ten o'clock Tuesday morning. She washed in bottled water and rinsed her underwear as best she was able to. She was curled up on the sagging settee that was the only other item of furniture, waiting for her body heat to dry her clothes, when the door opened. It was the thin one, thank God. She straightened her legs and sat up.

'Ham again,' he told her, apologetically.

'Thank you.'

He picked up her plate from last night and turned to go. Mrs Norris said: 'They said I might be released today. Do you know if I'm going to be?'

'Dunno. Might be.'

'When will you know?'

'When they come back.'

'The other two?'

'Yeah. They're, er, negotiating, like.'

'With my husband?'

'Yeah.'

'So I could be released today?'

'Could be.'

'Oh, thank God for that.'

She tried talking some more to him, but he was cagey, and sensed that he'd said too much already. Marina ate one piece of bread from the sandwich and drank the tea. For years she'd taken her tea without either milk or sugar, but there was something strangely comforting in the sickly brew she'd been given.

It was just after eight p.m. when the bolts on the door were slammed back, startling her from her torpor. It was the ugly one, and he meant business. Marina struggled to control her bladder.

'C'mon, on yer feet,' he ordered.

She pulled on her high heels and teetered unsteadily

across the floor and up the steps towards him. 'About time,' she said defiantly.

He grabbed a fistful of her hair and steered her through a big farmhouse kitchen and outside into the frosty night. He pulled so tightly she could feel her skin stretching in the corners of her eyes. 'You're . . . hurting . . . me,' she protested to his indifferent ears.

She was bundled into the boot of the Sierra, bashing her shins and finishing off what remained of her tights. The big one, who she had decided was the leader, was holding the boot-lid open, but this time he wasn't wearing a mask. The cataract of thoughts cascading through her head concluded that they must have come to some sort of arrangement with her husband. At least they hadn't tied her up for this journey.

It was a fast trip, all hard braking and tyres squealing round the corners. Soon she realised they were on a bumpy dirt-track, like last time. They were doing things in reverse, unwinding the nightmare – maybe her next ride would be in the Rolls-Royce. They stopped. She heard the two front doors slam shut and a few seconds later the boot-lid lifted.

The rear lights were still on, and she saw her two kidnappers standing over her, illuminated by the scarlet glow, like figures from the Inquisition. Behind them the branches of the trees were etched against the starry sky, and Shawn was holding the big gun that she was sure he'd shot Harold with.

They weren't taking her home. They were going to kill her.

'No!' she screamed. 'No! No!'

Bell tried to grab her legs but she was kicking them wildly, and punching at Parrott with her feeble fists. Bell hung on to one leg but couldn't get the other within his grasp. Mrs Norris's short skirt rode up over her hips as she twisted and fought with them.

'Cor! What a waste,' Parrott grinned, the Kalashnikov in

one hand as he wrestled her with the other.

'Grab her!' Bell hissed.

Parrott brushed aside Mrs Norris's death struggles as if he were dealing with a stroppy toddler, and his big mechanical-grab of a hand closed round her throat.

She kicked, and then twitched, for nearly a minute, with Parrott holding her down one-handed as effortlessly as restraining a playful puppy; the big Russian-made gun in his other hand, its butt languishing on his hip.

When she was still, and the spark had gone from her bulging eyes, he let go and straightened up. His own eyes were glistening with excitement; she was dead, but he'd never, ever, felt more alive.

He gazed, panting for breath and flexing the fingers of his right hand, at the pale limbs draped across the back of the car, like a broken swastika. 'I still say it's a fuckin' waste,' he mumbled.

Bell slapped him on the shoulder. 'I know, old pal. But we don't work like that. I'll get the carpet.'

Parrott grasped her wrists to pull her from the car and his fingers brushed over the watch she wore, partner to her husband's. Bet that's worth a bob or two, he thought, and slipped the expanding bracelet over her hand. He dropped the watch into one of his jacket pockets and buttoned down the flap.

They were on the edge of a municipal landfill site. Every day a procession of lorries brought a city's rubbish here, where it was tipped into a disused quarry and bulldozed and compressed back into the earth from whence all things come. They rolled the body of Mrs Marina Norris, born Miriam Scully, into an old carpet, and one-two-three-heaved her into the quarry. One day, in the distant future, she would briefly warm someone's life again, as a couple of therms of methane gas.

Chapter Four

I needed a haircut, a new pair of shoes and a talk with Marina Norris's boyfriend. The first two could wait. After the morning meeting I drove over to Northwich and tucked myself into a corner of the Royal Cheshire's car park. It had been a frosty night, and as I drove over the Tops the sun was driving the last of the mist away. The moors were etched like crystal, poking up through wraiths of cloud in the valleys, and I'd much rather have been tramping across them.

I was early, so could observe the build-up of the hotel's lunchtime trade. The guests appeared two-by-two, like the animals entering the Ark. Often it was an overweight gentleman in a suit accompanied by an attractive young lady with an infatuated, if slightly embarrassed, smile. The driving force was the same as that exploited by Noah: 'Mummy, what does a girl have to do to get a mink?' 'The same as a mink has to do.' I had that unhappy feeling that one day, when I look back on my life, I'll see a big hollow. It's called jealousy. I amused myself by ringing their numbers through to Heckley nick and checking them against the PNC, and soon had a list of potential blackmail victims as long as the Latvian national anthem. Maybe I could afford to retire, after all.

The Daimler swished into the car park just after noon.

He drove round a couple of times, as if looking for someone, then created an extra parking place for himself nearer to the front entrance than anyone else. That's when I decided I didn't like him.

He sat waiting for over half an hour. I saw his shoulders hunch, and thought he was about to get out, but the car's reversing lights came on and it began to move backwards. He'd realised she wasn't coming. I started my engine and streaked down the car park, wincing as gravel rattled under the wings. I reached the exit before he did and swerved across it, blocking it off. He stopped, and I walked over to him.

The police computer had confirmed that he hadn't lied about his name in the hotel register, but had given a false address. I showed him my warrant card and said: 'DI Priest, East Pennine Police. Are you Reginald Arthur Smith?'

He was probably in his late thirties, already podgy around the jowls, with two days' growth of beard and a pair of dark glasses. He looked like Yasser Arafat after an all-nighter.

'Er, that's right,' he replied, shaken.

'I'd like a word with you. Could you please park your car over there.'

I parked alongside him and told him to get into my passenger seat. By now he'd gathered his wits and started saying that he was in a hurry and would this nonsense take long?

'Why did you come to the Royal Cheshire today?' I asked.

'I had a business appointment,' he replied.

'Who with?'

'I can't tell you that. It's a commercial secret.'

'Was it the same person you saw last Wednesday, and all the Wednesdays before that?'

'I don't know what you're talking about.'

I turned on him. 'Listen, Mr Smith,' I told him, my face close to his. 'I'm investigating a serious crime. I'm not from the morality police and I don't give a toss about your little peccadilloes. I could take you down to the nearest nick and do a taped interview, and I could ask the bar staff at this overpriced knocking shop if they recognise you. Alternatively, you could give me some answers right here, then maybe we could both go home. So who are you supposed to be meeting?'

His suit was a fashionable three sizes too large for him and his shirt didn't have a collar. He put a hand inside his jacket and scratched his armpit. 'A woman,' he said. 'I can't tell you her name.'

I rolled my eyes. 'I've driven fifty miles to meet you, Mr Smith. Do you think I don't know her name? I'd just rather have you tell me first and not me ask you to confirm it. So would I be right in saying her initials are MN?'

'Well, yes.'

'So tell me. Mar . . . Mar . . . Maree . . .' I prompted.

He nodded. 'OK, you obviously know who she is. Mrs Norris – Marina.'

'Thank you. How long have you known her?'

He shuffled about uncomfortably and asked: 'Is this to do with her chauffeur?'

'What can you tell me about him?'

'Just what I read in the papers. I never met him.'

'Did Mrs Norris ever mention him?'

He shook his head. 'No.'

'So how long have you known Marina?'

He let out a long sigh. 'Do you know who I am, Officer?' he asked.

'Reginald Arthur Smith?' I suggested. I was supposed to be asking the questions.

'Have you ever heard of Rats?'

'Rats?'

'Yes, Rats. I am Rats, the photographer. If you'd ever opened a newspaper loftier than the *UK News* you would be familiar with my work. I've photographed collections for all the big fashion houses, and taken several Royal birthday portraits.'

'You're a fashion photographer?'

'I do fashion work, yes.'

I'd heard of him, but not for a long time. The last time he'd merited a brief mention in the gossip columns was when he'd been outed as a bisexual. 'I'm afraid I usually ignore the fashion pages,' I confessed.

His eyes flickered over my jacket, slacks and rather nice Marks & Spencer's shirt in a blue lumberjack check. 'Yes,' he sighed.

'So how long have you known Mrs Norris?'

'A long time. Thanks to me, Marina was once the Face of the Year. I discovered her. She was only fifteen at the time, still at school. I'd just finished college. Girls with the right looks are ten-a-penny at that age, but to get to the top they need three things: ambition, dedication, and, above all, a sympathetic photographer. One who can see the real woman within, unlock the sexual creature waiting to blossom into—'

'OK, I get the message,' I interrupted. 'So you unlocked this sexual creature and she became famous and married a millionaire. When did your latest affair with her start?'

'You're pathetic!' The words exploded on me like one of those old-fashioned flashguns going off. 'You rub your nose in your grubby little world and think everybody is like you. You couldn't begin to understand how it was between Marina and me.'

'Then tell me.' I resisted mentioning that I'd been an art student myself – in the *sixties*. That would've rocked him.

'I've told you enough. Can I go now?'

I ignored the question, and decided some goading might provoke a reaction. I'd remembered something Nigel had written in his reports. 'Did Mr Norris know you were screwing his wife?' I asked.

The contempt overflowed. 'That's all you can imagine, isn't it, Officer. Two people meet, they screw. It's all you are capable of understanding.'

Nigel had called at Norris's home in Lymm, on the off-chance of not catching him there. He'd had a word with his domestic staff and was surprised to learn that the gardener knew all about Mrs Norris's assignations at the Royal Cheshire. He'd related in vivid detail Harold Hurst's account of rescuing her the previous week. Her eyes, Hurst had told the gardener, were black and sparkling, and she'd chatted all the way home.

'Seems reasonable to me,' I admitted. 'So what else did you get up to?'

'I'm not saying any more.' He folded his arms like a defiant Just William.

'Mr Smith,' I said, 'Mr Norris's chauffeur was murdered in a particularly brutal way. Mrs Norris vanished on the same day, hasn't been seen since. Have you any idea where she might be?'

'She's vanished?' He looked shocked.

'Didn't you know?'

'Of course not, how could I? I wouldn't have come here today if I'd known.'

'Didn't you try to ring her?'

'No. We only talk on the phone if we can't make it.'

'So you were expecting to see her today?'

'I'd have thought that was obvious.'

'Quite. So maybe now you'll tell me if Norris knew you were having an affair with his wife.'

'I resent your assumption, Officer, that I was having, as you so quaintly put it, an affair with Mrs Norris.'

'So what *did* you get up to, all afternoon?'

'You've a mind like a bloody cesspit!'

He was swearing now. That proved he was angry. Soon he'd be stamping a foot. I had an appointment to keep, so I cut it short. I said: 'Reginald Arthur Smith, also known, appropriately, as Rats, I'm arresting you on suspicions of carrying drugs. You don't have to say anything, however, it may harm your defence if you do not mention, when questioned, something which you later rely on in court. Anything you do say may be given in evidence. Do you understand?' I assumed that his open mouth and bulging eyes indicated the affirmative. 'Give me your car keys,' I told him. 'I'm taking you to the local station for an interview.'

'You . . . you . . . I want to ring my solicitor,' he gasped.

'You can do that from the station. And if you're a good boy, answer all our questions, tell us where you get your goodies from, I might be very kind and not charge you with having sex with a child. Put your seat belt on.'

He was carrying four spliffs and a couple of grammes of heroin. Mrs Norris's behaviour with Hurst had given him away. Once he realised we couldn't do him for indecent assault without a complaint from Mrs Norris he reverted to his normal uncooperative self, but it was all an act. The big investigation hadn't moved forward, but it was good to have an arrest, even if I did arrive home too late to keep my appointment with Doc Evans.

The little girl, nearly nine years old, sat on the edge of the bed, engrossed in watching her mother apply her make-up.

'Me, please,' she demanded, puckering her lips.

Mother reached across and with three deft strokes

converted the tight little rosebud into a gaudy dahlia. She blinked the surplus mascara from her eyes, checked that her false eyelashes weren't dislodged, and smoothed her short leather skirt.

'Will Uncle John be coming home with you?' the little girl asked.

'I don't know. But if he does I want you to stay in bed. Otherwise he won't leave you any sweeties. Understand?'

The little girl nodded gravely. She'd never met Uncle John, but he was very generous with the sweeties. She thought she would have liked him.

Mother did a twirl, arms outstretched. 'Ta da! How do I look?' she asked.

'Beautiful!' her daughter confirmed enthusiastically.

She pulled on a denim jacket that had a sequinned guitar and the word *Elvis* on the back. Woven into the pattern were several tiny light-emitting diodes that used to sparkle at random, but they had long since ceased to work.

'Right,' she said. 'Now I want you to be in bed by half past nine. No later, or it's no sweeties. And if little Joshua wakes up or starts to cry, dip his dummy in the sugar. All right, darling?'

The little girl nodded. All of a sudden she didn't want her mummy to go out and leave her; she stood with her head bowed.

Mother bent down and pecked her on the cheek. 'And turn the telly off before you go to bed,' were her last words.

Outside, she click-clacked on her highest heels along the concrete corridor and down the stairs of the block of flats. Five minutes later she was on the bus into town.

The pub where she began her evening's trade was nearly deserted. 'Match on,' the barman explained. 'Replay. Be packed later.' He gave her a half of lager and she dropped a pound coin into his hand. At the till he pressed the No Sale button and whanged the drawer back home. She reached out her painted fingers and he gave her the same pound coin back. A free drink brought the toms in, toms brought the punters in.

'Ta, love,' she said, and went to sit with the only other woman in the place.

The other woman was eight years older than her, but looked more like her mother. She confirmed what the barman had said about a football match. 'Thank God I've got a regular on Tuesdays,' she said. 'I warn you – don't get mixed up with any football 'ooligan. He'll probably 'ave ten mates waiting in a Transit van somewhere. Gang bangs is all right if they pay the going rate, but they'll just dump you on the motorway. It's all a joke to them.'

The first woman, who became Danielle as soon as she stepped across the threshold of her flat, shuddered. 'I don't like the sound of that,' she confessed.

They made their drinks last for over an hour. ''Ere's my regular,' the older woman told her as a little man came in. He was wearing a flat cap and a cardigan under his jacket. Danielle thought that he probably had something going with his meals-on-wheels lady and giggled at the thought.

The other woman read her mind and smiled. 'He's a good payer, love, and that's all I ask.' She stood up to leave, then leaned across and said: 'Mark my words about what I said. No football 'ooligans.' She nodded towards the bar. ''Ow about 'im in the Army jacket? 'E's interested, if you ask me. Seen 'im looking at you. Tara, love.'

Danielle had seen him too, and noted how ugly he looked. You didn't have to kiss them, though. Kissing was for friends, kissing was intimate. She went to the ladies' for a pee and to replenish her Youth Dew. She straightened her skirt, checked her image in the tarnished mirror, lifted her chin high and walked back out through the bar.

'Good night, Danielle,' the barman called after her, drawing the attention of the few men in the pub. If she pulled a trick he was in it for a fiver. If she didn't, and it was still raining at closing time, he might get a freebie in exchange for a lift home.

'Night, George,' she replied, and stepped out into the darkness.

The rain had turned to snow, but she'd only walked about two hundred yards when a red Sierra pulled alongside. The driver leaned across and the door swung open. It was him.

'It's twenty-five quid,' she said, settling beside him and pulling the door shut.

''Ow much without a rubber?' Shawn Parrott asked.

'I don't do it without no rubber.'

He nodded. 'Fair enough. You got a place?'

She made an instant decision. You have to, in her trade. 'No. Old man's at home. Do you know the glassworks?'

'I know it.'

'Go there. It's dead quiet.'

They parked in the deep shadows at the back of the abandoned factory. A thin film of snow was beginning to settle on the dereliction, muffling the roar of the traffic at the other side of the wall. Danielle stroked the back of his neck and raised one leg so that her foot was against the dashboard. 'Doesn't the snow look lovely,' she whispered, trying to inject some romance into the transaction.

'Get in the back seat,' Parrott responded.

They undressed the lower halves of their bodies and embraced. Parrott tried to kiss her, but she turned sideways and he roughly mouthed her ear. She went through the preliminaries like a robot, making moaning noises and arching her back as if this was the lover of her life in a cheap B-movie. Parrott's coat was draped over the back of the driver's seat and she explored it with her free hand. There was something in one of the pockets. She flicked the button open and delved inside. It was a watch, made from a warm smooth metal. It felt expensive. She put her arms more tightly around him, faking interest in his attentions, and slipped the watch over her wrist. That would do for a nice little bonus – she'd give this one his money's worth. Her hands wandered downwards, feeling for him, so she could help him enter her.

It was a disappointment. She was going to have to earn her fee tonight. 'Who's been working too hard?' she cooed. 'Relax, everything's all right.'

But it wasn't, and he didn't look the sort who'd pay her for nothing, even if it wasn't her fault. She poked her tongue in his ear and said: 'Tell me what you like best. Tell Danielle what turns you on.'

His hands fell to her waist and started to grope their way under her sweater. He's a tits man, she thought, with relief. He's just a bloody tits man.

But the big hands didn't stop at her breasts. They skimmed over them and up through the neck of her jumper.

'What do . . .?' she protested, as his fingers tightened round her throat, choking off the rest of the question and, a few desperate seconds later, the rest of her life.

Reginald Arthur Smith, better known as Rats, had the last laugh. He rang his agent as I drove him to the station and told her about Mrs Norris's disappearance. Next day, the *UK News*, known as *Yuk! News* to its enemies and emulators, claimed a front-page exclusive. A few weeks later they were to print the full Rats story, with pictures, allegedly paying him about twice my annual salary. I wouldn't care if I could sleep at nights, but I can't.

Gilbert banned me from the Thursday-morning meeting, telling me not to come back until I had a note from the doctor. He changed his mind as soon as he saw the story in the paper, and I spent the rest of the day with our press liaison people and talking to the media. I repeated: 'At this stage of our enquiries we have not established a link between the disappearance of Mrs Norris and the death of Harold Hurst,' until I almost believed it. Now that the story of the Vanishing Lady was public knowledge, we had to capitalise on it, so we asked for their help. Norris issued a statement about the stress he'd been under, appealed for anyone who knew anything to come forward, and fled to America on business.

Annabelle had never been to my house. I'd first met her about four years earlier, when she was newly widowed, and my clumsy advances were about as welcome as an old flame at a will-reading. Things were moving fast, though, and now we were getting on really well. But she couldn't forget that she was the widow of a bishop, and the thought of having a strange car parked on her drive all night, with the neighbours listening for some man scraping the ice off the windscreen before he left for work, really disturbed her. I didn't mind. I probably loved her all the more for it.

It would just have to be my house. And my house was a dump. I neglected it. The same way as I neglected everything except the job. The same way as I'd neglected my first wife, until she upped and left me. One of the reasons I'd thought about retiring, finding something else to do, was because I was determined not to make the same mistake twice.

It was a common-enough scenario. Maybe it's a special occasion – anniversary or birthday. A table is booked or someone has toiled over the stove all day. The clock says six p.m. and you are comforting a family whose home and life have been wrecked by burglars while they were at work. These people are strangers, and the person you love is waiting for you. The SOCO is on his way and you know he hasn't seen his kids for a week. You have to decide who to hurt, and it isn't easy.

I called in the DIY store and picked up some colour charts and a pack of vacuum-cleaner bags. At home I surveyed the task and decided that ruthlessness and military precision were called for. Stage one, throw away everything that hasn't been used or read in the last twelve months. I filled the wheelie-bin and a couple of plastic bags. Next I dusted, finishing off with the long pipe on the vacuum, reaching into all the crevices and corners, rendering several spiders homeless.

Finally I hoovered every carpet in the house. At ten o'clock I poured myself a well-earned shandy and looked around. The difference was unbelievable, and I resolved to keep up with it. Little and often, I told myself.

The phone rang just as I stepped into the shower. I dried my hands on one of the fresh towels I'd put out, leaving filthy marks on it, and dashed downstairs.

'Hello,' I said, trying to wrap myself in the towel using only one hand.

'Hello, Charles. It's Annabelle. Have you been out?'

'Hi, Superwoman! This is a pleasant surprise. No, I've been in all evening.'

'Oh. I've tried ringing several times, but there was no answer.'

'Sorry about that. I've had the vacuum on, catching up with my cleaning. It's a bit noisy.'

'What a pity. You should have given me a ring.'

'Why, would you have dashed round to help me?'

'No, but I could have loaned you a quieter vacuum.'

'Listen, lady,' I drawled into the phone. 'In any relationship there's only room for one comedian, and it's me. Understood?'

I heard her giggling at the other end, and in my mind I could see the dimples in her cheeks and her nose wrinkling in the way that gave me an unfamiliar ache in the sides of my jaw.

'Charles,' she said, stifling her laughter.

'Yes, ma'am?'

'I've rung to tell you that I think I've got a job.'

'A proper one, paying money?' She worked hard for her charities, but they didn't pay her anything and I knew she was having to be careful.

'Yes. With a salary.'

'Hey, that's good news. Congratulations. Tell me all about it.'

'Heard about it on the old girl network. Someone I know is pregnant, so she'll be taking maternity leave from April, and probably won't go back after the baby is born. And I can have her job. Guess what she does?'

'Er, test pilot at the supermarket trolley factory?'

'No. She's a researcher for Tom Noon.'

'The MP?'

'The one and only.'

'Wait a minute!' I demanded. 'Wait a minute! This MP's researcher is pregnant and now he wants you as her replacement. Over my dead body!'

'Have you seen him?' she laughed.

'Have you seen all the others?' I countered.

'Actually, he's a sweety, but I think you're safe.'

'Good. I'm happy for you. Well done. I'm a bit worried about your job security, though. They had to have about ten recounts at the election, didn't they?'

'Ah, yes. He won by sixty-two votes, but he overturned a government majority of nine thousand to win the seat.'

'Mmm. And the way things are going with this lot he'll probably wipe them out, next time.'

'Hopefully. But I haven't told you the best bit.'

I hitched the towel up again. 'You mean there's more?'

'Yes. Apparently he's a close friend of Andrew Fallon.'

'The Leader of the Opposition?'

'*We* prefer to call him the Prime Minister-in-waiting. They worked down a coalmine with each other, or something.'

'Nearly, but not quite. He was Fallon's fag at Eton.'

'Was that it? Well, when I told him about my Africa trip he said that Andrew would be very interested. One of Fallon's hobby horses is the exploitation of the Third World by the tobacco industry. He was a founder member of FATE, the Forum against Tobacco Exports, and is violently anti-smoking and everything to do with the industry.'

'I was wondering if this affected your Africa trip.'

'No problem. Or *hakuna matata*, as we say in Swahili. Mr Noon thinks I might be able to combine some research for Mr Fallon with my charity work; maybe even receive a little sponsorship. The thing is, I've been invited to Westminster in the near future, for an audience with them both. Isn't it exciting?'

'It sounds it. Listen, Annabelle, I'm really pleased for you. Maybe we should have a celebration.'

'Well actually, Charles, I was wondering about this trip to Cornwall. Do you think we could settle on some dates in the near future, just in case I'm asked when I can be available? If I'm still invited, of course.'

It was crunch time. Annabelle or the job? In the cold light of my kitchen it was no contest, but when I was back in the office, with the phone ringing and the paperwork piling up and a suspect waiting in an interview room, would I be able to turn my back on it? I've never been good at walking away from anything. I said: 'Right, I'll see what I can arrange. Oops! Hold on a second.'

'Charles? Are you all right?'

'Yes. Sorry about that. My towel slipped off.'

'Your towel?'

'Yes. You dragged me out of the shower.'

'You mean you are standing there with just a towel round your middle?'

'And it's a very small towel.'

'Ooh! I'd have come round if I'd known.'

'Annabelle,' I intoned in my most serious voice. 'Will you make me one promise?'

'Yes, Charles, if I can.' Now she sounded serious.

'Promise not to say anything like that again. Unless, of course, you mean it.'

'Oh. Yes. I promise.'

I was happy for her, but I was also struck by the unfairness of things. Annabelle had a better brain than anyone else I knew. As a seventeen-year-old she should have gone to Oxford, but worked in a refugee camp in Biafra instead, and later she'd mixed with the highest and the lowest in the land with equal grace. Noon and Fallon should have been working for her, not the other way round. She was worth more than the two of them added together.

Annabelle was tall and striking-looking. She created a bold impression, but she'd lived in someone else's shadow for too long. She undervalued herself. I resolved to do my best to steer her through the doldrums, and into the trade winds at the other side, even if they did blow her towards Africa. Who knows? Maybe I'd look good in a safari suit.

And then I wondered if her going out with the longest-serving Police Inspector in the North of England was a symptom of that same reticence, and that thought made me sad. When I closed the bedroom curtains I noticed the first flakes of snow sliding down the window.

★ ★ ★

I made it to my next appointment. Sam Evans, the Police Surgeon, peered at me over his half-spectacles and asked how I was.

'Me? I'm as healthy as an aardvark,' I replied. 'How are you?'

Sam looked in pain, as if his hernia had hiated. 'An aardvark? Why an aardvark?'

I smiled smugly at him. 'It was just the first thing that came into my encyclopaedic mind,' I said.

'I see,' he replied gravely, and made a note. I found it worrying, as if I'd just declared some irrefutable symptom. 'And how are you sleeping?'

'Sleeping?'

'Mmm. You know – put your head on the pillow and lose consciousness, that sort of thing.'

'Oh, so-so.'

'I take it that means not very well?'

'I've never been a good sleeper.'

'Mmm. Any more dizzy spells?'

'I didn't have a dizzy spell; I stumbled.'

'You fell down a flight of stairs, and told me afterwards that you'd had a dizzy spell.'

'I didn't think you'd attach so much importance to it.'

'Well, I do. Classic symptom of stress. There are others there, too.'

'What others?' I demanded.

'That's for me to know; I'm the doctor. How's your appetite?'

'Great. I eat everything that's put before me.'

'Good,' he said, nodding. 'So jump on the scales, let's have a look at your weight.'

'Aw, come on, Sam!' I protested. 'There's a murderer out there. I've been working a week – all I need is a note from you to make it official.'

'Get on the scales.'

I took my jacket off and stood on the scales, glowering at him. Sam moved the slider across. 'You've lost three pounds since last time,' he told me.

'I had my long johns on.'

We sat down again and Sam took a pad from a drawer and unscrewed the top of his fountain pen. He said: 'In my professional opinion you should have some more time off. But I'll leave it up to you. What do you think?'

I pursed my lips and drummed my fingers on his desk. I had the feeling that I was at a crossroads. 'You're right,' I admitted. 'Deep down, I know I'm not a hundred per cent, and when I'm like that I make mistakes.'

He started scrawling on the pad. 'Good. Glad you can see sense. You know what they say about the graveyard being full of indispensable men. This life isn't a practice run, Charlie, it's the real thing.' He slid the note across to me. 'Here, I've given you another four weeks. And I still think you ought to see the force's counsellor.'

'Thanks, but no thanks,' I replied, folding the note and putting it in my wallet.

'Fair enough.' He sat back, relaxing now that the formalities were over. 'So what will you do with yourself? Some more painting?'

'No, not really. Gilbert has offered me the loan of his cottage in Cornwall, so I might go down there for a couple of weeks.'

'Smashing, just what you need. Tell you what – why don't you invite that rather attractive lady that I've heard you're walking out with? Do you both good.'

'Gosh!' I exclaimed, clapping a hand to the side of my head. 'Why didn't *I* think of that?'

From the doc's I went straight round to Heckley police station. First call was in the typists', where I ran off a couple of photocopies of the sick note. I breezed into the CID office and handed them out. 'Sick notes,' I announced. 'Four weeks for ten quid. Guaranteed authentic, no offers.'

Dave Sparkington tilted his copy towards the light and studied it. 'Malingering? What's that?' he asked.

'Eh?' I examined the original. 'That says malignant,' I declared.

'Oh, that's all right, then.'

Nigel pushed away the papers on his desk and swivelled his chair round. 'Morning, Mr Priest,' he said. 'You're not really having another month off, are you?'

''Fraid so, Nigel, but from what I've heard you were coping quite well without me.'

'Coping isn't the word I'd have used, boss.'

'Improving? Succeeding?'

'Mmm, something like that.'

'Flourishing?'

'That's the word.'

'I see. I am suitably chastened. Still, it's nice to know the shop is in good hands. Tell you what, why don't you have a go at the budgets? That would really earn you some Brownie points with Mr Wood.'

'All done, boss.'

'Great. In that case, you could do next year's, while it's all fresh in your mind.'

'Done them.'

'Oh. Good. Good.'

'And last week we caught a sheep rustler, so that will please a few people.'

'Did you? Great.' I was feeling less wanted by the minute.

'How's Annabelle?' he asked.

'Whaddya mean, how's Annabelle?' I demanded.

Nigel, Acting Detective Inspector, blushed like a naturist

who'd walked into a naturalists' convention. He was saved by the telephone. After listening for a few seconds he waved a hand to hush the rest of us. He was making notes, but I couldn't read his hieroglyphics. 'OK,' he said, after a few minutes. 'We'll be over there as quickly as possible.'

He replaced the phone and looked at me. 'A woman's body was found in Liverpool early this morning,' he said. 'They started the PM about an hour ago and found she was wearing an expensive wristwatch. Solid gold. A local jeweller has said it could be worth ten thousand pounds. The bit that interests us is that it has the initials MN engraved on the back.'

'Marina Norris,' I said.

'Could be. Dave, you dig out the descriptions, and see if Mr Norris is in this country. I'll pop up to tell Mr Wood.'

They dashed off, going about their business, leaving me sitting there remembering the time I turned up for the Cubs only to discover that they'd all gone to the circus without me. I'd been away the previous week, when it had been organised, and nobody told me. I was nine years old.

As soon as the dust settled I trudged upstairs to see Gilbert Wood, my Superintendent. 'Hello, Charlie,' he said. 'Put the kettle on as you're passing.'

I tested the kettle's weight, decided it was full enough and flipped the switch.

'Have you heard the news?' he asked.

'Yes. I was downstairs when the call came.' When we were both armed with a brew I passed the sick note across to him.

'Another four weeks,' he read out loud.

''Fraid so.'

'And how are you feeling?'

'Guilty. He's given me a note for terminal guilt, and the

more I'm off work, the more guilty I feel.'

Gilbert shook his head in sympathy. 'That's a hell of a catch, Charlie.'

'Best there is, Gilbert.'

'So,' he said brightly, walking over to the table in the corner to fetch the milk. 'Does this mean you're going down to the cottage?'

'Please. If you don't mind.'

'Of course not. Want you to go. Do the place good to have someone in it. Actually . . . I've been thinking about it. Why don't you take Annabelle with you? Be a nice break for both of you.'

'Ah! I was going to ask you about that. So it's all right if she joins me for a few days?'

'No problem. There's everything there you could need. Central heating is on very low, so it should soon warm through.'

'Great. Smashing. Thanks. What about, er, bed-linen? Is there a duvet or something for the spare bed?'

Gilbert's head jerked up and he stared at me as if I'd asked him for a donation to Hezbollah. 'The spare bed! Why should you want a duvet for the spare bed?'

'C'mon, Gilbert. You know what I mean.'

'What's wrong with the big bed?'

I looked him straight in the eye and pronounced: 'My relationship with Mrs Wilberforce is not of that nature.'

He shook his head and chuckled. 'Jesus Christ, Charlie. If the rest of the world were like you two, the human race would have died out fifty thousand years ago.'

Before I left Gilbert's office he suggested I wait a few days before venturing to Cornwall.

'Oh. I was thinking of going at the weekend,' I told him.

'Wouldn't advise it. Have you seen the weather they're having around New York?'

'Yes. Twenty feet of snow. But that's three thousand miles away.'

Gilbert shook his head. 'We always get it a week after them. Mark my words.'

Daft old bugger, I thought, as I came out of Heckley nick and found my car in one of the visitors' places, where I'd left it because Nigel had commandeered my DI spot. I drove into town and had a Chinese Lunchtime Special, followed by some shopping.

Chapter Five

If I'd known I was going to find a body on the beach I'd have worn my wellies. From the top of the cliff it looked like a giant tadpole, stranded where the morning tide had dumped it. A sinister circle of black-backed gulls stood round it, like Pharisees at a stoning. They weren't eating it yet, so maybe it wasn't dead. I decided to find a way down and take a closer look.

Gilbert had been right about the weather. It had snowed for a week, and everything came to a standstill. Then we had floods, so everything stayed at a standstill, but floating; and I topped off the misery by catching flu, so it was late February when I eventually drove down to his cottage in Cornwall.

Leaving the murder enquiry behind wasn't a wrench because it had slipped away from us. The wristwatch had once belonged to Mrs Norris, but the body hadn't. A little girl had wandered into a Liverpool station pushing a baby in a buggy and said their mother hadn't been home since the day before. The kids were sent to a foster-home and their mum's background investigated. There was the usual deafening silence, but it looked as if she'd been a part-time street girl, bolstering her social security giro. Nobody had seen her, but whoever strangled her had a taste for necromania and a reckless disregard for forensic science. He'd left a sperm sample inside her that would have stuck the wallpaper in a small attic. Everything led to Liverpool, apart from Hurst's body being found on our patch, so they took over the bulk of the investigation.

I found a path about a quarter of a mile further on, leading to the beach, and picked my way down it, trying to avoid the worst of the mud. I'd had a good morning. Sam Evans, the Police Surgeon, had been serious about me seeing a counsellor, but I hadn't wanted to consult the one who worked for the force. It was supposed to be confidential, but someone paid him, and I was concerned that a little note would appear on my record. Irrational? Maybe. Outdated prejudice? No doubt about it. But that's the way I felt.

More importantly, Annabelle agreed with Sam about counselling, so I found one of my own. I'd just been to see her, in St Ives, and was walking the three miles back to the cottage along the cliff-path. It had been a good experience and the sun was shining, so I was in a happy enough mood.

Her consulting rooms were in an old imposing house that had been converted into a centre for various therapeutic activities, mainly of the alternative variety. Acupuncture, homoeopathy, that sort of thing. After a short wait I was directed by a receptionist to the surgery.

She shook my hand warmly. 'Hello. I'm Diane Dooley. Please call me Diane. And you're . . . Charles Priest, I believe. May I call you Charles?'

'Charlie,' I mumbled, settling in the chair I had been directed towards.

It was a pleasant airy room, with prints of flowers on the walls. The chairs were neither high nor low, and were both in front of her desk. The clock on the wall was behind me, and the window, through which I could see only the bare branches of trees, was to my left. The whole place was planned to offer the minimum of distraction to the client, but they'd wasted their time.

Diane had long Titian hair and the peaches and low-cholesterol double cream complexion that goes with it. She was wearing a full-length skirt and an ethnic blouse in bright greens that showed off her hair. Diane Dooley was a five-foot-two stunner.

She was explaining about charges. I think she said the first session was half-price, but I wasn't listening. I have difficulty concentrating in the presence of attractive women.

'. . . and each session lasts about fifty-five minutes,' she concluded.

'Er, right.'

'So, Charlie, perhaps you'd like to explain why you are consulting a counsellor?'

'Er, yes, well, mainly because my doctor told me to see one.'

'I see.'

She was waiting for me to go on, but I decided not to. I wanted to do the full fifty-five minutes, but doubted if I could spin things out that long.

Diane broke first: 'But what about you, Charlie? Do you think you need a counsellor?'

'No.'

'Mmm.' Then: 'Go on.'

'I, er, fell down some stairs.'

'You fell down some stairs?'

'Yes.'

'Why was that?'

'I had a dizzy spell.'

'Just one, or do you have many?'

'A few, but not too many.'

'I see. And what do you think brings them on?'

'Stress.'

'Stress?'

'Mmm.'

'So you fell down some stairs when you had a dizzy spell, and your doctor thinks that these are caused by stress and has suggested that counselling might help?'

'Yes.'

'I see.'

No enlargement from yours truly. Diane went on: 'What about you? Do you think counselling might help?'

The setting was carefully planned so that the balance of power was evenly shared. Equal chairs, no desk between us, first names all round. Trouble was that I was a good foot taller than her. I tucked my legs under my chair, shrank down into it and said: 'No.'

She nodded, almost approvingly. 'Do you know how counselling works?' she asked. 'Have you any experience of any sort with it?'

'I've read a book about it,' I offered.

She looked relieved. 'Oh, yes? Tell me about it.'

'Something about how to choose a counsellor. I forget who wrote it.'

'I know the one you mean. Did you find it interesting?'

'Mmm, fairly.'

'And did it help you?'

'A little.'

'In what way do you think it was helpful?'

This took some thinking about. I decided to increase the stakes, go on the offensive. I said: 'There was a long chapter in the book about the relationship between the client and the counsellor. It said that the client was in a very vulnerable position, and often fell in love with his – or her – counsellor. Sometimes, but more rarely, it happened the other way round, too.'

'Yes, it does happen,' she confirmed.

I said: 'I was worried that it might happen to me.'

She pursed her lips and told me: 'You could easily have chosen a male counsellor. There are plenty on the register.'

I stared straight into her eyes – they were green, with big brown flecks in them – and said: 'Maybe that's why I chose a female counsellor.'

Diane Dooley didn't flicker an eyelid. 'Of course,' she said. We fenced around for another five minutes, before she declared: 'It looks to me, Charlie, that counselling isn't for you. There's nothing unusual in that. Most people rely on the natural healing process to overcome their problems. After all, that's what we've been doing for thousands of years. If, after a suitable passage of time, you haven't made any progress, it might be worth giving counselling another try. Meanwhile, it's been nice meeting you and I'll wish you good luck. We haven't been very long, so there's no charge.'

That was it. I was dismissed. 'But, I, er, don't mind paying,' I blustered.

'No, not at all.' She stood up to see me off the premises.

'I'd like to pay,' I admitted. 'I, er, need a receipt for my doctor; to prove I've seen you.'

'That's soon solved. I'll give you one of my receipts, for nil payment. How's that?' She moved round her desk, to the side where the drawers were.

I felt a complete louse. She signed a receipt and passed it across to me. Still in my chair, I folded it into a long spill and placed it in my wallet. 'Mrs Dooley–' I began '–Diane – how long is it before your next appointment?'

She looked up at the clock. 'About forty-five minutes.'

'Could we start again, please?'

She sat down and waited for me to talk.

'I've been a prat,' I confessed, 'and I owe you an apology.'

'No, Charlie, you don't owe me anything. Counselling is a two-way process, and requires a willingness to take part from both parties. But if it isn't for you, it – isn't for you. There's no right or wrong way of doing things.'

'Please. Let me explain. May I?'

'Of course.'

'I'm a police officer. Detective Inspector. I had a bad time. A little girl had vanished, and we were fairly certain that she had been murdered, but it took us six months to prove it. I had pictures of her all round my office walls. Have you any children?'

She nodded. 'A son.'

'I haven't. She was a plain Jane, wire spectacles and a gap in her teeth. But she had a smile that would have melted a chocolate cake. Every day she was there, grinning down at me. And at night, too. I think I grew to love her, wish she were my daughter. I've never admitted that to anyone before. It was me that found her body, what was left of it, wrapped up in a plastic bag. And it was all a bit too much for me.'

Diane looked across her desk at me. 'It must have been a horrible experience,' she murmured.

'So–' I smiled and lifted my hands. 'That's it. I don't think I need counselling. I'll get over it, all in good time. Thanks for listening.' I stood up to leave.

'When did all this happen?' she asked.

'Three, four months ago.'

'That's not very long. You are probably right, but you always know where you can find us.'

'Thanks.'

The body on the beach was a porpoise, I thought, or a small dolphin. Or a very very small whale. I threw a pebble at the gulls as I approached. They stretched their wings and were instantly airborne, landing thirty yards downwind without a single flap.

'Bloody show-offs!' I shouted at them.

It looked dead, but they hadn't started to peck at it. It would have been a heck of a job trying to roll it back into the sea. I found an empty Fairy Liquid container and used it to pour some water into the poor creature's blowhole. No bubbles – it was a gonner.

The gulls were growing braver, sneaking up on us. I yelled and waved my arms and chased them off. This time one or two paid me the compliment of shaking a wing. As soon as I'd left they would gorge themselves flightless. Those big limpid eyes, deep as oil wells, would be first to go. It didn't seem right.

I decided to bury it. Some people climb Everest, others walk backwards from Land's End to John O'Groats. I decided to bury a porpoise on the beach, just outside St Ives.

On the sea's strand, where all the rubbish collects, I found a discarded fertilizer sack and draped it over the porpoise's head, held down by some big pebbles. Then I went back to the cottage for a shovel and a pair of Wellington boots.

There was a message for me on Gilbert's ansaphone. Would I ring Mr Fearnside when I had the opportunity? He was a Chief Superintendent with the Serious Fraud Office. That could wait.

When I arrived back at the beach, I found that someone had beaten me to it. A boy, aged about sixteen, was digging a hole next to the porpoise. I clumped towards him in Gilbert's size ten wellies, a spade and a shovel over my shoulder. As I reached him he looked up from his task.

'Hi,' he said, with a nervous smile.

'Hello.' I nodded at the dead beast. 'You beat me to it.'

He was puffing with exertion, and took the opportunity to have a rest, leaning on his shovel. 'Was it you who covered its head?' he asked.

'Yes.'

'That was a good idea. Protect it from the gulls. It's a lot more difficult than I expected.'

'In that case,' I told him, 'two of us will do it quicker. Move over and let's have a go.'

He stepped out of the hole and I extended my hand towards him. 'My name's Charlie,' I said.

He shook my hand. 'Guy. Pleased to meet you.'

I liked this youth. He had good values. 'My pleasure, Guy. Now let's get this goddamn critter buried.'

It was a lot harder than I had expected, too. An hour later the hole was about two feet deep and full of water. I was climbing out at the end of my stint when I left a wellie behind. I balanced on one leg for a few seconds, sock flapping in the breeze, before plunging my foot back into the freezing water.

'Sh-sh-shilo!' I cursed.

My boots were slightly taller than Guy's. He stepped gingerly down into the hole and the water came over the tops. 'Aw, shit!' he complained.

We buried the porpoise with all the dignity we could muster. When we rolled its body in, it sent up a tidal wave second only to Krakatoa, drenching the pair of us.

'Would you like to say a few words at the graveside?' Guy asked solemnly, dirty water dripping off the end of his nose.

'Good riddance?' I suggested. We weighted it down with a few rocks and shovelled the sand back over it. When we looked around there wasn't a seagull in sight.

I straightened my aching back and nodded at Guy. 'Well done,' I told him.

He grinned back at me. 'You don't half look a mess, Charlie.'

'I know. Burying porpoises always does this to me. Did you have any lunch?'

'No. I missed it.'

'Me too. Fancy a bite in the Jolly Burger?'

Guy hesitated, looking embarrassed. 'Come on,' I told him. 'My treat. You deserve it. Don't forget your shovel.'

We put all the stuff, including our wet socks, in the car boot, and drove barefooted to the café, the heater blowing full blast on to our freezing feet. I'd rolled my trousers up around my calves.

'Oh, that's better,' Guy sighed as the heat came through.

At the café he walked round to the back of the car, stiff-legged and toes pointing skywards, expecting to put his boots back on. 'You don't need them,' I told him, and we padded silently into the Jolly Burger.

'Smoking or non-smoking?' the seating hostess asked, glancing nervously down.

As there was nobody else in the place it was rather academic. 'Near a radiator,' I growled.

We'd warmed through by the time the food came. Guy's face was glowing pink and I could see steam rising off him. I suspected we both smelled fishy. He took a bite of his Superburger and mumbled: 'Are you always doing crazy things, Charlie?'

I looked affronted. 'Me? No. Never.'

'So this is normal?'

I swallowed a morsel of one hundred per cent beef which felt like hoof. 'Yeah. Just an average day.'

Guy squeezed another dollop of ketchup over his fries. 'What do you do for a living?' he asked.

He was a talkative bugger. 'Oh, this and that. What about you? Why aren't you at school?'

'Half-term.'

'Already? You've only just gone back. How do you spend your spare time, apart from burying the odd stranded fish?'

'Oh, all sorts. Birdwatching, mainly. I've seen a chough near where we've just been. And football. I play goalie for the school team.'

I had a captive audience, so thought I'd do some showing off. 'I used to be a goalkeeper,' I told him. 'Had trials with Halifax Town. Played for the A team a couple of times, but they didn't sign me on.'

You'd have thought I'd admitted to scoring a hat-trick in the World Cup final. 'Wow!' he exclaimed, wide-eyed. I don't think he was taking the piss.

At the pay desk a youth with acne that must have been hell to shave round asked me if everything was satisfactory.

'The buns weren't toasted,' I complained.

He gave me my change and ordered me to have a nice day.

Guy only lived about a mile from Gilbert's cottage, in a similarly styled, but larger bungalow. There were clematis and honeysuckle that would look a treat in summer growing all over the fences and walls, and standing on the drive was a Volkswagen Golf convertible that looked uncomfortably similar to one I'd seen earlier that day.

As I opened the boot-lid to retrieve his stuff I asked: 'What's your second name?'

'Dooley,' he replied.

Great. He was Diane Dooley's son. 'Well, it's been nice meeting you, Guy,' I told him, and I meant it. 'Maybe I'll come and watch you play football sometime.'

'Aw, come in and have a coffee,' he protested, adding: 'Mum's home.'

I'd noticed. 'No, thanks. I'd better be off.'

'Saturday, then. Ten o'clock kick-off at the Grammar

School. You can give me some tips. You can play for us, if you want.'

'That might be fun,' I laughed. 'OK, see you Saturday.' Annabelle was coming down on the train on Saturday. I was looking forward to that, too.

I hate goodbyes; always drag them out too long. I was just opening the driver's door when Mrs Dooley arrived at the gate to see who had brought her pride and joy home.

'Mum, this is Charlie,' Guy enthused. 'There was a dead porpoise on the beach, and we both decided to bury it, so the gulls couldn't eat it. And guess what? He used to play in goal for Halifax Town. Tell him to come in for a coffee, Mum.'

She opened the gate for Guy and looked across at me. 'My, you have been busy,' she declared.

I shrugged my shoulders. 'It's not often you find a porpoise that played for Halifax,' I replied. Maybe it wouldn't have let seven in.

'Why are you both in your bare feet?'

'Our wellies filled up,' Guy informed her before I could think of a devastatingly witty response.

She gave me a long-suffering look that her son had no doubt received thousands of time. 'You'd better come in,' she said. 'The least we can do is find you some dry socks.'

A big pair of white sea-boot socks that probably belonged to the one-time Mr Dooley were produced for me, and we perched on high stools in the kitchen, sipping real coffee.

'I'm Diane,' she told me. 'And I believe Guy said you're called Charlie.'

I realised that as a counsellor she would have to have taken vows of chastity and confidentiality and God knows what else, so I went along with the charade without putting my rapidly warming foot in anything. No doubt a disclosure that I had consulted his mother professionally would have lowered my esteem in Guy's eyes by a couple of light years, so I suppose I was grateful for the pretence.

'Yes, that's right. Pleased to meet you, Diane.'

'What do you do for a living, Charlie, or are you a professional grave-digger?'

'No, I have a proper job.'

She was playing games, enjoying making me feel uncomfortable. Her eyes opened wide, inviting me to continue. Did she expect me to lie?

'I'm a detective,' I stated, feeling foolish.

'A cop! Honest?' Guy blurted out.

'Yes.'

'Wow! Fantastic.'

'Guy wants to become a policeman,' she informed me. 'Would you recommend it to a lazy smelly boy, who never does his homework?'

'Mum!' he protested.

Careers advice, that was it. She'd had me worried for a while. I shook my head. 'No, I wouldn't recommend it to anyone.' Guy looked crestfallen, as if he'd just discovered that I tortured small animals for amusement. I expanded: 'Everyone has to make up their own mind. Tell you what I'll do, though. I'll call in at the local station and introduce myself, and ask them if Guy can have a day with them; maybe go on patrol. How does that sound?'

From the expression on his face it looked as if I was back on the rostrum, but his mother deflated him.

She said: 'Tell me, Charlie, do many policemen have tattoos?'

Guy's face turned the colour of my last bank statement. 'That's not fair!' he exclaimed.

I took pity on him. We men have to stick together when the odds are against us. 'Sure,' I confirmed. 'Lots of them in the Drug Squad have tattoos. They might wash them off when they go home, though. I'm not certain.'

Diane said: 'There's a boy in Guy's class whose father has a tattoo parlour. He's persuaded several of his classmates to be done. He's into all sorts of things, but it's always the others who get the blame. He knows all the right things to say, always gets away with it. Wouldn't be surprised if he isn't dealing in drugs.'

She sounded worried, and not without reason. Guy was a good lad, but he was impressionable. I'd proved that.

'Aw, Mum, not now,' Guy pleaded.

'You're all like sheep,' she went on. 'And he's the one who leads you all to market. He's a Judas sheep, that's what he is.'

'A what?' Guy demanded.

'A Judas sheep.'

'You mean a Judas goat.'

'Do I?' she laughed, instantly changing the mood, much to my relief. She turned to me. 'Sorry about this touching domestic scene, Charlie, but you can see what a problem I have.'

'Yes, well, thanks for the coffee and the socks.' I stood up to leave, but turned and spoke to Guy. 'Did you see the youth who took the money at the Jolly Burger?' I asked him.

'Yeah. Oh Mum, he had acne like pick-your-own strawberries.'

'The same. Did you notice the backs of his fingers?'

'Er, no.'

'Well, he had scars, where he'd had tattoos removed. Probably *Love* and *Hate*, or something equally edifying. No doubt they were impeding his progress up the Jolly Burger management ladder.' In Heckley they would have said Fuck Cops, but I didn't tell them that.

Diane nodded her approval. They walked me to the gate.

Halfway there Diane turned to Guy and said: 'A bell-wether, that's what I was trying to think of.'

'A bellwether? What's a bellwether?'

'It's a sheep with a bell round its neck, that all the others follow.'

He pushed her playfully. 'A Judas sheep!' he mocked.

They were good to be around. As I drove away I wondered if it would be sensible to introduce Annabelle to them. Could we all be friends, or would I be playing with fire? On a February afternoon a warm homely blaze can be very tempting . . .

There was another message from Fearnside waiting for me. By the time I'd had a shower and put on some comfortable clothing it was dark. He'd probably gone home by now, which made it a good time to ring him.

'N-CIS,' said the girl who answered the phone. The National Criminal Intelligence Service are the big boys, but Fearnside was supposed to be in the Serious Fraud Office. They're big boys too, but wear better suits.

'Chief Superintendent Fearnside, please,' I intoned.

'It's Commander Fearnside,' she told me. 'Who wants him?'

I confessed to being a mere DI, but she eventually put me through. He hadn't gone home.

'Charlie!' he bellowed, as if greeting a long-lost basset hound. 'How are you?'

'Fine, thank you. Congratulations on the promotion.'

'Oh, that. Long service award, I'm afraid. Nothing exciting. We leave all that stuff to you. Seriously, Charlie, how are you?'

'I'm OK, sir. Never felt better.'

'But Superintendent Wood told me you were off sick.'

'Yeah, but I'm all right. Should be back in harness soon, if the doc'll sign me off.'

'So you're not going out on ill-health?'

'No, I don't think so. Everybody seems to be pushing me to, but I don't want it.'

'Not your style, eh?'

'Perhaps.' I wasn't sure how much one ought to admit to a Commander.

'You sound bored, Charlie.'

'Yes, I think I am.'

'Well, I've a little proposition that is just up your street.'

I'd walked straight into his trap, innocent as a sparrow. I said: 'Oh, dear, this sounds ominous.'

'Not at all, not at all. Firstly, you'd stay on sick leave. Any expenses you incurred would come straight through to me. No problems there. It's a surveillance job, up in East Yorkshire. Your neck of the woods. We can't afford to have anyone permanently on site, but as you are twiddling your thumbs, so to speak . . . The target is a drugs courier. We've been picking his compatriots off one by one, but we've left him dangling, see what he leads us to. He lives in a little house near the Humber estuary, and it just so happens that the one next door is up for sale or rent. We'd like to put a tenant into that house, and you'd be perfect, Charlie.'

'Because I'd come cheap?'

'As you are already being paid, yes, we could afford you, that's true. More importantly, you're the right man for the job. Shall I send the file down to Heckley, eh?'

Up to Heckley, I thought. Up, up, UP! It sounded like bloody blackmail to me. I was twiddling my thumbs, doing nothing, so I might as well twiddle them and do some observations at the same time. Trouble was, it wouldn't end at that. I'd become involved, embroiled. I knew it, and Fearnside knew it, too.

'My sick note runs out next week,' I told him, lamely.

'The doc would give you another.'

Through the window I could see that the dark sky was rent by a jagged slash of duck-egg green, like an undergarment visible through a ripped tunic. If they could put sunsets on the rates, this place would cost a fortune. I said: 'Sorry, Mr Fearnside. I intend going back on operations as soon as possible.'

We went through the usual pleasantries, and he wished me all the best, but I knew he was annoyed – people like him are used to having their way. It was a standing joke at Heckley that I was the longest-serving Inspector the force had ever had. Now it looked as if my record would be unassailable, and I didn't give a monkey's.

Annabelle wasn't answering her phone, so I had a beer and investigated the remote control for the telly.

Annabelle didn't answer her phone all next day, either. The cottage garden had not been tidied since last summer, so I attacked it with determination and all the sharp implements available in Gilbert's garage. I massacred the perennials without fear or favour: if it was brown, I dug it up; if it was green, I chopped it down. The snowdrops were out and the daffodils in bud. Blackthorn in the hedge around the adjacent field was in full blossom, and a robin and several bluetits followed me round as I gave the borders a hoeing. When I'd finished, it all looked pretty good, ripe for another season of burgeoning fecundity. I decided to leave cleaning out the gutters for another day.

I suppered on boil-in-the-bag rogan josh and thumbed the last-number-redial button at regular intervals. It was about ten o'clock when Annabelle finally answered the phone.

She sounded breathless and excited, and picturing her cheered me up. It didn't last.

'Oh Charles, I've just arrived home. I was wondering whether to call you.'

'If in doubt, ring,' I told her. 'So, what have you been up to?'

'I've been to London – Westminster – for an audience with Andrew Fallon. Tom Noon took me, and we all had lunch together. It was lovely.'

'Smashing. Haven't you been before? I'd have thought that . . . that when you were . . . er, married . . .'

'When I was married to Peter? Yes, I went a couple of times. That was fun, too. But somehow, this time, it was different. Then, I was Peter's partner; today, it was me they were listening to. Does that make sense?'

'Yes, it does.' It pleased me, too. 'So,' I asked, 'is Mr Fallon still interested in sponsoring your holiday in Africa?'

'Oh, Charles. This is the part you won't like. I don't like it, either.' She sounded awkward and embarrassed. I wondered if the deal was that she share a sleeping bag with him.

'Go on.'

'Well, apparently he can find some money to sponsor the whole trip, in return for me doing some additional research on his behalf. Trouble is, it's one of these silly accounting situations where we have to be there and back before the end of the financial year – April the sixth. So we provisionally fly out next Wednesday.'

She was right, I didn't like it. I felt like the man who'd wangled a cancellation on the *Titanic*. 'Oh,' was the best I could manage.

Annabelle must have sensed my disappointment. She said: 'So I won't be able to spend the week with you, but I was thinking that maybe I could come down on Saturday and return on Monday. It's a bit of a rush, but at least we'll have a couple of days together.'

So there was a place in a lifeboat for me. 'No,' I

mumbled. 'It's too far to come for two days.'

'But Charles, I can't go off for a month without seeing you.'

'Thanks, that's kind of you. I feel the same. I'll come back, back to Heckley. It'll have to be Saturday, though. I've promised to watch a football match on Saturday morning – might even turn out for them.'

'You don't have to, Charles. I was expecting to come down there.'

'No. I've finished here. I'll come home. It's all right.'

'If you're sure. Another reason I want to see you is so you can help me buy a camera.'

'A camera? What do you want a camera for?'

'Er, would you believe, to take photographs with?'

'Yes, it was a stupid question, wasn't it? What I think I meant was: wouldn't a video be more useful?'

'Ah, now for the exciting bit.' She was back to her cheery self again. 'I told you that Mr Fallon is violently anti-smoking?'

'Yes.'

'Well, apparently one of his pet campaigns is to prevent the tobacco companies exploiting the Third World. He's already tried once to have a Bill passed that would tax the trade until it was uneconomical. It really is disgraceful what they do, Charles. The cigarettes they sell over there are much more addictive than the ones available in Europe, and there are no restrictions or health warnings whatsoever.'

'Yes, I've read about it.'

She went on: 'If I can take some decent photographs – children smoking, cancer patients, advertising hoardings . . . that sort of thing – he'll either use his influence to have them published in one of the heavies, or we'll produce a booklet on the subject. Isn't it exciting?'

It was exciting all right, like poking a rattlesnake in the nostril with a cocktail stick.

I said: 'Annabelle, are you serious?'

'Serious? Why, what do you mean? she asked hesitantly.

'It's called spying!'

'Spying?'

'Yes! Spying!'

'Oh, Charles. I never thought of it like that. I just thought . . .'

'These tobacco manufacturers,' I interrupted. 'They might wear blue suits and be quoted on the stock market, but they also bribe governments and cause hundreds of thousands of deaths every year. They won't let an article by an amateur journalist stand in their way.'

There was a long silence. I heard her say: 'No,' very softly, adding: 'So you think I should refuse to do it?'

I didn't know. I wasn't sure about anything any more. I said: 'Maybe I'm overreacting. I'm pleased for you, Annabelle, honestly I am. But I'm worried, too. Now you know what a selfish old bugger I can be.'

'Yes.'

'Look. You'll be all right. It's just that . . . I'm missing you. Can we discuss it at the weekend?'

'Mmm.'

'And before you go away, will you promise me one thing?'

'What's that?'

'That I can see you in your white-hunter outfit?'

I pictured her smiling, with that wrinkle-nose way of hers that would soon be making the natives restless.

'Only if I can see you in your football kit,' she countered.

Chapter Six

As soon as the driver of the Volvo articulated lorry saw the light for the cylinder pre-heaters flicker off he turned the key all the way and the big diesel engine rumbled into life. He watched the display of lights and dials as the air and oil pressures built up, telling him that everything was OK for his long journey to Marseilles.

'Polish the bike for me,' he shouted down to his traffic manager, nodding towards the Harley Davidson parked in the corner of the garage.

'Might take the wife for a run on it tomorrow,' the comfortably-shaped manager yelled back, with more than a hint of yearning in his voice.

'She's too fast for you.'

'Then I'll take someone else's wife.'

The driver grinned down at him. It was the fiftieth time they'd had that exchange. 'I'll bring you some fags back.'

'Don't bother. Safe journey.'

He pre-selected first gear and eased the accelerator down. There were seven and a half million fags in the container he was towing, and the best part of quarter of a billion stacked nearby. He raised a hand in farewell and spun the steering wheel, easing the lorry forward through the big doors of the bonded warehouse and out into the night.

He stopped again at the gatehouse. The man there double-checked the customs seals on the container, glanced at his paperwork and raised the barrier. He was on his way.

This was the part he liked best: setting off on an overnight run to Dover, with the roads and the weather as clear as his new baby's complexion. He'd make the ferry before dawn, and the two-hour crossing would qualify as a rest period.

In three miles he'd be on the motorway network that would take him all the way to Folkestone. That was OK in the Volvo rig, but on the Harley he'd have chosen the byways. The bike would have to be sold, now that he was a dad. It was sad, but it was only fair. They'd had some good times on it, but a family meant responsibility, and there were too many nutcases loose on the roads these days.

A motorcycle was waiting at a junction on the left. He looked across at it. Two headlamps, probably a Suzuki. It pulled out behind him and followed, waiting for an opportunity to pass. They were on a long left-hand curve, so he flashed the lorry's indicators to signal the road was clear and the motorcycle slipped effortlessly by, the rider raising a hand in acknowledgement.

I wish I were going to the South of France on that, the lorry driver sighed.

Two minutes later he was rounding the junction that would take him up on to the M62. A car was parked on the slip road, hazard lights blinking. He changed down through the sixteen-speed gearbox and eased over on to the hard shoulder, so he could pass the stoppage on the left. A man was standing in the road, directing the traffic that way. He was probably from the red Sierra with its flashers going.

It was the motorcyclist. The bike was laid in the road, with the rider nearby. Another man was trying to remove the stricken rider's helmet, pulling and twisting at it.

'Hey! Don't do that!' the lorry driver yelled, hitting the

brakes. The heavy rig juddered to a standstill and he jumped down from the cab. 'Don't do that! You could paralyse him.'

He pushed the man aside and bent over the rider. He lifted the visor, unfastened the chinstrap and loosened the top of his leather jacket.

'Lie still,' he said calmly. 'You'll be OK.'

There was a metallic click near his right ear, a double *ker-chink* that he'd heard a thousand times before in TV thrillers, but never in real life. He turned slightly, and felt the cold metal of the gun barrel press into his neck.

The motorcyclist opened his eyes. 'I'm OK,' he said, 'but you're in the shit.'

The passing motorists were mildly relieved to see the young man in leathers jump to his feet. They assumed he'd been riding like a madman; how else could one fall off in a slip road? They accelerated away from the scene and promptly forgot all about it. The lorry driver saw that the man who'd been directing the traffic was particularly unpleasant-looking. He wouldn't be too difficult to describe. The ugly one climbed into the cab of the lorry, and the other, the big one with the gun, ordered him to follow. The driver's legs felt as if they were made of blancmange as he hauled himself up.

'Follow the red car,' the ugly one ordered, 'and don't try anything. I can drive this thing, so it makes no difference to me if you're dead or alive.' His argument was reinforced by another evil-looking automatic pistol.

They left the bike neatly parked at the side of the road and drove away in convoy. At the next exit they left the motorway, and half an hour later the red Sierra led him up a narrow lane and into a disused farmyard. The farm had been cut off from its fields by the development of the roads, and was now isolated and run-down. Frank Bell had bought it a few years earlier at a knockdown price. Literally. When the old farmer argued, he was knocked down.

The Volvo rig just fitted in the barn. The driver and Shawn Parrott jumped out and met the other two at the back of the container.

'Right,' Bell said. 'Let's get it unloaded.'

Parrott attacked the lugs for the padlocks with an oxy-acetylene torch while the ex-motorcyclist, Darren Atkinson, snipped through the seals with a pair of pliers. As the locks fell smoking to the floor Parrott turned, waving the cutting torch, and boasted: 'Easy as pissing on yer feet, eh?'

Not as easy as using the keys I have in my pocket, the driver thought. How did they expect the customer to get in?

He needed time. He was scheduled to ring in at about six a.m., when he reached Dover. They'd give him an hour, maybe, then start asking questions. The police would be informed, and also Lorry Watch, the informal network that circulated the number of a stolen vehicle to nearly every driver on the road. But it would all take time. He knew exactly where he was, would have no difficulty coming here again, and that was a worry. They couldn't let him go until the load was well away from this place, and them with it. Unless they didn't intend to let him go . . .

'C'mon, you,' the big one growled at him. 'Start lifting boxes out.'

They toiled through the night, and it was well after dawn when they finished. The driver worked inside the container, passing the boxes to the other three. Slowly he mined his way into the solid wall of brown cardboard, easing each carton out and carrying it to the tail of the lorry.

The other three took them from him and stacked them somewhere round the front of the vehicle. Each one would wait until his colleague returned empty-handed before staggering off under his load, making sure that the driver was watched all the time. After the first hour they all stripped to the waist.

At one point Darren was waiting for the Skipper to replace him. As the driver dropped the heavy carton into his arms he said: 'You ride a motorcycle well.'

Next trip he said: 'I have a Harley Davidson.'

'I know,' Atkinson replied.

When there were only about six cartons left the ugly one dropped out of the sequence, leaving them to the Skipper and Atkinson. The driver didn't know it, but he'd gone to fetch his beloved Kalashnikov.

'Last one,' he declared as he carried it from the far end of the container. He'd expected Darren to be waiting, but it was the ugly one. He couldn't see the gun over the top of the carton he held in his arms.

'Put it down,' the ugly one said ominously.

The driver stopped, and as he lowered the box he saw the Russian-made assault rifle, favoured weapon of a thousand armies and a million terrorists, pointing at him. Now he knew, with a clarity denied to most of us, what his fate was to be.

He hurled the box, containing thirteen thousand cigarettes, at the face he knew he could never forget.

Parrott moved his head sideways, like a boxer slipping a punch, and the carton flew over his shoulder. He pressed the trigger and gave the driver a burst of three bullets, SAS-style. The impact carried the driver's body backwards. He hit the far wall of the container and turned as he pitched forwards, landing on his back. His right knee bent and straightened three times, then he lay still. Outside, the birds stopped their singing at this sudden intrusion of noise, cocked their heads quizzically for a moment, and resumed saluting the new day.

The following evening Parrott drove the rig fifty miles down the M6, with Atkinson following in the car. He parked at a services, between a Texaco tanker and one carrying an indeterminate, but probably highly toxic, load. He lit a cigarette and took a couple of long drags, making sure it was well alight. He emptied a box of matches on the passenger seat and formed most of them into a bundle, held by a rubber band, with the lighted cigarette passing through the middle.

'Now for the tricky bit,' he mumbled to himself.

Every motor mechanic will tell you that a lighted cigarette will not ignite petrol vapour, but only the foolish ones make a habit of putting it to the test. Parrott unscrewed the stopper from a two-gallon can and doused a rag. He placed it on the floor of the cab and carefully rested the improvised fuse in a fold of the sodden cloth. The can was left upturned, gurgling the remainder of its contents over the high-quality upholstery of the £100,000 Volvo. Parrott climbed down and calmly walked round the back of the rig, as if checking his load. Darren was waiting at the other side, in the Sierra.

Eleven minutes and fourteen miles later the cigarette burned down to the match-heads and the lorry exploded. The fire brigade managed to save the Texaco tanker, but they couldn't help the poor chap who'd been resting in the Volvo's sleeping quarters. The overworked pathologist found the bullets the following day, and said a little prayer of thanks that he hadn't jumped to the obvious conclusion.

I decided that I'd drive home to Heckley straight from the football match. I loaded the car, went through the checklist for locking up the cottage – windows shut, thermostat down low, that sort of thing – and set off to look for the Grammar School playing fields.

The match was well under way when I arrived. I'd seen some sports fields during my travels around town, but they were the wrong ones, and I had to ask directions. About twenty spectators were down one side of the pitch, and a little solitary figure stood apart from them, near the goal where Guy was bobbing up and down to keep warm, as if he were suspended by a spring from the cross-bar.

'Good morning, Diane,' I announced briskly as I approached her. She was submerged in a big navy-blue coat that nearly reached the ground, its collar up over her ears.

'Good morning,' she mumbled, without enthusiasm.

'What's the score?'

'Nil nil, I think.'

'How long have they been playing?'

'About two hours.'

'A game of soccer only lasts ninety minutes,' I informed her.

'Does it? Well, they must have been playing for nearly that long.'

'So they've had half-time?'

'Half-time?'

'You're not really a fan, are you?' I chuckled.

'No. This is the first time I've been to a game. Probably be the last, too.'

I turned away from her, as if to watch the play, but really it was to hide the self-satisfied grin on my face. If Diane Dooley hadn't come to see the football, what, or who, had she really come to see?

Guy's team were on the attack, with every player in their opponents' half. It was typical schoolboy kick-and-rush, but no less passionate for that. Their goalkeeper gathered the ball and punted it downfield. It went to their centre-forward who booted it towards Guy's goal, and the chase was on.

Their player was a big lad. One of those genetic freaks

who has a five o'clock shadow at seven. Seven years old, that is. He streaked towards Guy, kicking the ball well forward to keep his speed up. Big kids like him have it easy at school, but when the others catch up they fade away. Then it's the little tough ones, who know what it's like to struggle, who make the grade.

Guy saw him coming and moved off his line. He was nervous, and so was I. The centre-forward came charging towards the goal, and Guy wasn't sure how to tackle him. At the last second the ball ran away from their player, and his shot was feeble. Guy stuck out a leg and deflected the ball round the post. He'd saved it, but it wasn't a move he'd read about in a textbook.

'Well saved, goalie,' I shouted, and Diane applauded with her gloved hands. The referee gave a long blast on his whistle and waved a hand in the air – the signal for the teams to change ends.

'That's half-time,' I told Diane, who looked less than enthusiastic at the news. 'Only another forty-five minutes to go.'

Guy came running over to us. 'Morning, Charlie,' he greeted me, smiling happily.

'Morning, Guy. That was a rather unorthodox save, if you don't mind me saying so.'

'Clean sheet, so far,' he responded.

'Fair enough.' I nodded towards the other players, who were gathered around their games master. 'Go see what the coach has to say,' I told him. 'Then I want a quick word with you.'

Guy trotted off towards the others, Diane and I following him at a more leisurely pace. 'Guy's a smashing boy,' I told her. 'You must be proud of him.'

'I am,' she answered.

'I'm surprised you haven't watched him play before.'

'Is that meant to be a reprimand?' she demanded.

'No. I'm sorry, is that how it sounded?'

I was receiving mixed signals from Mrs Dooley. Maybe I was wrong in my assumption that her motive for coming to the match was to see me. I chuckled to myself as I remembered our first conversation in her office, 'specially the bit where I'd said . . .

Oh shit! Oh shit and corruption! With great big spikes on and wired up to ten million volts! How stupid could I get?

'Aw God!' I exclaimed, clapping my hands to my head.

She looked at me, without saying anything.

I let out a big sigh. 'I've just remembered what I said,' I told her.

'Said? When?'

'In your office. When I came for a consultation. The bit about choosing a counsellor. I told you that I was worried that I might fall in love with my counsellor, and I said . . . you said . . .'

'I said you could always have chosen a male counsellor,' she interrupted.

'That's right. And I said . . .'

'You said that was why you'd chosen a female one.'

'Er, yes. Oh God! What must you be thinking? Well, I wasn't telling the truth. I was trying to wind you up, plus pay you a concealed compliment. I really did feel vulnerable. You're a very attractive woman.'

'With a very attractive son?'

The answer to that was yes, but not in the way she thought. I said: 'Look. I'm straight. I've been married once and have a girlfriend that I'm devoted to. I'd like it if we could all be . . .'

'You two arguing already?' Guy interrupted. He was carrying the ball, and tossed it towards my head. I nodded it twice, caught it on my instep and flicked it back to him.

'You never lose class,' I boasted, holding my hands wide for the applause. It was the first time I'd kicked a ball for fifteen years. 'What did the coach tell you?' I asked.

'Oh, him. He's only the English master. Something about "And gentlemen in England, now a-bed, Shall think themselves accurs'd they were not here." He's a right tosser, he is.'

'Guy!'

'Sorry, Mum. But he is.'

'Right. So listen. The main danger is that big centre-forward—'

'Lurch?'

'Yes – when they break away. You were lucky to save that last one. Forget him, just go for the ball. Throw yourself at it and try to turn sideways. That way you cover as much of the goalmouth as possible. Understand?'

'He'll kick my head off!' Guy protested.

'Very probably,' I admitted. 'But the good news is this: you won't feel a thing. If you go in half-hearted, you'll get hurt. Go in like a kamikaze buffalo, determined to go straight through him, and you won't feel a thing. Not until next day. You'll have some bruises, but you'll be proud of them. Ask any rugby player – he'll tell you the same thing.'

He didn't look convinced, and neither did his mother.

The second half was just like the little bit of the first that I'd seen. Guy's team did most of the attacking, but couldn't score, the others making the occasional break down the field. Guy made a couple of flashy saves from long-range efforts and did a lot of dancing about. With about three minutes to go his side were peppering the other goal with shots, every player except Guy packed into their half. Then the inevitable happened. Their goalkeeper gathered the ball and punted it over the halfway line to where Lurch was waiting. The referee, who taught history through the week, had never heard of the offside rule and kept his whistle in his pocket.

Lurch charged towards Guy's goal like a Rottweiler after a rent collector. I felt Diane grab my arm, then let go. Guy crouched, bobbing about, and moved forward to narrow the angle. Lurch had the ball under better control this time – he wasn't about to make the same mistake twice.

I waited until he was nearly on Guy then screamed: 'Go gerrim, Guy!'

Guy threw himself at the flashing feet of the big youth, blanketing the ball with his chest and arms. Lurch's legs flew into the air as he cartwheeled over Guy's body and he crashed down in the back of the net. Guy jumped up, bounced the ball twice, and booted it back up the field.

The other team had raced after their centre-forward, leaving Guy's players stranded in their half, but now fortunes were reversed yet again. The referee was consistent in his disregard of the offside rule and eight of Guy's team managed to manoeuvre the ball around what was left of their opponents' defence to score the only goal of the match. Diane danced a jig and shouted her congratulations down the length of the field. Lurch, stars revolving around his head, was still trying to find his way out through the netting when the final whistle blew.

'I'm on my way back to Yorkshire,' I told Diane as we walked slowly back towards where the cars were parked. The two teams had gone for a shower. We never had showers in my day. A bucket of cold water between twenty-two of us, and we thought we were lucky.

'Oh,' was all she said.

'Will you say goodbye to Guy for me?'

'He'll be sorry you didn't say it yourself.'

'I know, but it's a long drive. Should have been off hours ago. Tell him I'll be back, in the summer.'

'Very well.'

'That's if I'm welcome,' I said, with a sideways smile at her. She didn't smile back.

I fished an old envelope out of my pocket. 'Here,' I said, handing it to her. 'That's my address, and a couple of numbers where I can be reached. The name and number on the back is one of your local police sergeants. He's expecting Guy to ring him to arrange a day with them. Tell him to mention my name. He'll be OK.'

She slipped the envelope into a coat pocket without any comment.

We'd reached the cars. I was wearing my big Gortex anorak that I wear for serious walking, half-open at the front because I'd overdone the warm clothing. 'Look,' I said, turning to her. 'I want to tell you that I am not gay. I have never been gay and never want to be gay. I have no inclinations in that direction whatsoever. Understood?'

She reached up and pulled the collars of my jacket together, snug around my neck. I gazed straight into those eyes that caught the winter sun and shattered its rays into all the unnamed shades of green.

'I don't believe you,' she said, and jammed my zipper tight up under my chin. I swear there was a challenge in her words, and I swore not to accept it.

It's a long way from St Ives to Heckley. You drive east for two hundred miles, then turn left and drive north for another two hundred. Most of the roads are motorways, which are fast but boring, and the caravans are still hibernating in February, so I was home by nine o'clock. Highlight of the journey was playing a tape of Glass's *Itaipu*, extremely loudly. Annabelle gave it to me at Christmas. I rang her, arranging to see her for Sunday lunch, read my mail, had a shower and crashed out.

Annabelle insisted on cooking lunch herself, and out of

deference to my tastes it was roast beef and Yorkshire puddings.

'Nearly as good as Mother's,' I told her with a contented smile, raising my wine glass and lowering my head in respect.

'Praise indeed,' she replied.

I was looking forward to spending a relaxing afternoon stretched out together on her settee, listening to Elgar, or . . . Max Bygraves, but Annabelle had other ideas. She wanted to know all about photography.

'So you're still taking the tobacco pictures, for Andrew Fallon,' I said.

'Yes.'

'OK. So let's make sure they are worth the risk.'

'Charles, they are worth the risk. I have to take them, don't you see?'

'No, not really. I'd have thought there were hundreds of correspondents who could take them.'

'Then why aren't they doing it? How many of them are truly independent? If the papers take an anti-smoking stance they will lose millions in advertising revenue. Did you know that before the 1989 General Election, the tobacco companies loaned all their prime advertising sites to the Government, free of charge? And the Prime Minister was on a six-figure retainer for a consultancy fee, in return for which we vetoed the European Parliament's attempts to ban all tobacco advertising?'

'Yes, Annabelle,' I sighed. 'I read all about it, in *Private Eye*.'

'And doesn't it make you angry?'

'A little, but I've other things to be angry about.'

She blushed, and looked abashed. 'I'm sorry, Charles. I had no right to say that. I know how much you care about other people.'

'But you don't know how much I care about you,' I declared.

I explained all about film speeds, exposures, depth of field; the full ten-dollar lecture. Annabelle understood it all, but at the end she said: 'Gosh, there is a lot to remember.'

'Put your coat on,' I told her, 'and I'll take you to see my camera. And it's about time you visited *chez Priest*.' The place was still tidy from my blitz on it, and I didn't want to have wasted my efforts.

When we swung into my cul-de-sac we saw the scarlet Jaguar E-type sitting outside my house. 'It's my old car!' I gasped with delight.

My father was a Jaguar enthusiast, but he could never afford to own one. When he retired he bought a clapped-out E-type with the intention of restoring it, but he died and it came to me. I spent a fortune on it, did a good job, and then sold it for a minor pop star's ransom. It was a fabulous motor, the only car I could ever enthuse over, but it deserved a better home than I could give it. And now it was back.

The man I'd sold it to extricated himself and we shook hands. I introduced him to Annabelle and gave her a brief history of the car.

'I was just passing,' he claimed. 'Hope you don't mind me calling like this?'

'Of course not,' I told him. 'You're welcome any time. How's the old bus going?'

'Like a dream.'

'Smashing. Let's go in for a coffee.'

'Er, no thanks, Mr Priest. I'd better be on my way. I'd just like a quick word with you though, if possible.'

'Sure.' I unlocked my front door and gave Annabelle a wink as I ushered her inside. 'Make yourself at home, I won't be a second,' I told her, turning to see what he wanted.

He gathered his breath and said: 'I've decided to sell her. Thought I'd give you the first refusal, as you were pretty decent with me. I've spent over eight grand on new tyres all round, gearbox overhaul, re-spray and new leather. She's better than new, and you can have her back for what you sold her for. Interested?'

'Phew!' I exclaimed. 'That's a temptation.'

I walked round the car, and squatted down in front of it to see it from the most advantageous viewpoint. The E-type Jaguar is the most uncompromisingly beautiful vehicle ever made. From certain angles the windscreen looks a shade too high, but would Sophia Loren be the loveliest woman in the world if her mouth wasn't just a nibble too wide? It looked as if it were doing a ton just standing there.

I stretched upright again and shook my head. 'I'm sorry,' I said. 'My heart would love it, but the fact is, I don't like messing with cars; especially cleaning and polishing them. It needs someone who'll look after it better than I can. It's certainly a good offer, though. You should sell it easily enough.'

His disappointment was obvious. 'To tell the truth, Mr Priest, I need the money. The business is in trouble and the bank's putting pressure on me. We desperately need an injection of cash. We're caught in the negative equity trap with the house, so it looks as if the car has to go. Would you be interested if I brought the price down a couple of grand?'

'Have you tried advertising?'

'Not yet, but you know yourself how that just attracts posers and dreamers with no money.'

'Yeah, that's true. Do you mind if Annabelle has a look?'

'No, of course not.'

I tapped on the window to attract her attention and beckoned for her to join us.

'Let's see how you look in the driving seat,' I said, opening the door for her. She looked as if she were born to it.

We hummed and hawed for a while, and I told him I was doubtful but would think about it. He went away looking dejected. Annabelle and I watched the car as the brake-lights came on at the end of the street, and the long bonnet swung into the main road and slid away.

'Do you think I should buy it?' I asked her as we went back inside.

'Ooh, definitely!' she declared.

'The bank is foreclosing on his business. Poor bloke needs the money desperately.'

'Can you afford it?'

'The money he gave me for it is still in the building society, earning about one per cent interest. It would probably be enough to build a couple of hospitals, where you are going.'

'You can't draw comparisons like that, Charles. It's your money to do what you want with.'

'Mmm, I suppose so. The question I ask myself is: was I looking for a new car before he came? The answer is no. So let's get our feet back on the ground and give you your lesson in photography.'

My old single-lens reflex is good quality, but you have to do everything manually. Annabelle still thought it looked complicated.

'Don't worry,' I said. 'Technology will come to your assistance. Now let's see. If you are going away on Wednesday, that only leaves two days. Presumably you need some time to yourself for shopping and packing?'

'Yes, I'm afraid so.'

'OK. Will I be able to see you Monday afternoon? Then you can have Tuesday to yourself and I'll take you to the airport on Wednesday. How does that sound?'

'It sounds a terrible imposition on you.'

'Oh, it is. Terrible,' I laughed. 'The latest cameras,' I continued, 'are fully automatic. You just compose the picture in the viewfinder and press the button. Anybody could do it. Even a woman.' I screwed up my face in concentration as I reconsidered that final statement. 'Well, some women,' I decided. Before she could fight back I said: 'Am I right in believing you have a birthday on March the third?'

'Yes. How did you know that?'

I tapped the side of my nose. 'Just doing my job, ma'am.'

Annabelle blushed. She blushes very easily. If she could control it I'd think she used it as a weapon. It certainly worked on me. 'You look quite young for your age,' I teased.

Rod Stewart was on the CD player, croaking his version of *Waltzing Matilda*. Annabelle took a back-handed swipe at me and declared: 'You mean, I'm older than you thought!'

I grabbed her wrist and pulled her towards me. 'I like older women.'

We lay on the settee, listening to Rod. He's a romantic so-and-so. It grew dark around us, the glow from the fire casting soft shadows. I stroked the down in the nape of Annabelle's neck and said: 'I wish you'd stay here tonight.'

She didn't answer with words, but her head, buried in my shoulder, gently shook from side to side.

'Why?' I whispered, running my fingers into her soft fair hair.

She moved up, so we were cheek to cheek. 'I . . . I don't know. Please don't be angry with me.'

I kissed her nose. 'It's not important,' I told her. It was what I wanted most in the world, but I'd settle for what I wanted second-most.

On the way back to her place I drove along making vroom-vroom noises at every gear change.

'You're longing to buy it, aren't you?' she laughed.

'No, not at all,' I lied. I went on: 'The Yorkshire puddings you cooked were very superb, and very appropriate. Remind you of what you'll be missing in Africa. How about me taking you for a nice English cream tea tomorrow afternoon, just to make you even more homesick?'

'Ooh, that sounds like an offer I can't refuse.'

'Have you ever been to Shirley's Café?'

'In Harrogate?'

'Harrogate, York and Bath. Mmm.'

'No, never.'

'Good. Shirley's it is. I'll pick you up about one.'

First thing in the morning I rang the police photographer, to learn his recommendations on cameras and films, but mainly to find out who'd give me thirty per cent discount. Then I went into town and purchased the latest state-of-the-art, until the new one comes out next week, Olympus with a zoom lens. It was a superb piece of work, and small, too. Like the man in the shop said, 'Just point and shoot; and pray they don't shoot back.' I bought twenty films and a few odds and ends to go with it.

I was a few minutes late arriving at Annabelle's place, so I caught the first item of the one o'clock news on the car radio. Through the night there'd been a big fire at a DIY store in Manchester. Millions of pounds of damage and a couple of hundred jobs gone. Now a group calling itself TSC – The Struggle Continues – was claiming responsibility. Someone with an Irish accent had rung a newspaper before the fire, but had not said where it would be. The editor had decided it was a hoax. The DIY chain was in the process of opening new stores in both Northern and Southern Ireland, and all the combined political pundits of the BBC could not agree whether the blaze furthered the Republican cause or the Nationalist. Neither could I. I drew to a standstill outside the Old Vicarage and switched it off.

'Happy Birthday, a bit early,' I told Annabelle as I presented her with everything.

'I . . . I don't understand,' she uttered.

'It's called a present.'

'For me?'

I looked over both my shoulders. 'Yes. For you.'

'Oh Charles, it looks frightfully expensive.'

'They gave me a discount.' A measly ten per cent, but when they are handing out the life jackets you don't argue about the colour.

'You shouldn't have.' She embraced me, squeezing so hard I could scarcely breathe. 'You are so good to me, Charles.' When she released me she said: 'Thank you. I know you are not happy about me doing this, but I promise to be careful.'

I said: 'Just don't draw attention to yourself, and don't tell anyone what you are doing. Understand?'

She nodded and squeezed me again.

It was a bright but breezy day. Just outside Harrogate I saw a large advertising billboard and pulled off the road.

'Lesson one,' I said. 'Let's see you put a film in.'

I read the instruction book while Annabelle fiddled with the camera. It was easier than buying a timeshare.

'OK. Out of the car. We'll have a photo of the hoarding.' It was for Benetton. They make racing cars, I think, but I couldn't see the relevance of the picture.

I showed her how to use the tripod, or something solid,

like a tree, to eliminate shake; and how to use the zoom to compose the shot.

'Move in close,' I told her, 'then move in closer just to make sure. And take several shots at different settings.'

When she'd mastered that, I had her set me up for a portrait, with the camera on the tripod.

'Now press the self-timer and come and join me.'

'Where's the self-timer?'

'Should be a button somewhere.'

'Is that it?'

A red light had appeared on the camera. 'Yes. It's running. Hurry up!'

She dashed towards me and I lifted her off her feet. It was a long wait, but the camera clicked before a vertebra did.

At Shirley's we had Earl Grey and a cream tea each. The waitresses wore black uniforms with little white hats and aprons, and some of them looked as if they might have manned the Red Cross tent at the Siege of Mafeking. I enjoy sculpting great dollops of butter, cream and strawberry jam, balanced on crumbling pieces of pastry, and then popping them into my mouth. The secret is to keep your nose well out of the way. A certain piquancy is added by the element of danger in all that cholesterol. It's like bungee-jumping for the sedentary.

Annabelle ate hers with delight, making a lot less mess on her plate than me, and I decided that even though this might be what I wanted second-best in all the world, it was still pretty good. When the bill came it looked as if they charged by the calorie.

Walking back to the car, Annabelle took some pictures of the Pump Room and the Old Swan Hotel, where Agatha Christie accidentally locked herself in a wardrobe for three days and swore she'd been abducted by aliens. Annabelle didn't believe me, but it's true.

Leaving Harrogate, I wondered if we had time for a small diversion. The sun was low but the sky was still bright, so I decided we had. Trouble was, we were in the wrong lane at a set of traffic lights. I set the left-hand indicator flashing and looked over my shoulder. The driver behind gave a nonchalant lift of the hand and I pulled across, into the lane signposted towards Wetherby.

On the outskirts of town we drove alongside a big cemetery, with ornate gates and Gothic tombs visible over the hedge.

'We didn't come this way, did we?' Annabelle asked.

'No. I want to show you something.'

'Oh. Are you allowed to tell me what?'

I gestured towards her left. 'A graveyard,' I said.

At the end we turned down a narrow lane, and I parked half on the grass verge, half on the road. We entered through a well-maintained wrought-iron gate, and I turned to see Annabelle's reaction.

In front of us were row upon row of identical white headstones, casting long shadows across the tailored lawns. Blackbirds, foraging for worms, flew off, chattering angrily at our intrusion.

'War graves,' she said quietly.

'It's called Stonefall. They're all bomber crew, mainly Canadian. I think it must be Yorkshire's best-kept secret. My father brought me once, when I was about eleven. I'd kept pestering him to tell me about the war. He brought me here.'

We walked up the slope, over the grass, to the first stone and read the inscription. It said: *J.L. Hodgson, aged 23, pilot, Royal Air Force, 30th June 1943*. A few days later they laid W.C. Taverner, a twenty-one-year-old Australian, next to him; and a couple of days after that it was the turn of a Canadian, C.M. Johnson. He was also twenty-one. They continued until there were forty of them, side by side, and then they started a new row. When there were fifteen rows the field was half-full, so they turned around and filled the other half.

Annabelle lingered, reading all the details. I walked ahead, just scanning them. The pilots were the oldest – usually about twenty-five, but a couple were only twenty. The gunners were seventeen-or eighteen-year-olds. Sometimes a whole crew of seven were buried together.

One grave had faded flowers on it. When I saw the date I realised that we'd just had the anniversary of his death. I bent down and read the note on the blooms. He'd been a navigator, and a lady in Winnipeg was still carrying a torch for him. She'd be in her seventies, now.

I wandered back to the car and leaned on it, waiting for Annabelle. She returned about fifteen minutes later, looking pale. I unlocked her door.

A few miles down the road she said: 'That was a strange place to take me, Charles, but I'm glad you did.'

I said: 'Did you see the one with the fresh flowers on it?' My voice sounded as if it belonged to someone else.

'Yes. I read the note. It made me cry.'

'You're a softy.'

'And you're not?'

She reached across and placed her hand on my knee. I dropped my left hand from the steering wheel and took hold of it.

After a while I said: 'What I think I'm trying to tell you . . . in my clumsy way . . . is that we don't achieve anything in this world unless we are prepared to take a few risks. So you'd better make sure that these pictures you bring back from Africa are good ones.'

She gripped my hand tightly, and shook it from side to side. 'It's a promise,' she said.

I wanted to seal it with a kiss, but the Harrogate Road has a fearful reputation, and we were doing over sixty miles per hour.

Two days later, early in the morning, I took Annabelle to Manchester Airport and saw her on to a British Airways 767 bound for Nairobi, via Athens. Goodbyes are like listening to people discuss their vasectomies – they make your eyes water. I didn't let the side down, but it was a close thing.

The plan had been to breakfast at the airport, but I wasn't hungry. Commuter traffic was building up as I drove towards the motorway. We were travelling at about fifty up the slip road, bunched too close to the traffic in front and behind, when I caught a movement in my wing mirror. Some idiot in a Peugeot was making a do-or-die effort to overtake us all, driving on the shaded area where the lanes narrow. He came by me and dived into the gap I'd left, slapping his brakes on to get down to our speed. I hit my anchors and leaned on the horn.

He glanced up at his mirror and gave me two fingers.

I slammed the gearbox down into third and shot out of line. Alongside him, I held my warrant card at arms' length and pointed at the hard shoulder. His expression changed from arrogance to fear, and he pulled over.

I parked behind him. 'Oh, Charlie,' I said to myself, drumming my fingers on the rim of the steering wheel. 'What the fuck are you playing at?' My windscreen wipers were swishing from side to side, even though it hadn't rained for three days.

The driver of the Peugeot was sitting ashen-faced with his window down, waiting for me. The car was a typical rep's vehicle: bog standard, with his jacket on a hanger behind his seat. He looked about sixty and should have known better. That made two of us. Traffic was tearing by barely five feet away, the wash from a lorry nearly knocking me off my feet.

'DI Priest,' I yelled over the noise, poking my ID up his nose. I leaned in through his window and looked at the mileage on his speedo. He'd done twenty-two thousand miles, and the car couldn't be more than six months old. Rather him than me.

'Not very considerate driving, sir,' I said, mustering my reserves of restraint.

'Er, no, Officer.'

'Well, mind how you go. We're all in a hurry, you know.' I walked back to my car, and thought I heard him call, 'Thank you,' after me. I followed him in the slow lane for a couple of miles, before he sneaked away to resume his mad chase to wherever.

I wasn't proud of myself. It wasn't the sort of behaviour expected from one of Her Majesty's police officers. I'd lost control. Once upon a time I arrested a kid of fourteen who'd mugged a seventy-year-old lady. He'd knocked her over and she'd broken her thigh. She spent six months in hospital and seven in an old people's home, which she hated. Then she died. The youth skipped bail and gave us the runaround before we got him in court, by which time the old lady was in a happier place. Because she took longer than a year and a day to die we could only charge him with robbery.

He was given a probation order, and as he left the dock he gave me a one-fingered up-yours gesture, carefully shielding it from the magistrates with his body. I'd shrugged my shoulders and concentrated on the next job.

And now, here I was risking my life to bollock a motorist who'd carved me up. What would I do if faced with a youth like that again? Tear his legs off and play hockey with him? Very probably. I reluctantly admitted that maybe I wasn't ready to go back to everyday policing yet, but I had to do something.

At home I put the car in the garage and made myself a giant bowl of cornflakes, with a chopped-up banana and additional cream. A quick calculation told me that Annabelle's plane would be approaching Athens by now, for refuelling. It was going to be a long four weeks. After I'd emptied the teapot I sprawled on the rug in front of the fire and listened to Dylan's *Blood on The Tracks*. It's my favourite routine when I'm feeling sorry for myself, but I don't make a habit of it.

Fearnside was in when I rang him. 'It's DI Priest,' I said. 'I've changed my mind. What's the address of this house in East Yorkshire that you want me to rent, and the name of the drugs courier?'

'Good man, Charlie,' he responded. 'Good man. I'll send you the file.'

Chapter Seven

When Nigel called for me the following Saturday morning I was surprised, and pleased, to see that he had Dave Sparkington with him. Sparky's a good cop – the best – but he takes a delight in rubbing people up the wrong way. Nigel was learning how to handle him. It's easy enough – just let him do what he wants.

'Where's the Harold Hurst enquiry going?' I asked as soon as I was settled in the back seat.

'To Liverpool,' Sparky replied. 'Or Northern Ireland.'

'Why? What's happened now?'

'The gun that killed him – the AK47 – it's been used again. Back end of last week, a lorryload of fags were hijacked from Shenandoah. It was found burned-out and empty at a service centre outside Birmingham. The driver was in the back with three bullets in him from the AK.'

I said: 'Shenandoah? Norris's company?'

'Norris's company and Harold Hurst's, too, in a way.'

'So Hurst may have been an inside man for the hijack?'

'Possibly,' Sparky replied. 'Or maybe he had wind of it, so they eliminated him. Either way they're a bunch of ruthless bastards.'

'So it's out of our hands now.'

'That's right.' He gestured towards Nigel. 'The Brain of Britain here pops over to Liverpool now and again for a morning out, don't you, Sunshine?' He punched him on the shoulder. 'Otherwise it's in the hands of the Scouses and Special Branch.'

There was a big brown envelope on the seat beside me. I caught Nigel's eyes in the rearview mirror and asked: 'Is this the file from Fearnside?'

'I imagine so, boss. It came yesterday.' He was wearing cavalry twill trousers, a hacking jacket and a spotted bow tie.

'Cheers. Haven't you had a look?'

'It's marked for your eyes only.'

'Right. What's with the tie? Brightening up your image?'

Nigel straightened the tie. 'You told me to dress like an estate agent,' he replied.

'Oh, good. For a moment I wondered if I'd said theatrical agent.'

'Looks more like a bloody gynaecologist to me,' growled Sparky. After a few seconds' silence he added: 'Hey, do you know why gynaecologists always wear bow ties?'

'Yes, thank you,' we chorused.

The file wasn't very thick. The address of the house was 2, Longdyke Cottages, Wickholme, North Humberside. My new neighbour was Kevin Jessle, small-time drug smuggler, with form for receiving and possessing. The gang had been picked off, one by one, but Kevin had been left untouched, to increase his credibility and act as a focus for when they regrouped. Word was that he was active again, and this time we wanted the big boys.

Dealing is a serious offence, but the courts have their own criteria to differentiate between dealing and possessing for your own use. The gangs know the figures, and split their holdings into small quantities, inside the limit, and disperse them. The big men who finance the operations do their deals on mobile phones and never touch more than a single snort at any time. 'Don't look at me, man,' they protest, holding their hands up. 'First time I've ever tried it.' And we let them out on police bail and their flashy girlfriends drive them home in the Porsche and six months later a magistrate fines them fifty quid.

'M62 to Hull,' I directed Nigel. We were in the middle lane, doing about seventy, when a brand new Range Rover came steaming past, its spray making it necessary for Nigel to switch the wipers on for a few seconds.

'Look at that!' Sparky enthused. 'Now that is what I call one-upmanship.'

'What?' Nigel queried.

'A Range Rover *without* a personal number.'

'He might be called Ulysses Yorath Xylophone,' I argued. 'Take the A1033 out of Hull, past the jail, heading towards Spurn Head.'

'It's called Spurn Point,' Sparky insisted.

I peered at the map. 'It says Spurn Head here,' I told him.

'Well, it was always called Spurn Point when I was a kid. Flamborough Head, Spurn Point.'

'Maybe they changed it.'

'Why?'

'To confuse the Germans.'

'How would that confuse the Germans?'

'Well, it's confusing us. If they landed, they'd think they were in the wrong place.'

'Big deal. So they'd get back in the landing craft and bugger off somewhere else. "Achtung! Vee are all in zee wrong plaitze. Let's invade Sveeden instead." '

'Which way?' Nigel cried. We were rushing at a roundabout.

'Up here,' I said, unhelpfully.

'Up where?' he protested, swinging on the wheel.

'No, not this one.'

The car rocked from side to side as he changed direction.

'I think it's this one, unless they've altered all the names.'

Historical influences are heavy in that part of the world. The villages have neat nameplates as you approach, brightened by the local coats-of-arms. Some of the names, such as Roos or Hedon, look as if they've lost a few letters off one end. Others, like Thorngumbald, look as if they've found them. The land is a rich alluvial plane, sodden wet in early March, the tractor tracks in the fields reflecting the pale sky. We passed a church that had a spire every bit as elegant as Salisbury Cathedral, contrasting sharply with the solid Norman blockhouse of a building in the next village. Nigel commented that he might come back to do some exploring, and I wondered about bringing Annabelle.

Near our destination, the familiar sign of a Jolly Burger came into view and I suggested we have a coffee. I couldn't believe it: the youth who showed us to our places had terminal acne, just like the one in Cornwall. I wondered if Spotted Cow disease could pass through the food chain to humans. We decided to leave Sparky in the café while Nigel and I reconnoitred Number 2, Longdyke Cottages. 'He'll pay,' I told the youth as we left, nodding towards Dave.

It was one of a pair of white-walled semis, perched on the roadside in the middle of nowhere. They were both neat and tidy, but Number 2 had the slightly forlorn look of the unoccupied. A dilapidated Opel Manta stood in next door's garden. The Manta was once a desirable car, rival to the Capri amongst a certain group of enthusiasts, but this one was pock-marked with rust and sagging on its suspension. Drugs trafficking was evidently going through a recession in this part of the world. Maybe we could revive it.

'OK, Nigel, do your estate-agent act,' I told him, as we got out of his car.

'Right, Mr Priest. First of all I'll show you the delightful aspect of the rear, if you'll just follow me.'

I followed him, but found nothing delightful about his rear, I'm pleased to report. We stood in the back garden and Nigel pointed upwards. 'That,' he said, 'is what we call a roof.'

'A roof?'

'Yes. All decent houses have one. My advice to you is: never touch a house without a roof.'

'Thank you. I'll remember that.'

'Those things there . . .'

'With the glass in them?'

'Yes. Now they are called windows.'

From the corner of my eye I saw a face briefly appear at one of the windows next door, then vanish. He was in – we weren't wasting our time.

We walked round the front, and Nigel told me all about drainpipes and gutters. He read the name of the person he was supposed to be, from the *To Let* sign, and noted the address. His Head Office was in Withernsea. Across the low-lying fields we could see the River Humber, with one of the big ferries moving slowly towards Hull docks. The sun made a brief appearance, turning the river into a long bar of silver that looked to be higher than we were. After wandering round and chatting for a few minutes we went back to collect Sparky.

We used the Jolly Burger toilets and I gave the cashier a fiver, saying, 'I'll get these,' to the other two.

'That will be seven pounds twenty, sir,' he said.

'For three coffees!' I exclaimed.

'Four coffees and an American breakfast,' he replied.

'I, er, was hungry,' Sparky mumbled.

I swapped the fiver for a tenner.

'Was everything satisfactory?' the youth asked as he handed me my change.

'No. His grits were cold,' I told him.

'Thank you. Have a nice day.'

I was about to let him know that I was determined to have a bloody awful day, but Sparky dragged me away.

We took the coastal route to Withernsea. Nigel had never been there.

'Jewel of the Yorkshire coast,' I informed him as we headed north. 'You're in for a treat.'

'Lovely place,' Sparky agreed. 'Me and the wife spent our honeymoon there. Thought about going to Torremolinos, but in the end Withernsea won, hands down.'

'Torquay's nice,' I said.

'Very nice,' Sparky nodded. 'Very nice indeed.'

'But not as nice as Withernsea.'

'Oh no. Not as nice as Withernsea.' After a few moments he said: 'The Yorkshire Riviera.'

'That's what it is,' I agreed. 'The Yorkshire Riviera. Well, it would be, if there was a river.'

'But that's not the point, is it? Eh, Charlie?'

'Of course not, David. There's not a river at Torquay.'

'Exac'ly. Exac'ly. That's just what I'm trying to say. There doesn't have to be a river to qualify as a riviera.'

'It's just an expression.'

'Exac'ly.'

'Exac'ly.'

'Like . . . Dennis.'

'Dennis?'

'Yes. Have you noticed that firemen always call their engine Dennis?'

'That's true. I'd never realised it before, but now you come to mention it . . .'

Nigel protested: 'Dennis isn't the name of the engine. It's what they call the company that makes them.'

'Is it?'

'Gerraway.'

When you are not driving you can observe the scenery. The sea, to our right, was the colour it gave to battleships, with blue-black cloud shadows dappled across it. Wind-whipped waves crowded towards the shore, flags flying, in a ceaseless battle to reclaim the land – a battle they are winning.

Withernsea in winter is where the astronauts practised for landing on the dark side of the moon, before they decided that it was too inhospitable and called off the mission.

'Was that it?' Nigel asked as we drove out of the other side.

Sparky made a clicking noise and said: 'Glorious!'

We turned round and looked for the estate agent. It wasn't difficult to find, tucked between a launderette and Kurl Up 'n' Dye hairdressers, both closed for the winter. The bored girl behind the counter seemed astonished that I wanted a three-month lease on Number 2, Longdyke Cottages. I had no references, but my story was that my wife had kicked me out and I needed somewhere desperately. I needn't have worried. She accepted my cheque, including a month's rent as bond, and gave me the key. While I was waiting for her to write me a receipt I studied the photographs on the wall. They were big in caravans and did a nice line in 'shallies'.

Sparky complained that he wasn't hungry, but still managed a sirloin steak and chips in one of the local pubs. Over a pint we brainstormed a new persona for me, so that I could ingratiate myself with Mr Kevin Jessle, drug smuggler and neighbour.

'I think you should borrow a Rottweiler,' Sparky said. 'He's bound to be into Rottweilers.'

'Or a big snake,' Nigel enthused. 'A boa constrictor. I had a glimpse of him through the window and he definitely had a look of the herpetologist about him.'

I shook my head. 'Uh uh. No dogs, no snakes. I might run to a budgerigar, though.'

Sparky said: 'Nah, unless you could find a particularly evil budgerigar.'

'With a foul mouth,' Nigel added.

'And then you ought to have a few tattoos,' Sparky told me.

'Definitely,' Nigel agreed. 'LUFC on your forehead and some barbed wire twined round your neck.'

I wiped my last chip in the remnants of French mustard on my plate and popped it into my mouth. 'Look,' I said, pausing to swallow. 'This is serious.' I placed my knife and fork on the plate and picked up my empty glass. 'Same again?'

'Yes, please.'

'Better not, if I'm driving,' said Nigel.

'Something else?'

'Er, tonic water, please. I can't say that I enjoyed that beer.'

Me too. I studied the various refreshments on offer and by way of a complete change ordered half a pint of draught cider. It was worse than the beer, but it gave me an idea.

Back on the M62, heading west, Sparky turned round and said: 'So what's it to be, Charlie? A souped-up XR2 with *Sharron* and *Charlie* on the sunshield?'

I'd been deep in thought, thinking about Annabelle. After Kenya she was making a circuit round Lake Victoria that would take her through Tanzania and Uganda. Then it was up into Somali and Ethiopia. It was a gruelling schedule – she wouldn't be having a picnic.

'Sorry, I was miles away. No, more subtle than that. The draught cider I had – it was called Crossbow. Don't suppose you know anyone I could borrow one from, do you?'

★ ★ ★

Policemen have a variety of options open to them when they retire from the Force, which is fortunate, because most need to maintain their income. PCs and Sergeants retire at fifty-five, and Inspectors, because their role is supposed to be less physical, can keep going until they are sixty. If you have your full thirty years in it's not too bad for Inspectors and above, but lower ranks receive lower pay, and a drop to two-thirds salary, just when the kids are at university, can be awkward. So some are forced to find jobs in security, social services or insurance. Others, who have always had a hankering to work for themselves, become painters, cabinet-makers or chiropodists. I never cease to wonder at the varied talents of my fellow officers. Eric Dobson, one of our motorcycle patrols and a two-wheeled enthusiast, started a firm of couriers called Merlin, specialising in delivering bits and pieces for the various hospitals in the area. Bits and pieces of people, usually, like hearts and kidneys. Business was good, and when he expanded to four wheels he asked me to design a logo for the sides of his vans. I gave him a ring.

'Merlin Couriers,' he sang into the phone.

'Two hedgehog vindaloos to 12, Woodland Avenue, quick as you can,' I said.

'Charlie Priest! You old skullduggar. What on earth are you up to these days?'

I gave him the full story, and asked if I could hire one of his vans for the occasional weekend.

'You're too old for that sort of caper,' he replied. 'Why don't you pack it in and come and work for me? You could learn the ropes on the Kawasaki, then maybe graduate to a Transit.'

'No thanks, Eric. You cured me of motorbikes for ever.'

I was a young PC at the time, dashing out of the station to

investigate a domestic. Eric was leaving to go home on his Norton. 'Hop on,' he'd said. I clung to him like a mating toad, my shoes scraping on the road as he leaned over for the corners. We arrived safely, but trembling, to be told to mind our own business by the lady of the household. I walked back to the station.

'I'd rather take my chances with drugs barons,' I told him.

'Fair enough. Tell you what, our first van – the one you painted – has been pensioned off. Done nearly two hundred thousand miles. I just keep it for sentimental reasons. It's a bit tatty, but a good runner. You can borrow that for as long as you want.'

'Super. I'm on expenses, so we can afford to pay you something. And can you give me some sort of cover in case anyone rings up asking about me?'

'No problem, Charlie. How about if you are on our London and South Coast run, twice a week? That should keep you out of the office.'

'Great. Will I be able to collect the van Saturday morning?'

'We'll have it ready for you.'

After ringing Eric I drove into town and visited the market. One of the butchers had been very helpful in our investigations into sheep rustling. Without saying much I led him to believe I was hot on the trail again, and ordered a whole lamb from him, neatly cut into joints and packed in two separate bags. I paid for it, and told him I'd collect on Saturday morning. Then I went to the newsagents and looked for a magazine that might tell me something about crossbows. They didn't have one.

On the outskirts of town, south of the tracks, where expectations are low and so are rents, there is a shop that sells guns, just along from Help the Aged and another shop that deals in second-hand furniture. I threaded between the three-piece suites on the pavement and opened the reinforced door of Guns 'n' Ammo.

The proprietor's T-shirt bore a skull on the front, wrapped in the legend: *I will give up my gun when they prise it from my stiff dead fingers*. That could be arranged, I thought. A poster on the wall boasted: *A Smith & Wesson beats four aces*. Brave words, but mainly they sold airguns.

'Afternoon,' he said. He arms had seen more tattooists than Edinburgh Castle.

'Hello.' I wandered round his shop, taking it all in. I was out of touch – some of these airguns looked as if they could kill. I turned to him. 'Do you sell crossbows?' I asked.

'Crossbows?'

'That's right. William Tell, all that stuff.'

'No, sorry. No call for crossbows. Got one for a feller about a year ago.'

'But you haven't got one in now?'

'No.'

'Do you know anything about them? What to look for if you buy one: that sort of thing?'

He looked mystified and shook his head. 'Nah, sorry.'

'So you won't have any arrows – bolts – for them?'

More head-shaking.

'OK. Thanks a lot.' I turned to go, but changed my mind. 'Don't suppose you sell bows, either?'

'No. We don't sell no bows, or crossbows. No call for 'em, round 'ere.'

But presumably there was a call for air rifles with telescopic sights that a Bosnian sniper would swap his samovar for. 'No arrows, either?' I repeated, already shaking my own head in anticipation of his answer.

His brow furrowed with concentration, as if the act of thinking caused him pain. 'Yeah, we did 'ave some arrers, somewhere.' He started opening drawers at his side of the counter; then looked in several cupboards.

They were in a big drawer under the window display, in two bundles wrapped in newspaper. He spread them out on the counter, pleased with his success. There were about a dozen fancy aluminium ones, carefully painted with bands of colour, and a few cheap wooden ones that looked nowhere near as professional.

I inspected a wooden one, holding it carefully between finger and thumb and sighting along it. The varnish was peeling and the feathers were crooked. 'I'll take that one,' I told him, passing it across the counter.

Bradley T. Norris approached the Ivy League cheerleader behind the front desk of Jefferson Industries and wondered why he'd ever left America. He felt comfortable in his lightweight mohair suit and regular underwear, instead of those damned thermals he needed in England. And then there were the girls. There was nothing like an earthy Southern belle to warm the parts that British ice-maidens didn't know existed. He smiled at her and let his eyes wander. She returned the smile, apparently grateful for his appreciation.

'Could you please let Mr Jefferson know that Brad Norris is here,' he told her.

'Er, yes, sir. Is Mr Jefferson expecting you?' She'd never been asked to call the President of the company before.

'Yes, he is.'

She relayed the message, via a secretary, then said: 'Mr Jefferson will be with you in a moment, sir. Would you care to take a seat?'

'Thank you.' Norris didn't sit down, but wandered round the large marble-clad foyer, examining the works of art on the walls. There were prints by Rothko and Pollock, and posters for various events sponsored by

Jefferson Industries, from the ballet to stock-car racing. Norris nodded his approval.

The elevator door hissed open and the huge frame of Jefferson J. Jefferson III emerged, pulling a checkered jacket on over a short-sleeved shirt.

'Brad, old buddy. How're ya doin'?'

They clasped hands in a four-handed shake. 'I'm fine, Jeff, just fine. You sure look well.'

'Oh, you know . . .' They walked out through the revolving door without a backward glance at the girl. Jefferson's car was already waiting for them. 'Ruth's Chris,' he told the driver. Turning to Norris he said: 'I've told Krystal we'll meet her there. We can always move on to somewhere else, if you wish.'

Ruth's Chris is a well-known chain of steakhouses. Fortunately their steaks slide over the tongue more easily than their name.

'Ruth's Chris is fine by me, Jeff,' Norris told him.

Jefferson said: 'Look, er, Brad. I'd just like to say how sorry we all are about Marina.'

'Thanks, Jeff. It's good of you to say so.'

'You know that if there's anything we can do . . .'

Norris wondered about a formal introduction to Jefferson's receptionist, but decided against it. 'Thanks. Everybody's been so kind.'

Jefferson rambled on: 'If you don't want to talk about it, Brad, just tell me to button up, but we're all mystified over what happened to her. We heard she just vanished. Haven't you any idea where she went?'

'Well, there's a bit more to it than that, Jeff. First I knew was when someone phoned me to say my Rolls-Royce was in a certain parking lot, and would I collect it. I thought it was the police, but it wasn't. I collected the car, and Marina never came home that night. Fact is, Jeff, things hadn't been too good between us, so I wasn't surprised. A couple days later they found the body of my chauffeur, with his head blown off. Those limey cops play with their cards close to the chest, but I think they're working on the theory that it was a bungled kidnap attempt. Deep down, I know she's dead.'

'Jesus H. Christ! That's a helluva thing to happen to a guy.'

They rode the rest of the way in silence. As they waited to be seated in the restaurant, Jefferson said: 'So what do you think of the Rolls-Royce? Is it as good as the Brits reckon?'

Jefferson Tobacco was founded by the first J.J.J.'s father, who was called Schmitt but was eager for Americanisation. 'Tobacco' in the title was dropped in favour of 'Industries' in the late 1970s. Diversification of interests was the excuse, but the real reason was to change the company's image – tobacco products still provided eighty per cent of their profits.

They declined to order when the waitress introduced herself. 'Not just yet, thank you,' Jefferson told her. 'We're waiting for a colleague.'

'Did Krystal fly in last night?' Norris asked.

'Yeah. Phoned me this morning.'

'So how is she? Still as big and outrageous as ever?'

'She doesn't change none.'

Krystal Wallach was head of the LMW Group, formerly LMW Tobacco. Once again the family firm had passed down the line, but it jumped a generation when Krystal's father, last of the LMWs, found igniting space rockets more exciting than lighting cigarettes. He was a prominent physicist, and became a bigwig at NASA, allowing the company to pass from his father to his daughter. Ethics had nothing to do with it – he was still a major shareholder.

'Any men in her life?' Norris asked.

'Not so as anyone has ever noticed.'

'Seems a helluva a waste to me,' he declared, shaking his head.

'No disrespect, Brad, but she'd eat you for breakfast and spit the pips out.'

'I was thinking about you. You're more her size.'

'Me!' Jefferson laughed. 'Hell, no. I once tried bull riding at Carson City Cowboy Daze. Lasted two-point-four seconds and couldn't pee straight for a week. Krystal Wallach is more than I'd care to try taming.' They both threw their heads back and guffawed.

'She's here,' said Norris, wiping his eyes. The hostess was directing her towards the booth where the two men sat.

In the Land of Big Women, Krystal Wallach was regarded as tall, standing six feet two in her bare feet. She was wearing jeans tucked into snakeskin cowboy boots and a white silk shirt. The jeans cost three hundred dollars and the boots well over a thousand. Dangling from her ears were baubles that looked as if they were looted from Montezuma's treasure house and her black hair flounced over her shoulders. Every head in the restaurant turned to follow her, and the two men rose to their feet.

'Brad,' she said, holding out her hand.

'Krystal. It's good to see you.'

'Jeff.'

'Krystal.'

Norris said: 'Glad you could make it, Krystal. I don't think you'll have wasted your time.'

'Oh, I'll fly five hundred miles for a free steak any day.'

'Good girl. Shall we order?'

It was lobster and steak all round, with salads. It's a myth that American steaks are bigger than European ones. Cows are much the same size all the world over. The Americans just cut the meat thicker, and don't incinerate it.

While they were waiting for the lobster hors d'oeuvre to arrive, sipping Californian Chardonnay, Krystal said: 'Brad, I have to say something about Marina. I'd like you to know how sorry we all are. Have you any idea what happened to her?'

Norris coughed and shook his head. 'No, er, no. Thanks for asking, though; I appreciate your concern. I've told Jeff about it all, so maybe he'll fill you in with the details. I'm sure you'll both want to discuss what I have to say to you.'

'OK.'

On the surface their three companies – Shenandoah Incorporated, Jefferson Industries and the LMW Group – were deadly commercial rivals, who between them stitched up over half of the tobacco sales in the USA. They knew the difference between competition and destroying each other, though, and in the face of a common enemy they showed a united front. That enemy was all around them, for the industry that made them wealthy was now regarded by many as the pariah of the Free World. In the United States alone, an estimated 300,000 people died each year from smoking-related diseases, and the number was growing. The worldwide figure was probably approaching three million.

Fortunately for Norris, Jefferson and Wallach, the trade had one powerful weapon in its favour. Money. No government or political party so far could manage its books without the colossal contribution made by the sale and taxation of tobacco products. Health warnings and restrictions on advertising were merely cosmetic inconveniences. Tobacco was King; long live the King.

They cooperated with each other in many other ways. Jefferson sponsored classical music and car racing, so LMW supported rock concerts, and Shenandoah poured large amounts into horse racing and football. They didn't compete in advertising, one using billboards, the others magazines and newspapers. At a recent meeting they'd carved up the Third World markets to save duplication of effort.

Shipping billions of cigarettes across the Atlantic Ocean is expensive, so arrangements had been made. Red Wing, Shenandoah's market leader, was now made in England; but to save transport costs, Jefferson made a cigarette with the same name right there in North Carolina. In return, Shenandoah rolled, packaged and marketed Garfields for Jefferson. LMW were involved in a similar agreement.

They finished their steaks and ordered a bottle of Bordeaux instead of puddings.

'We've seen the figures, Brad,' Krystal said. 'The Liverpool plant is on stream and achieving its targets. It was a good move, so why have you called this meeting?'

It would have been natural for the men to light cigars, and Krystal to have smoked one of the long dark cheroots she was often photographed with, but they didn't. This wasn't a public performance. Norris waited until the waitress had delivered the second bottle and left them, before saying: 'We could have trouble brewing. The injuns are restless.'

'Would this be one particular injun called Andrew Fallon?' Jefferson asked.

'Got the bastard in one, Jeff. He'll be British Prime Minister in less than a year, carried along on a floodtide of woolly intentions and lofty prose. He's big on foreign aid, but says it should be a hand-*up*, not a hand-*out*.'

'Reagan said it first,' Krystal interrupted.

'Oh, I wish he were Reagan, Krystal, I wish he were. Where on earth are we finding these guys? He says the poor nations should be growing food to feed themselves, not tobacco to export and then buy back as cigarettes.

Cigarettes that will, he claims, ruin their health.'

'It still hasn't been proved,' Krystal asserted, shaking her head and enjoying the feel of her hair brushing her neck. 'And there's no other crop that will give those farmers the returns they are guaranteed from tobacco.'

'Heroin? Marijuana?' suggested Jefferson with a grin.

'Yeah, you got it, Jeff. Illicit drugs. Tobacco is legal.'

'The bottom line,' Norris said, 'is that we need them to grow the stuff, and they need to grow it to survive. We provide them with a market for their crop, earning good ol' American dollars for them. Fallon disagrees, of course. He's promising to cut off aid to tobacco-growing countries. Then he's going to tax our exports and tax our profits. He won't be happy until he drives us extinct. He's on a crusade, and right now Britain is looking for a crusader.'

The other two thought about what he'd said until Jefferson broke the silence. 'You make it sound real bad.'

'It is.'

'So what are you suggesting?'

Norris twirled his glass between his fingers. 'I don't want to be too specific,' he said, 'but I'd like you both to contribute to a fighting fund.'

'A fighting fund?'

'Yeah. I've been talking to some guys. Professionals. For a price, they can solve our little problem.'

'How much are we talking about?'

'Three-quarters of a million bucks each, plus a few expenses.' They took the news as if they'd enquired the price of a new hat. Norris went on: 'You'd have to lose it somewhere. Would that cause a problem, Jeff?'

'No, no problem. I'd just give the race team an extra million and tell them I wanted eight hundred grand back, in used tens. They can spend that much on tyres.'

'Krystal?'

'No problem, Brad. I'd lose it in the advertising budget.'

'OK. Are you both in, then?'

Jefferson looked puzzled. 'So what's it to be?' he asked. 'A dirty tricks campaign?'

Norris said: 'No, Jeff. Dirty tricks are not straightforward enough for a simple country boy like me.'

Krystal turned to face Jefferson. 'I think what Brad has in mind, Jeff, is solving our problem – how shall I put this? – the American way.' She pointed at him with a forefinger and raised her thumb, imitating the hammer of a pistol.

Jefferson said: 'Oh. Jeez!'

'All I want is your money,' Norris told them, quietly. 'For that, I'll guarantee our problems will go away. You won't need to know anything about anything. Can I count you in?'

Jefferson nodded. 'Count me in, Brad.'

Krystal Wallach raised her glass. 'I'd like to propose a toast,' she said, pausing for the others to raise theirs.

'To the American way.'

They clinked glasses. 'The American way.'

Chapter Eight

Saturday morning I collected the Transit from Merlin Couriers. Eric wanted to chat, but I escaped as politely as I could. The butcher handed the two bags of lamb over to me and I went home. Nigel had left a message on the ansa-phone. I rang him at the station and he told me that he had dropped the key off at Number 1, Longdyke Cottages. Kevin Jessle would be in all day.

I snapped the arrow into three pieces, leaving the pointed end about six inches long, and the bit with the feathers about two. I trimmed the feathers to half size with the kitchen scissors. Carefully removing the white Sellotape from around the neck of one of the bags of lamb, I selected the largest piece of meat in there. I pinned it down on the kitchen worktop with my left hand and drove the pointed end of the arrow through it. It would have been easier to have broken it after I'd stabbed the joint, but you live and learn – all this was new to me. I rubbed the short piece of arrow, with the feathers, in blood and dropped it into the bag, putting the large piece of meat back in with it. I washed my hands and re-sealed the bag with my own, clear, Sellotape. The fish and chip shop was open, so I lunched before driving the ninety miles to the cottage.

The Merlin Couriers Transit wandered about on the motorway like a drunkard in a gale. It had done 187,000 miles. I did some mental arithmetic. That was nearly eight times round the world. More, if you didn't count the oceans. It rattled like an RSPCA collection tin at a foxhunt, and a draught from around the window threatened to sever my head. I pulled into the drive at the side of Number 2 with a raging pain behind my right eye and frostbite in my ear.

I sat for a few minutes with the engine running and slowly thawed out. The headache subsided, too, I'm pleased to say.

Jessle came to the door before I knocked. I started to ask him if the estate agent had left a key with him, but he just held it out towards me. He hadn't done too well in the Good Looks Grand Prix. He was about five-ten and podgy with it, with a face like a suet pudding, framed by lank mousy hair. Age? About thirty-five, gone to seed.

'Er, cheers,' I said, taking the key before he closed the door on my outstretched arm.

The cottage was nice inside. 'Cottage' is a bit grand. It was a two-up, two-down semi, but it had a certain charm. The morning sun would catch it, and you could see the river in the distance. Could be spooky when the fog rolled in.

The place was rented as being furnished, and there was nearly everything you needed to get by. In summer it was let to holidaymakers, but the owners were wanting a more permanent arrangement. I had a good look round, making a note of things I might need.

The bed had a mattress on it, still with a plastic bag covering it. That made me feel more comfortable. I had a look in the other, smaller bedroom, and found a single bed in there. Good, I thought. No water came out of the taps when I tried them, which is a sensible precaution in winter. The stop tap was under the sink. I turned it on, then turned it off again, as hard as I could.

This time I knocked, but he still answered it as if he'd been waiting, hand poised on the doorknob. 'Sorry to trouble you again,' I told him, 'but I can't get the water on. I've found the tap but it's too stiff for me to move. You haven't a pair of pliers or a wrench I could borrow for a moment, have you?'

'Wait a minute,' he replied, and disappeared back inside. A few seconds later he handed me a pair of pliers with red plastic handles.

'My name's Charlie, by the way,' I said, taking them. 'Looks as if we'll be neighbours for a while.'

'Kevin,' he mumbled.

I held out my hand and he offered his. It was like shaking hands with a corpse. Nigel was right – there was something herpetological about him. Maybe it was the scales.

'I'll be straight back,' I told him. I dashed in, turned the water on by hand and immediately returned with the pliers.

'Cheers. There's nothing like having the right tool for the job.' As he turned to leave me I said: 'You're not a vegetarian, are you?'

'A vegetarian? No, why?'

'Do you like lamb?'

He looked puzzled. 'Lamb? It's all right. Why?'

I winked at him. 'I have a supplier. I'll bring you some. Thanks for the loan of the pliers.' It was my turn to leave him standing there.

I finished my list, checking the heating and the meter readings, and went home to Heckley. It had been a good day, except that I realised I could have managed with just half a sheep. I called in at the supermarket and bought lots of vegetables and jars of sauces. At the checkout I impulse bought a cookery magazine that was running a feature on ten delicious things to do with lamb.

In the evening I opened the bag with the white Sellotape

still round it and played at being Sweeney Todd. When I'd finished, the kitchen looked like a charnel house. I threw the biggest pile of bloody fragments in the dustbin and cooked the rest. I made lamb casseroles, lamb hotpot, lamb stew, lamb rissoles, lamb curry, lamb pudding, lamb trifle, lamb jam. I stuffed the lot in the freezer, using every container and dish I possessed, and fell into bed after midnight. I couldn't sleep, so I tried counting sheep, but they kept chasing me.

I was up early but instead of going to church I visited the local DIY store and bought four miles of heavy duty draught-sealing strip and attacked the van doors with it. Just in case it didn't work, I wore an old tracksuit top with a hood. After I'd loaded surprisingly few belongings into the van, plus the bag containing the left half of an assemble-it-yourself sheep, I drove to the cottage again. I was going to grow very familiar with the M62 and the road through Hull in the next few weeks. I wore the hood over my ears for the first few miles, but once the interior of the van warmed through it wasn't too bad.

Kevin Jessle's Opel was still outside his house. I grabbed the bag of meat and knocked at his door.

'Stick that in your freezer,' I told him when he came, thrusting the bag forward.

'What is it?' he asked, taking it.

'Lamb. I asked you if you liked it.'

'Oh, ta. Smashing. How much?'

I shrugged my shoulders. 'Eight quid, if it's any good to you. Pay for my petrol.'

'Right.'

He gave me the exact money and went back inside to check if he'd been ripped off, while I unloaded my van. Most of the stuff I'd bought was bedding. The invention of the duvet was the answer – well, part of the answer – to a bachelor's prayer. Cornflakes were a big help, too. I plugged in the little black and white telly, that I'd probably never watch, and my rasta-blaster, which I'd listen to non-stop. I stuffed an old Jimi Hendrix tape into it and wound the volume up loud. Might as well test the acoustics of the dividing wall.

It was half an hour later that I caught his knock at the door, between the wailing chords of *All Along the Watchtower*, but he hadn't come to complain about the noise. He held his hand towards me, and laid across his palm were two pieces of wood. The longer piece had a steel point at one end, and the other had narrow feathers. He'd found my pretend crossbow bolt.

'Ah!' I said, looking, well, sheepish. I took the bits from him. 'You, er, weren't supposed to see that.' He was grinning as if he had a toothless ferret up his trouser leg. I went on: 'I thought it had gone straight through. The butcher must have found it. He joints them for me. Half for him, half for me. Forget you saw it, eh, Kevin?'

'Never saw a thing, Charlie,' he replied.

'Great.' I opened the door wide. 'Kettle's just boiled. Fancy a brew?'

'Some other time, if you don't mind.'

'OK.'

Shit, I thought, as I flopped on to the little settee, this is hard work. He was biting, but not hard enough. Maybe I'd have to buy that Rottweiler after all, to get through to him. Hendrix was hurting my ears, so I swapped him for Joan Baez. My musical development ceased with the demise of split-knee flares.

I stayed at the cottage overnight. Further exploration revealed one of those poles that allows you to play tennis with yourself, and a couple of board games – Monopoly and Scrabble. The double bed was extremely comfortable.

Eating my breakfast of toast and marmalade in front of the gasfire, I caught the final summary of the news on Radio Four. The group calling itself TSC was claiming another victory. They'd admitted planting a firebomb in a restaurant in Liverpool. It had been quite a blaze, and the manager and his wife, who were Irish, were missing. Remains of two bodies were being examined. I shook my head at the futility of it and hoped they'd stay away from Heckley. Drugs pushers I could handle, terrorists were something else.

There was only one item of mail lying on the doormat, but it was what I'd been waiting for. I felt like a change, so I had roast chicken for tea. Lamb is very nice, but you can have too much of it – I was beginning to speak with a New Zealand accent. Afterwards, when it had been digested, I jogged to the letterbox about three-quarters of a mile away and posted my expenses to Commander Fearnside. I was worried about my fitness, and also about the money I was spending on my journeys to Wickholme, so I'd decided to submit expenses forms weekly, and jog to the postbox with them.

With perfect timing, the phone rang as soon as I started to shampoo my hair, under the shower. I dashed down the stairs and grabbed it – it might have been a long-distance call, you never know.

'Charlie Priest,' I said.

It was the E-type man, wondering if I'd come to a decision. I wiped the foam from my eyes with the corner of my wrist and asked him to ring back in ten minutes.

I was sitting there, all neat and shiny in clean clothes when he did. The postcard from Annabelle was in my hand. She'd arrived safely, had met up with her colleagues, but was missing me. That was nice of her. She thanked me for my birthday card and promised to write a long letter when she had the chance. I'd made the birthday card myself and smuggled it into her hand-luggage. It was a long water-colour sketch of all the animals of Africa wishing her a happy birthday, with a little policeman at the end adding his own greeting. As a PS she asked: *Did you buy the car?*

Secretly, I think she was quite keen. I had to admit that she looked gorgeous sitting in it. It was a lot of money, though, and a car like that was wasted on me. I picked up the phone, prepared to disappoint someone.

'Hello, Mr Priest. Sorry to keep bothering you,' he said.

'It's no bother,' I assured him.

'Fact is, Mr Priest, I have an appointment with the bank manager tomorrow afternoon. After that, it's down the tube for me. I can afford to let you have the Jag back for five thousand less than I gave you for it. That's as low as I can go.'

We fenced around for a while, me making sympathetic noises, him saying that I was his last realistic hope of selling it in time, and apologising for making it sound like black-mail. He was a good bloke, banging his head on the wall of the recession. I couldn't believe it when I heard this voice telling him to bring it round in the morning – I'd make a decision then. I replaced the handset and bashed my own head against the kitchen wall.

It was a beautiful spring morning when he pulled into my street – even nature was conspiring against me. He'd obviously given it a good waxing, and it shone like a supermarket tomato as it sat there on the drive. Just before he switched off he gave the obligatory blip on the accelera-tor. It sounded like a lion giving a warning growl: come any closer at your peril, was the message. I went out and walked round it, absorbing the smells of polish and hot oil, listening to the clicks and hisses of contracting metal.

He'd driven up from Nottingham, so I invited him in for a coffee. 'I've brought all the documents,' he told me, 'and the receipts for the work I've had done on it.'

I gave them a perfunctory once-over. He'd certainly spared no expense, and it was as near to new as a car made in 1962 could possibly be. 'Take me for a drive,' I said.

The intention had been to turn right at the main road and head up on to the moors, but I'd made my decision before we reached the junction. I told him to turn left, into Heckley. We parked in a pay-and-display and I led him into my bank.

It was the biggest single cheque I'd ever drawn, but it still left five grand, plus interest, in the high rate account I'd opened specially for his cheque, a year ago. And now I had the car back, so I don't suppose it was a bad morning's work, although my shaking knees weren't convinced.

Back at my house we drew up a contract, signed the documents, and I telephoned the insurance broker and had the E-type put on my policy.

When I handed him the cheque he said: 'I loved that car, Mr Priest, but this will save . . . this will save . . .' He couldn't say the words, and lowered his head, embarrassed, so I never found out what it would save.

I carried our cups into the kitchen and took my time washing them. When I went back I said: 'Look, I'll probably keep the Jag a couple of years, then sell it. If you get turned around, want it back before then, you can have it at the same price. How does that sound?'

'It sounds very fair, Mr Priest.'

'Right. So how about ringing your wife to tell her you found a sucker to take it off your hands, then I'll drive you home in it.'

I rearranged the stuff in the garage – lawnmower, broken lawnmower, half-empty tins of magnolia emulsion – so that the ketchup torpedo would fit in, and relegated the Cavalier to the drive. Friday morning I swapped them around again and drove the E-type into town. I called in at the travel agents and the bank, then drove to the cottage. The travel agent had managed to squeeze me in on the evening ferry to Rotterdam, and we boarded at five-thirty.

I skidded into the drive of the cottage with a flurry of revs and scrunching gravel. This was my no-time-to-waste entrance. I slammed the Jag door moderately hard and dashed inside. *Readers' Digest* had tracked me down, otherwise nothing had changed. I ran up the stairs, making as much noise as I could, then flopped on the bed, listening, for several minutes. Nothing.

I flushed the toilet, put a toothbrush in my shirt pocket, and went outside. Kevin was squatting on his heels alongside the Jaguar, one extended arm resting on a wheel arch.

'Want to buy it?' I asked.

His eyes were as big and round as those on the little furry animals you always see on the front of nature magazines, calculated to twang the heartstrings. 'Is this yours?' he enquired, in the tone of voice the Pope reserves for Easter Sunday.

'Yeah. D'you like it?'

'It's fabulous. Brilliant. Best-looking car ever made.' He stretched upright.

I said: 'Yeah, well, this and maybe the Corvette Stingray.' I had an old *Classic Car* magazine somewhere that I stole from my barber's shop, with an article comparing the E-type and the Stingray.

Kevin shook his head. 'Nah, no contest,' he assured me.

'I have to go,' I told him, threading myself back into the driving seat. 'I'm booked on the ferry in half an hour. I'll take you for a ride when I get back Sunday morning.'

'The ferry?' He sounded interested.

I wound the window down so I could talk to him. 'That's right. Something cropped up – sudden, like.'

'What, to do with your courier job?' He'd seen the *Merlin Couriers* sign on the side of the Transit van.

I dithered visibly before answering. 'Mmm . . . you could say that,' I told him. My arm was dangling outside. 'Work,' I said, patting the door. 'That's the trouble with having expensive tastes.' I reversed into the road and drove away, giving him the briefest of waves.

The name came to me just after I'd joined the trickle of vehicles turning into the King George dock. Those furry creatures are called bush babies.

There was plenty of parking space and the car park looked relatively safe. I managed to find a bay at the end of a row, leaving a big gap between the Jag and its neighbour. I showed my ticket inside the terminal and was given a boarding pass, as with aeroplanes. It's a procedure that baffles me, but no doubt someone has put a lot of thought into it. Upstairs, past the *Passengers Only* signs, was a lounge with refreshments on sale. I found a seat and observed my fellow travellers.

It was amazing how many people wanted to visit Holland during that weekend in March. I played at 'Spot the Drug Smugglers', and decided that ninety per cent of them looked likely candidates. My police training told me that the other ten per cent were probably the real smugglers. The Customs Officers might have their successes, but they were only sniffing the gleanings.

An announcement in four languages invited us aboard, and I joined the shuffling queue. Most people were loaded down with hand-luggage and children. We went through a passport check and crossed a gantry on to the ship. There was a strong smell of fresh paint. A ship's police officer, doubling up on his duties, looked at my ticket and directed me to the appropriate desk. The hum of the engines could be felt through your feet. I put my tickets and passport safely in my pocket and went exploring.

The ferry was a bit like I imagine a cruise liner to be, but with a slightly less select clientèle. There were duty-free shops, a big dining room, casino, cinema, the works. Maybe I'd bring Annabelle if I ever did another trip, if it would be safe. I'd made myself a promise that I would try to involve her in my job as much as possible. Maybe that way I could avoid neglecting either her or it.

It had been a doddle so far. Show ticket and passport, obtain boarding pass. Show boarding pass and have tear-off strip taken. Customs Officer standing by, like a small boy with a fishing net, wondering which goldfish to catch. Presumably the vehicles coming on board were also under scrutiny, each driver praying: 'Please don't let it be my car they decide to strip down to its basic components and leave for me to put back together.'

I imagined myself in the Customs Officers' shoes and wondered what category of vehicle I would choose to pull from the line and humiliate. Easy. Anything with bullbars and stupid numberplates. I might not find any drugs, but I'd have fun.

The fare included what was described as an airline-type seat, in which one was expected to sleep. I found the lounge where they were. The seat was bigger than I had thought it would be, not too bad at all. I had considered an upgrade to a cabin, but objected to the usual rip-off that we singletons always encounter when travelling alone. The meal in the restaurant was OK, with plenty to choose from, but the bars were crowded. A couple of hours in the cinema appealed to me, but the films were aimed at the children on board, so I gave it a miss. This was one area where I'd been disappointed to learn that Annabelle's tastes were different from mine. She enjoys films by Ingmar Bergman, and most of Bertolucci's output; my favourites are Westerns and thrillers.

The big seat wasn't as comfortable as it looked, but I managed to get some sleep. A grey dawn found me peering through a window as a green and white navigation light slid by; we were entering Europoort, Rotterdam.

Guy Dooley reached out and cancelled the alarm clock ten seconds before it chirruped into life. He swung his legs out of bed, yawned and rubbed his eyes, and shuffled towards the bathroom in the dark. He could hear his mother's half-snores coming from the other bedroom. He chuckled and closed the bathroom door as silently as he could, trying not to disturb her.

Ten minutes later he was striding down the lane, stuffing a jam sandwich into his mouth with one hand and carrying all his birdwatching paraphernalia with the other. Away to his right the sky was just beginning to lighten.

The chough, *Pyrrhocorax pyrrhocorax*, resembles a rook, but has startling red legs and beak. Its normal habitats are coastal cliffs and mountainous heathlands, but changes in agricultural methods have driven it to the edge of extinction in most of its traditional haunts. Guy had seen one last year, and was hoping that it might return to breed. Now was the time for nest-building.

Wooden steps led down the cliff to the beach. At the bottom he glanced to his left, to where he'd helped Charlie bury the porpoise, then turned right. In a quarter of a mile he scrambled up the sloping cliff to a natural shelf, pulling himself along with handfuls of grass and the dead stalks of sea thrift. When he reached a level place he erected the little canvas hide he'd brought with him and settled down on his folding stool, binoculars at the ready.

He was well-hidden, surrounded by gorse bushes that

were already in full leaf. From this spot he'd seen basking sharks cruising along, and porpoises leaping for the sheer joy of it. On a couple of occasions he might even have seen a whale. His mother would smile tolerantly when he arrived home starving hungry, to tell her of his latest sighting; and she'd privately wonder if her son was inventing a world to compensate for the loss of his father.

Guy scanned the horizon with his binoculars. The morning star should have been at its most glorious, but there was too much cloud. The sky was lighter now, the colour of pigeons' wings, with butterscotch clouds torn into small fragments and scattered from horizon to horizon. The surf was thumping into an outcrop of rock with a sound deeper than any rave band could produce, throwing plumes of spray into the air. The teenager surveyed it all, and felt happy.

A movement away to his left caught his attention. 'Oh shit!' he cursed – two men were walking down the beach. They'd scare away all the wildlife. The secret of good observation was to be very still and quiet, and let the animals and birds come to you, but these men would cancel out all the patience he had invested in this.

Guy trained the binoculars on them as they walked towards him. They were wearing combat jackets, and the smaller of the two had a slight limp. As they passed below him he could easily see the man's facial features, and he gave an involuntary shiver. He looked as if he'd had some sort of accident that had left him disfigured. A boxer, maybe, with a bad record. He looked out of place on the beach, at this hour of the morning. The baseball bat he was carrying only added to the incongruity.

They were walking close to the bottom of the cliff, and passed within fifty yards of Guy. Neither of them spoke. After they'd gone he lost sight of them, hidden by the gorse and the outcrops of rock. Guy looked at his watch. The man with the Labrador would be here in fifty minutes. He was Guy's signal to pack his belongings and go home for breakfast.

The chough didn't show itself, and no sea monsters were observed. Highlight of the morning was a bird that alighted on a bush about twelve feet in front of Guy and gave him a concert. At first he thought it was a yellowhammer, but he suddenly realised that it might be a cirl bunting. He was trying to consult his guidebook with as little movement as possible when it flew away.

The man with the Labrador came every Saturday morning. No other day, just Saturdays. He was on the beach at least an hour before all the other dog-walkers. Guy saw the Labrador first, dashing towards the sea after being let off its lead at the bottom of the steps. It dashed into the waves, sniffed them, and galloped back towards its master.

He came into view and strolled along just beyond the reach of the tide, throwing stones for the dog, which it never recognised once they had come to rest amongst all the others. Guy trained his binoculars on him, and noted, not for the first time, that he was extremely well-dressed for dog-walking on the beach. As Guy watched, the man glanced back over his shoulder, and a look of apprehension gripped his face.

Guy lowered the binoculars and saw why. The taller of the two men he'd seen earlier had emerged from the foot of the cliff, behind the dog-walker, and was walking towards him. Now the other one, with the baseball bat, appeared in front of him. Guy stood up.

The man had turned back the way he came, taking a course to avoid his assailants, but the tall man moved to cut him off. Ugly Face, with the baseball bat, was running towards them. The man started to flee, trying to dodge round the tall one, but he couldn't. He fell to the ground as the other one dashed up, raising the bat above his head.

'Hey! Stop it!' Guy was on his feet and shouting.

Three faces turned towards him. 'Stop it!' Guy screamed, and jumped down the first few feet of cliff between him and the men. Ugly Face froze, the bat still held aloft.

His colleague grabbed him. 'Forget it! Let's go!' he yelled. They started running towards the steps. Guy stumbled and rolled the last few feet on to the beach. He leapt to his feet and started after them. When he reached the wooden stairs they were nearly halfway towards the top. Guy took the steps three at a time. He knew he had no chance of tackling them, but thought he might get the number of their car. They had to be in a car.

The tall one stopped. He delved inside his jacket and pulled out a gun. Guy saw a puff of smoke from it, whipped away by the wind, and above the pounding of the blood in his ears he heard a crack and the buzz of the bullet going past his head. He turned and ran back down the steps.

The well-dressed man was on his feet, dusting the sand from his overcoat, the dog jumping around as if it were all a game.

'They got away,' Guy told him, puffing from the exertion. The man's face was the colour of the surf. 'Are you all right?' Guy asked.

He nodded, struggling for his breath. After a while he managed to say: 'You saved my life.'

Guy helped him up the steps, back towards where his car was parked. When he was more composed, the man said: 'They shot at you. You could have been killed, too.'

'Missed by a mile,' Guy told him with forced bravado. 'What do you think they wanted?' he asked.

'Don't know. Probably just a mugging. Drug addicts, that sort of thing.' They'd reached his car. It was a big Rover, and brand new. 'What's your name?' the man asked.

'Guy Dooley.'

The man extended his hand. 'Thanks again, Guy. You were the right person in the right place. I'm grateful to you.'

Guy shook his hand. 'What about the police?' he asked.

'Yes, I suppose we'll have to tell the police. Will you do that?'

'OK.'

He drove away, leaving Guy to go back to retrieve his birdwatching apparatus. As he drove off Guy wrote the number of his Rover in his notebook. It was a personal number, the letters being RJK. 'Don't mention it,' he said after the retreating vehicle. Now he felt scared. He daren't go back down to the beach, so he walked home. He'd have to come back later for his stuff, when there were more people about.

A bus ride from the dock to the centre of Rotterdam was included in the fare. We drove in on the A15, past ten miles of oil storage tanks and a forest of windmills. Sadly, they were the modern propellor-driven type. I read the road-signs: *Ring Road Nord*, *Utrecht*, *Den Haag*. We passed huge depots belonging to Mitsubishi and Wang, and were overtaken by a van with *Slagboom* written down the side. I'd visited Holland before, when I was an art student, and it was still the same bewildering mixture of the familiar and the totally foreign.

Rotterdam was bustling. I discovered how to use the underground system and spent three hours in the Boymans-Van-Beuningen Art Gallery. When I was lost, I asked, and people were very helpful. I lunched the easy way, in a department store self-service restaurant, and couldn't resist having an *warme appelbol* for pudding. Scrumptious!

The novelty had worn off for the journey home. The meal wasn't as good and the airline seat was even more uncomfortable. I had a couple of drinks in the bar and fell into a conversation with two girls from Bradford who'd caught the train to Amsterdam and visited the Rijksmuseum. They'd wandered into the red light district, and couldn't tell me about it for giggling. Maybe I should have gone with them.

The Jag was right where I'd left it when we docked at eight o'clock on a bright Sunday morning. I wasn't sure what to do next. In theory, I had a kilogram or two of an illegal substance on my person, so I ought to be disposing of it, somewhere. I drove into the centre of Hull and did some exploring, learned my way around. Early Sunday morning is the best time for that. Then I went for a spin in the Jag.

I drove over the Humber Bridge, into no-man's-land. It was fun driving the E-type across the bridge, but I'd have liked to have been down on the river, watching it go by. I pushed the tape into the machine and waited for the music. It was the Karelia Suite; just right.

The roads were deserted. The only other vehicles I saw were the occasional police traffic cars perched on their ramps at the side of the motorway, the driver with his head down, engrossed in the *News of the World* on his knees. I shot by at about a ton without attracting any attention. The M180, M18 and M62 took me to the A1 services and breakfast. It was just after eleven when I revved the engine in the drive of the cottage, hopefully awakening Kevin from his slumbers and dreams of the Big Time.

At ten past twelve, shaved and showered, I knocked on his door. He emerged blinking, like Mr Hedgehog on the first day of spring. It soon would be, I thought, and a week later Annabelle would be home.

'Hi, Kevin. Fancy going to the pub for Sunday dinner?' I asked.

'Er, dunno.' He was tucking his shirt into his trousers.

'C'mon, do you good. My treat, I'm feeling flush. We'll go in the Jag.'

'Oh, all right then. Ta.'

'Good lad. Come round when you're ready, but don't be too long: my stomach thinks my throat has a knot in it.'

He came in about twenty minutes, looking quite smart in a suit but no tie. I was restricted to jeans, clean shirt and my trusty leather jacket. I drove us over the Humber Bridge again to a big pub I'd seen on the outskirts of Brig. Maybe I showed off just a little on the way. Kevin beamed like he was coaching a team of synchronised swimmers.

'What will she do?' he asked, inevitably.

I shrugged my shoulders and sucked a long breath in, like a cowboy plumber surveying someone's flooded kitchen. 'It's supposed to do a hundred and fifty,' I told him, modestly adding: 'but I've only ever had a hundred and thirty-five out of her. That's plenty fast enough for me, though.'

'And me. What does she do to the gallon?'

Kevin asked questions all the way. Anything I didn't know I invented. All part of the training, some might say. What do macho drug smugglers have for Sunday lunch? Something different, like trout and salad, would have been very nice, but I had an image to cultivate.

'Roast beef and Yorkshire,' I told the waitress, dismissing the proffered menu.

'Yeah, me too,' Kevin agreed. 'So,' he said, sipping the froth off his pint. 'How did the trip go?'

'Pretty good,' I replied. 'One package collected and delivered. Charlie paid, cash on delivery. That's how I like it.'

'Where did you go?'

'Just to Rotterdam. No sweat. You ever been?'

'Yeah. Yeah, I've been a few times. So where did you have to deliver to?'

I plonked my glass down hard. 'Come off it, Kevin. You'll be asking me what was in the package next. And if you do, the answer is: "I don't know".'

He grinned and said: 'I bet you've a good idea, though.'

The waitress was hovering with two heaped plates. I leaned across to him an whispered: 'Well, I don't suppose it was friggin' Edam cheese.'

It was my treat, so I fetched the drinks each time and was able to order myself low-alcohol lager. Strange thing is, you feel just as drunk on it. I didn't quiz Kevin about his activities, being content to concentrate on winning his confidence. He'd open up, do some boasting, all in good time.

He insisted on buying a final round, so I told him to make mine an LA. 'Don't want pulling over by the filth,' I said, strangling a burp.

I drove back well within the speed limits, and laughed a lot. When Kevin got out, in my drive, he said: 'Thanks for the meal, Charlie. I appreciate it. I'll get the next one, if things buck up a bit.'

I adopted my grave, empathic look. I did a course on it, once, but the pretend booze helped. 'Why?' I asked. 'Aren't you doing too well at the moment?'

He looked embarrassed. 'No, not really. Things have dried up a bit. It's just temporary, though.'

'Oh, I'm sorry to hear that, Kevin,' I said, in tones you could have sweetened porridge with. This was my fatherly bit. 'These are rough times for everyone, it's not easy. Look, I might be able to direct something your way. Would you be interested?'

'Er, no. Thanks all the same though, Charlie. I've heard there's something in the pipeline for me, in the next few days. Like I said, it's just temporary.'

I was glad about that. The plan was that he recruit me, not the other way round. I said: 'I hope so, Kevin,' adding: 'Well, I don't know about you, old pal, but I'm going to crash out for four hours, catch up on my sleep.'

And that's what I did.

In the evening I drove home, to Heckley. There was a long blue envelope lying on the doormat, with four stamps with elephants on them, nearly obliterated by the wavy lines of the franking machine. I made a pot of tea and opened a new packet of custard creams. When I was nice and comfortable in front of the gasfire, I sliced open the envelope and unfolded the pages.

It was a long letter, and I'd been looking forward to receiving it, but now I felt a strange reluctance to read. Sometimes, distance changes one's perspective, throws you into decisions that you might not otherwise take. She'd be visiting new places as well as familiar ones, meeting interesting people, finding a purpose. Maybe Heckley and its inhabitants couldn't compete with all that.

The phone was ringing, but I ignored it. Annabelle had arrived safely and was met at the airport as planned. After six rings the tape on the ansaphone clicked into action and I heard my flat tones inviting the caller to leave a message. Annabelle's schedule was hectic, no time for sightseeing, so she hadn't seen any wildlife.

A faraway female voice said: 'Hello, Charlie, this is Diane Dooley . . .'

Annabelle had written: *I'm missing you; wish you'd been able to come, too. Maybe next time?*

'. . . could you give me a ring, please. It's about Guy.'

I'd read what I wanted to hear, so I jumped up and grabbed the phone. 'Hello, Diane, it's me. How are you?'

'Oh, hello, Charlie. I'm all right, I think.'

'You said something about Guy.'

'Yes. I hope you don't mind me ringing you . . .'

'Of course not. Has something happened?'

'I'm not sure. He says someone took a shot at him.'

'Well, that sounds serious enough,' I told her. 'When was this?'

I heard a big sigh come down the line, then she said: 'First of all, he went out with a patrol car one day last week. The school let him have a day off – work experience, they called it. Needless to say, Guy came back determined to be the next Chief Constable; he was full of it. By the way, he's in the middle of writing you a thank-you letter.'

'No problem,' I interrupted. 'Glad he enjoyed it.'

'Oh, he enjoyed it all right. They were very good to him – gave him the full treatment. In fact, I felt quite envious when he told me all about it.'

'So who shot at him?'

'This was Saturday morning. He often gets up before dawn to go down to the beach, birdwatching. Then he comes home filled with fanciful tales of what he's seen: killer whales, eagles, all sorts of things. Saturday he came home and said he'd saved a man's life, and someone took a shot at him.'

'And you don't believe him?'

'I'm not sure. He was certainly scared when he came home – he'd left all his stuff at the beach.'

'Do you want me to have a word with him?'

'I'd be grateful if you could, Charlie. You know how impressionable he is, but he seems to look up to you.'

That sounded like being damned by faint praise, but I don't think it was intended that way. 'Tell me the full story,' I suggested.

When she'd finished I asked if she had the number of the Rover.

'Yes, it's here on the pad.' She read it to me.

'And the police haven't been back to you?'

'No.'

'Do you think they believed him?'

'I'm not sure.'

I drew a doodle on my pad, of a stranded whale alongside a hole in the ground, with shovelfuls of sand being ejected from the hole. 'Well, I believe him,' I told her. 'Leave it with me; I'll see what I can find out and come back to you. It might be tomorrow.'

I rang Heckley nick and asked them to run a PNC check for me. 'Don't you ever give it a rest, Charlie?' the duty Sergeant protested.

'Just find out who he is. Nobody gives me a dirty look like that and gets away with it.' A few minutes later I knew that the Rover belonged to one Richard J. Kidderminster, of an address in St Ives. He had no convictions. Technology is wonderful.

I rang Diane straight back and asked her if the name meant anything. 'No,' she replied. 'Never heard of him. Shall I look in the phone book – see if he's in?'

'Mmm, good idea.'

But unfortunately he wasn't.

'Never mind,' I told her. 'I'll have a word with the local police and see what they say. If I learn anything interesting I'll let you know.'

It was late, but I didn't want to sleep on it. I dug out an ancient copy of the *Police Almanac* and found the number of the station where I'd arranged for Guy to have his visit. The PC who answered had been on the early shift when I'd called in to make arrangements for Guy's visit, and he'd read the reports of the shooting.

I said: 'His mother is worried that he's romancing, carried away after his ride in a squad car. Is his story being taken seriously?'

'Oh yes, sir, very seriously. We checked with Mr Kidderminster and he made a complaint. Said young Guy probably saved his life.'

'Good, I'm glad about that. Who is this Kidderminster?'

'Sorry, don't you know? He's an MP.'

'A military policeman?' I queried, being my normal awkward self. Ambiguity is the mother of confusion.

'Er, no, sir. A Member of Parliament. He lives in St Ives, but he's MP for North Dorset. Apparently he comes down from London every Friday evening and takes his dog for a walk on the beach early Saturday morning. It looks as if they were waiting for him. We've notified the Special Branch and are awaiting further instructions. It's in their hands now.' He added: 'I'm not sure if I ought to be telling you all this.'

'Don't worry about it. So presumably the Special Branch or the anti-terrorist people will contact Guy as soon as they find a map with St Ives on it.'

'I imagine so.'

'OK, thanks for your help. I won't say anything to him, leave it all to the big boys. One last thought: is anything being done about Guy's safety?'

'Yes, we're keeping a discreet eye on him.'

'Smashing. I'm very grateful.'

So, somebody was trying to pop off an MP. Speculation was pointless – I didn't even know which party he belonged to, though I could have a good guess. I'd never heard of him, so he can't have held particularly outrageous opinions about anything. I wondered about the group who'd claimed credit for the fires, but the name wouldn't come to me. TLC? No. The Struggle Continues, that was it – TSC. They were probably the favourites. I picked up Annabelle's letter and started to read it again, from the beginning, and all thoughts of St Ives and MPs and terrorists went from my head.

When I'd had lunch with Kevin he'd said that he was expecting some work in the next few days. Presumably he didn't mean laying tarmac on the M62 extension. I needed to know what he did mean, and if possible become involved. In cases like this you have to think while you are running, take advantage of any little snippet that comes your way.

I was switching round the TV channels, trying to find something worth watching. It was a choice between a couple arguing in cockney accents; a couple arguing in Liverpudlian accents; a pair of giraffes mating; and a commercial for a car, designed to appeal to elderly vineyard owners with plain but wilful daughters. Someone should have a word with their advertising agents. I stayed with the giraffes until the news came on. Then I grabbed the van keys and my jacket and drove the ninety miles to the cottage.

First item on the news, read out over the introductory fanfare, was details of a drugs bust, up in Tyneside. A ton of cannabis and an estimated million pounds' worth of heroin and cocaine had been found on a Russian fishing boat. Gleeful Customs Officers were interviewed, claiming that this was their biggest-ever haul. A lot of dealers were going to be disappointed; prices would soar.

It was nearly midnight when I reached the cottage, but there was still a light on downstairs at Kevin's. I made a lot of noise with the van, then knocked softly on his door.

'Who is it?' he called.

'Charlie,' in a loud whisper.

He slid back a bolt and opened the door. 'What's the matter, Charlie?' he asked.

'Not sure,' I told him. 'But if anyone comes asking after me, you never spoke to me. And you never saw the Jag, OK?'

'Er, yeah.'

'You never saw the Jag. Remember?'

'I got it. Don't worry.'

'Fair enough. I might see you at the weekend. If not, you can come and visit me at one of Her Majesty's holiday camps. They say the food's good. Take care.'

'Yeah, thanks, and you.'

He closed the door and I climbed back into the van. It had been a long drive to deliver a short message. I hoped I hadn't wasted my time.

Chapter Nine

Shawn Parrott picked up the mobile phone at the first ring. ''Ello?' he said tersely.

'It's me,' Frank Bell told him. 'I'll be on the seventeen thirty-five. Meet me at Huddersfield at twenty twenty-seven, but stand by just in case I decide to catch a taxi from Leeds.'

'Understood,' Parrott replied, and folded the phone, breaking the circuit. 'C'mon,' he ordered Darren Atkinson, the third member of the gang. 'You've nearly three hours to get us to Huddersfield. Even you should be able to manage that.'

In the car, Atkinson asked: 'So what's 'appening?'

'The Skipper's followed Noon on to the Leeds train at Kings Cross,' Parrott told him. 'He'll probably catch the connection from Leeds to Huddersfield, where we'll pick him up. If he catches a taxi from Leeds, Frank will ring us with the number. Then we'll just have to watch out for him.'

Atkinson grinned across at him. 'Me and you should do this one, eh, Shawn? Make a better job than you and the Skip did in Cornwall.'

'Yeah, well, we were disturbed. A stupid kid jumped up out of nowhere.'

'So why didn't you just kill them both?'

Parrott pulled a folded magazine from within his jacket

and started to look at the pictures. It was called *Viet Vet Monthly*, and was filled with lurid details of the killing power of the accoutrements of war. 'Because, Darren, old son,' he explained, 'there's no point in killing anyone unless it looks like an accident.'

'Dead's dead. What difference does it make?'

Parrott lowered the magazine. 'This first one is just the bait – sprat to catch a mackerel, if you're knowing what I'm meaning. Then we go for the big one. That'll make Operation Nimrod look like a bunch of girls' blouses at a tea party.' Operation Nimrod was the freeing of the hostages by the SAS in the Iranian Embassy Siege in 1980.

Atkinson looked confused. 'What's Operation Nimrod?' he asked.

'Just fuckin' drive,' Parrott ordered, burying his face in the magazine.

They stopped for a burger at the Birch services on the M62, but still made it to Huddersfield station with nearly an hour to spare. 'How about that?' Atkinson boasted, nodding towards the station clock as they came to a standstill. 'Fast but safe, that's what the Skip calls me.'

'Not bad,' Parrott grudgingly admitted. It was a fact that Atkinson had a flair for driving fast, but with the minimum of fuss, never attracting attention. He was the slowest of the three in other ways, but a useful asset. And every gang has to have a driver. At twenty-five minutes past seven the phone rang again.

'Hello?'

'It's me. I've decided to catch the connection.'

'Understood.' Parrott turned to his colleague: 'He's coming on the Huddersfield train, making it easy for us.'

Parrott wandered inside the concourse to check the arrivals. 'Be here in three minutes,' he said when he returned.

A better parking place became available, one that gave them a good view and a decent getaway, so Atkinson manoeuvred into it. A trickle of people began to exit through the ticket barriers.

'There's Frank.' Atkinson gave a single flash on the headlights, attracting his attention. Bell saw them and sprinted over.

He climbed into the back of the Sierra. 'That's him,' he said. 'Third in the queue, in the light coat, carrying the big pilot's briefcase.' The two in the front focused their eyes on Tom Noon, Member of Parliament, for the first time, and recorded the appearance of the man they intended to kill.

The taxis shuffled forwards and picked up their fares. The Asian driver of the second one recognised the man who represented him in Her Majesty's Government. 'Hello, Mr Noon,' he said, enunciating his words. 'Have you had a busy week?'

Noon muttered a silent curse – now he'd have to give a big tip. 'Yes, thank you, we're always busy. And you?'

'Oh, so-so.'

'Wife and family well?'

The car slid into the traffic flow, the driver hardly noticing the red Sierra that pulled out behind him. 'Yes, very well, sir, thank you.' He smiled. Now he'd be able to go home and tell his wife that his friend Tom Noon, Opposition Spokesman on Foreign Affairs, had asked after the welfare of her and the children.

Noon lived in a select new housing development on the outskirts of Heckley. Just before the last General Election, the seat he'd held for fifteen years vanished in a vindictive reorganisation of the constituencies. With characteristic grit he'd contested a nearby Government-held seat and overturned a 9000-vote majority to win the place at Westminster by the slenderest of margins. At the next election, due in less than a year, he was confident of consolidating his position.

The taxi stopped outside his five-bedroomed executive-style house, complete with its two-point-four *en suite* bathrooms. A Land Rover Discovery stood beneath the carport at the side of the house, glistening like a funeral car. A hundred yards away, Darren Atkinson switched off his headlights.

Tom Noon fumbled with his wallet and handed over a twenty-pound note and a fiver. 'Call that right,' he said.

'Thank you, sir. Thank you,' the taxi driver gushed.

'And remember me to your wife. Good night.'

'Yes, sir. Good night.' As he drove away he radioed his controller to say that he was available for hire. It was fifteen minutes past nine.

'What now?' Atkinson asked.

'Watch and wait,' Bell told him. Parrott tried to sleep.

Periodically another vehicle would drive into the development. Three men sitting in a darkened car looked suspicious, so Atkinson would start his engine and turn on the lights, as if they were about to drive off. Once, they did a tour round the immediate district, and saw a pub, the Royal Oak, about a quarter of a mile away.

'I could murder a drink,' Parrott said.

Atkinson agreed. 'Not here,' Bell told them. 'We'd be noticed. We'll find somewhere later, if we get chance.'

They watched the lighted windows of Noon's house, guessing his behaviour from their patterns. Kitchen, stairs, bathroom, bedroom. A few spots of rain fell on the windscreen, and every few minutes Atkinson gave a short burst on the wipers to improve their vision.

'He's either gone to bed or he's getting changed,' Bell guessed.

At twenty minutes past ten a beam of illumination from

the side door caused all three of them to sit up. 'He's coming out,' Parrott declared.

Tom Noon walked down his drive. He'd changed into casual clothes, and was now wearing a padded jacket with big pockets, in a subdued colour that immediately identified the store from which it came. Trotting in front of him, pulling on its lead, was a pedigree King Charles spaniel. Most MPs agree that owning a dog is good for at least a five per cent swing, providing of course that the Opposition doesn't own one. Some dog-hating politicians have been known to make a pairing arrangement with their rivals – I won't buy one if you don't. Tom Noon, alas, had failed to do so, hence the King Charles.

When Noon reached the pavement he turned up his collar and gazed skywards for a second. It was raining – he'd go in the Discovery. The dog leapt in ahead of him, for he too preferred riding to walking.

'Shit! He's driving,' Bell exclaimed. 'If he'd walked we might have been able to run him down, here and now. That would have been perfect.'

There were no fences or gates around the houses, demarcation between the properties being indicated by red-paved driveways and large areas of lawn. A few rebels had declared independence by planting hedges of miniature conifers, which would soon blot out their neighbours' daylight. The large all-terrain vehicle, which, like most of its cousins, never encountered anything more challenging than the speed bumps in Sainsbury's car park, trickled out into the road. As soon as it was out of sight Atkinson started the engine of the Sierra and caught up with it.

'He's going to the pub,' Parrott guessed, correctly.

The parking area in front of the Royal Oak housed several cars, but Noon drove round the back, where it was quieter.

'Great,' Frank Bell declared. 'He's playing right into our hands.'

'Are we going in?' Atkinson asked.

'No, we've seen enough. Let's talk tactics, then we'll have a drink somewhere in the town. Be less conspicuous there. Any suggestions, Shawn?'

'No problem. If he walks, we run him down. Accidental death, if you're knowing what I'm meaning. If he drives, we meet him here. Darren and me invite him to take us for a ride in his Land Rover to somewhere quiet. You follow in this. Somewhere along the way he meets with a nasty accident. He really did ought to be more careful.'

'Good. Well done,' Bell agreed. 'Except that Darren drives the Sierra, me and you take Noon.'

Parrott nodded his approval. 'And we're talking about next Friday?'

'Yeah, next Friday.'

'And where are we taking him?'

'I know the perfect place,' Bell said. 'Boy, do I know the perfect place.'

Darren Atkinson drove the three of them into the centre of Heckley and from there they gravitated, like dross, to the less savoury corner of town. It was just before eleven o'clock, and the youth of the area were making their way from the public houses, which closed at eleven, to the town's only night club, which didn't. Two Panda cars were watching the action, and several taxis cruised by. Nobody wore a coat, despite the drizzle. The males swaggered along, anaesthetised by alcohol; the girls folded their bare arms as protection against it.

'It's buzzing wi' cops,' Atkinson observed.

'We're just out for the evening,' Bell told him. 'Don't worry about them.' It was good advice. The police, hopelessly outnumbered, were looking for a quiet night. They'd only intervene if absolutely necessary.

Two girls, similarly dressed in borderline-obscene mini skirts, white blouses and denim waistcoats, watched the car pass them. One was attractive, in a waiflike way, the other was overweight from a surfeit of chips. They were standing in a shop doorway, self-consciously smoking. Parrott turned to inspect them, and the slim one caught his gaze.

'Looks like it's the Copper Banana,' Bell declared, nodding towards the neon sign above the door of the ex-cinema. 'Who knows, we might be able to do some business here.'

Once, Randolph Scott and Dorothy Lamour had excited its clientèle, now it was house music and Ecstasy. Atkinson reversed expertly into a parking place, between an elderly Ford Capri with all the trimmings and a Skoda with none, and the three of them got out.

Although they were well above the average age of the majority of customers, they knew what to expect: dim lights, thick smoke, and a constant throbbing beat, as if an aneurism in the brain was about to go critical. Bell pointed to some empty tables at the rear of the hall, and mimed a drinking action. Speech was impossible. He and Parrott sat down while Atkinson fetched three pints of lager.

It was marginally quieter here, the beat reduced to a rumble in the furniture, like on a ship at full speed with a grossly unbalanced propellor. Young men stood around, clutching their pints and swaying. The girls, most of them hardly nubile, dashed to and fro, pulling each other, as if on the most important business in the world. To them, it was.

Atkinson returned, three unappetising pints held between his hands. 'Two-fifty a bleeding pint,' he complained.

Parrott took a sip. 'And it's watered, if you ask me.' He

pulled a pack of Red Wings from his pocket and fumbled with the cellophane wrap.

'Here, 'ave one of mine,' Atkinson told him, throwing an opened pack on to the table. They all took one and lit up.

Bell studied his lager, swilling a good draught of it around his mouth. He swallowed and said: 'You're right, this beer's watered. Maybe we should have a word with the management.'

Parrott grinned. 'Want me to find someone, Skip?'

'Yeah, please, Shawn, if you don't mind.'

He was back in a couple of minutes. 'One of 'is penguins has gone to fetch 'im,' he said.

When he arrived, the owner of the club looked more Hollywood than Heckley. Above white skin-tight jeans he wore a lilac leather jacket with its sleeves rolled up to just below the elbow. The zipper was unfastened, to avoid trapping the blond forest growing on his chest, for he wore nothing under it. His long bleached hair was pulled back into a ponytail and he peered at them through tiny spectacles whose lenses could have been made from the bottoms of iodine bottles. A yard behind him walked a bow-tied bodyguard with a chest like bulldozer pushing a snowdrift. Bell gestured towards a chair, inviting the owner to join them.

'Good evening, gentlemen,' he said, turning the chair round and sitting on it the wrong way, cowboy style. 'Not having any problems, are we?'

Bell pushed his pint forward. 'My driver,' he said, 'is worried about breaking the drink-driving laws, and wants to know how much of this piss he is allowed. I reckon about eight pints, but he says fourteen. What do you say?'

'Oh dear,' replied the owner. 'If my manager is doctoring the booze again, then I want to know about it. Mister . . . Smith, I believe your colleague said?'

'Just call me Frank.'

'Right, Frank. And I'm Georgie. What would you gentlemen like to drink?' He'd assessed his three visitors from the first moment he saw them, and come to a number of conclusions: they weren't the filth; they weren't here for a night out; and they weren't complaining about the beer. No, they were here to do business. It might be good business or it might be bad. Either way, he'd listen to what they had to say and act accordingly. The bodyguard was despatched to fetch four full-strength drinks.

'Actually,' Georgie confessed with a conspiratorial wink, 'we're doing everyone a favour by serving weak drinks. The police prefer it, the parents approve, and the kids themselves don't seem to mind. They need the fluid, not the alcohol. Dancing all night takes a lot out of you.'

'Yeah,' said Shawn. ''Specially when you're zapped on XTC.'

Georgie shrugged philosophically, like a Jewish mother at her son's wedding. 'You're so right,' he said. 'But what can we do? How can we stop them bringing these things in? We thought about intimate body searches – I even offered to do them myself – but it wouldn't work.' He laughed, and the others joined in.

'What about stronger stuff?' asked Bell. 'Are any of them sneaking anything else past your tame gorillas?'

Georgie shook his head. 'No. Prices are too high. Maybe some pot, smack now and again, but snow and base are over the roof, even if you can get it.' He smiled and raised his glass of blue fluid. 'Even Saturday-night users are having to find alternatives. It's back to good ol' sex and alcohol. Cheers!'

Bell looked thoughtful, not sure how forward to be. 'So it's a sellers' market,' he said.

'Sure.'

Parrott finished his drink. 'Do you need me, Skip?' he asked. 'I could use some fresh air.'

'No,' Bell replied. 'I'm sure Georgie will keep us company. Are you all right?'

'Yeah, it's just too stuffy for me in here. Give me the keys, Darren. I'll wait in the car.'

Atkinson handed the keys over.

'I'll be back in about an hour,' were Parrott's parting words.

'What's wrong with him?' Georgie asked as Parrott departed.

'Women,' Atkinson explained. 'All these young birds has made him feel randy. Me too.'

Georgie waved an arm in the direction of the dance floor. 'Be my guests,' he invited.

'Shawn doesn't do too good at pulling birds,' Bell told him. 'He has better results when he pays for it. But never mind him, let's get back to business.'

'With a face like that, I can understand his problem. OK, Frankie, what have you to offer?'

'Let's just say we might have a shipment coming in next week. Small but tasty. Will you be interested?'

A girl, about eighteen, with long hair obscuring half of her sulky face, slinked by, looking sideways at Georgie.

'Talking about small but tasty . . .' Atkinson murmured.

Georgie turned to follow his gaze. 'Hi, Trish,' he called to the girl. She pretended she'd just noticed him, and smiled. He extended an arm and she walked into its embrace. As he was sitting in a low chair this meant that it was wrapped round her legs, and he stroked her bare thigh with a hand that bore three gold sovereign rings and a bracelet that might have kept the Welsh goldmining industry viable for a couple of years. She draped an arm around his neck and let her fingers explore the undergrowth of his chest. 'Next week?' he commented, unmoved by the girl's administrations. 'You disappoint me, Frankie. I was hoping you could do better than that.'

Bell produced a new pack of Red Wings from his pocket and tossed them towards Georgie. 'How about cigarettes?' he asked.

Georgie picked them up and rotated the packet between his fingers. They looked genuine. 'How many are we talking about?' he wondered.

'More than you can handle.'

The owner of the Copper Banana untwined the girl's arm from around his neck. 'Trish,' he said, 'why don't you take this young man – Darren, isn't it? – for a dance, eh?' The sulk returned, like a bad smell at a picnic. 'Be a good girl; I'll see you later.' His hand flicked upwards and briefly goosed her. She set off walking towards the dance floor, not waiting to see if Darren was following. He rose awkwardly, adjusting his jeans, and chased after her.

'Right, Frank,' Georgie said. 'Now the children are out of the way, let's talk about prices and deliveries.'

Shawn Parrott eased the driver's seat forward a notch and started the engine. He was about the same height as Darren, but preferred a more hunched driving position. And his legs were shorter. He didn't readjust the mirrors. Cruising round the one-way system he passed a police car, which was still in the same place, and the doorway where the two girls had been standing. They were no longer there. Two streets further along he saw them, arguing with three boys. The youths were following behind, hurling insults, but Parrott couldn't tell if it was good-natured or deadly serious. They wore back-to-front baseball caps and bomber jackets with incomprehensible slogans emblazoned across the backs. He drove a few yards past them, stopped the car and got out.

'Fag?' he said to the slim girl, as the pair drew level with him. The three youths stopped in their tracks, a respectful thirty feet away.

'Yeah,' she replied, throwing a triumphant glance at them.

'What about you?' he asked the podgy one.

'Ta.'

He held his lighter towards the girls, and soon they were blowing clouds of smoke into the blackness above the drizzle slanting through the streetlamps' glare.

'They causing you any bother?' He nodded towards the youths, who'd turned their backs and were rapidly losing interest.

'No, they're just pests,' the overweight one told him, gazing straight into his face. It was an ugly face, but she didn't mind.

'What about you?'

'Yeah,' said the other girl, smiling. 'They're causing me a lot of bovver. What you going to do about it?'

Parrott accepted the challenge. 'I could give them a good thumpin', if you wanted. Or you could come with me and we'll just forget them, if you're knowing what I'm meaning.' He liked the look of her. She reminded him of a film star – the one that married Frank Sinatra and that weedy American comedian.

'What about me?' the big one protested, realising that she was being abandoned, yet again.

'You'll be all right,' her friend assured her. 'Go with them – you know that Baz fancies you.' She turned to her new-found white knight. 'Where you taking me, then?'

The less attractive half of the couple walked after the boys, who turned to accept her into their group. She wasn't too disappointed, for now she'd have their undivided attention, free from the shadow of her better-looking friend. They'd flirt with her, until they found themselves lost among the empty stalls of Heckley Market. She'd share her favours, allowing each a quick grope and a feel, accompanied by French kissing, until two of them left her and Baz alone together. Then they'd explore the roller-coaster delights of fumbled sex, where, earlier in the day, Asian traders had sold cheap clothing, and white ones had peddled pirate videos.

'What's your name?' the slim one said, pulling the car door closed.

'Shawn.' He started the engine.

'I'm Nicky.' She was disappointed that he hadn't asked. 'What you got, then?'

'What do you want?'

'Dunno. I 'aven't scored for a week. What you got?'

'Nothing.'

'Nuthin'! Not even any adam?'

'No.' He swung away from the kerb without signalling, causing the taxi behind to blow its horn, and headed out of town. 'I've got plenty of money, though.'

Nicky shook her head and smiled across at him. 'You're a disappointment to me, Shawn. I fought I'd found me the man wiv the golden arm. Never mind.' Never mind. So it was to be sex again – sex for money. Unlike her friend, she had no romantic illusions about the sexual coupling of two members of the human race. All those notions had been destroyed when she was ten years old, under the grunting beer belly of her mother's second husband.

Shaw bragged: 'Next week. We'll 'ave some stuff then. All sorts. Anything you want. Big shipment coming in from Amsterdam.'

Her eyes widened. 'Are you a pusher then, you know, big time?'

'Look,' he said, reaching across and grasping the back of

her neck between his thumb and fingers, 'smart people don't take it, not all the time. Maybe just a bit, say once a week, if you're knowing what I'm meaning. Smart people *sell* it. Make a lot of money that way.' He sounded almost fatherly. Nicky rotated her head, so that his fingers moved against her skin. She wouldn't take his advice, but she appreciated it. She liked him.

He was ugly, but – in a perverse way – that made him more attractive to her; brought him within reach. And he was fairly young, with a good body. Not like the drunken friends of her stepfather, who'd come up to her after playing cards into the early hours of the morning, and leave him a fiver for the privilege. Shawn was a loser, like her. She could give him a lot, and he could give her more than he dreamed possible. They'd be two outlaws, battling against the world. It was a potent combination.

'Is this your car?' she asked.

'Yeah.'

'Nice, innit?'

'It's OK. Got a new one coming next week. A BMW.'

'Why? What's wrong wiv this one?'

'Nothing. It's just been seen around too much. It's time for a change. It doesn't do to be seen around too much. They watch, if you're knowing what I'm meaning, on videos.'

'Who does?'

'The filth, that's who.'

'Bloody 'ell. So you just swap your car to keep them guessing?' She was impressed.

'Yeah.'

'Will you take me for a ride in your BMW?'

'If you're a good girl.'

The lights of the town had fallen behind and below them. Parrott turned left, into a narrow steep lane. He noted an isolated cottage, completely in darkness, with *Withins House* written on the gate, and an estate agent's *For Sale* board lying on the ground, a victim of the prevalent winds. 'So 'ow old are you?' he asked.

She leaned towards him, provocatively pursing her lips and feeling her breasts dangle against the front of her blouse. ''Ow old would you like me to be?' she whispered, in a way that she thought was seductive.

There was a clearing at the side of the road, housing a large mound of road salt, left over from a mild winter. Parrott parked the car behind the heap and switched off the engine and lights. 'I asked you your fuckin' age,' he growled.

Nicky giggled. 'My fuckin' age?' she mimicked. 'My fuckin' age is sixteen, but I 'aven't seen that many Christmasses.'

'So 'ow many *'ave* you seen?'

She didn't like being asked her age. 'Fifteen,' she admitted. 'What difference does it make?'

Parrott's hand was on her shoulder, his thumb roughly flicking back and forth across her cheek. 'None,' he told her. 'Get in the back seat.'

He needed a pee, so he walked over to the pile of salt and relieved himself into it, the steaming stream of urine carving a deep canyon in the pink crystals. Nicky climbed over into the back of the car. She removed the waistcoat and her shoes and waited for him to return, wondering how much she should sting him for.

He climbed in with her, throwing his jacket over the back of the seat and unzipping his jeans. Bloody hell, he don't hang about, thought Nicky, as he started to strip her.

Shawn Parrott, failed soldier, drug pusher and murderer, never knew what he had in his hands. Nicky was the best thing that nearly happened to him, but he threw it all away.

He strangled her, and when she was dead he violated her body like all the others before him; on the back seat of a Ford, in a layby, with the moon blazing brightly, then fading away, as the rainclouds fled across its face.

I decided not to see Kevin over the weekend, after all. The M62 to Hull was becoming a hair shirt to me. I drove over on Tuesday, instead, in the Transit.

'False alarm,' I told him, with my broadest smile.

'What happened?'

'Customs got lucky. They used a sniffer dog, and a bag had burst. Arrested everyone, but they'll have to let them go. The captain's Russian, but he speaks no English and doesn't know a thing. Lot of money down the drain.' It sounded convincing to me. 'Trouble is,' I continued, 'my lords and masters have decided to cool things for a while, so I'm in the same boat as you, Kevin, old pal. Looks as if I'll have to do some freelancing, or the Jag'll have to go back. It's a bit risky, though.'

Kevin looked what I took to be thoughtful. Less blank than usual. He said: 'I could maybe 'ave a word with someone, if you like?'

I shrugged. 'Beggars can't be choosers,' I declared.

'Where can I get you?'

'You can't, unless you leave a message at Merlin.' I pointed to the van, with the swooping bird of prey that I'd painted years ago. The telephone number was written underneath it. 'It'd be a shame to lose business now,' I told him. 'Prices will be sky-high, and the Customs will be feeling over-confident. Should be a piece of cake.'

Kevin looked puzzled. Things like that never crossed his mind. 'Yeah. Just what I thought. I'll see what I can do.'

'Cheers.' I wrote the number down for him.

Christmas Day fell in late March that year. Early on Thursday morning Annabelle's plane landed at Heathrow. She caught the shuttle up to Leeds and Bradford Airport and I was there to meet it.

I was the only person waiting at the Arrivals exit. There was no sudden flood of self-conscious holidaymakers in Bermuda shorts and silly hats; just a trickle of po-faced businesswomen and men, carrying bulging briefcases and heavier newspapers. And a tall lady in jeans and Stewart Grainger jacket who looked ridiculously healthy compared to her fellow travellers.

She let go of her suitcase and threw her arms around my neck, nearly throttling me. I squeezed the rest of her to me.

'I've missed you, Charles,' she said.

'You've lost weight,' I observed. I kissed her on the lips, and told her that I'd missed her, too.

It was a bright spring day, but the breeze had been sharpened by the polar icecap. When we reached the automatic doors I put her suitcase down and told her to wait inside while I fetched the car. I sprinted across to where I'd left the E-type and drove it to the front of the terminal.

We were well on the way home before the power of speech returned to her. 'I didn't think you would buy it,' she admitted.

'Good. I like to keep people guessing.'

'Maybe you are not the old fuddy-duddy that I thought.'

I looked across to check for the dimples in her cheeks. They were there – she was teasing me.

'I have two weaknesses,' I told her. 'Wimmin 'n' cars. I like 'em fast and flashy.'

'Then you should be well content.'

I nodded. 'Yep, I think I am. Well content.'

We were at her home in about forty minutes. Everything was intact, with the usual pile of mail inside the door. The only letter of interest was from Tom Noon, asking her to go for a formal interview on the following Saturday.

'So you haven't got the job yet?' I asked.

'No, there are probably lots of other applicants. I must be in with a good chance, though.'

'A dead cert, if he's any sense.'

'Thank you, kind sir.'

We had a cup of tea, then I left her to have a shower and catch up on her rest. At the door I suggested we went for a meal in the evening. As usual, she volunteered to cook something.

'No,' I insisted. 'We'll go out. There's a new vegetarian restaurant in town. Shall we try that? Unless, of course, you have a craving for a T-bone.'

She looked surprised. 'Vegetarian is fine by me, but what about you? Won't you develop rickets or something if you are deprived of your daily dose of roast beef and Yorkshire pud?'

'Mmm, possibly, but I'm fed up of eating meat. Let's have a change. Then you can tell me all about Africa.'

The beeper on my ansaphone was going. I pressed the button and heard Eric Dobson's recorded voice asking me to contact him at Merlin Couriers.

'Somebody called Kevin has been after you, Charlie,' Eric told me when I called him. 'Wants you to give him a ring. I told him you were on the South Coast run, but that I'd try to raise you.'

'Fantastic, well done.'

I tuned the radio to a pop music station and turned the volume up high. Kevin was in.

'I'm on my mobile,' I yelled into the phone, over the din of the music. I said it, I really said it. I couldn't resist saying it again: 'It's Charlie, I'm on my mobile. I'm just outside – er – London. What do you want?'

Kevin had watched too much TV. He said: 'Hello, Charlie, this is control. We've another run for you, if you can get back in time. Friday night, OK?'

I entered into the spirit of it. 'Message understood, control,' I told him. 'Will comply. Over and out.' I was sitting on the floor, close to the radio. I clicked it off and did a backward roll, jumping to my feet and shouting, '*Yes!*'

The meal was enjoyable, but it would've had to be pretty awful not to be. Annabelle told me all about the poverty and deprivation she had witnessed, and the overwhelming optimism of the people. She'd taken her photographs and was looking forward to seeing the results. I'd been worried about the danger, but she assured me that the only threat had come from a military attaché with amorous intentions, and she'd soon discouraged him. The influence of the tobacco barons was everywhere, she claimed. Their stranglehold on the countries was twofold – economic and narcotic. She was animated and enthusiastic as she related her story, and I wished I'd gone with her. Africa was obviously my chief rival for her affections, and I wasn't happy that it was a fair contest. Maybe next time I'd have to go, for I felt sure there would be a next time.

I told her about my new cottage, and she wanted to see it. I briefly mentioned the drug smugglers, making them sound like the Famous Five, and said I would be on duty over the weekend, 'Just on observations, on the ferry to Holland.' I said I was working part-time. Annabelle needed to write a lengthy report, so wasn't too disappointed that I would be away for a couple of days. I wanted to stay the night with her, but didn't suggest it, and she didn't invite me to.

Kevin gave me a sports bag of indeterminate make and told

me to put a few things in it that I might need over the weekend. 'Towel, sweater, that sort of thing. We'll swap it over there for one with the goods.' He had an identical one.

'Where's "over there"?' I asked.

'You'll find out.'

'What are "the goods"?'

'Only shit, this time. It's a practice run. Good stuff, though – Ukrainian gold, it's called.'

'How much are they paying us?'

'Two hundred and fifty quid each.'

'Two hundred and fifty lousy quid! You gotta be joking!'

He looked devastated. 'C'mon, Charlie,' he protested. 'I stuck my neck out for you. It's all arranged.'

I gave him my morose look and hooked the bag over my shoulder. 'OK, I'll do it this time. For you, Kevin, because I'm grateful. But I want to talk money with someone before we go again. Understood?'

'Right, Charlie. Right. I knew you wouldn't let me down.'

We made our separate ways to the docks, pretending that we didn't know each other. I suppose it lessened the risk of us both being caught, but I couldn't see much point in it – there were plenty of men travelling in small groups, as well as the usual couples and families. This time I didn't enjoy the meal and the airline seat was even less comfortable.

Not until we were in Rotterdam did we speak to each other again. 'So where are we going?' I asked.

Kevin produced a minute slip of paper from his pocket and read from it. 'Delf-shaven. Then we find a big red barge called *Orion*. We ask for Villie and tell him that we had an unpleasant trip.'

I said: 'It's haven, not shaven. Delfshaven.'

'Is it? Let's find a taxi.'

'No,' I insisted. 'We'll go on the tram. It's cheaper and

doesn't attract attention.' He looked impressed.

I force-fed the ticket machine with coins as if I'd been doing it all my life and handed Kevin his ticket. 'I take it you've been 'ere before,' he said. I glowered at him for a few seconds, without speaking.

Delfshaven is a smashing little place. The rows of houses look as if giant hands have compressed them together, leaving them tall and impossibly narrow. They front on to the canal, spanned by one of van Gogh's bridges; and a magnificent windmill – the traditional type – stands guard over everything.

Kevin wandered up and down, looking for the boat. 'You look like a bloody tourist,' I told him. 'Let's walk down to the end, as if we know where we are going. Otherwise some kind Dutch policeman is going to ask you if you need any help.'

'Yeah, see what you mean.'

It wasn't on the first length of canal. We walked round the end of the houses and back along a parallel stretch of water. There were plenty of boats, mainly barges with sails to assist them and conserve fuel, but not the *Orion*. Most of them didn't have names at all, just numbers. We crossed the main road at a bridge, and there she was.

'Bingo!' I exclaimed.

'Thank Christ for that,' Kevin said. 'I was starting to get worried.'

'Do you want to collect the stuff now,' I asked, 'or go for something to eat and come back later? Save us carrying it around.'

He looked worried. 'I think we should get it now. I'd feel 'appier.'

'OK, you're probably right. Let's go meet Villie, then.'

He was fat and dirty, wearing a fisherman's sweater that looked as if the dog slept on it at nights. 'I am Villie,' he admitted. 'Kom on board.' We ducked into a low doorway, down some steps, and entered the living quarters of the barge. It was beautiful, all carved wood and shining brass, with fancy oil lamps – the real things – fastened to the walls. 'Haf you had a good journey?' he enquired.

Kevin's mouth opened like a stranded flounder, but I beat him to it. 'A very unpleasant trip, Villie,' I told him. 'Very unpleasant indeed.'

'Very unpleasant,' Kevin agreed.

'Good. Vould you like a trink?' He gestured towards a bottle on a tray, surrounded by tiny glasses.

I swung the bag off my shoulder and placed it on a bench seat. Kevin did the same. 'Not for me,' I said, 'but a cup of tea would be very welcome. Or coffee.' I sat down.

'OK, von tea. And you, my young friend?'

'Er, coffee, please,' Kevin said.

Villie shouted something in Dutch – well, it was Dutch to me – and another man, skinny and much younger, appeared through a doorway. He paused, taking his instructions, then disappeared again, taking the bags with him.

I looked round the cabin we were in. It was cosy, and the sunshine was being reflected on to the ceiling, dancing and swirling like some electronic light-show. I felt like curling up and going to sleep.

'What do you normally carry?' I asked.

'Consumer goods.'

He didn't elaborate, so I didn't ask him where he took them from and to. The tea came.

'So how's business?'

'Business eez bard.'

I nodded my agreement. 'Same everywhere,' I told him.

It was obvious that polite conversation wasn't required, so I closed my eyes and dozed, with my face in a patch of light coming through one of the little windows. After about fifteen minutes I heard the door again, and opened my eyes to see another man enter, with our bags. 'Hello, Kevin,' he said.

Kevin looked happy for the first time since we landed. 'Hiya, Darren,' he greeted the newcomer. 'You get around a bit.' He'd have wagged his tail if he'd had one.

Darren was medium height, medium build. Lank hair, didn't get much sunlight, needed a bath. Kevin introduced me.

'Wotcher,' I said.

'Kevin reckons you're a professional,' he replied.

'Me? Nah, I just like sailing.'

He put a bag similar to the one I'd brought on the bench beside me. 'Well, don't fuck us about, and don't lose that. If you do, you'll find yourself feeding the fishes. Understood?'

He terrified me, like a spider frightens a teddy bear. The arrangement was becoming clearer. The drugs were brought in by barge, possibly from somewhere in the Eastern bloc; Darren came over to pay and supervise the handover, make sure the English end wasn't swindled; Kevin and I were the mugs who took the risks. It was a lot of trouble to take for a couple of kilos of marijuana.

I hooked the strap of the bag over my shoulder and stood up. 'C'mon, Kevin,' I said. 'We've a boat to catch.' Going across the little gangplank I shouted back: 'Thanks for the *tea*, Villie,' but it was wasted.

Kevin trotted after me. When he caught up he cautioned me against crossing Darren. 'He 'as some dangerous friends,' he warned.

'Who is he?' I asked.

'One of the gang. He usually collects the stuff off me.'

'So who normally looks after this end?'

'Another one of them. Bloke called Shawn. He scares the shit out of me. Darren must've been promoted.'

We caught the tram back into Rotterdam. The bags we carried were the same ones we'd brought, but now they were heavier. Kevin didn't fancy a ride to the top of the Euromast but I managed to drag him into the Imax cinema. We saw an astronaut called Book Musgrave repair the Hubble telescope, floating about like a speck of dust in a sunlit room. He had a shaved head, and could have stepped straight out of *Star Trek*. You felt as if you were holding his screwdrivers. When it was over and our feet were back on solid ground, I pretended to forget my bag. Kevin nearly had a cardiac arrest, so I introduced him to a *warme appelbol*, but he didn't appreciate it.

I banged my holdall straight into one of the left-luggage lockers that the ferry owners thoughtfully provide. Kevin and I were travelling separately again, and I occasionally saw him wandering around the various bars, clutching his bag as if his life depended upon it, which was a reasonable assumption. I was sipping a lager, putting off my date with the airline seat, when I saw Darren.

He was leaning on the bar, pint glass in front of him. I guessed that he'd driven over to the continent, probably by a different route. I wandered over and whispered into his ear: 'I want a word with you. Now!' I walked away, out through one of the heavy doors and on to the deck. We were batting across the North Sea, guided by faith and a radio signal. I shivered as a gust of wind dashed rain and spray against the cliff-like side of the ship. Darren followed me almost immediately.

'What the fuck at you playing at?' he hissed.

I leaned on the rail and peered into the blackness, imaging what it must have been like when there were U-boats out there, waiting with their torpedos. There'd be no warning – just an explosion and a juddering shock, followed by pant-wetting terror.

'Two things,' I said, quite calmly. 'First of all, don't make threats on behalf of other people.' I turned to look at him. 'You might get hurt that way. I'll deliver the stuff to the best of my ability, but if a third party moves in and takes it, it's everybody's problem, not just mine. Tell that to your masters, otherwise I'm not playing.'

'That's just, you know, insurance,' he mumbled.

'If they want insurance, tell them to see Eagle Star.' I liked that. I felt a smile coming on, down in my stomach, but managed to strangle it before it passed my neck. 'And I want more money. I don't believe it's pot we're carrying, and I don't like being lied to. So if they want my services again, the price is a thousand pounds. Tell 'em that.'

'A grand! They'll never pay you a grand!' He sounded shocked.

'OK, call it seven-fifty, plus expenses. That's my final offer.'

He looked miserable, as if going back with an ultimatum would be considered failure. I said: 'Don't worry about it, Darren. They can afford it – prices are sky-high at the moment.'

'Yeah, I suppose so.'

'Want another beer?'

'No, we're not supposed to be seen together.'

'Fair enough. When's the next run likely to be – any ideas? I've a social life to organise.'

He considered it for a few seconds. 'Could be a fortnight,' he told me.

'So I'm safe to arrange something else for next weekend?'

'Yeah.'

'Cheers. Well, it's too cold out here for me. I'm going back inside.' I walked off, leaving the deck and the night to him alone.

I wanted the number of his car, but following him around

was difficult, and if he'd seen me it would have made him suspicious. I abandoned the idea and went to bed, but I couldn't sleep. Next time I'd take a cabin.

We disembarked dead on schedule and the old van started first try. I drove back to the cottage with the bag of dope on the front seat, beside me. I'd let Kevin get away first, hoping that I might see Darren again, but I couldn't afford to linger too long. Kevin was waiting at his door for me.

'Bring it in 'ere,' he said.

I followed him into his home. It smelled of stale food and cigarette smoke, and there was a huge poster above the fireplace of one of the supermodels proudly showing her nipples, as if nobody else in the world had a pair.

'A good job well done,' I declared, unzipping the bag.

'You didn't ought to have left it in the lockers,' Kevin warned. 'They'll kill you if you lose the stuff.'

'No, they won't,' I told him. 'I've sorted it out. No more threats; seven hundred and fifty quid each; and next time we share a cabin.' I lifted my stuff out, including a couple of decent bottles of claret from the duty-free shop, and held it in my arms. 'Keep the bag,' I said, and went next door.

Darren called to collect the drugs from Kevin about an hour later, and I took the number of his red Sierra without any trouble. As soon as he left I went next door and Kevin gave me my money. I counted it, checking each note against the light. Darren had a ten-minute start on me as I drove towards the M62. At ninety miles per hour the Merlin Couriers' Transit rattled and shrieked like a witches' sabbath on crack, but I didn't catch him.

Chapter Ten

'So how did the trip go?' Annabelle asked when I saw her in the evening. She was wearing a pin-stripe suit. I think she's at her best when dressed fairly formally, but I'd hate to do business with her. She'd put me through the mangle and hang me out to dry, and I'd love every second of it.

'Oh, you know. Routine and boring. Never mind that, though. What about your interview with Tom Noon?' She was supposed to be seeing him at eight-thirty on Saturday morning, before his constituency surgery began.

Annabelle raised her eyebrows and sighed. She looked disappointed, which was unlike her. 'It didn't happen,' she said.

'Why?'

'He didn't turn up at the office. I was there bright and early, with my best suit and a smile, but he failed to make an appearance.'

'No apology?'

She shook her head.

'Was his secretary there? What did she have to say?'

'Oh, she was full of apologies. Said he must have been detained in London. She tried ringing his wife, but there was no reply. Later in the day she called me and said that Mr Noon appeared to have gone missing. Didn't want to enlarge upon it, though.'

'Missing, just that?'

'Mmm.'

I pointed towards the telephone. 'Want me to see what I can find out?'

'Er, yes, if you can.'

I dialled Heckley nick. 'Hello, Arthur, it's Charlie Priest.'

'Hello, boss. We thought you'd died.'

'An exaggeration, Arthur. What can you tell me about Tom Noon, MP? Apparently he's gone missing.'

'That's right. His wife reported him missing Saturday morning. Went out for a drink, Friday evening, late on, like he usually does. Took the Land Rover and the dog with him, never came home. That's it.'

'Are you looking into it?'

'Have to, with him being an MP. Nothing coming up, though. Doesn't appear to have a girlfriend; no business worries that anyone knows about. Nothing.'

'OK, Arthur, and thanks. Will you let me know, please, if anything comes to light?'

I filled in the other side of the conversation for Annabelle, and her disappointment turned to concern. 'We are not fair to our MPs,' she told me. 'We make them the butt of jokes, and complain about them, but they work hard, and take a lot of risks.'

'Some of them,' I conceded.

I was cleaning my teeth in my own bathroom when the phone rang. It was Arthur.

'Why haven't you gone home?' I asked.

'Can't get the staff, Charlie. Too many sick, lame and la . . . You know how it is.'

'I see. Am I included in one of those groups?'

'Not you, boss. You've nothing to prove to anyone. Are you still interested in Tom Noon?'

'Yes. Have you found him?'

'Not him, the car. It's at Bolton Abbey, in the Strid car park.'

The Wharfe is a modest river at Bolton Abbey, but at the Strid its character changes. It narrows dramatically from about fifty feet across to rip through a two-foot-wide crack in the rocks. A simple step can take you from one side to the other, but if you slip, there's no escape. The rocks are undercut, and bodies can be lost for days in underground whirlpools. It's a sinister place.

'Oh sugar!' I said. 'That looks bad.'

''Fraid so. We start dragging the river at first light.'

I called Annabelle at ten o'clock next morning. It was the first Monday in a new month, and she could have been starting her new job. I told her about Noon's car being found and drove round to collect her.

Bolton Abbey isn't in our patch, but as Noon was one of my parishioners I had an excuse to find out what I could. I rang Superintendent Wood and told him that I had a personal interest in the man. He'd already sent young Caton along to the scene to demonstrate our interest, but had no objection to me going, too.

'Two heads are better than one, Charlie,' he stated with all the authority his rank held. 'Even if they are sheep heads.' I didn't mention that I had Annabelle with me.

The local police had cordoned off the Strid car park and large areas of wood at either side of the river, much to the consternation of the walkers. I couldn't believe how many people were out in the woods on a Monday morning. I left the car on the road, behind several Pandas and a couple of police horse-boxes, and showed my ID to the Constable vetting visitors.

'Mrs Wilberforce – she's a friend of the missing man,' I told him when he looked expectantly at Annabelle.

'Thank you, sir. Will you keep well to the right, please, then within the tapes.'

'Cheers. Keep close to me,' I told Annabelle. 'Have you ever been here before?'

'This area, but not actually to the Strid.'

I'd told her of the place's reputation on the journey up. Once in, nobody ever came out alive. With one notable exception. About fifteen years earlier a man had tried to murder his wife by pushing her in. By some freak of the current, or maybe due to the clothing she was wearing, she was carried straight through, and survived. He was charged with attempted murder, but she changed her story and they were reconciled. I bet she keeps the carving knives in a locked drawer.

Noon's Land Rover stood forlornly in the bottom corner of the car park, tucked under a chestnut tree that was just breaking into a pale leaf. Another Land Rover, a proper one from the Underwater Search Unit, was near the entrance to the woods. We'd asked for the Mounted Police to scour the riverbanks, and the Task Force were standing by in case we required an extensive search of local properties, outbuildings and suchlike. I led Annabelle along the track between the red and white tapes, down to the riverside.

You can hear it booming long before you arrive, and the sodden trees, dripping with ferns and lichen, create the atmosphere of a Lost World. When you see the river it looks like the aftermath of an explosion at a brewery – a demented torrent of peat-brown madness and churning foam. Nothing could survive that, you tell yourself. Downstream, the river widens, flowing serenely between twisted oak and thriving willow. Only rafts of froth, drifting aimlessly, indicate the agitation the water suffered merely seconds earlier. A dipper flew across and landed in the shallows.

Several people were standing around, one in a diver's dry suit, attached by a line to his attendant, ready to go to the assistance of his colleague in the water should an emergency arise. Jeff Caton saw me and walked over.

'Hello, Jeff. Anything happening yet?' I asked.

'No. There's a diver down, but they haven't found anything.'

He'd met Annabelle before, on the walking trip. 'Annabelle knows Tom Noon,' I explained. 'She should have started work for him this morning.' I'd give her the job, even if Tom Noon wasn't in a position to.

'I'm sorry,' Jeff told her. 'Did you . . . do you know him well?'

'Not really,' she replied. 'I have only met him three times. Did you say that there was a diver down, in that?'

'That's right. Rather him than me.' He pointed to an officer in a boilersuit, wearing a headset and holding a line that led tautly into the river. 'He's on the end of the rope.'

'Anybody local here, Jeff?' I asked.

He pointed a Sergeant out to me. I went over and introduced myself and told him who Annabelle was. I made it sound as if she could have identified Noon, if they'd found him. Taking one's girlfriend to the scene of a crime is not generally regarded as good police procedure.

The diver came to the surface, in the deep pool on the low side of the Strid, and was helped out. He had a long conversation with his colleagues, pointing into the stream and describing the shapes of the rocks with his hands. The next diver listened intently, before wading into the icy water.

A Constable came over and asked if we'd like mugs of tea. Jeff accepted the offer, but I told him that Annabelle and I were going shortly. The Sergeant and the Diving Supervisor joined us, and the Constable brought Jeff his tea. As he handed it over the diver's attendant called to us: 'He says he's found something!'

He drew in the line, walking downstream, planting each foot carefully on the slimy rocks. We followed him part of the way, and caught sight of the diver's red suit beneath the broken surface of the water. He swam slowly into the shallows and stood up, holding something, towing it to the side. His diving colleague waded in to help him.

They lifted the body of a small dog, skinny as a whippet, on to firm ground, a lead trailing down from its neck. We resisted the temptation to crowd around, standing back until the Diving Supervisor and the local Sergeant had received the corpse. Fumbling fingers undid the dog's collar. The Sergeant peered at the engraved disc that hung on it, wiping it dry and holding it towards the light that slanted through the branches. When he'd read it he stepped from boulder to boulder, back up to the rest of us, and handed the collar and lead to me.

The weak sun caught the meniscus of tears under Annabelle's eyes, making them appear larger than they were. I passed the collar to Jeff and put my arm around her shoulders. 'It says *Bobby Noon*,' I told her, 'with a Heckley phone number.'

We had a cup of tea each and I managed a toasted teacake in a café in the village and drove home. I stayed at Annabelle's through the afternoon and read her reports on Africa. I was stunned into silence, even though I'd expected them to be good. One report examined a number of projects that the various charities had sponsored, evaluating their effectiveness and suggesting improvements. She understood all the angles, and wasn't afraid to comment on economics or practical aspects. She knew all about crop rotation, medicine, and the merits of plastic, concrete and iron pipes. They'd sent the right person.

The other report was about the impact of tobacco on the economy and health of the region. It was a complicated story, told better by the pictures she'd taken. My pupil had done me proud, but it nearly broke her heart. One photo was of an old man dying of cancer, the only relief available being from the cigarettes that were killing him. Others showed little kids, urchins, with stalls selling a few packets, and all the time they puffed away at the weed. Annabelle bought what she could from them, to bring back for analysis.

She was on the best picture, a tiny figure against a huge advertising hoarding. On it, a Michael Jackson lookalike straddled a Harley Davidson. He was half-turning, to light the cigarette of the beautiful girl on the back. 'Smoke Red Wings and you too can have all this,' was the message to a population whose *per capita* income wouldn't pay for his Ray Bans.

Annabelle was in the kitchen, emptying cupboards. I wandered in and said: 'Your reports are superb. Andrew Fallon will be delighted with the tobacco stuff. I'm sorry if I was boorish before you went. Now I see how worthwhile your trip was.'

She came to sit on a stool next to me. 'Do you know what my favourite part was?' she asked.

I shook my head.

'Your birthday card. It was the best one I've ever had.'

'It was very expensive,' I told her.

'I know. It positively oozed expense.'

'And taste?'

'Taste more than expense.'

'Thank you.' I decided that the time was right. 'Annabelle?'

'Mmm.'

'You know you were going to come down to Gilbert's cottage in Cornwall?'

'Yes.'

'Well, I've been thinking. East Yorkshire isn't exactly Cornwall, but it's still very nice. And the cottage there is OK, too. It's not really a cottage, more a little house. But it can be very pleasant, and you'd never know you weren't in a cottage. So we could, you know . . .'

Annabelle tipped her head to one side and tried to look puzzled. 'Could what?' she asked.

'We could, well, walk on the beach; spend some time together. And you can skim pebbles on the North Sea just the same as any other sea. So . . . what do you think?'

'I think you have such a way with words, Charles.' The smile had defeated the puzzled look, and her cheeks were pink, showing off her dimples.

I nodded several times, perched on the high stool, sitting on my hands. 'I know,' I agreed. 'We have intensive training, for when we appear in court. So can I take that as affirmative?'

In the distance I could hear a noise like a budgerigar gargling. We both froze, listening. It was my mobile phone, in my jacket pocket, hanging in the hallway. The world had caught up with us again.

Halfway through, Annabelle joined me to listen to my end of the conversation. My tone probably gave away the content of the message. I said: 'Thanks for ringing, Jeff. Will you let me know what the pathologist has to say?' I folded the phone and clicked the aerial home.

She was leaning on the door jamb, arms dangling. 'They've found a body,' I told her. 'It fits Tom Noon's description.'

All the newspapers were filled with eulogies for the dead politician. The local rag said he was one of the greatest Prime Ministers we never had. Their quota of originality is expended on the football scores. Andrew Fallon, PM-in-waiting, was widely photographed and videoed in a distressed state. His other passion, apart from knocking tobacco, is railways. He is a great advocate of expanding the system, and heard of his friend's death while opening an extension to a private line somewhere near his home town of Dumfries. Pictures of him on the footplate of a steam locomotive, rivulets of tears cutting through the grime on his cheeks, appeared on all the front pages.

I was more interested in the pathologist's report. Tom Noon had drowned, but had been unconscious when he entered the water. A wound on the back of his head was consistent with him slipping and banging his head on a rock. People who should have known better nodded wisely: the rocks were slimy with moss . . . it had happened before . . . it was a dangerous place to take a dog for a walk on a lead.

At eleven o'clock at night! Twenty-five miles from home, without telling your wife where you were going! I didn't believe a word of it. I asked to see the body, and examined the wound on his head. It wasn't as bad as I'd expected, with little indentation to indicate the shape of whatever had caused it. I revisited the Strid and tried to reconstruct a possible scenario. It could have happened, but I wasn't convinced. I waited for some organisation, like The Struggle Continues, to claim responsibility, but nobody did.

The inquest heard evidence of identification and was adjourned. It looked as if an open verdict was on the cards, with a rider about walking the dog near deep water after dark. Mrs Noon was given permission to dispose of her husband's remains, and I made plans to entertain my favourite person in the whole world at my cottage on the coast, on expenses.

I couldn't face the journey in the Transit, and I didn't want Kevin to know about the Cavalier, so it had to be the

E-type Jaguar. Sometimes I feel I'm just a victim of circumstances. I loaded it with everything off the spare bed, down to the electric blanket, and took it all to the cottage on the Thursday afternoon. I made the bed, vacc'd round everywhere, washed the windows and plumped up all the cushions. I stocked the fridge and made sure there was a corkscrew. Annabelle's photographs had prompted me to develop the film in my camera. The picture I'd taken of her on Ingleborough, with Batty Moss viaduct in the background, was a smasher. I propped it on the mantelpiece above the fireplace, to add a personal touch to the room, and just to be on the safe side I went to see Kevin.

'Hi, Kev,' I said when he opened his door. 'I, er, just thought I'd tell you that I'm bringing a visitor over for the weekend. Female, you know. So, er, stay away, eh?' I gave him a knowing wink.

'OK, no problem. You still all right for the following weekend?'

'Yeah, great. Where are we going?'

'Not sure, yet. How long 'ave you known this bird?'

I hadn't expected him to ask that. 'Since yesterday,' I improvised.

'Blimey, Charlie, you're a fast worker.'

I pointed towards the Jag. 'Not me, Kevin, the car. See you.' I drove home, wondering how much of this conversation I ought to relate to Annabelle.

I told her it more or less verbatim, while we were driving over on Saturday morning, and she feigned indignation. 'He'll think I'm a tart,' she protested.

'Kevin probably thinks all women are tarts,' I told her. 'I've warned him to stay away, so hopefully he won't meet you.'

'Thank you very much!' Annabelle jerked her hand away from mine and turned to study Drax power station as it slipped by on her side of the car. I shrank into my seat and put my foot down – speed is supposed to be an aphrodisiac.

She liked the cottage. 'It's sweet,' she pronounced, surveying the whitewashed exterior.

I pulled a face. 'Sweet? What does *sweet* mean?' I asked, lifting her overnight case out of the boot.

'Well, it is ordinary – unprepossessing – on the outside, but with the promise of hidden delights, providing you are willing to modify your expectations.' She leaned over and pecked me on the cheek. 'Bit like you,' she added, and skipped out of my reach.

The April sun was shining straight into the front room, making it warm and homely. Annabelle saw the photograph on the mantelpiece of herself standing in front of the Batty Moss viaduct, and observed: 'That's a sturdy piece of Victorian architecture if ever I saw one,' inviting further comment from me.

I accepted the offer. 'Yes, and the bridge looks quite substantial, too,' I smirked.

'This is the kitchen,' I said, holding the door open so she could see through into it. 'I think you'll find everything you need in there.' I was rewarded with a scowl.

'Bathroom,' I said, pointing, when we were upstairs. 'And this is your bedroom.' I put her case on the bed. 'There's a wardrobe if you want to hang anything up.' Annabelle nodded her approval and followed me out. 'And this is the master bedroom. I sleep here.' The sun was in this room, too, and it looked much more inviting than the small back bedroom. I demonstrated the springiness of the mattress with my fingertips.

After a cup of tea we drove into Hull and had a fun afternoon, dodging the showers. It's a fascinating place, the only disappointment being the Land of Green Ginger, which Annabelle discovered was a street of solicitors' offices. The indoor market was a delight, and we bought a fresh salmon, for tea.

We had the fish with new potatoes and garden peas, followed by bread-and-butter pudding, all washed down with two bottles of Riesling. I made coffee and we watched some TV, with the fire on at full blast, cosy as two hermit crabs sharing one shell. The television wasn't very entertaining, so we switched it off and talked. Annabelle told me more about her trip to Africa, I told her about growing up with a policeman for a father.

About ten o'clock I drained the last of the wine into our glasses and said: 'How about . . . a game of Scrabble?'

Annabelle's eyes lit up. 'Scrabble? Do you have a set?'

'Yes, ma'am, we certainly do.' I rose to fetch it from the cupboard in the kitchen.

'I have to warn you that I was the Mombassa junior champion,' she called after me.

'In that case,' I declared rashly, as I returned with the box, 'you should be able to give me a good game.'

We arranged the chairs around the little coffee table and spread the pieces out on the board. I was playing upside down, so Annabelle had to keep score. 'Marquis of Dewsbury rules,' I suggested. 'Anything goes?'

'Of course. Two spelling mistakes and you are off the field?'

'Oh, absolutely.'

I slid seven plastic tiles towards me and turned the first one over just as the phone started ringing in the kitchen.

'Jeez!' I muttered under my breath, managing to abbreviate the blasphemy as I rose to my feet. It was Heckley nick.

'Sorry to trouble you, Mr Priest, but a lady's just been after you. I think she expected this to be your home number. Asked if you could ring her, sometime.'

'No problem, Arthur. Presumably she left her name?'

'Mrs Dooley. Do you want the number?'

'I know her. Yes, please.'

I'm not very good at holding back, waiting for a more opportune time. I rang the number with the Cornwall code that Arthur had relayed to me. She was still there.

'Hello, Diane,' I said. 'It's Charlie Priest. You've been after me.'

'Hello, Charlie. Hope I haven't caused you any embarrassment – I didn't realise it was your station number.'

'My fault, I must have written the wrong one down.' I might have added something about being confused in the presence of an attractive woman, but the kitchen door was ajar. 'What can I do for you?'

'I've just been watching a chat show on local TV, and guess who was on it?'

'Er . . . no idea.'

'None other than Richard Kidderminster, the man who Guy saved. He's an MP.'

'Ah, yes. I found out he was an MP,' I confessed. 'I didn't say so because I knew that we'd be sending someone to interview Guy. Didn't they let you know?'

'No, never mentioned it. They were a pair of real smoothies.'

'We're all smoothies,' I told her. 'What did Kidderminster have to say?'

'Oh, usual stuff. They were talking about Tom Noon falling in the river. That was near you, wasn't it?'

'Yes.'

'Well, apparently, Tom Noon had a very small majority – second smallest at the last election. Two or three recounts. The smallest majority just happened to be Mr Kidderminster, with a magnificent twenty-three votes. That is his major claim to fame, hence the invitation to be on TV.'

'Sounds like riveting viewing. How are you both keeping?'

They were well. I promised to ring Guy and prised myself away as politely as possible. Annabelle looked resigned when I returned to the front room.

'Sorry about that,' I apologised. 'Lady with some information she thought I might be interested in.'

'And were you?'

'Not really.' I placed my Scrabble pieces on the little holder. There was only one vowel. 'She'd just learned that Tom Noon had the second smallest majority at the last election, pipped for that doubtful honour by Richard Kidderminster with twenty-three votes. He's MP for somewhere in Dorset.'

Annabelle was frowning, peering at her letters. 'Fascinating,' she mumbled.

'It's a long story. I'll tell it to you some rainy Sunday afternoon, when conversation is flagging. This is a terrible hand.'

Terrible was putting it politely. I'd drawn A – that took care of the vowels – followed by J, V, K, Q, Z and F. 'You start,' I generously suggested.

'We'll draw for it,' she insisted. 'Nearest to the beginning goes first.' She lifted a tile, not allowing me to see the letter. 'X,' she sighed, and placed it face-down back with its fellows.

I chose one, flipping it right over. 'M. My go.'

I was in trouble. Intellectually, Annabelle could have me for hors d'oeuvre, I had no illusions about that. I wasn't thick, but it might take some proving. I studied my row of little plastic squares with growing panic.

'This is a dreadful hand,' I complained again.

'Mine's rather depressing,' she told me, preoccupied. There was no sympathy for me there.

Five minutes later I said: 'I, er, don't think I can go.'

Annabelle smiled. 'Nonsense, you must be able to.'

Ah well, I thought, when in difficulties, play it for laughs. It was a philosophy that had done well for me so far.

I placed a single tile on the star in the middle of the board. 'A,' I said.

'A?'

'Yes. Indefinite article.'

'It should have at least two letters.'

'I can't do a two-letter word.'

'Of course you can.'

'No, I can't.'

'Then exchange your tiles.'

'C'mon, it's your turn.'

Annabelle studied her hand and I studied her. The corners of her mouth kept twitching upwards, as if she were trying to contain a smile, and the pinkness of her cheeks ebbed and flowed, like a glowing coal when you blow on it. I drummed my fingers in feigned impatience.

Slowly and deliberately she laid her letters next to my A, one after the other, until only a single tile remained in her hand. 'There,' she said, triumphantly.

I read her word, upside down, with undisguised dismay. 'AXOLOTL?' I said.

'Yes. Its a South American lizard.'

'I know.'

Annabelle totted up the score and wrote it next to the point I'd earned. 'Fifteen-one to me,' she declared with a wicked grin.

'My word scored two,' I complained. 'One for vertical, one for horizontal.'

'Gosh, yes. I am sorry.' She made the correction. 'That makes it only fifteen-two.' She giggled and fell back into her easy chair.

I put up a brave fight, but never recovered that early

deficit. And I was subjected to some terrible distractions. Nearly two hours later we were filling the top of the board, Classic FM playing softly, earning odd points where we could. I was holding BELL, hoping for an opportunity for a big finish, but it looked unlikely. Earlier, in a burst of inspiration, I'd put THE. Annabelle had promptly made it into ETHER and now, with her last play of the match, converted it to WHETHER.

'Right into my trap,' I declared with glee. 'Priest wins with the last kick of the game. How about this: BELL-WHETHER. Triple score.'

Annabelle looked puzzled.

'It's a sheep,' I told her. 'With a bell round its neck, like a Judas sheep.'

'Judas goat.'

'Same thing.'

She shook her head. 'Sorry, Charles. A brave attempt, but there is no H in the middle.'

'Honest?' I asked, downcast.

She looked sorry for me. 'Honest,' she confirmed. 'But I'll let you call it a draw.'

I took my pieces back. There was a stray D over on the right-hand side. In that case,' I said, 'how about . . . BED?'

'Yes,' she agreed. The fire in her cheeks had caught hold. 'That is a good idea.'

I turned the board round to study it. All the best words were hers. I read the little table at the bottom that told you how many times each letter occurred. There were twelve Es, nine As, but only one each of X and Z.

'Wait a minute!' I declared. Annabelle was now bright scarlet, and her nose was wrinkling. 'According to this, there should only be one X. You said you'd drawn an X at the beginning, but you put another one down, in AXOLOTL.'

She collapsed back into the chair and wrapped her arms around herself. 'Oh Charles, your face!' she spluttered.

I reached over and grabbed her wrist. 'Of all the cheatin', lyin', connivin' wimmin I've ever met . . .' I squeezed into the chair and held her in a bear hug, crushing her. She smiled up at me and we kissed. 'You play a helluva game of Scrabble,' I said, when we came up for air.

'You bring out the best in me,' she replied.

'Dammit. That wasn't the intention.'

We put the game back in the box and washed our glasses. 'You go up to bed,' I suggested. 'I'll check that everything is secure.'

Annabelle pecked me on the cheek. 'Good night, then.'

'Switch your electric blanket off,' I called after her as she vanished up the stairs. 'It's been on about four hours. Good night.'

I locked the front door and carried the Scrabble box into the kitchen. Plumbing noises came from above, followed by the creaking of floorboards in the back bedroom and the click of the electric blanket switch. I checked the back door and put the glasses away. More creaking of floorboards. I turned the gasfire off and pushed the chairs back. I checked all the lights, double-checked the fire. When I couldn't find anything else to check I went upstairs.

In the bathroom I stripped off all my clothes and wrapped them in a bundle. I gave my teeth the best cleaning since I had a crush on the school dental hygienist and washed myself all over with smelly soap. I pulled the lightswitch and padded silently, in the dark, into the front bedroom.

There was no electric blanket on the big bed. I slipped under the duvet but never noticed the chill of the sheets, because Annabelle was there, waiting for me.

Chapter Eleven

Everything worked, for both of us. It all worked again, when the shape of the room was slowly being revealed like a grainy print in a developing tray, and the first blackbird was clearing his throat on the rooftop. In between, I lay wide awake, not caring to sleep, arms and legs wrapped around Annabelle, as if I were scared that she'd escape if I relaxed for a second. I listened to her breathing, feeling her body rhythmically moving in my arms, and wondered which god I'd pleased, and if I could hold on to it, this time.

Lots of thoughts passed through my mind. Most of all, I was glad that I hadn't become involved with Diane Dooley. The slate was clean for once, the cupboard empty of skeletons. There was still work, of course. That wouldn't go away. I was learning to adjust my priorities, but I was still a detective. The rat-like body of Bobby Noon floated across my thoughts, as did Tom Noon and Richard Kidderminster. I drove them away by re-playing the game of Scrabble, and chuckled to myself. That had been fun.

'Bellwether!' I said out loud. Annabelle stirred, shifted her position, and slumbered on.

I did fall asleep, much later. I woke to find an empty place next to me, and heard the scrape of a pan on the hob coming from downstairs. Annabelle reappeared, bearing a tray loaded with orange juice, coffee, and neat little bacon sandwiches. She was wearing my clean shirt and little else. There was a mirror on the far wall, and as I watched her reflection she stooped to place the tray on the bedside table and a tiny white triangle of her knickers winked at me.

'You look uncommonly pleased with yourself,' she said.

'Happy,' I confirmed. She slipped back under the covers and passed a plate across. 'This is wicked,' I told her. 'What would your neighbours think?'

'I know – bacon sandwiches in bed. They would probably organise a petition to have me drummed from the street.'

When we were sipping our coffee Annabelle asked what we were doing for the rest of the day. I brushed a few crumbs off the duvet, on to the floor. 'I'll go and buy all the Sunday papers,' I suggested, 'and we'll spend the morning reading them and drinking tea. Then we will go to a local hostelry for lunch, and afterwards – this afternoon – we could always come back here and – try for the hat trick.'

She turned and smiled at me. 'I'm not sure that that is a good idea,' she said. 'You are at a dangerous age, Charles. You should practise restraint in these matters.'

I pulled my glum face. 'True,' I admitted. 'Sad, but true.'

We went for a walk. It was a bright breezy morning, and we wandered off like a couple of teenagers on honeymoon. We headed for the shore, but were frustrated by fields with no paths, and a wide dyke.

'You talk in your sleep,' Annabelle told me.

We were on a bridlepath, my arm across her shoulders, hers around my waist. 'Oh heck,' I said. 'I hope I didn't mention any girls' names.'

'No, just sheep.'

'Sheep!' I laughed.

'Yes. What's so funny?'

'Nothing. You don't accuse a Yorkshireman of dreaming about sheep, that's all.'

'Why not?'

'Because.'

'You're blushing!'

'No, I'm not.'

'What is so funny about Yorkshiremen and sheep?'

'Nothing.'

'Tell me!'

'There's nothing to tell. What did I say?'

'You just said: "Bellwether".'

I hadn't been asleep. I said: 'Oh yes. I remember.'

'So what *were* you dreaming about?'

Once, I would have avoided the discussion, made an evasive reply, but I was determined to change, be different. I didn't want to exclude Annabelle from my work as a policeman, and I wanted to be a part of her work, her life. We'd reached a five-barred gate, a big solid custom-made one, a sign of prosperity. I rested my arms on it and Annabelle did likewise, looking towards the silver streak of the Humber, which didn't appear to be any closer.

I said: 'Do you remember the Brighton bomb?'

Annabelle looked puzzled. 'When the IRA tried to assassinate Mrs Thatcher?'

'That's right.'

'Yes, I remember. Tory party conference, about, oh, nineteen eighty-four. Several people were killed by it.'

'That's right. The IRA were successful because they knew exactly where Mrs Thatcher would be at a given time. So, three months, maybe six months earlier, they planted a bomb with a long time-fuse. Probably put it behind a bath panel, or under floorboards. They nearly did what Guy Fawkes failed to do.'

'And where is this leading us?'

'OK. Let's say that someone, possibly this organisation called TSC – The Struggle Continues – wants to murder the current Prime Minister. How might they go about it?'

Annabelle shrugged her shoulders. 'I don't know. They would have to be very familiar with his movements.'

'That's right,' I said. 'They'd have to know where he would be at a given time. But security is intense at all the usual functions he attends. We learn by our mistakes. So instead of following him, they might try to lead him.'

'Sorry, Charles, I don't understand.'

'Neither do I; this is just me thinking aloud. The phone call I had last night, when you fixed the scrabble pieces—' I looked across at her and she blushed and smiled. 'It was from a lady I met in Cornwall. Her son foiled an attempt to kill Richard Kidderminster. No, not to kill him – they could easily have done that. To kill him and make it look like an accident – that was their intention, if my theory is correct. Kidderminster had the lowest majority recorded at the last General Election. Right now the Government needs a by-election in a marginal seat like Saddam Hussein needs his legs waxing. If one were called, all the big guns would flock to support their local candidate, including the Prime Minister. Most of all, the Prime Minister. It wouldn't take a genius to guess where he would address meetings, or stay overnight. Two months after the attempt on Kidderminster, the Member with the second smallest majority dies under suspicious circumstances. It looks like an accident, but it could be murder. Maybe it was another attempt to dictate the Prime Minister's movements, lead him to the slaughter-house. That's what I meant by bellwether. Tom Noon was a Judas goat, but this time the goat had to die.'

Annabelle looked doubtful. 'It . . . it seems so unreal,' she said.

'Yes, I agree. Out here with everything so fresh and new, it's hard to believe that there are men plotting daft schemes like this. But there was nothing unreal about what we saw at

Bolton Abbey; that was real enough.'

'Yes, it was. So what will you do?'

'Pass on the information, that's all. I have friends in high places.' I put my arm back around her. 'They'll probably have a little chuckle amongst themselves and put a cryptic comment on my secret file in the personnel department: *Prone to believing in conspiracy theories*.'

We turned to walk back, and were met by a wall of black cloud, building up like burning-tyre smoke, with Persil-white gulls wheeling against it. The storm hit us before we reached home, and there wasn't a tree within three miles. It was brief and savage. Annabelle's coat had a hood, but mine didn't and she didn't offer to lend me hers. In two minutes it was over, but cold water was running down my neck, under my leather jacket, to merge again with the rain soaking through my jeans.

'Brrr!' I shivered. 'The weatherman didn't warn us about this.'

'Or even the bellwetherman,' she teased, in spite of the discomfort.

The last half-mile was made bearable by thoughts of drying each other with big warm bath towels, but I don't know what sustained Annabelle. I was worried when I saw the red Sierra parked outside Kevin's cottage.

We dashed inside and warmed ourselves by the gasfire. I fetched towels and rubbed my hair. 'Go have a quick shower,' I suggested. 'That will warm you up.'

'You go first, you are soaked to the skin.'

Before we could fight over it, or, better still, come to a compromise, there was a knock at the door. It was Darren.

'Hello, Charlie, mind if I come in?' he said.

I rubbed my neck with the towel and held the door wide. 'No, be my guest.'

'I was in the area, so thought I'd call to see you and

Kevin, know what I mean?' He stared at Annabelle.

'Yeah. This is, er, Sharron, I said. 'Sharron, this is Darren.'

'Hi, Sharron.'

''Ello, luv.'

I dropped the towel. This was not what I had planned.

'You all right for next weekend, Charlie?' Darren asked. He turned to Annabelle, a.k.a. Sharron. 'Business,' he explained with an expansive gesture.

'I'm all right, if the terms are.'

'Mmm. I think we'll be able to meet your requirements, but you drive a hard bargain.'

'You know what they say, Darren. If you pay peanuts, you'll get monkeys.' With a nod of my head towards the dividing wall I added: 'Like Kevin.'

'Hey, that's good,' Darren laughed. 'I like that. If you pay peanuts you'll get monkeys. I'll remember that – thanks.'

'You're welcome.'

He turned to Annabelle. 'He's a great one with words, you know.'

'I 'adn't noticed, luv,' she said, with a flick of her eyes at me. The dimples were back in her cheeks – she was enjoying this. She moved away from the fire, and Darren saw the photograph on the mantelpiece at the same instant as I did.

'Hey, that's, er, don't tell me, er, Batty Moss viaduct,' he said.

'That's right,' I agreed. He seemed more interested in the bridge than in the beautiful lady in the foreground. 'Do you know it?'

'Yeah, we were there last week. Just for a look, if you know what I mean.'

I hadn't a clue what he meant, if anything. I said: 'It's a big so-and-so.'

'Yeah. Hundred feet high, four-forty yards long and twenty-four arches.'

'You know some stuff, Darren.'

'Yeah, well, I like to know what I'm talking about.'

I managed to get rid of him, on the understanding that he would make the arrangements for the next run with Kevin. As soon as he was out of the door I patted Annabelle on the bottom and said: 'Go get a shower, love. Right now. I'll do the potatoes,' I couldn't resist calling: 'Sharron,' after her as she headed for the stairs.

We were having jacket potatoes and lots of trimmings for lunch. I loaded the spuds into the microwave and brought my change of clothing downstairs. I dried myself and dressed right there in the kitchen. My clean shirt smelt nice. The conversation taking place next door wasn't hard to imagine: Darren would tell Kevin what a smashing piece of crumpet Sharron was; Kevin would say it was the car she was after, and Charlie only met her two days ago; Darren would say: 'That's funny, he has a photograph of her on the mantelpiece, taken when there was frost on the ground.' That's the trouble with lies. They go everywhere with you, like loose shoelaces, waiting to trip you up.

The weather made it easy for me. Another freak storm rattled the windows, and there were a couple of loud thunderclaps. It looked, as we say, set in. After lunch I suggested that we went home, maybe calling at the multi-screen cinema on the way. Annabelle agreed. I didn't want to frighten her, but Darren wasn't the cuddly simpleton that I made him out to be. He could be dangerous, and I wanted her far away from him.

I wrote my reports and phoned Fearnside, telling him that I'd had enough of being off sick and suggesting that we try to lift the gang the following weekend. After discussions with the Technical Support Unit it was decided that we would plant tracking devices in the holdalls and set up an operation to follow them. When all that was settled I called in at the nick to let Superintendent Wood know that I was intending to resume duty.

He was absorbed by the crossword puzzle in one of the tabloids when I strolled into his office.

'Good morning, Gilbert. You look busy,' I said.

'Boss's perks. Morning, Charlie, do I detect a new spring in your step?'

'Possibly.' I pointed at the paper. 'Any you need help with?'

He looked down at it again. 'Yes, there is one. How's your Shakespeare? Here we are, four down. "Falstaff's page". Any ideas?'

I said: 'Bottom?'

'No, can't be. Starts with an R.'

'Rectum?'

He removed his spectacles and folded the paper. 'Yes,' he sighed, 'I can see that you're back in the Land of the Living again.'

'I've come to see if you need a new detective, lots of experience?'

'Great. Start tomorrow, on nightshift.'

'Oh. I was thinking about next Monday, and only part-time.'

'Is that what Dr Evans suggests?'

'I don't know. I haven't told him yet.'

I explained about the drugs bust, and there might be a few loose ends to tie up, and he agreed for me to have a low-profile return to duties. 'Young Newley's doing a great job,' he declared. 'First time we've ever been in front with the budgets.'

'Then we'll let him keep doing them,' I suggested.

Downstairs, Nigel was engrossed in a serious conversation with Dave Sparkington about the deprivations of Sparky's childhood, growing up in the cobbled streets of Old Heckley.

'And on Tuesdays it was always tripe and onions,' Sparky was saying, 'unless our mam could find a nice cow heel.'

'There's gonna be some changes in here,' I declared, as I marched in.

Nigel looked up and said: 'Hi, boss. Are you back with us?'

Sparky swivelled in his seat. 'Hello, Charlie. I was just telling Nigel about when we were young 'uns. You used to have pigs' trotters when you were a kid, didn't you?'

I looked down at my hands and said: 'No, little fingers and toes, like all the other children.'

I rang Eric Dobson and arranged to borrow the van again at the weekend. He promised to relay any messages from Kevin straight to me. I read a few files, to bring myself up to date, and made another appointment to see Sam Evans. Annabelle was down in London presenting her paper to the charities, and leaving the one about tobacco with Andrew Fallon's office in Westminster. It was doubtful if she would see the man himself. It was a sunny day, so I drove home and polished the Jaguar.

Nigel called in to see me, for a meaningful, quality time, man-to-man talk about his prospects. He was well regarded, and due for a full Inspector's job, but he'd have to move. Promotion would almost certainly mean a spell back in uniform, too. I warned him that he was being sucked in by the cosiness of Heckley, and advised him to make the break.

When I'd finished he gave *me* some advice. I'd been in the middle of two days' washing up when he arrived. 'Why don't you buy a dishwasher?' he suggested.

'For one person?' I replied. 'It'd be a waste of money.'

He shook his head. 'You don't understand. The main advantage of a dishwasher isn't that it does your washing up.'

'You could've fooled me.'

'No. What it does is keep your kitchen tidy. You just stuff your crockery into it until it's full, and every three or four days switch it on. No more dirty dishes in the sink. Ever.'

I nodded my approval. 'Mmm. I'd never thought of it like that. Which powder do you recommend?'

He'd have told me, but his mobile phone was warbling. 'Excuse me,' he said, pulling on the aerial.

I watched the expression on his face change from interested to anxious. 'Where did you say it was?' 'I'm at Mr Priest's.' 'OK, I'll ask him. Be there in ten minutes.'

'Someone's found a body,' he told me, putting the phone back in his pocket. 'Can you direct me to Withins House, somewhere on High Moor Lane?'

'I know it,' I said, and drew him a sketch.

He studied it for a moment, before suggesting: 'Alternatively, you could come with me.'

'I thought you'd never ask,' I said, and grabbed my jacket.

We went in separate cars, me leading, via the back lanes that led to Withins House. A Panda car was outside and all the house windows were illuminated. A uniformed PC, aged about twenty, was standing at the gate. His face glowed luminous in the darkness.

'She's in the dustbin, sir,' he gulped. I directed his attention to Nigel.

'Who found her?' Nigel asked.

'The householders, Mr and Mrs Myers. They've just come back from a three-week holiday. Mrs Myers went to throw some sandwiches they hadn't eaten into the bin. She's in a bad way.'

'Where is the bin?'

'At the back.' He didn't volunteer to show us.

It was a large black wheelie bin. Nigel lifted the lid with his fingertips and the light from a window fell inside it. She was naked, and had been dropped in head-first. Her legs were pushed down, so the lid would close, and she was now in a grotesque parody of the foetal position. We looked down on her with no sense of her humiliation, then moved our heads back in unison as the smell invaded our nostrils.

'You do the necessary,' I told Nigel. 'I'll keep the Myerses company.' The Necessary was to inform Divisional HQ and the duty DS. That's how you launch a full-scale murder enquiry.

Mr Myers had made some tea, so I accepted a cup. Words of comfort were no use, so I bombarded them with the details about how the enquiry would proceed. Their home would be crawling with various experts for the next couple of days. 'In fact,' I said, 'it might be better if you went into an hotel, at least for tonight. We could pay, if you'd like that.'

'We could always stay at my sister's in Halifax,' Mr Myers suggested.

'I think you should. Why don't you give her a ring?'

It was agreed, and they re-packed a few things. Their holiday was already a distant memory, a waste of money and time.

The queue of vehicles in the lane outside was growing. I introduced the Myerses to ADI Newley and told him where I was taking them. While he was asking for a few details I had a word with Dr Evans. The photographer was assembling his equipment.

Sam observed him with distaste. 'Does he have to take

her photo, like that?' he asked.

I ignored the question. 'Book me off, Sam,' I said. 'I want to start work again.'

'You must be crazy.'

'What, *moi*?'

Mr Myers's sister lived in a leafy suburb of Halifax, in one of a row of grand stone houses that had once belonged to prosperous tradesmen and minor civic dignitaries, in an age when such people had status in the community. They couldn't thank me enough for spiriting them away from the apparent chaos unfolding at Withins House.

After that I drove home. I had a small glass of port, because I fancied one and felt I deserved it, and went to bed. Gilbert and Nigel, with assistance from Division, could handle the case. It would be a struggle not to interfere, but I'd sit in the wings and watch.

I lost the struggle. Seven-thirty next morning found me in Heckley General Hospital, negotiating my way through the basement, to the place where I knew the post mortem would be taking place.

In a room of white, she still looked pale, stretched out on the table like a fish after the filleter has finished. The pathologist raised his head and gave me a wink of recognition. Nigel was standing nearby, absorbing every gruesome detail.

'Morning Professor, Mr Newley,' I said.

Thankfully all the major cutting had been done. The assistant was sewing the skin back, making the body as presentable as possible, before relatives, if found, were asked to identify her. 'About to take vitreous humour sample for time-of-death indication,' the Professor droned into the microphone, hovering over her with a syringe at the ready.

I tapped Nigel with the back of my hand. 'Don't look,' I

said, turning away from the grim scene.

Nigel ignored me. After a few seconds he hissed: 'Jeeesus Christ!'

One of the most valuable pieces of information that the pathologist can tell us is time of death. It's an imprecise science, but the latest development is the analysis of the fluid that fills the eyeball – the vitreous humour. Someone has discovered that chemical changes take place in it at a steady rate after death. The fluid is drawn off through a needle directly into the eye. This causes the eyeball to collapse, like a deflating balloon. Injecting distilled water soon brings it back to normal shape, but it is grotesque to watch, as Nigel could now verify.

The preliminary report said that she was about fourteen, had been dead a couple of weeks and took drugs. Her arms bore nearly-healed injection scars, but analysis of her organs would tell us what she'd used lately and her hair would give us the longer picture. She'd been strangled with such violence that her larynx was ruptured, and then raped. The rapist had left a full sample inside her.

None of the missing girls on our books fitted her description. We widened the net, but kids usually ran away from Heckley, not towards the town. A description of her and her clothing was published in the local paper, and on Friday morning George Leach stumbled into the nick and claimed that the body could be that of his stepdaughter Nicola McGann. An hour later he made a positive identification. She had gone missing nearly three weeks earlier, but he hadn't reported it. She was almost sixteen, and he assumed that she had gone to live with her older sister, as she had threatened to do many times.

I had unfinished business with Darren and his gang. The Area Detective Superintendent took overall charge of the murder investigation, with Nigel doing the donkeywork, ably assisted by most of the Heckley complement and about twenty bodies imported from neighbouring divisions. They investigated Nicky's background, looked at known suspects, listened to information and made house-to-house enquiries. No one leapt into the frame.

Drug running was becoming boring, and I would have preferred to have stayed on the murder enquiry. This was to be the last run, hopefully resulting in the arrest of the people who employed Darren. Fearnside had set the whole thing up; all I had to do was go along for the sail. Gilbert would be pleased to have me back. Nigel was competent enough, but didn't carry any clout with Division. If we didn't get a quick result for Nicola they might move in and take over. I'd be glad to be back on the case, too – I hadn't liked the smell of Nicola's stepdad, and didn't rate a person who could let his daughter vanish and show such little concern.

This time it was Amsterdam. Kevin showed me a grubby scrap of paper with the address on it. We were to collect the goodies from a patisserie on Jordaanstraat, ten minutes' walk from the town centre. I grabbed the paper from him and passed my hand across my mouth, pretending to chew and swallow the address. Then I ripped it into sixteenths and dropped the bits into a litter bin.

'You don't learn, do you?' I reprimanded.

'I can't remember stuff like that,' he protested.

We were on the ferry, outwardbound. We'd travelled together to the docks, in Kevin's car, and were booked into a cabin.

I took the top bunk and slept like a three-toed sloth. It was important that I didn't spend any time alone with the bags, so when he went to the toilet, I decided to go, too. He didn't wash or clean his teeth, but I managed a refreshing few minutes in the bathroom as we docked at Europoort.

Everything went smoothly. A lady who'd stepped straight out of van Gogh's *Potato Eaters* fed us coffee and a pastry in the back room of the bakery while the bags were switched, and we were out of the place in fifteen minutes. Whoever did the checking for the English side didn't show himself.

'What happened to Darren?' I asked Kevin as we strolled back to the station.

'Dunno. 'Spect it was Shawn who did it this time. Usually is. Darren just collects it off me and brings the money.' He turned to me. 'Don't meddle with Shawn,' he warned. 'He's a nasty piece of work.'

'So you keep saying. I can be fairly disagreeable myself.' I smiled at him, trying to look manic, like Jack Nicholson does.

Because of the hour's train ride in each direction, plus a compulsory warm apple-ball, there was not too much hanging around. My taste for art galleries was suppressed, and I disappointed Kevin by suggesting that a stroll through the redlight district with a couple of kilograms of heroin in our possession might be unwise. At six o'clock we sauntered up the gangplank, kitbags at a jaunty angle hiding our tension, like a slightly dishevelled Noël Coward and Michael Wilding in *In Which We Serve*.

We dossed on our bunks until the dining room opened. I managed a wash but Kevin didn't bother. We left the bags on the beds and joined the queue at the restaurant, where he had two helpings of trifle for pudding and declared that the food was smashing. It was OK. A middle-aged woman briefly made eye contact with me. She was accompanied by someone much younger, could have been her daughter, but it wasn't.

We were in the bar, sipping halves of lager, when they joined us. 'These anybody's seats?' the young one asked.

'Saving them just for you,' I told her.

'Where are you from, then?'

'I'm from Chipping Sodbury, Kevin's from Highgrove.'

'Chipping Sodbury? Where's Chipping bloody Sodbury?' she laughed.

'It's a nice place. I'm Charlie, by the way. What are you called?'

We talked nonsense for half an hour, Kevin's blank gaze switching from one to the other of us as we spoke. 'I'll get some drinks,' I said, standing up. 'What would you like?'

When I returned they'd dragged Kevin into the conversation, and were chatting like old friends. He was enjoying himself.

'Cheers, Charlie,' said the older one, raising her glass.

'Cheers, love.'

Kevin was telling the 'daughter' seated next to him about the car he wanted to buy. I tapped my companion on the knee, under the table. Her hand came down to mine and I passed the key for our cabin to her.

'I'll have to go to the loo,' she announced, rising. 'You coming, Josie?'

'Yeah, suppose so. Save our drinks, we'll be back.'

While they were gone Kevin and I discussed our prospects. He thought I was in with a chance, but didn't rate his own. I assured him that the opposite was true. The thought intrigued me – I'd never had sex with a Sergeant from the Drugs Squad.

We had another drink with them, then they announced that they had tickets for the cinema, and left us. Kevin didn't look too disappointed. When we finally hit the hammock the bags were exactly where we'd left them, but with one slight, invisible difference. If Kevin had possessed a radio receiver, tuned to the right frequency, he would have discovered that they were now emitting regular electronic beeps, like Sputnik I, courtesy of the East Yorkshire Constabulary Technical Support Unit.

★ ★ ★

Darren arrived at the cottages in the afternoon, but didn't stay. I was just about to go next door to join them when I heard the engine of the Sierra start and he was away.

'He was in a hurry,' I said to Kevin when he answered my knock. He looked uncomfortable.

'Yeah. He, er . . . he couldn't wait.'

I walked in without being invited. 'But he left the money, I presume.'

'Yeah, well, some of it.'

'Whaddya mean, "some of it"?' I growled.

He produced a slim roll of notes with a rubber band round them. 'Two-fifty quid, same as before.'

'Two hundred and fifty! We agreed seven-fifty. Give me his number. Tell me where I can find him.'

Kevin raised his hands in appeasement, carefully keeping his settee between us. 'L-look, Charlie,' he stuttered, 'D-Darren says they're a bit sh-short. They've a big job coming up, need all the readies they can get their hands on. He says they'll pay us, but it might not be in cash.'

'Not in cash! What the fuck are they playing at, Kevin? Where can I get hold of them?'

'If I knew I couldn't tell you, Charlie. I'd be a dead man.'

'OK. Well, next time you hear from Darren tell him that I want my money. There'll be no more trips until I'm paid in full. Meanwhile, if I see him first, I'll beat the marrow out of him. Understood?'

'I'm sorry, Charlie. I'll tell him.' The poor bloke looked heartbroken.

I went back to my half of the building and rang Commander Fearnside. My career as a drug smuggler was now terminated. He said: 'Well done, old boy,' and hinted that he might have more work for me. I told him to watch out for my expenses landing on his desk. After that I flopped on the bed, pulling the pillow over my face in case Kevin peeked through the window and caught me laughing. When I was ready I left for home, spinning the van's wheels as I shot out of the garden. I tuned the radio to a music station and drove sedately back to Merlin Couriers for what I hoped was the last time.

The Monday-morning case conference for Nicola McGann was held in the big lecture room. Nigel chaired it, after Gilbert made a few opening remarks. Nicola's movements were well-documented until late Friday evening, eighteen days before her body was found in the dustbin at Withins House – right up to when she'd left a friend and gone off with a man in a car. After that, *zilch*. The friend wasn't too bright, not the most observant person to have witness your last movements. The man was stockily built and indescribably ugly. She hadn't fancied him. She couldn't remember anything about the car, except that it was not a little one. To be fair, the sodium lights in the town centre make it difficult to recognise colours. We don't like them.

The stepfather was in the frame, although he wasn't the man Nicola was last seen with. He'd married Nicola's mother ten years earlier, but it wasn't much of a marriage. Mother was an alcoholic and possibly schizophrenic. Most of the time she was either undergoing treatment or pursuing oblivion. She had two daughters, but the older one had married and moved away. My twisted mind wondered if the daughters were the real reason George Leach had married a drunkard. When I saw his record, I was convinced – he'd done six years for indecent assault on a minor.

He also had a cast-iron alibi. On the weekend in question he was admitted to Heckley General with acute appendicitis. Neither he nor the mother expressed much grief at the death of their daughter, but that's not a crime. I told Nigel that a conversation with the sister might prove profitable.

Pauline lived in Bristol, we discovered, when Leach eventually found a torn-off corner of a letter in a drawer full of dirty socks. A female detective from the local force went round to confirm that she lived at that address, and made an appointment for me to visit her the next day.

It was a long way to go, and we could have asked the local people to do the interview, but the offences were serious and I wanted to talk to her myself. There wasn't a pool car available so I went on the train. The lady 'tec, called Jean, met me at the station and drove me to a mushroom farm of high-rise flats that made Heckley look like Palm Springs. We parked outside a block that was evidently the right one, although I couldn't see why, and rode up in the toilet to the sixth floor.

Simple mathematics told me that Pauline was twenty-two, but she could have passed for a young forty. Every few seconds she brushed her hair from her face, and I saw a bottle of two-coloured capsules on the table. The flat was cheaply furnished and untidy, but clean. A photograph on the wall betrayed the reason for the clutter: she was the mother of two mixed-race imps with grins like angels.

'What a lovely picture,' I told her, after Jean had introduced us and I was seated in a sagging easy chair. I meant it, but it still sounded like the opening gambit of a double-glazing salesman.

She smiled her appreciation and asked if we'd like a cup of tea. I said we would.

'How did you learn of Nicola's death?' I asked, after a few sips.

'In the paper. Friday, I think it was. It was a shock.'

'I can imagine. I'm sorry it happened that way but we didn't know you existed. Your stepfather should have let us know.'

At the mention of her stepfather she pulled the mug of tea towards her, clutching it against her stomach as if it were a teddy bear and gazing down at the carpet. 'Him,' was all she said.

'When did you last see Nicola?' I asked.

'When I left 'ome, five years ago. I was seventeen, Nicky was only ten.' Her eyes filled with tears and the DC handed her a tissue. They always carry a supply.

'Did you write?'

She nodded. 'Christmas, and her birfday, that's all. She wanted to come down 'ere, but we don't 'ave no room. We tried for somewhere bigger . . .'

'It's difficult,' I said. 'In her letters, did Nicola mention any friends? We think she was into drugs. Did she say anything about that?'

Pauline shook her head, as if she were elsewhere in her thoughts, and swept some non-existent hair to one side.

'What about George Leach, did she mention him?'

I saw her knuckles whiten as she clenched the untouched mug of tea, but she didn't answer my question. Maybe a change of tack was called for. 'What does your husband do, Pauline?' I asked.

She looked at me and said: 'He's an electrician. Just got 'is first job on 'is own. Probably be working late tonight.'

'On his own,' I said. 'That's a big step. Should be plenty of work for a decent electrician, though. What's he called?'

'Leon.'

'Where did you meet him?'

'A club in Bradford. He 'as relatives down 'ere.'

'So he took you away from the bright lights of Heckley?'

She nodded.

'And from George Leach?'

She threw me a scared glance and the knuckles whitened again.

'Pauline, did Nicky ever write and tell you that Leach was abusing her?'

She relaxed a little, now that the cards were on the table. 'No,' she replied.

'So do you think he was?'

She nodded and blew her nose.

'What did Nicky say?'

'Just . . . just 'ow rotten he was. He used to beat her, an' was always drunk. 'Ow she 'ated him, and wished he was dead.'

'But she never wrote that he was abusing her, sexually?'

Pauline raised her head and looked me in the eye for the first time. 'You don't write to your big sister and say that your stepdad is doing it to you summat rotten, do you?'

I shrank into the chair and felt a spasm in the muscles of my lower jaw. 'No,' was all I could say.

The DC came to the rescue. 'And was he?' she asked.

Pauline nodded.

Very quietly, the DC asked: 'Did George Leach ever abuse you, Pauline?'

She started to cry. When she had regained some composure I said: 'Pauline, this is obviously very upsetting for you. We don't want to force you into anything against your wishes, but poor Nicky didn't have much of a life. George Leach didn't murder her, but he hurt her enough. Maybe we can get something back for her, give her some justice. I'm going now, but you know where you can get in touch with Jean if you need to. Just remember this, though. It's your life; don't let us push you into anything you are not happy with. Think of yourself, and what's good for *you*. Nothing else matters.'

I rose to my feet, but she reached out and grabbed my sleeve. 'Don't go,' she said. 'I want to tell you.'

The pattern had been set the night before George Leach

married her mother. When the bride-to-be was unconscious in bed he went next door and raped her twelve-year-old daughter. For the next five years he plied the mother with alcohol, or waited until she was having one of her many spells in hospital, and satisfied his cravings for young flesh on Pauline. He was almost pleased when a young black stud ran away with her, because she had a ten-year-old sister . . .

We sat in stunned silence for a couple of minutes. It was what we'd expected, but hearing it told, first-hand, turned the blood to ditchwater.

'How much of this does Leon know?' I asked.

'Everything. He got me away from it. He . . . he's so patient and understanding. I don't know where I'd be without him.'

In Nicola's place, I thought. 'If you testified against Leach,' I told her, 'the papers wouldn't be allowed to print your name, but they'd make it pretty obvious that you were Nicky's sister. And some twisted barrister for the defence could give you a hard time – say you were promiscuous, led him on, that sort of thing. It could be rough for you.'

She looked up at me like a mouse studying a cat, wondering which way to jump. I wandered over to the photo of the kids and examined it for a moment. They illuminated the room like a ray of sunshine. Maybe the cycle of abuse had been broken. That was the good part of the day.

I said: 'Think about what we've said, Pauline; discuss it with Leon. Don't do it to please me, or even for Nicky. Do what's best for you.'

She said she'd think about it, and Jean took me back to Temple Meads railway station. I'd never make a salesman. He'd have closed on her, to use the jargon. 'What time would you like to come to the station to make a statement?'

he'd have asked, making the bigger decision for her. That's not my style, but I usually have my way.

I arrived home earlier than expected. It had been one of the warmest April days of the century and was developing into a pleasant evening. I rang Nigel about my trip and he told me that Fearnside had been chasing me. I thought about ringing him, but called Annabelle instead.

'I thought you were in Bristol,' she said.

'Been, bought the sherry, come back,' I replied. 'Do you fancy going out for a bite?'

'I could cook.'

She always says that. 'No,' I insisted. 'I was thinking of driving over to the cottage to pick up my things. I'm afraid my sojourn there has come to an end, but we could have a pub meal on the way.' Even as I spoke a development occurred to me. 'If you're not doing anything first thing in the morning, we could stay overnight . . .'

Annabelle was afraid of headlines in the tabloids – THE COP AND THE BISHOP'S WIFE – if I slept at her place. Being dropped off at the door at seven-thirty in the morning, if she had stayed with me, or furtively letting me out of her house, were not for her. It wasn't priggishness. She did it to protect her late husband's reputation and his family's feelings, and that was all right by me.

'Mmm,' she replied. 'Yes, that would be nice.' It looked as if I'd have to buy a little place at the seaside.

I had a lightning shower and swapped the cars around. As a special treat, we'd go in the E-type. I was giving the results of my labours a final check in the mirror when the phone rang. I assumed it was Annabelle with some last-minute arrangement. 'Yes, darling,' I cooed into it.

'Er, is that you, Charlie?' asked a rather puzzled Commander Fearnside.

'Ooops! Sorry, boss, I was expecting someone else.'

'I'm relieved to hear it. Thought I'd better give you an update on the drugs thing.'

'Right, fire away.' I slid my sleeve back to see the time, and hoped he wouldn't be long.

'They blew it. The idiots blew it. The tracking devices were working beautifully, and an unmarked car had picked them up. Somewhere over in Greater Manchester it all went pear-shaped. The tailing car decided to overtake and wait for them again at the next junction. Just at that moment some hawk-eyed bloody motorcycle patrol who knows more about cars than I know about my cock happens along and notices that the numberplate on the Sierra doesn't tally with the design of the tail-lights, or something equally obscure. So he gives chase.'

'Shit,' I said.

'You haven't heard the half of it. Laddo drives off, but stops on a bridge, somewhere called . . . is it Irlam?'

'I know it.'

'Right. He throws two holdalls off the bridge, then runs over the motorcycle patrol and makes his getaway. West Lancs are dragging the canal, but haven't found the bags yet.'

'What about the pursuit car?'

'Bah! They were listening for a signal. Apparently they can't listen and watch at the same time.'

'Mmm. Like you said, they blew it. The tracking devices – do you think the car driver realised they were there? It could be important for my future health.'

'Can't be sure, but I doubt it. I'm paying them a visit tomorrow, to kick a few arses. I'll let you have a copy of my report. You did your bit, Charlie, and I'm grateful for your contribution.'

'You're welcome.' Cushiest job I'd ever had, and the most rewarding. 'How's the motorcyclist?' I shouted into the phone, but he'd gone.

When Annabelle saw the Jag she forgave me for being late. I told her about my trip to Bristol and dropped a few titbits about the Nicola enquiry. This was my new policy, and I knew she wouldn't gossip. I didn't say anything about the bungled drugs bust.

We took the motorway system to the south of the river, which led us over the Humber Bridge. Annabelle had never crossed it, and looked pleased. I liked to inject a little geographical interest or local history into an evening out with a girl. The sky wasn't yet dark, but all the lights were on, and it was like driving through a magic spider's web.

There was nothing magical about the pub meal we had, but we still lingered over it, and the landlady's cherry pie compensated for the tough steaks. The moon hadn't risen, so it was as dark as the inside of Dave Sparkington's wallet when we left the street-lights behind and picked up the Withernsea Road towards the cottage.

'Will all your stuff fit in here?' Annabelle asked, turning in her seat to survey the luggage-carrying capacity of the Jaguar.

'I think so,' I replied. 'There's my radio and portable TV, plus a few kitchen items. The only bulky stuff is the bedding. Oh, I mustn't forget the electric blanket off the spare bed.' I glanced across at her and she smiled at me.

'That was a waste of electricity,' I teased.

'What was?'

'Warming the spare bed for six hours, and then you didn't use it.'

She reached across and took my hand. 'No, it wasn't,' she said, giving it a squeeze.

'Wasn't what?'

'Wasn't a waste of electricity.'

'How do you make that out?'

'Oh, never mind.'

I pulled my hand free to drop the Jag into third for a tight bend – the land might be as flat as a motorway hedgehog, but the roads zig and zag like Alpine passes. 'Why wasn't it a waste of electricity?' I repeated.

Annabelle twisted in the seat and leaned against her door, facing me. 'Because,' she said.

'Because what?' I insisted.

She gave a long exasperated sigh. 'Because . . . because it showed you weren't taking me for granted.'

'Oh.' I wouldn't have dared to take her for granted. It looked as if Lucky Charlie had done the right thing for the wrong reasons once more, but I'd settle for that. I reached across and took her hand again.

Twenty-eight years in the Force and I still wonder what I've done wrong when a blue light comes up behind me. I saw it when he was way back, flashing on the telegraph wires like distant lightning. He caught me quickly, and I pulled over to let him through.

'He's probably been for the fish and chips,' I explained as he raced away from us.

Before he'd vanished, another blue light was visible in my mirrors. The road was narrow, so I pulled into a gateway and waited for him. This one was an ambulance.

'Traffic accident,' I surmised.

We could see the glow from the lights when we were about a mile from the cottage, flickering on the night sky like a television screen on the curtains of a darkened room.

'It looks as if something has happened quite close to the cottage,' Annabelle said, but I was a long way in front of her.

Three fire engines were drawn up outside, with a police car behind and the ambulance trying to turn round in the narrow lane. A uniformed Constable stopped me while the ambulance completed the manoeuvre and sped off, siren strangely silent, back towards Hull.

The pulsating lights illuminated the front of the building as if it were a stage-set for some modern opera. Black smoke-stains streaked upwards from all the windows, including mine, and the chorus of firemen in oilskins and yellow helmets could be seen inside. No soprano appeared, belting out one of the tear-jerkers from *Madame Butterfly*.

I opened my mouth to say: 'Wait here,' but changed it to 'C'mon,' as I stepped from the car. We edged our way to the front of the house, skirting behind the appliances and assorted vehicles. First in the queue was a Rover with a blue light on top and a fireman with fancy epaulettes clipped to his sweater standing alongside, talking to a policeman. I let go of Annabelle's hand and asked her to wait while I had a word with them.

The fireman was the Assistant Divisional Officer. When I asked if I could have a few seconds of his time the Constable excused himself and left us. When he'd gone I showed my ID and introduced myself. 'I don't want to become bogged down with the local Force,' I explained, 'but I was keeping an eye on the occupant of Number one. He's known as Kevin Jessle, and is a suspected drug runner. I'd rented next door and was hoping he'd lead us to the bigger fish. Was that him in the ambulance?'

'No, Inspector. We've sent the ambulance back empty and your colleague has informed the local CID that you have a murder on your hands.'

'So poor Kevin's dead?'

'No doubt about it, if it's him.'

'Does that mean you think the fire was deliberate?'

'Off the record, you understand? Almost certainly. An accelerant has been used in several places, probably petrol.'

'Where was Jessle's body found?'

'Upstairs, on the bed.'

'So the smoke got him?' That was a relief – I had a soft spot for Kevin. Anyone who appreciates the E-type like he did can't be completely beyond hope.

'Do you think his gang were on to you, Inspector?'

I'd been wondering the same thing. 'It's a possibility,' I replied. 'What makes you ask?'

'Because he didn't die peacefully of carbon-monoxide poisoning. You see, Inspector, his hands and feet are tied to the bedposts.'

I wended my way back to Annabelle, stepping over hoses and squeezing between appliances whose engines were running to generate power, their radiators blasting hot air into the night. She looked smaller, vulnerable, amongst all that activity. Her face was pale, the African tan washed away by the lights, and there was something else there. She looked scared.

'Let's go home,' I said, running my fingers into her hair and pulling her towards me. Several cars were slinking by, under the control of the PC. When the lane was clear he stood in the middle while I did a seven-point turn, and flagged me away as if I were a Saudi royal. I gave him a wave and a wink.

'Kevin is dead,' I told her, bluntly. 'They found him laid on his bed.'

After a few moments she said: 'Poor Kevin, he didn't sound to be beyond redemption. So he wouldn't have known much about it?'

I shook my head. 'No, he wouldn't.'

The car behind had badly-adjusted headlights. The off-side was OK, but the other one shone straight ahead, dazzling me through my mirrors. I tilted my head to one side to avoid the glare, and we drove into Hull in silence.

'I'll have to put in an insurance claim,' I said. 'That should cause some confusion in the system.' It was only for conversation; I had other things on my mind.

At seventy miles per hour the E-type is running like a sewing machine at a lazy three thousand revs. I slotted into the middle lane of the motorway and settled down for a leisurely cruise home. I suggested that she looked for some music, but Annabelle said she didn't mind the silence. When I glanced in the mirror I noticed that the car with the odd headlights was coming this way, too. He was about four hundred yards behind, but not gaining.

Heavy lorries, carrying imports that we could make just as well ourselves, thundered by on their way from the docks to the motorway network. Sporty saloons rocketed past with complete disregard for the speed limit. Oddlights maintained his station, neither gaining nor falling back. I drifted into the slow lane and dropped speed slightly. So did he.

He was still behind me half an hour later as we approached the junction with the A1. There is a large service centre there. 'Let's check the price of the petrol,' I said, swinging into the slip road without signalling.

The exit I needed was at four on the clockface, over threequarters of the way round the roundabout. I crept across the forecourt, past the pumps, eyes fixed on my mirrors. A black saloon followed me in and paused in the entrance. The harsh lights of the station reflected off the chrome strip surrounding the familiar shape of a BMW radiator.

'Too expensive,' I decided, out loud, and steered towards the exit. So did the BMW, and as his headlights swung my way the nearside one dazzled me. There was no doubt about it: we were being followed.

Chapter Twelve

I hit the motorway at about eighty and pulled straight across into the fast lane. This time he kept closer. I deliberately hadn't brought the mobile phone, and cursed my stupidity. Traffic wasn't heavy, but there was plenty about. Two miles from Junction 28 I saw a lorry well ahead signalling that he was pulling across into the middle lane, and a VW Polo in that lane started to move over in front of me.

I blazed my full beams at him, intimidating him out of the manoeuvre. His brake-lights came on and I streaked by him. In my mirror I saw the Polo pull across behind me, blocking the fast lane until after he'd overtaken the lorry. I drifted back into the middle lane and when the lorry was between me and my pursuers I put my right foot down to the floor, with the accelerator pedal firmly beneath it.

The Jag set off like the second stage of a Saturn V booster kicking in, the boom of the exhaust filling the cab. Annabelle glanced across at me.

'Just giving the old girl a quick burst,' I told her as I flicked the headlights off. I didn't have an excuse for doing it in the dark – maybe I'm shy.

We flew past the Junction half-mile board at about a hundred and thirty, with me deciding that this was plenty fast enough. There was no traffic in the slow lane, so I slotted across into it. We dropped into the slip road at over the ton, a prayer on my lips and a foot hard on the brakes. Two cars were waiting, side by side, for the roundabout to clear. A lorry glided across in front of them and their brake-lights went out as they prepared to move off. I shot through on the left, on the hard shoulder, and had vanished round the island before they could say 'UFO!'

The road led into Leeds, but it looked as if the BMW had overshot the turn-off. Just to make sure I took a few lefts, tyres squealing, into an estate of terraced houses and parked outside a kebab takeaway that was serving the last customer of the night.

'Made it,' I said, pulling the handbrake on. 'I was afraid they'd be closed.'

Reports, reports, reports; that's what it's all about. I've instilled it into the men to write everything down – not just the facts that seem relevant at the time, but every other detail they can think of. If a pigeon bombs the witness while you are talking to him, put it in the report. Somewhere along the line someone might notice a man with pigeonshit on his shoulder. And it's a strange phenomenon, but courts tend to believe anything that is read out, but are doubtful if it comes from the witness's memory. Writing reports takes up an awful lot of time, unfortunately.

I wrote a long one to Fearnside, all about the fire and the chase. I enclosed *Fin 23* and *Fin 33* expenses forms and devoted the last chapter to explaining them. I imagined some little man in a windowless office allowing the ghetto-blaster to pass, but drawing a line through my electric blanket. After that I read everything on my desk about Nicola's murder, but didn't learn much.

I'd skipped the morning meeting to sew up the loose ends of the drugs case and ring the Driver and Vehicle Licensing Centre at Swansea, but now I was free to concentrate on catching Nicola's killer. I'd asked the DVLC to put a stop on the Jaguar number. That meant that if anyone rang enquiring about my address, they would be politely referred to the Police Liaison Officer. At just after nine o'clock the others started to wander in from the meeting.

Nigel was in earnest conversation with a DCI from Liverpool called Trevor Peacock and his DS. They'd taken the Harold Hurst enquiry off us. Peacock was built like a council skip, but he shook hands like a cocker spaniel. I suspected that this was deliberate, having crushed a few fingers in the past.

'Hello, Trevor,' I said. 'What are you doing here?' I think he'd have preferred me to call him Chief Inspector, which was why I addressed him as Trevor at every available opportunity.

'If you came to the meetings you'd know,' he replied, smiling, but he meant it.

'Sorry about that. I had a few loose ends to tie up with N-CIS.' Advantage Priest.

Nigel butted in. 'I'll fill in Mr Priest,' he volunteered, 'if you want to be on your way . . .'

'That's OK,' he replied. 'If we go over it enough times it might start to make sense to my small brain. It's a complicated story.'

'You mean, he's struck before?'

''Fraid so. The sample he kindly left inside Nicola was a perfect match with one we found in the dead prostitute in early January. The one wearing Marina Norris's wristwatch. That's, what – over three months ago. Same MO: strangled first, then raped. Incidentally, it's the first match we've had from the data bank; looks like it's starting to produce the goods. So Nicola is linked to the murdered prostitute by a DNA sample and the prossie is linked to Mrs Norris by the watch.'

Nigel said: 'And Mrs Norris's husband made the cigarettes that were hijacked, and the driver was shot with the same gun that killed Harold Hurst.'

'In other words,' I declared, 'the same gang hijacked the cigs, kidnapped Mrs Norris and murdered her chauffeur, strangled the prostitute and killed poor Nicola. We're looking for a necromaniac with a smoking problem. I wonder if there's a gene for that?'

'We can't be sure Mrs Norris was kidnapped,' Peacock said.

'True,' I conceded.

The Sergeant decided to have his say. 'Don't forget the gun has also been used in Northern Ireland, back in 1988.'

Nigel excused himself, to deploy the troops, leaving me with the DCI and DS from Liverpool. I suggested having a brew in the canteen, and they agreed. When we were settled, with mugs of tea and toasted currant teacake for me, bacon sandwiches for them, I said: 'Do you think there is an IRA link, then – turning their skills to something more profitable? Or the other lot, maybe?'

Trevor nodded. 'The so-called Loyalists? It's a strong possibility. We've sent the files to the appropriate people – Special Branch, RUC – but they haven't told us much.'

'Then there's our own side,' the DS said. 'We've plenty of disillusioned ex-Army on the streets. They have the skills, too, and a lot of them have difficulties when they're thrown back on Civvy Street.'

'That gives you plenty to go at. And think – up to this morning we thought we were looking for some psychopath who'd just discovered what makes the world go round and who lives locally.'

''Fraid not, Charlie,' Trevor said. 'We're looking for a gang of professionals, with some good contacts. It just happens that one of them is a psycho. Maybe he'll lead us to the rest.'

'I'd prefer it if they led us to him.'

'Yeah, that would be better, but he's the one who's making all the mistakes.'

I spent the rest of the day reading the reports on the other murders and the hijack, and discussing them with Gilbert and Nigel. Hijacks are usually inside jobs, so it might be useful to know of any employees of the transport company who had links with the Army – a lot of ex-soldiers become lorry drivers – or with Northern Ireland. Or who had criminal records, or took days off at the appropriate times, or whose eyes were too close together. No doubt Peacock would be handling all that.

Our end of the investigation was concentrated on Nicola's last movements, and trying to learn of any strangers in town on the Friday in question. Late in the afternoon I received a phone call from Jean, the DC in Bristol.

'Good news, Mr Priest,' she told me. 'Pauline came in about an hour ago, with her husband, Leon. She's made a full statement incriminating her stepfather, so you'll be able to pull him in as soon as you receive it.'

I'd enjoy doing that. Annabelle had invited me round for what she called vegetarian chilli con carne, so I left early and called at the florists on the way. She'd guessed we were being followed the night before, and was frightened, although I suspected that she was just a little bit excited by the chase. I'd driven straight to my house and taken her home in the Cavalier. She wouldn't stay the night with me. I'd handled the whole thing badly, but perhaps some flowers would make amends. I selected a small bunch of fuchsias that looked just right. As I was fumbling for the money I noticed the Interflora poster and said to the girl behind the counter: 'I'd like to send a bouquet to someone else, too, but I don't know the address. If I pay for them now, could I phone it to you in the morning?'

'Of course, sir, no problem.' She started to fill in the appropriate order form. 'Who shall we say they are from?'

'Er, leave that blank, please.'

'And what message would you like?'

'Er, no message,' I said, adding: 'They're for a lady in Bristol,' as if it explained everything.

As soon as I'd had a chance to have a good think about the case, I rang DCI Peacock and had a long chat with him. We'd come into it late, and were looking at things in reverse order. I needed some clarification.

'So presumably the first episode, from your point of view, was when we circulated details of the body we'd found. Harold Hurst's,' I said.

'Well, before that,' he replied, 'Hurst's wife had walked into her local nick and said that her husband hadn't come home the night before. We did nothing, as per, until she came in again the next day and became hysterical. Then we received your notification about the unidentified body and things fell into place.'

'Have you talked to Norris?'

'Yeah, a couple of times. He was quite open about things, more or less repeated what I'd read in your reports. Said their relationship was going downhill; she had a boyfriend, but he didn't know who; thought she'd walked out on him. He wasn't exactly cut up about it, and assured us there was nothing going off between her and the chauffeur.'

'Still no ransom notes?'

'He says not.'

'Do you think he would have enough day-to-day knowledge to be the inside man on the cigs hijack?'

'You've a wicked mind, Charlie. He probably would

have. He was a hands-on employer, the worst kind. Knew everything about everything and kept them all on their toes by working all hours and expecting everyone else to do the same.'

'I used to be like that,' I confessed.

'Yeah, me too. That's why they all love me.'

'And what about Hurst? How much did he know?'

'Good question. He took the Roller into the lorry depot nearly every day and washed it. Nobody is saying they ever saw him speak to anyone, though, and we can't find any links with other employees. He led a quiet life.'

Norris had no money worries by normal standards, but he was on a different planet to anyone else I knew. He was a ladies' man, but it was all hearsay, no names. I asked DCI Peacock if he had any objections to my straying into his patch and asking a few questions of my own.

'What have you in mind?' he asked warily.

'Well, to tell the truth, I'd like another go at the manager of the department store – Town & County – where his wife was last seen. And the security staff. A bit more background about Norris himself might be useful, too. I might pick up something new, maybe only a different nuance. You know how it is.'

'OK, be my guest, but keep us informed. And I'd like you to keep away from Norris himself. He knows more than he's admitting, but he's a crafty bird. Leave him to us, please. Mind you, he's in America at the moment, so you'll have to, unless your expenses allowance is better than mine.'

'You'd never believe me, Trevor, you'd never believe me. I'll keep you informed.'

I wrote down various addresses and drove over the Pennines into Lancashire – or should I say Greater Manchester and Merseyside? Injun country.

First stop was Norris's palatial mansion in Lymm. The

boundary wall and the electrically-operated front gate looked impressive, but that was as far as I got. A motor mower was buzzing away inside, but I leaned on the bell and shouted into the phone to no avail. A month ago I would have climbed over the wall, but I resisted the temptation. I was wearing decent trousers, all part of my new tidy-at-work image. Next time I'd come in jeans and trainers.

At least Town & County would be open, unless Thursday was half-day closing. I risked it, and was lucky. They probably stayed open on Christmas Day. The manager's secretary asked me if I would like a coffee and this time I said: 'Yes, please.'

He greeted me like a longlost cousin and invited me to sit down. No doubt he was hoping to learn some titbit that he could take home to his family to revive the sagging saga of his boss's wife. If I didn't disappoint him maybe he'd open up.

'Thanks for seeing me again,' I told him.

'Any time, Inspector. We were beginning to think that the trail had gone cold.'

'Lukewarm,' I replied, 'until now. Last week, a fifteen-year-old girl was murdered in Heckley. Incidentally, that's where Harold Hurst's body was found. You may have read about it in the papers?'

He nodded. 'Yes.'

'It was a particularly vicious crime. You may also know that we recently started a data bank for DNA samples. Well, it's beginning to show dividends. Samples from Nicola's body indirectly link her killer with the person who killed Mrs Norris's chauffeur. We are working in cooperation with Liverpool police, of course, and I know you have gone over everything with them, but I hope you don't mind answering a few questions for me.'

He leaned forward, interested. 'Certainly, Inspector,' he replied.

'How well did you know Harold Hurst?' I asked.

'Hardly at all. I didn't know his second name until after he was dead. I'd ridden with him a couple of times and we'd chatted about our families. Mr Norris would sometimes invite me over to Lymm for a meeting, and he'd send the Roller. He was like that.' He smiled at the memory.

I said: 'You sound as if you like Norris.'

'He's OK. Super-efficient, but you know where you are with him. You hear horror stories about American businessmen, but he seems keen to retain the family atmosphere we have amongst the staff. We hadn't expected that.' His cheeks were creased with amusement.

'What's so funny?' I asked.

Coffee and biscuits arrived. I'd forgotten to ask for it without milk. 'About a week before she vanished,' the manager said, 'Norris came in and the first thing he noticed was that we'd moved one of the security cameras. The ground-floor one. We'd redirected it so you could see the pavement outside the front door. He said: "Hey! Now you'll be able to see when Marina's paying you a surprise visit." We didn't tell him that that was exactly why we'd moved the camera, but I think he'd guessed.'

'He sounds a wily old goat.'

'Wily's not the word. He doesn't miss a trick.'

'I should have asked about the security videos then when I saw you before. Did they capture Mrs Norris?'

'Mmm. Worked a treat. Every floor knew she was here before she'd barely come through the front door.'

'Your early warning system.'

'Exactly.'

'Any chance of me having a word with the person who actually saw her arrive?' I asked.

He grinned sheepishly and pressed his fingertips together. 'It was me,' he admitted. 'I was down in Security, watching the monitors when she arrived.'

'So what happened?'

'Nothing out of the ordinary. The chauffeur, poor Harold, opened the door for her and she got out. That's all I saw.'

'What about when she left?'

'I walked out with her, saw her into the Rolls. Harold was dozing, didn't see her come. That didn't improve her temper.'

'She was in a bad temper?'

'Yes. She'd given a salesgirl a ticking off over nothing. She usually found something to complain about.'

'I see. Did she say where she was going next?'

'No, I'm afraid not.'

'What sort of a person was she?'

The secretary came in to collect the cups. 'The Inspector wants to know about Mrs Norris,' the manager said to her.

'Then tell him,' she threw back as she left.

He smiled again. 'She was a cow,' he declared. 'She'd been a model, so she thought she knew all about the business, but she was useless. God gave her a good figure and a nice face, but I'm afraid he economised on the brain cells.'

'What was their marriage like?'

'Can't really say. He had an eye for the ladies. I think he bought into this place just to keep her happy; give her an interest. Not bad, eh?'

'Not bad at all. When I saw Norris he told me that he called in on the Saturday morning and saw you. Did he want anything in particular?'

He looked puzzled. 'Well, yes. He wanted to see the security videos.'

Now I looked puzzled. 'The videos?'

'Yes.'

'Was that unusual?'

'Unusual, but not a surprise. It was his style to arrive unannounced and ask to see something out of the ordinary. One week it might be the figures for staff sick leave, another, the footwear accounts or the kitchens. He believed it kept us on our toes.'

'And did it?'

'You bet.'

'So what happened?'

'Not much. It's a twenty-four-hour recording system, switching round the cameras at five-second intervals, unless we want to stay with any selected camera. He sat down with the Friday's cassette and asked me how things worked, then told me to leave him to it, which I gladly did.'

'And by now it will have been recorded over a few times,' I suggested.

'Well, no. We thought you had it.'

'Us? The police? Why did you think that?'

The manager shook his head. 'We didn't realise it at the time, but he probably took it with him. We normally have seven tapes in use, and put a new one in at nine o'clock every morning. The day before's goes to the other end of the rack, so we hold a record for a complete week at a time. The following week we realised that one was missing. Security told me, but by this time we knew about Harold and the papers were suggesting that Mrs Norris had been kidnapped. It explained why Norris had called in, and we presumed he'd given the tape to the police.' Suddenly he looked unhappy. 'It was the last picture he'll have seen of his wife. Maybe he's kept it.'

'Yes. That's the probably explanation,' I agreed.

His in-tray was piled high with documents – some green,

some yellow, and a few an urgent pink; he'd been working late tonight. The back of a photograph frame was towards me, and I wondered how resigned the faces on the other side would be towards his absence. Sometimes I envy colleagues who have photos of their families on their desks; other times, I think they're pillocks.

'Did anyone else see the tape of Mrs Norris's arrival?' I asked.

'Yes, one of our security staff, Sylvia. She's been with us for years.'

'So you employ your own security?'

'Yes, always have done. Town & County had been in the same family for seventy years until five years ago. Most of us have been with them all our careers.'

'But times are changing?'

'Sadly, yes.'

'If it's any consolation, you've escaped for longer than most. Is Sylvia at work?'

He did some telephoning, then told me that she was on the early shift, and had therefore left for home.

'I'd like a word with her,' I said. 'Will she be working in the morning?'

'Yes, seven till three.'

'Fine. How about if I catch her tea break at, say, ten?'

'I'll tell her to expect you.'

We shook hands. At his office door I turned and asked him to treat our conversation as confidential. 'Particularly what I said about the DNA links,' I added conspiratorially. He nodded with enthusiasm.

Outside I tried to ring DCI Peacock, but he'd gone home, too, so I joined the crush of traffic and threaded my way back towards God's Own Country. Marina Norris had been a model, and fashion photographers shoot off films like Don King shoots off his mouth. Somewhere there would be drawers, trunks, attics, filled with glossy prints of her in every pose imaginable, wearing the latest offerings from the world's most expensive couturiers. The image of Bradley Norris poring over five seconds of flickering video, a lone tear trickling down his cheek to drop into his Jack Daniel's, didn't move me. So why did he need that video?

Next morning I did the journey again. Sylvia was not quite what I expected. She reminded me of my grandma, and had worked for Town & County for nearly forty years in various capacities, but never on sales. Her right arm trembled as she poured me a tea, splashing into the saucer, and I guessed that she suffered from a mild form of Parkinson's disease, or something similar. She was a loyal servant, and had been treated loyally. I accepted a couple of bourbons and held the saucer under the cup as I drank, so as not to drip on my trousers.

'So how do you like being in the law-enforcement business, Sylvia?' I asked.

'Oh, it's smashing. Best job I've ever 'ad. Are you sure you don't want milk?'

'It's fine, thanks. Just what I needed. How many people do you catch?'

'You'd be surprised, Mr Priest, you'd be surprised.'

'Call me Charlie,' I told her, popping half a biscuit into my mouth, 'Everybody else does. Tell me about this missing tape, please.'

She pointed to the rack of tapes above the VDU. 'Well, Charlie, as you can see, each tape is marked with a label, saying which day it is. I thought the label had fallen off Friday's tape, until I looked in the cupboard. See what I mean?' She delved under the desk and opened a door. There were two unmarked tapes inside. 'We 'ad ten tapes, so there should 'ave been three spares, but there's only two. It looked as if the unmarked tape was a new one, and Mr

Norris 'ad taken the Friday tape.'

'Why would he do that?'

'To give to the police, I suppose.'

'Has anyone else interviewed you?'

'No, but I couldn't tell you nothing, could I?'

'The manager tells me that you were with him when the camera caught Mrs Norris arriving, that last time.'

She smiled. 'Yes, I was.'

'Does he often come down here?'

'Just on a Friday morning, usually.' The smile reached her eyes, displaying a fine set of crows' feet.

'I get it,' I said, as if I'd just learned their little secret. 'He comes down here to watch for her arriving, so he is ready for her. Is that it?'

She nodded, spilling more tea into her saucer. 'As soon as we see her he rings Drapery. They ring Menswear and Fashion. In thirty seconds the entire store knows she has arrived.'

'He rings them? Don't you ring anybody?'

The smile vanished from her face, quick as the channels changed on the VDU. 'No. I'm too slow with the telephone. I operate the cameras, see where she's heading.'

'So you were watching the monitor while he was phoning?'

Now she looked worried. 'Yes.'

'What did you see that he didn't?'

'I . . . I thought the police had the video. I didn't think I'd seen anything important.'

The feeling I get in my loins when I'm on to something was growing stronger. It's a bit like dancing in fur-lined underpants, and the slower you dance, the greater the sensation.

'Your manager told me yesterday that Mrs Norris was a proper cow,' I said.

'He said that?'

'Yep. He has a very low opinion of her.'

'Is she dead?'

'We don't know.'

'Would you like some more tea?'

'I thought you'd never ask.'

The teapot was lighter, now, so she could manage it one-handed without spilling a drop.

'There was a man on the video . . .' she began.

'Yak!' I spluttered. 'No sugar! Sorry about that. Tell me about this man.'

She passed a spoon across to me. 'I was just about to switch to another camera, see which way she was heading, when I saw this man approaching the car, so I stayed with the front entrance. He walked up and spoke to the driver – that poor man whose body they found. I didn't like the look of 'im so I zoomed right in. The police – you – would've 'ad a really good shot of 'im. Close up.'

'Can you describe him?'

'He was a skinhead, wearing one of them old Army jackets, with the camouflage patterns on it.'

'I had one of those once,' I told her. 'Could never find it. How tall was he?'

She shrugged, unamused. 'Hard to say.'

I stood up. 'Whereabouts did the roof of the car come?' I asked, indicating various levels on my chest. She picked one that made him seven feet nine.

'That's excellent, Sylvia,' I said. 'You've been brilliant. Look, it's all been a misunderstanding about the tapes. If anything, the fault is with me, for not asking to see the right people. Now I'd like it if tomorrow I could send someone to talk to you and try to help you remember more about this man. One of our experts. He'll show you some pictures, and ask you to pick out the ones most like him. Will that be all right?'

She nodded.

I jumped to my feet again and grinned at her. 'You're a good witness, Sylvia. I wish they were all like you. Expect it's with being in the business.'

She still looked troubled. I didn't want to leave her feeling depressed, that's not my role in life. 'I'll tell the boss how helpful you've been,' I said. 'And that we'll need some more of your time. It might be easier if we invited you to the station, but if he grumbles, let me know.'

Her left arm was across her body, holding the right one steady. She looked from me to the floor, and back to me.

'I . . .' she began.

I pulled a chair across and placed it close to hers. 'What, Sylvia?' I said, softly.

'I . . . there was someone else. On the video. I don't suppose it's important, but—'

'It might be. Why not let me be the judge?'

She nodded. 'There was an old woman on the pavement. She turned and watched Mrs Norris la-di-da into the store. She's like a bag lady, except that she pulls one of them bags-on-wheels. I've noticed her before, on the VDU, but 'aven't seen her since. She . . . she . . .'

I let her lapse into silence. After a minute or so I asked: 'She what, Sylvia? What were you going to tell me?'

She smiled and shook her head. 'Oh, nothing.'

I didn't move. 'Please?'

She sighed and pulled her arm tighter. 'She reminded me of what I might have become, if it 'adn't been for Town & County. That's all.'

There was a proper café just over the road from Town & County, with tablecloths and portions that varied in size according to the whim of the waitress, so I had a decent lunch. My seat looked out on to the street, but no old lady pulling a shopping trolley shuffled by. It was the right time of the week, but maybe she wasn't a creature of habit. I'd asked Sylvia to keep a lookout for the woman on the video, and save me the tape if she saw her again.

DCI Peacock wasn't chuffed when I rang him from home and told him about the missing tape. No doubt he ruffled a few feathers amongst his staff when I rang off. He agreed to send someone sympathetic round to interview Sylvia, for a full statement of what she saw and a description of the mystery man in the combat jacket. I typed a report for the files and dossed on the settee for an hour, listening to Mahler's Fifth. How did he know that, a hundred years later, it would just fit on a CD? That's genius.

At the Heckley end of the enquiry into Nicola's death Nigel now had a comprehensive account of her last movements, and was starting to interview all known sex-offenders who were loose in the community. There were over ten thousand of them across the country, including fifty who'd been convicted for child murder. We'd interview them all, starting with those living locally, and ask for hair samples where necessary, to obtain a DNA profile. For the ones who'd been given life, we'd be able to store this information in the data bank, but all the rest would have to be destroyed. They'd paid their dues, asked forgiveness, changed their spots. After that lot had been sorted through there were all the others, without records. Everybody is a first-time offender at some point in their career.

We had some spin-offs. Dave Sparkington took a dislike to the creep who owned Heckley's new disco, the Copper Banana, and did him for possession and employing unlicensed bouncers. We drove the town's only full-time prostitute off the streets, and charged George Leach, Nicola's stepdad, with indecent assault and every related offence we could think of.

Under expert guidance, Sylvia described the mystery man as being about five-ten, stockily built, a skinhead with a round face. He was wearing a combat jacket and trousers. It was good. Liverpool CID circulated the description, but didn't release it. The following Friday Sylvia rang me at the station. She'd seen the old lady again and caught her on camera.

I was busy, interviewing a couple of youths for something that would have warranted a clip round the ear when Dave Sparkington was a kid. Mind you, they guillotined pick-pockets in Halifax in those days. I told Sylvia and asked if she would mind if an officer from the local nick visited her and collected the tape. She'd rather liked whoever it was who took the statement from her, and I promised to ask for him again.

Saturday morning DCI Peacock rang to say they had a hard copy for me, and I told him I would collect it on Monday. He had no objections to me coming on to his patch to track her down, but he sounded as if his teeth were gritted. On the way home I called in at the Electricity Board showrooms and picked up a few leaflets on dishwashers. One wall was covered with TV sets, all showing the same picture. A bomb had exploded inside an Army recruiting centre, damaging the furniture and ruining a scale-model of a Centurion tank. The group calling themselves TSC had claimed responsibility.

I was growing used to the drive to Liverpool, over the tops of the Pennines, backbone of England. It was a change from the flat drive to Hull. They may not be high hills, but the weather up there is extreme and variable. Thick fog, a gale and driving snow – all at the same time – are not unusual. Today it was sunny, but you still needed the car heater on. It's the fast lane up the hill, overtaking all the lorries grinding their way westwards. Down the other side it's every man for himself as they make up time, freewheeling at eighty miles per hour until you hit the roadworks.

The motorways on a map of England look like the veins in the back of your hand. The lorries and vans and salesmen's cars are the red corpuscles, carrying the nation's oxygen – trade – in a ceaseless merry-go-round, twenty-four hours per day. The leucocytes are white and fast, with coloured stripes down the sides and blue lights on top. They clean up the damaged cells, or any that are behaving abnormally. They can't see viruses, though, or spot the ones who lie in wait, ready to spread cancer when the opportunity arises. That's my job.

The picture of the old lady was built up from the lines of the video screen, with very little detail. It showed a stooped figure in women's clothes, pulling a shopping basket on wheels. Her coat was brown and the basket may have been green, but you couldn't make out any patterns on the material of either. She had almost escaped off the left-hand edge of the frame when the camera caught her, and was facing the wrong way, but the picture showed her essential characteristics, like a Lowry painting, and that's what I wanted.

DCI Peacock granted me the freedom of Liverpool. A couple of nasty racial attacks over the weekend were stretching his manpower beyond the limits of elasticity. A search of doubtful value, for a bag lady of uncertain reliability, was the last thing he needed. 'You find her, Charlie,' he suggested with strained resignation. 'Be my guest. You have quite a way with old ladies, I'm told.'

Fifty yards downwind of Town & County was a newsagent's kiosk. The proprietress had seen the old lady many times – she went thataway. A busker, a hairdresser and a waitress in a bistro had all seen her go by in recent months, but not lately. By now I was getting away from the shopping area. A greengrocer told me she sometimes bought oranges from him and a window cleaner had seen her around. He pointed me towards a residential area; rows and rows of terraced houses. I was growing warm.

Several people shook their heads and asked what she'd done. I told them she might have witnessed a crime. 'It's a long shot, but we have to take it,' I explained, over and over again. A man pushing a buggy with a little boy in it told me to get stuffed, wack, he wouldn't help the filth if we paid him. He was wearing a ring in one ear and had a mural of Walt Disney characters tattooed around his midriff. His dad looked a nasty piece of work.

I knocked at the first door at the end of every row of houses, without luck. About fifty per cent of the time nobody answered, in which case I knocked at the next door until I raised someone.

I was growing depressed by the time I climbed the three steps up to the front door of Number 11, Ladysmith Grove. The little yard was littered with plastic toys, and a big pile of fresh steaming dogshit decorated the iron lid that led down into the coal cellar. The hound started barking before I knocked.

A female voice shouted at the dog, and its barking grew even more frantic, but muffled, as it was evidently shut in a room where it couldn't savage unexpected callers. Bolts were slid back, a lock turned, and a skinny girl with bleached hair, wearing a pink quilted housecoat, opened the door. She had a snotty-nosed infant in her arms.

'Sorry to trouble you, ma'am,' I said, holding my ID towards her. 'DI Priest. I'm conducting a few investigations, and would like to know if you have ever seen this woman. We believe she lives near here.' I showed her the picture.

She took it from me and inspected it for about two seconds. 'It's old Missis Crowther,' she said, in an accent that sounded as if she had a jar of Vick up each nostril. 'Lives over there, where the windowboxes are.'

I followed her pointing arm. At the other side of the street, about fifty yards further along, were the only surviving plants within half a mile. 'Thanks,' I said. 'You've been a big help.'

She closed the door without another word, and went to try to stop the dog giving the furniture rabies.

The plants were geraniums, just breaking into bud. The paintwork on Mrs Crowther's house was just as dilapidated as all the others in the street, but the windows and curtains were clean, and her stone steps were freshly painted white at the edges. Tubs of wallflowers were scattered around, ready to give a colourful show in a few weeks, if the frost or the vandals didn't get them first. I knocked at the door.

There was a light on in the kitchen, so I was fairly sure that she was home. After a couple more knocks I heard some shuffling and the door opened as far as a safety chain would allow it.

'Mrs Crowther?' I asked the left half of the face that appeared in the gap.

'Vat do you vant?'

'I'd like a word with you.'

'Who are you?' She sounded frightened.

'I'm a police officer. My name is Charlie Priest.' I passed my ID through the gap and a surprisingly large hand took it from me. If she'd run off with it I'd have been in big trouble. I put my face close to the door so everyone in the street couldn't hear what I was saying. 'Last January, just after New Year's Day, you were seen walking past the Town & County department store. Do you know where I mean?'

Her hand emerged, offering my warrant card back to me, and the half-face nodded. 'A car drew up,' I went on, 'a Rolls-Royce, and a woman got out. Do you remember?'

She nodded. 'Yes, I remember. He sploshed me.'

'I'd like you to tell me all about it. May I come in, please?'

She closed the door. I heard the scrape of the chain and the door opened wide. 'I do not know vat I can tell you,' she said, nervously.

We went through into a heavily furnished sitting room, all dark wood and maroons. Some of the furniture looked expensive, but it was gloomy in there and I'm no expert. Her accent sounded East European, maybe German, but I'm about as good with accents as I am with furniture. Several watercolours adorned the walls, and they were excellent. I do know a bit about paintings. The one over the fireplace was of a young girl, playing a violin. The expression on her face was of profound concentration mixed with pleasure, and you felt that somewhere, sometime, you had met her, heard the music. She was a figure from your past.

When I approached the painting and peered at it, Mrs Crowther put the light on so I could see it better. 'That's a beautiful picture,' I told her, hoping that she had never been visited by a double-glazing salesperson. I meant it, dammit, I meant it. Is it my fault if they've usurped sincerity for the sake of a sale? The signature on the bottom said *O. Crowther*.

'She vos a beautiful girl,' she replied, gravely.

I sank into an easy chair and let the 'vos' register. 'You say the Rolls-Royce splashed you,' I said.

'Yes. I told the madam, but she just rushed by me. So I told the driver. "You sploshed me," I said, and he apologised.'

'That was big of him.'

'It vos more than I expected.'

At a guess she was about seventy, maybe a little older. I suppose I could have asked her, but it wasn't important. She was an intelligent lady, and that mattered more than her age. I remembered the overweight teenager who'd witnessed poor Nicola's last movements and couldn't describe the simplest detail, and vowed to fight ageism until I crumbled to dust.

I said: 'Another man was seen approaching the car, a few seconds later. Did you see this man?'

I could tell from her reaction that she had. Her hands began to tremble and she bit her lip.

'Tell me what you saw, Mrs Crowther,' I said.

'He scared me,' she mumbled.

'You've no need to be scared. Nobody is going to hurt you.'

'If they find I am here, they vill come round, paint things, evil things, on my valls. Break my vindows.'

'Who will?'

'The skinheads. The . . . the Nazis.' She spat the word out as if it were a draught from a poisoned chalice.

'So you think this man was a Nazi?'

'He haf the badges on his jacket. The SS. He vos a cruel man, I haf seen men like him before.'

'So you saw his face?'

'Yes, and I haf seen it many times since.'

'Where?' I demanded, sitting up.

'In my dreams.'

'Oh. What else did you see, Mrs Crowther?'

'They gave him a lift. Later, down by the traffic lights. The big car stopped vere he vos valking and he get in the back.'

'You saw him get in the car? The same Rolls-Royce that dropped the lady off?' I couldn't believe my luck.

'Yes, it vos like I say.'

'Who else was in it?'

'I don't know. It is impossible to see inside.'

I glanced round at the other pictures. They were done with a confidence that showed in the brushwork, or, more accurately, the lack of it. Each time the brush touched the surface of the paper it made a statement, then never went back. The artist was a professional.

'Who is the girl in the painting?' I asked gently.

She was silent for a while, before saying: 'She vos called Katrina Rosenberg.'

'Was she very talented?'

'Yes, fery.'

'Was she more talented than her sister, the one who paints?'

She looked at me, taken aback, and her glance fell to the carpet. 'Yes,' she whispered. 'She vos much more talented than her big sister, the von who paints.'

I stood up and wandered to the back of the room, examining the other pictures. Some were of landscapes, others of still-lifes and flower arrangements. I was trying to decide how much I could screw my expenses for.

'I'd like to buy one of your paintings,' I said. 'I can't afford to pay much, say, fifty pounds. Will you do one for me?'

She smiled for the first time and joined me, examining a basket of spring flowers. 'You are fery kind. These are just daubings. The hands, the eyes, they are not as good as they vere. Today I hardly paint at all. You are velcome to take von, for no charge.'

'No, it's fifty pounds, that's only fair. But I don't want one of these. I want a portrait – a portrait of the man you saw getting into the Rolls-Royce, the skinhead. Is it a deal?'

She raised a hand to her mouth. 'I . . . I don't know.'

'Paint him!' I urged, my face close to hers. 'Paint him for me. I know all about men like him. Not like you do, of course, but I can feel for you. Paint me his portrait, Mrs Crowther – Fraulein Rosenberg. Maybe then you won't dream about him any more. But I will. I'll dream about him until I put my hand on his neck and throw him behind bars, where he belongs, for the rest of his natural life. Help me do that to him.'

Chapter Thirteen

'Oh God! What do *you* want, Charlie?' DCI Trevor Peacock didn't seem pleased to see me, but at least we were still on first-name terms.

It was two days after my first meeting with Mrs Crowther, and I'd just been to visit her again. 'The bag lady, Mrs Crowther. She's come up with the goods,' I told him.

'You've seen her again?'

'That's right.'

'Well, we stayed away from her, just like you said. You certainly have a way with old ladies. How are you with the younger ones?'

'Just the same. They fall over themselves for me.'

'Lucky you. So what did she give you – his name and address and inside-leg measurements?'

'Almost as good as.' I unrolled a coloured photocopy of the portrait Mrs Crowther had done for me and placed it in front of the DCI. It tried to roll itself up again, so I pinioned it with his coffee mug and an ashtray filled with paper clips. 'That's the man you're looking for,' I said.

Mrs Crowther had done an excellent job. She was sure about the shape of the head, the eyes and the boxer's nose, and had portrayed them with all the flair she was capable of. The ears, mouth and chin she had hinted at, leaving them vague. It was a good painting, of an evil face. When you saw it you could understand her fear.

Trevor Peacock studied it in silence, nibbling at his fingernails. I noticed that they were eaten down to the quick. After a few seconds he said: 'He's a wicked-looking bastard. Usually, you wouldn't pick one out in a crowd, but this one looks capable of anything.' He realised what he was doing and put his hands under the desk. 'How accurate do you think it is?'

'I've shown it to Sylvia at Town & County. She says it's the man she saw on the video. It's him all right.'

A female DC came in and placed some papers in his tray. He asked her to fetch two coffees. 'You've done it again, Charlie,' he said, after she'd left. 'Made us look like a set of wassocks.'

I shrugged my shoulders. 'You have no reason to know anything has happened to Mrs Norris,' I said. 'Plus, due to circumstances, I have the freedom and time to move around a bit; follow my hunches.'

'Don't patronise me, Charlie – you've made us look like prats.'

'Oh, all right, if you insist.'

'So, are you going to leave it with me?'

'Be my guest, as long as he's behind bars as quickly as possible.'

'Behind bars is too good for him. I'd like to see him turning in the wind.'

The coffee came and we talked about the job as we sipped it. His problems were just the same as ours, but magnified. I was about to leave when I remembered something else. 'Oh, by the way,' I said. 'Mrs Crowther told me that he walks with a limp, but she didn't know how to paint one.'

I lunched on the motorway and listened to the one o'clock news as I drove the last few miles home. The writ had been moved for the by-election to fill Tom Noon's seat at Westminster. It would be held on the last Thursday in May, four weeks away.

The house where Nicola's overweight friend lived stank of chip fat. I'd decided to call there first, then write my reports at home. 'Have you ever seen this man?' I asked her, holding up one of the photocopies.

She raised her head from the butty she was constructing from the huge pile of chips on the plate in front of her. 'Dunno,' she said.

'Try to think if you have,' I urged.

'Dunno.'

I held it there, waiting for a better answer.

'Is it that feller that Nicola went with?'

That was more like it. 'That Nicola went with when?'

'When she was murdered.' She said it as if it were as consequential as going to the lavatory.

'Does it look like him?'

'Yeah, I suppose it does. A bit.'

'Did you notice anything else about him?'

'Such as?'

'Well, for instance, how he walked.'

'How he walked?' Her voice rose as she spoke, implying that he walked by putting one foot in front of the other, as any cretin ought to know.

'Did he walk with a limp?' It's called leading the witness, but this one needed dragging by the hair.

'I never noticed.'

'Thanks, love. You've been a big help.' I pinched one of the chips off her plate – she could afford it.

There was a letter lying on my doormat written in a strange hand. I picked it up, together with the electricity bill and one from a life assurance company touting for business, and walked through into the lounge. It was from the man who had sold the Jaguar back to me, and included an invitation to a rally at Chatsworth House, in Derbyshire, for all owners of E-types. There would be a procession of cars round the local villages, followed by a picnic; and the Duke of Devonshire had been invited to judge the *concours d'élégance*. His note said that it was no use to him now, so why didn't I go? He sounded cheerful, so maybe he'd turned the corner. I hoped so.

I placed the invite in my pocket, to show Annabelle. It might be fun. Then I took it out and looked at the date again. It was for the first weekend in June, straight after the Tom Noon by-election. No problem there.

The walking club had folded due to the pressures of the Nicola investigation. When you spend sixteen hours a day with your colleagues you don't feel like climbing a real mountain with them on your day off. I didn't mind. Annabelle and I discovered a bed-and-breakfast in the Lake District, Keswick, with a self-contained annexe that they let for weekends during the low season. We squeezed one in, between the May Bank Holidays, and enjoyed a blustery day on Skiddaw.

Annabelle was delighted with the invitation to Chatsworth House. She thought we should enter the *concours*, and insisted on us spending a whole Sunday polishing the Jaguar. I was back working full-time, poor Nigel being relegated to a humble DS again. He'd proved he could do the job, not that I had any doubts, so I piled most of the work on to him, reducing my own hours considerably. I was learning how to delegate. Liverpool had taken over the Nicola enquiry, as it was obviously part of the bigger scene they were investigating. We handed the files over to them and wound down our incident room and HOLMES terminal. Trevor Peacock rang me from time to time to update me, partly out of courtesy but also, I like to think, to bounce ideas around. They were making slow but consistent progress.

Norris was spending a lot of time back in the States, flying over there every week for about three days, dodging out of the way. That was OK by DCI Peacock – it made it easier for him to interview staff without having to go through their chief all the time. Norris's habit of being unpredictable, dropping in on every corner of his empire without warning, might be good management, but it could also be his undoing. Peacock discovered that Norris had visited the bonded warehouse adjoining the factory, where the lorries are loaded, just before Christmas. While he was there, a lorry driver arrived for work on his Harley Davidson motorbike and Norris had a long and cheerful chat with him. Six weeks later the same driver was murdered and his load stolen.

But the best was still to come. I was bogged down by a wave of burglaries and muggings, brought on by the shortage, and subsequent high price, of street drugs. Sometimes, legalising them makes a lot of sense. I went up to see Gilbert, for a moan and a decent cup of coffee.

'Just the man,' Gilbert greeted me.

'That usually means an unpleasant job that you want rid of,' I grumbled.

'Nonsense. I've just had a request from Region for as many men as we can spare. It's the by-election in a fortnight and they're in a bit of a panic. Apparently Special Branch have tipped them off that this TSC organisation might try something spectacular, so it's saturation policing for the Wednesday and Thursday. All the party bigwigs will be in town. Bear in mind that there's no paid overtime, unless they can screw the contingency kitty, so they'll have to come from the strength. Who've we got?'

I realised that my mouth was hanging open. 'It's, er, it's all my fault,' I said.

'Your fault? What's your fault?'

'The panic. You remember Commander Fearnside?'

'Your friend in high places? Of course I remember him.'

'Well, I told him that this by-election might be a good opportunity for TSC to assassinate the Prime Minister. It looks like he believed me.'

Gilbert put his hands to his head. 'Oh God, Charlie. What have you done now?'

'I'm not sure. Maybe I was drunk. It seemed like a good idea at the time.'

'I'm sure it was. You might be right. So why didn't you just keep your mouth shut?'

We were saved from a long discussion on impartiality in modern policing by the telephone. Gilbert listened for a few seconds before saying: 'He's here,' and handing it to me. 'DCI Peacock,' he added.

'Hello, Trevor, Charlie Priest. What can I do for you?'

'Shawn . . . Parrott,' he said, drawing the words out and enunciating the consonants, like a wine taster sampling a decent claret.

Had I known him better I'd probably have countered with: 'Seamus Sparrow,' or somesuch, but I didn't, and I hadn't observed any sign of a sense of humour in my dealings with him. 'Who's he?' is what I said.

'The man in the painting that Mrs Crowther did for you. He's been identified as one Shawn Parrott, late of Her Majesty's Parachute Regiment and various other of Her establishments.'

'Gerraway! Well done! Tell me all about it.'

It was a complicated story. Shawn Parrott was Liverpool-Irish and had been a regular soldier, in the Paras. He'd done several tours in Northern Ireland, and while his bravery was never in doubt, his loyalties were. Helped by his Irish connections he'd played one side against the other, and the Army against everyone. He hadn't always been ugly, but a massage with a baseball bat changed that. Peacock told me that whichever side it was, they were quite gentle with him, really, considering what they were capable of. They drilled a kneecap, too, but only used a small drill – just as a warning. While he was in hospital it was discovered that he was a drugs dealer, and suspicion about some stolen ammunition also fell on him. He served a year in the Army's prison at Colchester and three in ours at Walton. A retired Major had recognised him from the painting, and a couple of prison warders confirmed it.

'Sounds like your man,' I said.

'You bet. And we have another name. Parrott was buddies with a Captain called Frank Bell – always called him "the Skipper". No record, but he was implicated in the drugs and cashiered, all hush-hush to avoid bad publicity. He was born in Huddersfield – your neck of the woods.'

'So they both have reasons to be disaffected with society and the world in general,' I suggested.

'That's putting it mildly. Bell is said to be of above average intelligence. Parrott was described as a BFN.'

'A big . . . fine . . . newt?'

'No. A brainless fucking nutter.'

Every cop in the country had seen a picture of Parrott, and the original was framed and hung behind my desk. Pity I didn't insist on royalties for Mrs Crowther. Peacock's DS had tracked him down via the Ministry of Defence, following his hunch that he might be ex-Army. After a lot of thought they had decided not to go public with his identity. That would only serve to warn him, but if he killed again we'd be in big trouble. If our deductions were right they had about seven million cigarettes to off-load on the black market, so we concentrated on asking around for information about any shady salesmen offering big discounts, but nobody came forward. The next step would be to give his ID to the tabloids and see if a reward produced the goods, but that was a last resort. We have our pride. Being detectives, we like to detect, but it was a gamble – with someone else's life.

Annabelle was happier, and more beautiful, than I'd ever seen her. I was working reasonably regular hours and we spent most of our spare time together. We did all the usual things, like cinemas, restaurants and the theatre, but were quite content to sit and talk, or listen to music. She tried to convert me to Mozart but, with one or two exceptions, I still found him overfussy. Too many notes. She tolerated my Dylan collection, and wept at his tortured tones. I shook my head sadly and accused her of having no soul.

We were on our way to a concert at the Civic Hall when Nigel caught up with me on my portable. Some of the Opera North cast were giving a selection from their repertoire for one of Annabelle's charities. By way of a contrast I was playing *Blonde On Blonde* on the car's cassette system.

'It's Nigel, boss,' he said. 'I'm sorry to disturb you.'

'Pardon?' I shouted, holding the phone near a speaker and turning up the volume.

'I said it's Nigel, boss!'

'Nigel Moss? I don't know a Nigel Moss.'

'Nigel! DC Newley!'

'Hello, Nigel. Why didn't you say?' I steered into the side of the road and stopped. Dylan was at full blast, well into *Just Like A Woman*.

'Where are you?' Nigel bawled.

'I'm very well, thanks. How are you?'

'No, WHERE are you?'

'I'm at a rock concert, with Annabelle.'

'A rock concert, where's that?'

'It's a concert, with rock groups.'

'No, WHERE is it?'

'Oh sorry, they're a bit loud. It's in the park. What can I do for you?'

'I've had Fearnside on the phone. Wants you to ring him, as soon as you have the chance.'

'As soon as I've had a dance?'

'A CHANCE! As soon as you have the CHANCE!'

'Hang on, Nigel, I can't hear a thing. I'll just pull this big plug out . . .' I hit the eject button, and silence invaded the car like a winter fog. 'That's better. What were you saying?'

'Phew! Now I can hear you. Commander Fearnside rang. Wants you to contact him as soon as possible. He said it was important.'

'OK, Nigel, thanks. I'll ring him straight away. Look, I'd better put this plug back in, I'm getting some ugly looks.'

'Say hello to Annabelle.'

'Will do. *Adios*.'

I switched the phone off and placed it in the glove box. 'Nigel says hello,' I told Annabelle, steering out into the traffic.

'So who do you have to ring?' she asked, disguising her disappointment.

'Don't worry, it can wait,' I assured her, reaching across for her hand. I wouldn't have said that three months ago.

The singers were good, but they performed mainly lesser-known works, not the blockbusters. Most people knew them, though, and applauded enthusiastically. The tenor's big finale was *Nessun Dorma*, a true blockbuster, and he did a good job, so we were all buzzing with excitement as they took their final bows.

It was tea and biscuits with the cast afterwards. They

were smaller than they looked on the stage, and the men had bits of egg-yolk and God knows what else on the lapels of their tail-coats. I excused myself and rang Fearnside, from outside, leaning on one of the pillars that adorn the Civic Hall.

'Charlie! Thank goodness you're there,' he enthused.

'Sorry I didn't ring earlier, I was at a concert.'

'So your young Constable said. Didn't know you went in for that sort of stuff.'

'All in the line of duty, boss.'

'Say no more. The good news is that your friend Darren has surfaced. You know, the chap you met at Delfshaven. At least, Customs and Excise think it's him.'

'Darren! Where?'

'He's on the ferry from Rotterdam to Hull, right at this moment. They say he crossed the Channel last Tuesday and worked his way up to Holland. He's driving a black BMW; I'll give you the number. How do you fancy renewing your acquaintance with him?'

'I'd love to. Any ideas about how to play it?'

'Not really. It would have been nice to try another tracking device, attached to his car, but as you know, that's not admissable.'

Planting a bug in the drugs was OK, but if we'd attached one to his car it would have been an infringement of his civil liberties, and jeopardised our case. If the crooks had found the devices in their bags they'd have known that I was responsible, which would have jeopardised my breathing, but *that* was all right . . . It's a funny old world.

'You never recovered the drugs from the canal?' I said.

'No, I'm afraid not.'

'So we don't know if they found the bleepers?'

'No.'

'Somebody did for Kevin, and followed me, so it looks as if they'd sussed us.'

'Perhaps. If you think it's too risky, just say so.'

'No, leave it with me. I can handle Darren. I'll just play it by ear, see what he has to say for himself.'

'Good man, Charlie. And good luck.'

'Thanks. What time does his boat dock?'

I rejoined Annabelle and had a cup of coffee and ten biscuits, just in case I missed breakfast. As soon as politeness allowed I asked if she minded if we left. I told her that they were arresting someone on the ferry and wanted me to ID him in the morning. It was only a small fib.

An anticyclone was stationary over the county, so we were having sunny days and frosty nights, much to the delight of the garden centres. Everybody was stuffing their borders with bedding plants and finding them all dead next morning. The columns of steam from the three power stations along the lower Aire valley towered into the sky like nuclear explosions, glowing pink and gold in the morning sun. I wondered if observers of the real thing were ever struck by their beauty. The M62 was deserted, so I cruised at about ninety-five all the way without difficulty.

The ferry docked at eight a.m., and Mother – the DS from the Drug Squad – was waiting for me. She repeated what Fearnside had said, adding that it looked as if two teenage girls – one black, one white – were carrying the drugs.

'Are you going to lift the girls?' I asked.

'Yes, we'd like to. There's a limit to how much we can allow to go through.'

'And what about Darren?'

'He's probably not carrying, so he's all yours.'

'OK, so get me up that gangplank the second they touch

dry land. I'll pretend I've done the crossing with them, see what he has to say.'

The smell of new paint was still there. As soon as the door in the side of the ship opened we stepped across and pushed our way through the throng of pasty-faced travellers anxious to disembark. They staggered under the load of cheap booze, some in bags slung across their shoulders, a lot carried in internal belly-tanks. I was clutching one of the duty-free carriers I'd acquired on my first visit, stuffed with a couple of towels. The ship's police were expecting us and held the crush back so we could get through.

Mother knew her way around, for which I was grateful. She took me along a corridor and through a little door that led to an iron staircase down to the car deck. Most drivers were in their seats, waiting for the big doors to release them back on to home soil. A few impatient ones started their engines, while the seasoned travellers stood around, stretching their legs.

'He's in a BMW, third row, about six cars from the front,' she told me, pointing. We were towards the back of the phalanx of vehicles, looking over their roofs.

'OK, I'll go introduce myself, ruin his day. Thanks for your help, we'll let you know what happens.'

'Good luck.'

That was the second time someone had wished me good luck. Did they know something I didn't? I threaded my way along the lines of vehicles, keeping in his blind spots in case he glanced in the mirrors. They were doing well – it was a much better car than the Sierra, and almost certainly the one that had chased me from Hull to Leeds. It was Darren all right.

I slipped down the left-hand side of the BMW and yanked the passenger door open. He jerked round with surprise and his jaw dropped.

'Morning, Darren, old son. Any chance of a lift?' I asked, flopping into the seat alongside him.

'F-f-fuckinell, Charlie! You n-nearly gave me a 'eart attack. What are you doing here?'

'Same as you, I imagine. Life goes on, for some of us.' He was glancing from side to side, scared that my presence might be giving him away. 'Calm down,' I told him. 'Two men in a car is quite natural. It's you looking like Jesse James at a lynching that'll attract attention.'

'Yeah, well, you scared me. You're not carrying, are you, in that?' He pointed down at the bag between my feet.

'Of course I am. They don't check duty-free carriers. They're looking for stupid bags with false bottoms, hanging over the shoulders of amateurs. I hope the two girls – coffee and cream – weren't yours.'

He looked shocked. 'Why?' he blurted. 'What's happened to them?'

'The ship's filth collared them, just as we docked. I had them eyeballed as your likely carriers before we'd left Rotterdam. Looks as if I was right again. You're working for a bunch of jerks, Darren, believe me.'

'Shit!' He lolled back against the head restraint, staring at the roof of the car.

The big doors were opening, the light outside making me blink. 'Looks like you're having a bad day,' I said. 'Then there's the matter of the five hundred quid you owe me. I want my money, Darren. Like now!'

'No chance,' he boasted defiantly.

I opened the glove box of the BMW and saw his portable phone, so I pulled it out and pressed the buttons until a number came up on display. I started to write it on the back of my hand.

''Ere, what are you doing?' he demanded, making a grab for the instrument.

I yanked it out of his reach. 'Just writing down your stored numbers.'

'You can't do that!' He came at me, determined to reclaim his telephone.

Engines were starting all around us. I grabbed his lapels and lifted him off me, forcing him back against his door and scraping my shin on the handbrake. 'Or else what?' I hissed at him through gritted teeth. My shin was hurting like hell. 'What will you do? Tie me to the bed and set fire to it, like you did with Kevin?' His lips were turning blue. 'Go back and tell your masters this, Darren. Tell them that if I don't get my money they'll start something that'll make Desert Storm look like afternoon tea in a convent. Understood?'

Jesus, where do I get it from? I was glad Annabelle couldn't see me playing the tough guy – she'd probably wet herself laughing.

I let go of him and he flopped into his seat, gasping for breath and rubbing his throat. There were only two numbers stored, but I wrote them both down. The driver alongside was staring at me, his face a white mask. I winked at him and the car behind blew its horn. A big gap had appeared in front of us.

'You're holding everybody up,' I said.

Darren started the engine and we trundled down the ramp and on to solid ground. 'Stop in the car park,' I ordered.

When he stopped I asked: 'So whose are these numbers?'

'They're just phones. Portables. They won't help you.'

'So who owns them?'

'Nobody.'

'Listen, Darren. I liked Kevin. I've half a mind to beat the shit out of you for what you and your friends did to him. Who do these phones belong to?'

He looked in pain, as if thinking hard thrust a dagger into

his brain. 'Look,' he began, we'd like to pay you. It's just that . . . we don't have the readies. We've plenty of other stuff, like cigarettes, but the cash flow's not too good, if you see what I mean. Fact is, we've a big job coming off – and boy, do I mean big – middle of next week, and we need all the cash we can raise. There'll be no problem paying you after that. After that, we'll be rich.' The thought of it generated the beginnings of a smile.

Now it was my time to do some thinking. The word *cigarettes* had fired a circuit in my brain, like pushing one of those F buttons on the computer keyboard. Things were happening that I couldn't understand.

'I see,' I said. After a few moments I went on: 'If it helped, I might be willing to be paid in fags.'

'It'd be a big help, Charlie. We're not trying to do you – you're a good courier. The best. It's just that, like I said, we're short of the readies.'

I nodded, as if I fully understood their predicament. Small firms were going bust all over the country for exactly the same reason. I practised my mental arithmetic. Five hundred pounds, at, say, a pound for twenty, would be five hundred packets of twenty. I think. Or fifty cartons of two hundred. It sounded about right.

'I'll take fifty cartons,' I said. 'I'll give you my number, so you can let me know about deliveries.'

Darren was a lot happier now. 'Cheers, Charlie. I knew we could sort it out.'

'How many fags do you have?' I asked casually, as I wrote the number for my portable on the back of a pay-and-display ticket I found in the door pocket.

He grinned, like he'd fallen from a hotel window and landed on Raquel Welch. 'Oh, only about five million,' he bragged.

Bingo! it was them. The same bastards who'd hijacked

the lorry. And one of whom had strangled two women. Boy, was I going to make Trevor Peacock's day. I couldn't trust them, though. Paying me a few fags would be low priority for them, and like the saying goes, honour among thieves is thinner than a solicitor's smile. I needed some bait, and a decent hook.

'You said you'd be rich in a couple of weeks.'

'Yeah.'

'In that case, I might have a little proposition for you and your friends that'd make you even richer. I'd do it myself but, same as you, I've the old cash-flow problems.'

Darren looked interested. 'I'll put it to them, if you want.'

'Great. So listen to this. About two months ago, a Russian trawler was seized up in the North-East, loaded to the gunnels with pot, horse and coke. You might remember it.'

'Yeah. Did the world of good to the prices.'

'That's right. What the Customs don't realise is that there's another trawler going in and out of West Hartlepool every week with a million quid's worth of rock – crack cocaine – sealed in its hold. The captain doesn't know what to do with it because this end of the chain are all in jail. I've been offered it for two hundred thousand, which I'm a little short of. Two hundred thousand short of, to be exact. I reckon a firm offer of, say, a hundred grand might get it. Tell your friends that.'

He looked quite eager. 'Yeah. Yeah. I will do. Thanks, Charlie.'

The full story was beginning to unfold in my mind. 'It's from Russia,' I improvised. 'The Communists had a plan to release it in the West, to undermine our society. When they fell it was left in store for a while, at the KGB Headquarters. The KGB agents were all sacked, so they took the drugs as redundancy payments. Unofficially, of course. Nobody knew about them, so it didn't matter. Now they're finding their way on to the black market. One hundred per cent clinically pure, and there's plenty more where this came from.'

'Phew,' said Darren, obviously impressed. Now he, too, had a story to go home and tell someone.

I watched him drive away, careful that he didn't see my Vauxhall, and went round to the local nick to tell Mother the full story. They gave me breakfast in their canteen, but I'd have preferred to have eaten in the Jolly Burger. I could afford it for once – I was on expenses.

This was one appointment that I had to keep, so I forewarned Annabelle that I might have to dash off at a moment's notice. She didn't mind. She'd often said that it wasn't necessary for us to go somewhere every time we met, so we stayed in and enjoyed each other's company. We had a small disagreement about Nigel. Annabelle said I shouldn't tease him; teasing was the thin end of bullying. I didn't agree, but she gave me something to think about, and it hurt.

As it happened, I was having a night at home when Darren rang. I'd tidied the kitchen and was just about to start on the bathroom, so the warbling of the portable came as a relief.

'It's Darren,' he told me. 'Be at Burtonwood services, westbound, in an hour. What will you be driving?'

Burtonwood was at the far side of Manchester. 'I can't be there in an hour. I'm in the Merlin Couriers van, coming up the M1. Make it two hours.'

There was a silence. I listened hard, but he had his hand over the mouthpiece.

'Hour and an 'alf,' he said, when he came back on.

'It'll be a rush for me. I might be late.'

'Call it 'alf-eleven, no later.'

'OK, half-past eleven. I'll be there.' The fish were biting, and it felt like a big one.

Chapter Fourteen

I had some arranging to do. I rang Peacock and told him we were *go!* Then I rang Heckley, where we had a plain Armed Response Vehicle standing by to lend a hand. All I had to do then was collect the big van and hot-foot it to Burtonwood.

The two numbers from the memory in Darren's phone had been for an insurance salesman in Knutsford and a woman in Birmingham who worked, she said, as a travelling masseuse. We'd arranged to see their itemised bills to see who was receiving the calls that crooks were making on their behalf. A BMW with the same number as Darren's belonged, rightfully, to a bank manager in Hemel Hempstead. He said he could see it outside his office even as he spoke to me. We didn't learn much from these exercises, so a meeting was our remaining hope.

The ARV followed me all the way. A traffic car, lights flashing, was parked on a bridge near the M6. I flicked my lights at him and pulled on to the hard shoulder. A few minutes later he joined us, and three officers armed with Heckler and Koch automatics, made in Nottingham, piled into the back of my Transit.

'This had better be worth it, Charlie,' DCI Trevor Peacock warned me.

'No guarantees, Trevor. Your assessment of the information is as good as mine.'

They were rattling and sliding about in the back of the van, unable to hold on to anything. Fortunately for them it wasn't far. At Burtonwood I parked in the middle of a big space that gave me a good view of most of the car park and switched off the lights. The ARV had kept going when I stopped, and was already lost somewhere in a line of cars.

'Which are ours?' I asked.

'The furniture van and the minibus. Plus a cleaning van near the exit and the chopper's standing by.'

'That should just about cover it,' I said, glad that it wasn't coming out of my wages. Peacock radioed the others and told them that Vicar One was in position. It was the nearest he ever got to making a joke. Vicars Two to Four acknowledged.

At dead on eleven twenty-eight a Salford Van Hire Transit cruised into the services and wandered about, looking for the optimum parking space amongst the eight hundred that were available, before settling for one of the Disabled spots. I heard the scrape of metal behind me and Peacock clicked his transmission button three times.

'Are you armed, Charlie?' he whispered.

'No,' I replied, without moving.

'Christ, you ought to be.'

'Take a good look at my back. I'll be lying on the floor with my hands over my ears.'

There was a snigger from behind me. I didn't bother telling them that three years earlier I'd emptied a Walther into someone. Killed him. This time they could have the glory, and the pain.

A middle-aged lady climbed out of the van with great difficulty, before walking round to extricate a wheelchair from the back. She helped her crippled husband out from the passenger seat and into the chair and pushed him in the direction of the toilets. Fifteen minutes later they reappeared and went through the long and painful procedure in reverse, before driving away. Peacock clicked the radio once. Everybody relaxed.

There was a steady procession of vehicles. Some people just used the loo, others presumably had a meal or a snack. One or two had us on red alert. At about twelve-thirty I went for a pee and bought a morning paper. A footballer had been done for drink-driving and a star of one of the soaps had been reunited with her thirty-year-old love child. I hadn't heard of any of them. According to the latest Gallup Poll, the Government would be annihilated in the forthcoming by-election. I'd thoughtfully provided a plastic bucket for them to use in the back of the van, but they had strong bladders.

An hour later the sarcastic comments were coming thick and fast. At two o'clock Peacock declared: 'They're not coming. Let's go home.' They fell out of the back of the van and stretched stiff limbs. The rest were ordered to stand down, and little groups of figures in flack-jackets started doing callisthenics in the corners of the car park, automatic weapons hanging from their shoulders.

'Don't call us, Charlie. We'll call you,' Peacock wisecracked before slamming the back door and turning the handle. He was a wag underneath, after all. We drove off in convoy. At the next exit the ARV and I turned off to go round the flyover while the rest of them continued westwards. An hour later the ARV overtook me and headed back to the station. They gave me a friendly wave, which I needed. I returned the van to Merlin and went home to bed. It was broad daylight and the blackbirds were singing like lunatics.

Nigel was right – I needed a dishwasher. I collected all the leaflets and listened to the sales patter from smooth-chinned youths who didn't know the difference between dabbing it on and showering in it. 'May I just take a few details?' they'd ask, fingers poised over the keyboard.

'No, I'm just looking,' I'd reply, eyes watering.

At home I took a big sheet of paper and drew a rectangle on it, the same shape as my kitchen. Along one side I represented the worktops and the sink. The dishwasher would have to go in place of one of the cupboards. I drew a square for the washing machine, linked to the sink by a couple of pipes, and wrote WASHER in it. The dishwasher would need more pipes, and they'd need electrical connections. It was going to look like a Sellafield under there.

Did the dishwasher need to be near the sink? That was the big question. Or did the washing machine? Annabelle would know, but it was a feeble reason for ringing her. She'd be an expert in such things – all I knew about was being a policeman, but there were doubts about that.

I crossed out WASHER and wrote NICOLA. In the square for the sink I wrote PROSTITUTE, and on the pipe linking them I put DNA. The dishwasher became MRS NORRIS, linked to the prostitute by the expensive watch.

I drew three more squares, radiating out from Mrs Norris, and wrote CIGS, HURST, and LORRY DRIVER in them. Off to one side were Darren and his gang, with more lines joining them to the cigarettes and the two dead drivers. I tore the sheet into shreds and went to bed.

Dave Sparkington volunteered for unpaid overtime during the by-election. 'If somebody bumps off the Prime Minister I want to be able to tell my grandkids that I was there,' he explained.

'You're supposed to prevent it,' I told him, testily.

'Humph!' was his reply. Who'd be a Prime Minister?

The campaigns started in a civil-enough fashion, but soon

degenerated into personalised slanging matches. The candidates were cleancut newcomers, with impeccable credentials and winsome images. Then it was leaked that the Opposition hopeful had been sent down from his first university for shagging the Provost's daughter. His lead in the polls immediately leapt by a further ten points, much to the dismay of the Government's spin doctors. Annabelle went out distributing leaflets, and received much leg-pulling from me for it. She tried to persuade me to go with her, but I informed her that policemen weren't allowed to express a political standpoint. She called me a lackey of the State.

The day before the election, Heckley nick was like a stockbroker's office on Derby Day. Everybody was out playing. They'd all been seconded to our neighbours, and were now poncing about on rooftops or poking into manholes, looking for weapons of assassination. They were armed with pictures of Shawn Parrott and an armoury of equally lethal hardware. Particular attention was being devoted to grassy knolls.

I had a coffee with Gilbert and listened to the phones ringing unanswered. Eventually the system would bring the more persistent callers to him, unless, of course, I was at my desk, in which case they'd come to me first. I decided to go out.

A woman from Keighley had been mugged in the town over the weekend. We'd recovered a handbag which may have been hers, so I decided to drive over and ask her to identify it and make a statement. It was a bit feeble, but it would do.

'How's Annabelle?' Gilbert asked.

'Very well, thank you. Pass the spoon, please.'

He handed it to me and looked grave. 'I can't see us doing well in this election, Charlie. The PM's handled the whole thing very badly.'

'Us!' I protested. 'Speak for yourself.'

He shook his head, as if in despair. 'What are you doing today?'

'I have to go over to Keighley, to interview Mrs Webster, the woman who was mugged on Monday.'

'Good idea. Better show how keen we are, with her husband being Chairman of the Bench.'

I hadn't known that. 'Just what I thought,' I replied.

He dunked a chocolate digestive. 'Do you really think they'll have a go at the PM?'

'Nah. They just want to cause disruption, which they've already done. Still, you never know, do you?'

What was it Governor Conally said in 1963? 'Now you can't say we don't love you in Texas, Mr President.'

My next cuppa was from a china cup in Mrs Webster's sitting room. The bag was hers, but the contents were missing. Her assailant had a mohican haircut, which made him rather conspicuous, so an ID parade might not go down well with the brief of the youth we'd arrested. Ideally, we'd let them all wear hats. Failing that, we'd organise a street ident, where the victim tries to pick him out of the crowd. 'That's him,' she'd say. 'The one handcuffed to the policeman.' Mrs Webster was badly shaken by her ordeal, but was willing to cooperate in any way. I wondered how muggers would fare in her husband's court from now on.

It was a beautiful day, so I bought a sandwich and ate it in the car, parked near the river. I tuned in to the local station to catch the news, make sure mayhem wasn't breaking loose during canvassing. There was only one item, the full programme being devoted to the by-election. It was the biggest local story since the Queen opened the new Municipal Swimming Pool. She should have told them she couldn't swim.

'The Prime Minister and the Leader of the Opposition

are even competing in their modes of transport,' the newsreader was saying. 'The PM is already in town, having arrived in an Army Chinook helicopter which landed on the Grammar School playing field. Meanwhile, firefighters are standing by over the length of the Settle to Carlisle railway line in anticipation of Andrew Fallon's journey. He is travelling by train later this afternoon, demonstrating his support for the railways, and will be hauled by the record-breaking steam engine *Mallard*. The last time a steam train did this journey, over fifty grass-fires were started along the line.'

Great, I thought. The bloke can't stand cigarette smoke but has no compunction about igniting most of the North of England. Wait till I see Annabelle. The newsreader was rabbiting on: 'Trainspotters are expected to congregate at famous beauty spots like Dent and the Batty Moss viaduct to take advantage of this opportunity to see the legendary locomotive *Mallard* for what might be the last time. Thanks to Fallon, the Opposition candidate can now safely rely on the trainspotter vote.'

'Mmm.' I nodded in appreciation of the thought. Wouldn't mind seeing *Mallard* again myself. It was common enough on the local lines when I was a kid, but I'd never seen it on the Batty Moss viaduct. I'd never seen any steam train up there. It promised to be a memorable event. If I'd had my camera in the car I might have been tempted to play hookey and have a drive over. What was it? A hundred feet high and quarter of a mile long, with twenty-four arches?

How did I know that?

I walked over to the bin and dumped my litter, brushing the crumbs off my trousers. Who'd told me about Batty Moss viaduct?

Annabelle had been there, but it wasn't her. We were at the cottage, when . . .

It was Darren.

He saw the photo on the mantelpiece and knew all about it. What was it he said? They'd been 'just for a look' and he 'liked to know what he was talking about'.

I thought about my other conversations with him. He'd said they had something big planned for the middle of this week – something that would make them rich.

And that they had five million cigarettes.

It was them, the drugs gang! They'd hijacked the lorry and murdered the driver. They were responsible for the disappearance of Mrs Norris and Harold Hurst's death. One of them had strangled two women. And now they were planning an assassination, but it wasn't the Prime Minister they were after – *it was Andrew Fallon.*

Norris had been the inside man for the hijack, possibly as a down payment, and now he'd hired them to bump off the man who wanted to wreck the tobacco business. Maybe they'd had dealings before, hence the disappearance of Mrs Norris. They'd killed Tom Noon to set up the election, and put Fallon just where they wanted him. It made sense, and it was all going to happen at Batty Moss viaduct. Soon.

I dialled the Heckley number. 'Put me straight through to Mr Wood, please; it's urgent.'

'Superintendent Wood.' He sounded fed up. I'd soon alter that.

'It's Charlie, Gilbert. Listen. It's not the Prime Minister they're after, it's Andrew Fallon. He's coming down on a train from Carlisle. Get him off that train.'

Poor Gilbert sounded hesitant. I was only putting his reputation on the line, in front of the nation's press. He wanted an explanation.

'No time. I'm going to Batty Moss. Ring Fearnside. Ring anyone, but get Fallon off that train. At a guess they're going to blow up the viaduct.' I switched off before he could argue.

I made a tyre-squealing U-turn, causing a woman in a Mitsubishi Shogun to hit the anchors, depositing her two children and a Labrador pup on the floor, and screamed up through the gears. Ribblehead, and the viaduct, were about thirty-five miles away. I drove with the headlights on and used the horn a lot. I've done the advanced course, but I think my instructors would have disowned some of the manoeuvres I made.

It's a right turn in Settle, and then you're on a typical Yorkshire Dales switchback. I never actually took off, but I achieved weightlessness for several seconds over some of the bigger brows. A couple of lorries carrying limestone from the quarries slowed me for a while, but I bullied my way past them. I barely noticed Pen-y-ghent on my right and Ingleborough on the other side as I swept through Horton-in-Ribblesdale in a flurry of gravel and irresponsibility.

Where do they all come from? I negotiated the junction at Ribblehead and the roadsides were lined with parked cars. The train had obviously not gone through yet. I turned left towards Chapel le Dale, now driving slowly, assessing the situation. A police Escort was parked on the verge, and I pulled up behind it.

The local bobby had a boozer's face and a paunch to match. I wondered if the more liberal opening times had taken some of the attraction from his job, now that there was no need to steal a crafty pint or four in the landlord's kitchen with the door locked.

'DI Charlie Priest,' I said, waving my ID at him. 'What's happening?'

'Oh, er, dunno, surr. I've been told to get misself 'ere and look out fer anything suspicious. Can't be more specific than that.'

'When's the *Mallard* due?'

''Bout fifteen minutes, surr.'

'Are there always this many trainspotters for a steam train?'

'Don't rightly know, surr. One of them told me it's a special. Apparently it'll stop on the bridge for photographs, then go back and come over again, making a lot of smoke. Should be a proper spectacle, if you ask me.'

I scanned the valley between us and Whernside, spanned by the viaduct. The railway line ran above the road, near our position, so we couldn't see the tracks. The sun was at this side, and the flat area beside the railway was dotted with little groups of enthusiasts, cameras on tripods, waiting for *Mallard* to make an entrance. They wore bobble hats and anoraks to protect them against the ravages of a warm summer's day.

'OK,' I said to the bobby. 'I want you to radio in and get everybody available up here. Any ARVs within striking distance are to join us. Then tell the nearest helicopter to stand by. On second thoughts, get him airborne.'

His jaw fell on to his paunch. This was a bit different from his normal fodder of pig movements and sheep scab precautions. 'Yes, surr. Right away, surr.' He fumbled with his personal radio.

'It might be better if you used the car radio,' I suggested, 'just in case they're using a scanner.' It's too easy to monitor the personal radios.

'Yes, surr.'

'And stop calling me sir. Charlie will do.'

'Yes, surr. Charlie.'

I listened to him trying to raise help, saying: 'This Inspector Priest says . . .' to every query.

'They want to know what it's about,' he told me, looking up from the radio.

'Tell them we think someone is going to blow the bridge up, with the train on it.'

He gulped and turned pale, before repeating what I'd said.

I was standing alongside his car, talking to him through the window while I let my gaze wander across the scene, inspecting the viaduct from one end to the other. Suddenly a figure appeared in the middle, jogging towards us.

It's a single track over the bridge, the total width being about ten feet. A small wall, about eighteen inches high, gives a degree of protection to anyone walking across. I think the figure must have been kneeling down, concealed by the parapet. Now that he was nearer I recognised him as Darren.

As he reached our end of the viaduct he slowed to a walk, not in a hurry now that he was unlikely to be suddenly confronted by a train. He stepped off the track and descended the embankment at the other side, out of my sight.

'Lend me your handcuffs,' I told Dangerfield of the Dales.

'Handcuffs?'

'Yes, handcuffs.'

I vaulted the British Railways standard seven-strand wire fence and galloped down the bank at this side, towards the first span of the viaduct. Darren was in for a surprise.

He was leaning with his back against the stonework, under the massive cathedral arch, lighting a cigarette, when I breezed round the corner.

'Hello, Darren,' I said, still puffing from the sudden exertion.

'Ch-Ch-Charlie!' he exclaimed, aghast.

'Shawn sent me. Said to make sure you had a gun.'

'Shawn? Yeah . . .'

His hand moved towards the zip of his combat jacket, but my fist hit him in the face before he got anywhere near it. It was a beauty, starting right down in my foot and moving up through my leg and shoulder, just like we were taught. Darren flew backwards and fell in a heap, blood spurting from his nose and a bewildered expression on his face, like a pet dog that's just been whipped for the first time.

I had a cuff round one wrist before he realised what was happening. He jerked the other arm behind his back and took a kick at me. I grabbed his foot and slapped the other bracelet round his ankle. Unorthodox, but effective.

I took the gun, a standard-looking automatic, maybe a thirty-eight, from inside his jacket and ejected the clip. I put the bullets in one pocket and the pistol in another.

'Detective Inspector Priest,' I told him. 'Police. Sorry, Darren, but you're nicked. Don't go away.'

I climbed the embankment, pulling myself upwards with big handfuls of willowherb and ragwort. I knelt down for a rest at the top, waiting for my respiratory rate to catch up with the adrenalin rush. What had Darren been doing in the middle of the viaduct? They couldn't be attempting to blow the thing up – it would take an atom bomb to do that. The answer was somewhere in the middle, two hundred and twenty yards away.

Ten feet wide seemed suddenly narrow, like walking a plank. I jogged between the lines, leaning sideways into the stiff breeze that was blowing up there, hoping it wouldn't suddenly cease and send me staggering towards the edge. Every ten yards I looked back over my shoulder – I'd have felt silly if a train coming the other way had flattened me.

It wasn't what I'd expected. Two climbing ropes were neatly coiled at the side of the track. One end of each was looped under the rail and tied around the anchorage. So that was it. Two people were going to get off the train and abseil down off the viaduct. Presumably after killing Andrew Fallon. And then what?

The answer came immediately. Over the roar of the wind in my ears came the *chom-chom-chom* of a helicopter. I looked up and saw it over Whernside, and it wasn't one of ours. It swooped round in a big arc and hovered over the trainspotters. They gathered their gear and fled from the downdraught, holding their hats on while composing strong letters to various public servants.

And then I heard another noise; a sound guaranteed to wipe away the years from the most disenchanted, embittered, disillusioned grown-up in the land and reduce him to a starry-eyed, rubber-kneed schoolboy. It was the long mournful wail of the A4 Pacific steam engine.

Most American locomotives make that noise, but in Britain it is only the streamlined A4. The words of the old song flashed through my mind: *You can hear the whistle blow a hundred miles . . .*

But it wasn't a hundred miles away, it was less than one. And I couldn't get this bloody knot undone.

A cop in a film would have severed the rope with a single shot from his gun. If I'd tried it I'd have probably caught a ricochet in the balls. I grabbed a large pebble from the ballast between the rails and started to bash the crap out of the first rope. I was about halfway through, striking blindly into a mess of frayed ends, when the whistle blew again. I looked up and saw *Mallard* coming round the bend in the track, black smoke pouring from the stack and white superheated steam billowing around its wheels. It was a shot the trainspotters would have killed for, but for me it had lost all romance. I attacked the rope with renewed fervour.

I did it. When I was through I gathered the coils in my arms and cast the lot into space. 'A hundred feet high,'

Darren had said. It looked more like a thousand to me. I knelt down while the dizziness subsided and took hold of the second rope. *Mallard* was nearly at the end of the viaduct, creeping forward with the characteristic *CHUFF-chuff-chuff-chuff*, *CHUFF-chuff-chuff-chuff* of that type of engine. I threw the pebble down – there had to be a better way than this.

She was about fifteen yards away when I stood up and started running. I won the hundred yards in the school sports in eleven point two seconds. Afterwards I worked it out at nineteen miles per hour. *Mallard* can do a hundred and twenty-six, but she has lousy acceleration.

I was fleeing down the middle of the track, jacket flapping behind, glancing over my shoulder every two seconds at the clanking, roaring behemoth bearing down on me. Steel screeched against steel, and a sudden change in the breeze enveloped me in a cloud of steam and smoke and the smell of hot oil.

She'd stopped. I slowed to a jog and in a few seconds was at the end of the viaduct. I jumped off the track and rolled and slid to the bottom of the embankment.

Darren hadn't moved very far. I collapsed on the grass beside him, recovering my breath.

'It's too tight. I've got cramp in my foot,' he moaned.

'Just be grateful it wouldn't go round your neck,' I wheezed.

The gun had vanished from my pocket. I thought I'd felt it go when I was running. It was cold in the shade of the bridge, and a shiver shook my body. I grabbed Darren's collar and dragged him out into the sunlight. He said 'Ooh! Aah! Ooh! Aah!' as the end of his spine bumped over the outcrops of carboniferous limestone that recorded the origins of the region. I gave him a final spin and left him facing down the length of the viaduct.

I walked away from it, to obtain a better view. The chopper was about two hundred yards away, on the ground, its rotors idling. The spotters had regrouped and were clicking away like a convention of flamenco dancers.

Two figures appeared on the viaduct, running away from the train and peeling off their jackets to reveal the climbing harnesses they were already wearing. They paused for a few moments, clipping their figure-of-eight abseiling devices on to the two ropes they found, then stepped over the parapet.

I watched them as they leaned out at forty-five degrees, as if supported by only the breeze. The one on the right lowered himself a few feet and produced something from a pocket. His right hand moved up and down several times and then horizontally. He was holding an aerosol of white paint, and the letter T appeared on the stonework of the bridge, followed by S and C. When he'd finished he tossed the can over his shoulder, nodded to his companion and kicked away from the wall.

They were above one of the arches, so soon had no wall in front of them. They dropped alternately, about ten feet at a time, leapfrogging past each other.

Until they reached the loop in the rope. It was Shawn Parrott who reached it first, but I didn't know that at the time. A second later Frank Bell – the Skipper – landed on top of him, his crotch pressed hard into Parrott's face.

'What the fuck's happening?' one of them shouted.

'The fucking ropes are tangled!'

'Well, pull an end up!'

'I can't find it.'

Bell leaned sideways and looked down at the ground, fifty feet below. 'We're on the same fucking rope!' he screamed.

I'm not sure if Darren heard the rest of it, but it wasn't complimentary and contained a good number of threats.

His credibility in the gang was lower than a penguin's bottom.

I wandered back to him. 'I take it that's Bell and Parrott.'

Darren nodded. He'd wiped the blood away from around his mouth, but missed quite a bit and it had dried on his chin and cheeks. He looked miserable; ill, almost. He was having a bad day.

'Let's have a talk,' I said, but before we could start the helicopter engine speeded up and it took off. I dialled Heckley control and told them its registration letters and the direction it was headed.

'Who's in the chopper?' I asked Darren.

'Dunno.'

'C'mon, Darren. You'll have to do better than that.'

'No, it's true, Charlie. It's a pal of the Skip's.'

'Bell's?'

'Yeah. Army pal. I've never met 'im. My foot's killing me.'

'Sorry, I haven't the key. I'll get it in a minute. Is it hijacked?'

'Well, half-an'-half. Hired proper to start with – that's what we needed the cash for – then hijacked. The pilot thought he was going to Ascot.'

'I see. OK, Darren, listen to this. Parrott is going away for a long time. He'll be eating his meals off a tin plate for the next thirty years; maybe even the rest of his natural. Bell will probably get something similar. Now we have a simple rule in the police. We believe whoever tells us a story first. So you can tell us yours, or we can wait until someone else tells us. Understand?'

'I was just the driver, Charlie. Honest.'

'I believe you, Darren. But will a jury? 'Specially if the other two say you were an equal partner.' He looked scared. 'Then there's Norris. We'll be picking him up later today, and I can't imagine him taking the rap for any of you lot, can you?'

'It was his idea. Norris's.'

'I'm sure it was.'

The local bobby suddenly appeared beside me and I noticed that a ring of spectators had gathered around us, video cameras recording the action and a few of them telephoning their agents to get the best deal. 'I thought you might need some assistance,' he panted.

'Yes, I do, thanks.' I asked him his name and we shook hands for the cameras. 'This young man wants to make a statement. I put the cuffs on a bit tight, so do you think you could take the one off his ankle and place it round his other wrist, then take him in? He's an old friend of mine, so treat him properly.'

'Yes, surr. Charlie. Will do.' He fished a bunch of keys from his tunic pocket and bent over Darren. 'Let's 'ave a look at you, then.'

As we were walking up to the road I glanced back at Bell and Parrott, swinging gently from side to side. The breeze would be cutting, up there. I wondered if I ought to shout something clever at them, like: 'Hang around,' or: 'Sorry to leave you dangling,' but I couldn't think of anything worthy enough.

Traffic cars could be heard coming up the lane. Before the local bobby drove away with Darren he asked me what Darren was charged with.

'Oh, trespassing on railway property,' I replied.

Large policemen with serious faces were approaching me. Later, when I saw myself in a mirror, I was surprised I hadn't been charged with vagrancy. They melted a little when I showed them my ID, but didn't smile. We'll, if they did it was hidden beneath their moustaches. A uniformed Inspector arrived just after the helicopter carrying the

Yorkshire Television film crew, but well before the BBC. I suppose the BBC did have further to come.

'What's this all about?' he asked me.

'It's a long story,' I began. I told him the brief details and a bit about Bell and Parrott. 'The plan was to shoot Andrew Fallon on the train and escape in the helicopter. I think Fallon wasn't on it, but I'd check. Those two might look ridiculous at the moment,' I warned him, 'but they're armed to the teeth. Personally, I'd starve the bastards out before I let them down.' From this distance they looked like one big spider, dangling on two strands of silk. The front pair of the spider's eight legs were flailing about, as if it were trying to knock its own head off, and shouted obscenities drifted on the breeze.

Crowd control looked like being the Inspector's biggest problem. I told him about the gun I'd dropped in the viaduct, and while he was organising his troops I rang Shenandoah Incorporated, domain of Mr Norris, and spoke to his secretary.

'I'm sorry, Inspector, Mr Norris isn't here,' she said.

'Could you tell me where I can find him?'

'Yes. He's on his way back from the States. He's just spoken to me from the plane and asked me to have the car meet him at Manchester Airport. He will be available tomorrow, first thing. Shall I make you an appointment?'

'No, it's important. What time does his flight land?'

He'd conveniently arranged it so he would be airborne at the time of the planned killing. If he saw a television set in the near future he'd be on the next flight back to the good ol' U.S. of A., and we'd never get our hands on him. I needed him straight off that plane.

'He lands at seventeen-twenty,' the secretary told me.

Twenty past five. I could do it. I could dash to Manchester Airport and stand at Arrivals with a board that said

Norris and wait for him to come to me.

'Hi, Inspector,' he'd drawl. 'Are you waiting for me?'

'You bet, asshole,' I'd tell him. 'You're cotton-pickin' nicked.' And I'd grab him by the scruff of his silk suit and drag him through the crowds of travellers like the murdering little scumbag that he was.

That's what I wanted to do. But I was supposed to be seeing Annabelle at eight, and I wanted to see her more. I didn't have Manchester Airport in my book of numbers, so I rang Trevor Peacock. Might as well kill another two birds with one stone.

'Oh, so it's the ladykiller. What do you want this time?' he said, with no attempt to hide the sarcasm.

'A favour.'

'Such as?'

'I'm not in my office. Could you please arrange for someone to meet the seventeen-twenty flight from New York to Manchester for me, and arrest Bradley Norris as soon as he sets foot on British soil?'

'Are you joking, Charlie?'

'No. I already have Frank Bell and Shawn Parrott.'

'Parrott? And Bell? Where?' Suddenly he was interested.

'Have you a TV handy?'

'No, not in the office. There's one in the canteen.'

'Switch it on and you might see them.'

'Why, where are they?'

'Right where you wanted them, Trevor – turning in the wind. Turning in the wind.'

The good weather held, and when I peeked through the curtains on the morning of the picnic it looked as if it was going to be hot enough to crack the flagstones. I was freshly showered, crisply attired and had just put the workaday car out in the road when I heard the scrunch of tyres on the gravel. It should have been Annabelle's little flyer, but it was a shiny black Rover.

'Sugar!' I cursed. 'What does he want?'

Commander Fearnside climbed out and came towards me, beaming like the Fastnet Lighthouse. 'Morning, Charlie. What a beautiful day, eh?' he hollered, shaking my hand and patting my elbow.

'I'm going out,' I said.

'Don't worry, old boy, wouldn't dream of detaining you. I'm just going to see this Norris fellow to ask him a few questions. When politics are involved I get to do some interviewing. Of course, if you want to sit in you'd be more than welcome. Matter of fact, can't think of anyone I'd rather have there . . .'

'No thanks, Mr Fearnside. I've arranged to go for a picnic with my girlfriend. We haven't seen much of each other lately. Has the one from the helicopter been caught yet?'

'No, 'fraid not. As you know, he was dropped off somewhere in the Kielder Forest. He didn't get to their car, but he's on the loose, living rough. He's ex-SAS, so should be at home in there. We'll get him.'

'Good. Would you like a coffee?'

'No thanks, Charlie, I don't want to take up your time. Just thought I'd pop round to mention a couple of things, while I was in the area. Nothing like the personal approach, eh?'

I decided it would look rude if I glanced at my watch, and waited for him to continue.

'The results of the DNA tests have come through,' he said. 'Parrott murdered the girl and the woman, no doubt about it. Perfect match.'

I folded my arms and looked at him. 'I'm glad about that,' I said. 'Thanks for telling me. Now let's hope he gets what he deserves – stuck in a cell for the rest of his life, and not playing the system in some psychiatric hospital.'

'Out of our hands, old boy. Out of our hands. At least now we know he did it the Civil Liberties people should get off our backs.'

'Hrumph!' I snorted and chuckled at the same time.

'It was a big naughty of you, Charlie, leaving them hanging there all night.'

'I missed my date. And it was for their own protection – the train spotters were growing ugly. And it wasn't really *all* night.'

'Ha ha!' he guffawed. 'God, I wish I'd been there. Bloody good show, I say.'

It was as good a moment as any. 'You said two things,' I reminded him.

He blew his nose on a huge white hanky. 'Yes, I did, didn't I? It's just that . . .' For once he was almost lost for words. 'Not to put too fine a point on it, I wondered if you might be interested in coming to work for me. I know I've asked you before, but maybe you've changed your mind. You've what, three years to go? You could come on promotion, which would nicely enhance your pension. Might even make superintendent. It's worth considering.'

'I'll think about it,' I said, smiling at him in a way that meant no.

'If the pension won't attract you, how about the lifestyle? Just the ticket for a bachelor like you: all those fast cars and glamorous women.'

'I have a fast car,' I told him, turning the lock of the garage door and pulling at the handle.

'Ah yes,' he said. 'The famous three-point-eight Jaguar that inflated your expenses.' The door folded upwards, revealing the predatory nose of the E-type, gleaming like a bullet in the sunshine. 'Holy smoke!' he hissed through his teeth, screwing his eyes against the glare. 'I expected an old banger, not a bloody E-type.'

A movement in the road caught my eye as Annabelle drew up in her little car, and we both turned to watch her uncoil herself from the driving seat. She was dressed in a semi-safari style, to humour me, with a pair of her famous culottes showing off those long, tanned legs. She gave me a little wave as she unlocked her boot.

'Excuse me,' I said to Fearnside and went to meet her. As I lifted the picnic basket out I whispered: 'Don't worry, he's going.'

I put the basket on the wall near my garage and introduced them. 'Annabelle Wilberforce, this is Superintendent Fearnside,' I said, hoping I'd done it the right way round.

'Please, Roland,' Fearnside insisted, pumping her hand. 'Wonderful to meet you, Annabelle. Charlie tells me you're going for a picnic.'

'That's right,' she said. 'We're going to Chatsworth House.'

'Chatsworth, eh? Should I know where that is?'

'Derbyshire. It's the Duke of Devonshire's place.'

I opened my mouth to speak, then shut it again.

'Of course it is. Super. Well, I won't delay you any longer. Have a think about what I said, Charlie, but . . .' his eyes flicked from Annabelle to the Jag and back to Annabelle, '. . . I can see I'm wasting my time. Ring me Monday for an update, eh? Goodbye, Annabelle, enjoy your picnic. 'Bye, Charlie.'

'Goodbye, Roland. Lovely to meet you.'

'S'long, boss.'

We sat on the wall close together, and watched him shuffle into the driving seat and head off down the street.

'Please, call me Roland,' I mimicked. Then, in a higher voice: 'It's the Duke of Devonshire's place.'

As the Rover negotiated the corner at the end of the road